'James Harland' is the pseudonym of a well-known financial journalist who has worked on the *Sunday Times*, *Sunday Business*, as a columnist for *Bloomberg News* and on television.

Visit www.jamesharland.com for more information.

JAMES HARLAND

THE
MONTH OF
THE LEOPARD

SIMON & SCHUSTER
A VIACOM COMPANY

First published in Great Britain by Simon & Schuster UK Ltd, 2001
A Viacom company

1 3 5 7 9 10 8 6 4 2

Simon & Schuster UK Ltd
Africa House
64–78 Kingsway
London WC2B 6AH

Simon & Schuster Australia
Sydney

A CIP catalogue record for this book is available from the British Library

ISBN 0–7432–0975–3

This book is a work of fiction. Names, characters, places and incidents are
either a product of the author's imagination or are used fictitiously. Any
resemblance to actual people living or dead, events or locales is entirely
coincidental.

Typeset by Palimpsest Book Production Limited,
Polmont, Stirlingshire
Printed and bound in Great Britain by
The Bath Press, Bath

TO ISABELLA

PROLOGUE

Tallinn, Estonia, 9 December

TATYANA BRUSHED THE COLD AIR AWAY FROM THE SMOOTH, white skin of her neck, tightening the collar of her black felt coat into her cheekbones. Pulling her hat down, she tucked away her long black hair, making sure none of the remaining warmth of her body could escape. It had been many years, she reflected, since she felt the frozen air of an Estonian winter against her face. And yet, though the icy coolness might fade from your memory, she could never forget how to stay warm. It was an instinct, a reflex for survival, bred into her over generations.

Her leather knee-high boots trod into the crisp snow, and as she glanced down at the tracks she was leaving, the glimmer of a smile played upon her face. As a child, she had spent hours watching her tracks, always wondering whether they would be hidden by fresh flakes, or whether they might still be there, frozen and lifeless, in the morning. While she examined the footprints, half-recovered memories pulsed through her mind, momentarily making her forget what she was doing there. I am just visiting a friend, she told herself; the one friend who remains from my childhood. No one will recognize me. By tomorrow I will be safely back in London.

Her eyes rose from the tracks, glancing towards the rows of traditional Nordic buildings rising up from the side of the street. Each was finely decorated, ornamented in the style of a different time and place. Heavy stone steps led up to the solid imposing doors of each courtyard, their grand facades now weary and flaked with age. Weeds grew along some of the guttering, but each one, Tatyana reflected, was still a window on a better place in time; a memory written in mortar, of how this city had endured many changes, and a reminder that brick would always outlast flesh. A few, she noted, had already been transformed by Western money, the fresh coats of paint looking like new skin on old bones. The rest merely looked like corpses, abandoned to be eaten by the elements.

Fifteen yards behind her, a black Mercedes moved along the icy road, slowed down by the weight of its armour. Shading along the windows obscured from view the three men sitting inside the car. From the back seat, Henri Boissant leant forward, pointing to the woman standing alone on the side of the street. 'It is her,' he whispered softly to the driver.

Boissant watched carefully as her long, elegant legs stepped across the frozen pavement. A fine-looking woman, he thought to himself. He had seen pictures of her father – a tall brute of a man, with a face of iron and eyes like granite – but he knew nothing of her mother. It hardly mattered, he decided. The party bosses in those days had always married the best-looking women, and it was no doubt her mother's looks she had inherited. 'Closer,' he whispered to the driver.

The car ground to a halt five yards ahead of her. 'Take her,' said Boissant. The door locks sprang silently open. Both men eased out of their seats, standing on the pavement, leaving the doors open as they walked away from the car. Ahead, Tatyana watched them nervously. The larger man wore black jeans, a dark leather jacket wrapped loosely around his thick, animal torso. Over his head he wore a black woollen cap, and his black shades were pulled down over his eyes. The smaller man wore blue jeans, tucked into heavy military-style boots, a thick black sweater, and the same sort of cap and shades as his partner. She could see the breath from their nostrils escaping into the freezing air.

It took just three sharp paces for the men to reach her. She stood still, her eyes swivelling down the street; there was nobody in sight who might come to her aid. The smaller man held the back door open, pointing her towards the seat. 'A gentleman?' Tatyana said archly, looking into the man's shades.

He shook his head. 'Do as you are instructed,' he said, the words coming in a fierce monotone.

'And if I refuse?' she asked.

Boissant leant sideways, noting the delicate curve of her features, and the elegance of her expression; definitely someone who grew up as a party girl, he decided. In the deepest recesses of her heart, she would turn out to be one of us. 'Then he will kill you,' he said. 'But then you must already know that.'

Tatyana cast her eyes down. A French accent was not what she had expected on the lips of her captors. Why a Frenchman would come all the way here to Estonia to kidnap a tourist, she could not imagine. And yet she did not doubt his word. If she did not obey, he would kill her. She had seen his type before, and she knew what atrocities they were capable of.

Tucking her coat beneath her, she climbed into the back seat of the Mercedes, sitting as far as possible from Boissant. She could hear the clunk of the doors as the two men took the seats at the front, and heard the purr of the engine as it wheeled away from the kerb. 'Where are we going?' she asked.

'Not too far,' said Boissant softly. 'An hour's drive, maybe more. You'll find out when we get there.'

He leant towards her, and she noticed for the first time the deep scar running down his left cheek, and the shimmer of hardened steel in his eyes. 'You will need this.'

In his hand there was a long, narrow strip of black cloth. She fastened it around her eyes, tying a simple knot at the back. 'Why me?' she asked.

'You will find out soon enough,' answered Boissant.

For the next fifteen minutes she could hear the sounds of the city around her as the car breezed its way through the light traffic, but from then onwards the journey was completed in total silence. They were in the countryside now, she reasoned, and, from the slope of the car, probably heading to the gentle hills that stretched from the east of

Tallinn towards the Russian border. More than that she could not say. Listening to the car make its way through the hills, she realized there could only be one reason why they had kidnapped her. It was, for years, the thing she had dreaded most, the one thing from which she had always hidden.

By the time the car stopped, Tatyana had lost track of how long they had been travelling; she could not see her watch, and she had little natural sense of time. The blindfold was still wrapped around her face as an arm took her wrist and led her out. Engulfed in blackness, she could feel herself being led along a small path, through a creaking door, and then pushed down into a small wooden chair. She felt a rope being wrapped across her chest three times, its knots tightened securely behind her back. A hand moved up her neck and unwrapped the blindfold.

Her eyes blinking in the pale light, Tatyana looked upwards. There was straw on the ground, and a musty smell of animals pervaded the air. Light shone through two open windows, casting pale shadows across the floor. The larger of the two men knelt down at her feet, took her palm in his fat, greasy hand, and then from his pocket withdrew an ink pad. Carefully he pressed her left index finger into the pad, then onto a piece of paper, before standing and handing the print to Boissant.

The Frenchman examined it through an eyeglass, comparing the print to a small sheet of paper he had taken from his wallet. He nodded to himself, a thin smile playing across his lips. 'Collect the entertainment,' he snapped curtly.

Both men disappeared briefly from view. When they returned, they were dragging a girl and boy behind them, both with their hands and feet bound in ropes. Neither was any more than a teenager, Tatyana decided. Seventeen or eighteen, perhaps even younger; children grew quickly in this countryside. Both were simply dressed: the boy in faded jeans and a sweatshirt, the girl in a long skirt and a thick, grey nylon sweater. They were thrown roughly to the floor, where they lay, both panting for breath. Boissant approached Tatyana from behind, leaning closely into her ear, his breath warm against her cheek. 'Watch and learn,' he said softly.

A heavy boot swung into the boy's belly, doubling him up in pain.

Tatyana could see the contortions on his face as his hands tried uselessly to wriggle free from the ropes binding him. The other man knelt down beside the girl, slapping her hard across the face, bringing a trickle of blood to her lips. A low anguished moan escaped from her as the pain rattled through her frail body. The man turned her roughly on her side, drawing a knife from his hip and cutting through the ropes binding her legs, scratching her skin with the blade as he did so. A slow trickle of blood started to seep down to her ankles. 'Leave her, you bastard,' cried the boy, looking up at her attacker.

'Silence,' roared the larger man, swinging his boot into the boy's belly once more. The boy coughed violently, rolling over on his side in pain. With the back of his hand, the man crashed his knuckles into the boy's face. Even several feet away, Tatyana could hear the sound of the bones crunching beneath the force of the blow.

She looked up towards Boissant. 'No more,' she said. 'I will do what you ask of me. There is no need for this.'

The Frenchman smiled, his lips creasing and his chin swaying from side to side. 'It is necessary that you watch,' he said. His eyes rolled up towards the two men. 'Continue.'

The larger man knelt down beside the girl, pulling her legs roughly apart. A grim smile was evident on his lips; his brow was furrowed and a bead of sweat was dripping from his wide forehead. The girl was struggling, shaking her hips to try and wriggle herself away. Another blow caught her sharply on the side of the face, making her cough violently. 'Silence, peasant,' muttered the man.

Her skirt was scrunched up around her waist, and with a simple, sharp flick of his knife the man ripped aside her pants. The smaller man knelt beside her, punching her frail body in the side, making her recoil in pain, before pushing her thin legs roughly apart. Above her, the larger man started unbuckling the metal of his belt. He turned towards the boy. 'She'll enjoy this,' he said, his lips already creasing up into laughter.

The rape only lasted a few minutes. It was brutal and swift, a hard and cruel pounding against her helpless and battered body. The man grunted as he took her. His body jabbed downwards, and an expression of malicious pleasure contorted his face. When he was finished, he looked down at her contemptuously before spitting in her eye. 'Your turn,' he said.

The smaller man started running his fingers along her body, unbuttoning her tunic, exposing her small breasts to the cold air. He hammered his fist into her stomach, doubling her up in pain, and bringing more blood foaming to her mouth before pushing himself roughly inside her. At her side, the larger man was laughing. 'It is not elegant, is it?' observed Boissant, standing at Tatyana's side. 'My friends here have learned none of the subtleties of lovemaking. Crude, I am afraid. But effective, no?'

Tatyana remained silent. With their belts, the two men began whipping the boy. The leather straps crashed down on his skin with stinging force, leaving deep red lines where each blow had been struck. The metal buckles tore into his skin, tearing chunks of flesh, and blood began to seep from the open wounds, spilling onto the reddening straw. Whether the boy was still conscious after his beating, it was difficult for Tatyana to judge. A limp eye, clogged with blood, was still half open, but through the tattered skin surrounding his face it was impossible to tell if the pupil showed any signs of life. For his sake, Tatyana hoped the girl could not see what was happening.

To the side of the barn, the two men had collected a pair of shovels. They were digging, casting the damp mud to the wall. The shallow pit must have been no more than four or five feet long, judging by the amount of mud they had removed. It was two or three feet wide. When they were finished they looked up at Boissant. 'Now?' asked the larger man.

A curt nod signalled his assent. To what, Tatyana had no idea.

The shorter man picked up the boy by the back of his shirt, lifting him clear of the ground and leaving a pool of blood. The larger man slapped him roughly in the face a couple of times, as if to wake him up. The boy shook his head, blood spluttering from his mouth. Still alive, thought Tatyana. And conscious now.

'Leave him,' cried the girl from the floor, shattered teeth spitting from her lips as she struggled to pronounce the words. 'You can do anything you want to me. Just leave him.'

A look of fear accompanied the protest, as if she was expecting the boot that swiftly stamped down on her left arm, silencing her. The crunch of splintering bones sounded like the man had broken her elbow, but the will to cry had escaped her. Her elbow just lay on the ground, lifeless and deformed.

The shorter man took the boy to the pit, holding him above it with both arms, while the larger man took his head and pointed it downwards. He wriggled, struggling to break free, but he no longer had the strength left to fight. With a brutal thrust, the larger man pushed the boy's head towards the bottom of the pit, holding him up by his ankles. Behind him, the shorter man took one of the shovels, pushing the mud back down into the pit, surrounding the boy's head, burying him alive. Above the ground, his knees and ankles were still just moving.

The larger man knelt down beside the girl, turning her head in his hands so that she could see the boy's legs moving. 'We have a bet going,' he said. 'Fifty deutschmarks. My friend thinks we can both fuck you again before he dies. I think I'll still be fucking you when he stops moving. Who do you think will win?'

The girl remained silent, merely turning her head away. 'Don't ignore me, you bitch,' roared the man, the anger visible in the reddening of his face. Swiftly he unbuttoned his trousers again, kneeling down before the girl, pushing himself roughly inside her. He was starting to tire now, and his movements were slower, but there was still a grimace of cruel satisfaction playing upon his brutish face. The girl, with the strength she had left, was trying to look away, but the man kept turning her head back towards the two legs sticking from the ground. The movement was starting to fade as the boy's life ebbed away. After several minutes, the man pulled himself from the girl's body, emptying himself onto her face. His semen mingled with the blood still seeping from the cuts across her cheeks and mouth.

Boissant leant over, brushing his lips past Tatyana's ear. She could feel his cool breath on her skin. 'You are impressed, I believe?'

'I think it is horrible,' she replied, her eyes remaining rooted on the floor as she spoke.

Boissant turned on his heels, walking around the chair she was bound to, examining her, trying to gauge her reaction. 'There is nothing here that your family would not be familiar with,' he said slowly. 'Commissars, were they not? Yes, I am right, I think. Party men, your father, your grandfather as well. These things you have just witnessed, the game with the boy, these were all practised during the civil war, by the whites as well as the reds. Terror. That was always the way in this part of the world, and that is our trade. This is no different.'

Tatyana kept her eyes rooted to the floor. She could see no point in arguing with him. Whatever was about to happen now, it was surely no worse than the scenes she had just witnessed. Before her, the girl was watching as the legs sticking from the mud finally grew limp and lifeless, all motion ceasing. Her eyes rolled away, looking up towards the shorter man, now looming above her, his belt unbuckled. 'Finish her off,' barked Boissant.

The shorter man pushed himself into her body, his two hundred-pound torso thrusting between her bruised and aching legs. With his fist he started beating her face, slamming his knuckles into her cheeks and forehead until blood was streaming from the cuts. A few times she cried out in pain, but, before long, her voice shrivelled, and only a low, agonizing moan could be heard above the slow thrashing of her body against the ground. Eventually, still inside her, the man picked up her wrist, checking for her pulse. 'Nothing,' he said, looking up. 'She's dead.' He thrust his body into her a few more times, before eventually finishing with an ugly grunt. He pulled himself from her lifeless, wrecked body and started to buckle his belt.

'Not a pretty sight,' said Boissant coldly, looking down at the woman.

She could detect a glint of satisfaction in his dark, brown eyes. As if he was proud of his work, of the performance of his men, and the immensity of his ability to inflict suffering. As if he were an impresario of terror. Of guilt, remorse, or shame there was no sign. 'It was pointless,' Tatyana replied, struggling to conceal the fatigue, exhaustion and fear in her voice. 'You have done nothing that could not have been achieved with a simple threat.'

'I don't believe so,' said Boissant. He took one pace forward, standing closer to her bound feet. 'For you to follow my instructions exactly, it is necessary that you understand what will happen if you deviate in the slightest degree from what I tell you to do.' He walked forward, standing close to the dead girl, looking down, his expression one of mild curiosity as he examined the precise angles of her demise. 'It is interesting the way a dead body falls, is it not?' he continued. 'We have a choice in how we die, you know. Some people curl themselves into a tight ball, as if still hoping to protect themselves from the inevitable. They are the ones who are truly frightened. Others spread themselves outwards, as though they welcome the ending. They are the ones who have given up hope. You often find that among torture victims. Others lie limp, sprawled haphazardly, as though they did not know this was the end. They are the ones who have failed to realize what is really happening. I would say this girl comes into that category. I don't think she understood what was happening.'

He turned, walking back towards Tatyana. 'How do you think *you* would die?'

'Perhaps you will find out,' she said angrily.

Boissant laughed. 'Well said,' he replied. 'I suppose I may have that pleasure, but not today.' He leant forward, his eyes staring into her face. 'You see, death is not enough to frighten some people. Strange, I know, but true all the same. A quick painless death, after all, is not such a bad thing. A mere acceleration of what is anyway inevitable. Plenty of people are ready to face that, and for all I know you might be among them. But torture. That is the real terror.'

He turned away again, walking towards the buried boy, inspecting his upturned ankles, examining them as though they were slabs of meat on a butcher's counter. 'I don't believe that anyone could witness what has happened to these two young people and not be prepared to do anything, absolutely anything, to avoid the same fate for themselves.'

From the corner, Tatyana could see the two men smirking as they listened to their master's words. He was right, of course. He was an old practitioner of these skills, a craftsman of his ugly trade. There was, she knew, no way that she could contemplate ever encountering his anger. No way she could allow herself to become his victim. She would do anything that he asked, no matter how vile.

'Could you imagine seeing your husband upturned in the earth like this?' said Boissant. 'Buried alive, whilst the men who are killing him made love to you?' His tone was casual and cool, as though calculated to remind her of how little it would mean to him. 'Can you imagine being beaten and whipped, and then fucked to death by these two men?' He walked forward again, leaning down, looking into her eyes. 'You should try to imagine, because this is what I will do to you and your husband if you do not co-operate with me. Do I make myself clear?'

Tatyana nodded. A tear had formed in her eyes, one she would have wiped away were her hands free, and the salty liquid stung her skin. 'What do you want me to do?' she asked.

She is broken, thought Boissant. The way he thought she would be. The way they always were. 'Follow my instructions,' he said carefully.

'I will do as you ask,' Tatyana answered.

Boissant leant back against a wooden post, his feet digging into the soft earth. His eyes flickered across the woman's face, admiring the smooth delicacy of her skin, and the fine contours of her figure. To have to turn her over to the brutish desires of those two animals would be a shame. A waste of a fine body – one, no doubt, that with the right encouragement could be put to better uses.

He walked across the ground, standing closer to her, cradling her chin in his palm. He looked down into her eyes, hoping to read her expression, but was met with a blank indifference. That was sometimes the way, he reflected. When a person's spirit was broken, their will left them, and little remained except an empty, morbid dread of what the future might hold. But indifference could hide another message: a show of defiance, or a resolution to fight. I can peer into her eyes, but not into her soul, he reflected to himself. That was always impossible. 'You are a careful woman, I think,' he said. 'You will do as you are told. But remember, one slip, one mistake, and I will punish you instantly.

Perform your tasks well and you will be rewarded. That is a fair offer, I think.'

Tatyana looked up, meeting his eyes directly, and for a brief moment Boissant imagined he could catch a glimpse of the ice in her expression. 'Your work is done,' she said.

CHAPTER 1

Monday, 1 February

S ARAH LOOKED UP AT THE NUMBERS ON THE SCREEN, A HARD, impersonal row of pixels, each of them coloured red. The figures started to streak into each other as her vision blurred. I've just lost one million dollars, she told herself, the words sinking through her brain and stabbing at her chest. Not a great start to my first day in this job.

The clocks on the wall displayed the time in London, New York, Tokyo, Paris and Frankfurt. Just after 10.00, she noted. I have been an employee of the Leopard Fund for just over two hours and I have begun losing more money than most people make in a lifetime.

This, she told herself, can only get better.

Sarah had arrived at the gleaming modern offices of the fund at 7.45 that morning, precisely on time. Before stepping inside she had walked around the block twice to steady her nerves. The badge on the label the security guard gave her said Miss S. Turnbull, and it was from that the man who met her at the lobby had identified her. A tall, handsome American called David Sheldon, he took her towards her desk, then spent the next hour explaining Leopard Fund staff policies: no smoking inside the building, no drinking at lunchtime, no downloading porn from the web, a minimum twelve-hour working day, and no dealing privately without authorization from your department head.

'Ever done any actual trading?' said the next man, who introduced himself.

His name, he said, was Terry Semple. A tense, muscled character running to thirty-something plumpness, with fading hair and dark eyes slung back deep into his skull. Semple looked in his mid-thirties, but Sarah realized she could have been a decade wrong either way. As a senior trader with the fund, one of his jobs, he explained, was to show the new people how the system worked.

'I'm joining as a currency analyst,' said Sarah politely, tucking a lock of her thick blonde hair back under its clip. 'I don't think I'll actually have to trade.'

Semple grinned, took a packet of Polo mints from his pocket and popped one into his mouth. 'The Leopard is the biggest and most successful hedge fund in the world,' he said. 'Trading is what we do. It's sort of a ritual around here. When people join, we like them to do a bit of your actual real-life dealing. Nothing spectacular. Just so they get a feel for what the fund actually does.'

He leant over her desk, pointing to the Reuters and Bloomberg screens, both linked to separate keyboards. In less than two minutes, he explained the basics of using the machine to trade currencies. Sarah was familiar with the system from her last job, even though she had never tried it for herself. 'Have a go for yourself,' Semple suggested as he walked away. 'You'll soon get the hang of it. Anyone who makes a profit trading in their first morning gets to keep it,' he added. 'That's a house rule.'

Do they get to keep the losses as well? wondered Sarah gloomily. It was only fifteen minutes since Semple had left her, and she was already a million down. She had started with what she had thought would be a simple trade. The machine only dealt in units of ten million dollars, and Sarah had placed an order to switch three units of euros into Polish zlotys. That was thirty million dollars, but she knew the Polish central bank was due to publish inflation figures at nine; those, she expected, would show prices rising more swiftly than last month, raising pressure to hike interest rates, which should push up the currency. When she saw the announcement scrolling forwards on her Reuters screen, she could almost feel the blood stop pumping through her heart. Polish inflation was much lower than expected. The currency promptly sank by 3.4 per cent in the markets. Her zlotys were now worth $1,020,000 less than she had paid for them.

This can only get better, she reminded herself.

Cut your losers, and run your winners, Sarah decided. That was one of the few pieces of investment advice her father had given her, back when he was still a player in the markets. Using the keyboard, she sold the zlotys into dollars, then bought six units of Hungarian crowns. Should be safe enough, she told herself. Hungary's balance of payments figures were set to be released, which she calculated should be encouraging for its economy. The trade completed, she scanned the screen, anxiously waiting for the information. At 9:15 the numbers scrolled in front of her eyes. Hungary's current account had moved sharply into the red. In the next minute, the currency dropped by five per cent. Sarah had lost another three million dollars.

She looked out across the office. There must have been fifty, perhaps sixty, people. No more than ten women. Each person sat at a thin black desk, surrounded by three different computer screens: a Reuters and a Bloomberg terminal plus their own personal computer. Across the top of the hall, a continuous electronic ticker fed through the news and prices from the markets. The same information was scrolling across the desktop computers, but seeing it up on the wall, Sarah reflected, made it seem more vivid and more realistic. Each trader was looking intently at the screens, some of them talking at the same time into the mouthpieces hooked around their necks. None of them, so far as she could tell, spoke to each other very much.

She could see that the rouble had been falling all through the first thirty minutes of trading in London, and looked, she judged, as if it would keep going down. All the analysis she had ever done suggested that once the bears got a grip on the rouble it usually shifted down by at least ten per cent before it stabilized. That has to be okay, she told herself. Nobody ever lost money by selling the rouble. Her order this time was to short sell nine units, or ninety million dollars of roubles. The computer, she noticed, would not let her trade the other unit in her accounts, presumably, she guessed, because she had already lost three million. Never mind, Sarah told herself. This should make it up.

Sarah looked at the man at the next desk. About thirty she guessed, okay-looking if you liked computer nerds, which she didn't very much. He was wearing expensive but mismatched clothes, that suggested he shopped for effect rather than pleasure. When she caught his eye, she smiled in his direction. 'You new?' he said curtly.

Sarah nodded. 'You could show me the ropes,' she said, attempting a smile.

The man swivelled in his chair, looking back towards his screen. 'Nothing in it for me,' he said, turning back towards his terminal.

Nice attitude, thought Sarah to herself, turning back towards her own screen. The IMF had just announced it had reached agreement on the latest phase of its Russian debt rescheduling programme. Sarah could feel her heart sink. The rouble had just jumped by thirteen per cent against both the euro and the dollar, and it was still climbing. On the sell contracts she had placed ten minutes earlier, her losses now came to $11,700,000.

Her total losses for the morning, she calculated, were now almost sixteen million dollars.

For a moment she fell absolutely still, paralysed by indecision; the blood was starting to pump furiously through her veins and, beneath her, she could feel her legs starting to tremble. There was, she decided, no possibility she could admit to losing sixteen million dollars in her first morning with the fund. Only a certain amount of humiliation could be endured. One more trade, she told herself, the words echoing through her mind like bullets through a gun barrel. That is what I need to dig myself out of trouble.

It would have to be a derivatives trade, she realized. It would be risky, she knew, but nothing else could make enough money quickly enough to recover her losses before anyone found out. Looking at the screen, she noticed the weakness in the Czech crown seemed to be turning. It was up almost two per cent against the euro this morning, and looked to be starting a sustained rally on the back of encouraging unemployment statistics. You just have to move with the opportunities, Sarah told herself. Great traders forget their losses instantly, just as every great striker immediately forgets a missed penalty. That was something else her father had taught her.

Her fingers moved swiftly across the keyboard, placing an order to purchase seven and a half billion dollars-worth of Czech crowns. The buy options for that amount of money cost one per cent of the entire contract, seventy-five million dollars, which was just about what she had left in her Leopard Fund account. I'll sell them in a few minutes, thought Sarah to herself. Just as soon as I have made good my losses. Taking a deep breath, she closed her eyes and tried to calm the nerves rippling through her stomach. This should work, she told herself. It has to.

'Setback to Czech EU hopes,' read the story scrolling across the Reuters screen two minutes later. She switched over to the Bloomberg display. 'Czech Republic rebuffed by EU,' it read. She called up the information. 'The European Commission this morning said the Czech Republic's application to join the EU was likely to be delayed because the country was making slower than expected progress in harmonizing its legal system with that of the EU, according to a report released in Brussels today,' it began.

Sarah looked up to the currency board. The crown had already slipped almost two per cent against the euro. Smashing her fingers into the keyboard, she attempted to trade. I have to sell those contracts before this gets any worse, she thought to herself. The machine refused to respond, ignoring every command she keyed into it; even as her fingers battered the keyboard, it felt as if it had been unplugged. She could feel a sweat starting to form on her forehead, and a dull ache began to throb within her heart. A message flashed onto the screen. 'Your trading account has been suspended as the account is now empty,' it read, the words displayed in neat black lettering on a shimmering blue background. 'No more trades will be accepted. Thank you for using the system today.'

One hundred million dollars, she thought to herself. Turned into dust.

A silence seemed to descend upon her, as if she had suddenly disappeared into a vacuum. Around her, Sarah could see people talking into mouthpieces, hitting their keyboards, and walking quickly along the corridors, but she could hear nothing, as though she was trapped within an insulated bubble through which no sound could penetrate. She glanced towards the clock, watching as the second hand clicked towards 10.00. Only just over two hours since I walked though the door, she thought to herself. And I have just lost more money than most people could even dream about.

Sarah stared blankly at the computer screen, aware of her reflection caught in the glass of the monitor. Her skin, she noticed, had turned whiter, and her eyes had crept deeper into her face, as though they were retreating from the moment. Better not to look at anyone, she thought to herself. If I catch their eye they might ask me what is happening. The minutes seemed to tick painfully away, each second a prolonged, tortured agony. Sarah could feel her limbs begin to stiffen under the desk, but she was, for now, too frightened to move. Better just to sit here, she thought to herself, repeating the command again and again. Better not to say anything. Better not to move. Perhaps the whole situation will just go away.

Terry Semple looked at her curiously for a moment, leaning forward on the edge of his desk, but she ignored him, looking straight ahead, her eyes fixed on her computer screen. He offered her a crisp from the packet in his hand, but she said nothing; she could feel her lips starting to move, but no sound emerged. 'You've either done something brilliantly clever or amazingly stupid,' he said, leaning into her face, his expression suggesting he was betting on the latter. 'Because the chairman would like to see you.'

'Ten million?' said Tom, his tone betraying his surprise. 'You dropped ten million in a single week?'

From the look of anxiety fluttering across the man's face, Tom could already tell the answer was going to be yes. 'That's right,' answered John. 'The question is, how am I going to make it up?'

The other three men around the table nodded, but their lips remained motionless. Their silence roared through Tom's head, opening up seams of memory. 'And since it falls into my territory, I suppose it's up to me,' said Tom.

'It would be a big favour,' said John.

'Club rules, Tom,' said Andrew.

Rules, Tom reflected. In every community there were always codes that people lived and worked by. In today's business world, the main rule was very simple: be loyal to, and true to, your friends, not your company or your client, since there is a chance your loyalty to your friends might be repaid one day, whilst your loyalty to your company or your client will be forgotten by the end of the week. That much had always been agreed between them. It was the code on which they had forged their careers. 'Of course, of course,' said Tom, a grin spreading out across his lips. 'The only question is how.'

The Breakfast Club, named after one of their favourite films of the mid-eighties, met every Monday morning at the Bankside Grill, a small, old-fashioned cafe just off Cheapside, populated almost exclusively by spotty teenage traders from the nearby futures exchange, all of them with pale white skins and bright jackets with the names of their firms emblazoned across their backs. The club included Andrew Taylor, who now worked as a senior bond analyst at Morgan Stanley; Ian Fletcher, now the head of derivatives trading for Credit Lyonnais; Alan Gibson, now the equity strategist at HSBC; John Dundee, a senior fund manager at Mercury Asset Management; and Mark Jones, a colleague of Tom's at Samuelson & Co, the London subsidiary of Germany's giant KrippenBank. The five of them, plus Tom, had all started at what was then Morgan Grenfell on the same trainee intake fifteen years ago, and although they had since all gone their separate ways, they had remained friends ever since. For the first few years, they had met up one evening a week for a few drinks and a curry, but three years ago they had switched it to breakfast after both Taylor and Fletcher became fathers and their wives started to cut up rough about their staying out late, drinking. Now they all had children, apart from Tom, and breakfast together once a week was the best way of staying in touch. 'That and christenings, of course,' Tom had remarked when the idea of switching to the morning had first been suggested.

'Our European fund has tanked out on some Hungarian pharmaceuticals stocks,' continued John. 'Nothing much wrong with the companies, they'll come good in time. Sentiment is against them right now. It needs a boost.'

'We could advise some of the German and Dutch funds to move in there,' said Jones. 'That wouldn't be too much trouble.'

'I'll get the derivatives boys to starting pepping up the currency,' said Fletcher. 'That should help a bit.'

Tom looked across the table at Dundee, noticing how much better the man was looking already. A memory started to meander through his mind; they were all in the first-year graduate trainee intake in 1982, fresh from Oxford and Cambridge. They were naive and ambitious, the most lethal combination Tom could imagine. In an attempt to impress the firm, they had cooked up between them a ridiculously optimistic series of trades in the gold futures market they believed would make a fortune. It hadn't, and only by covering it up between themselves, then painfully working the position out over the next six months, had they saved themselves from certain dismissal and possible fraud charges. Ever since, the club rule had been strict: when anyone is in a jam, the others help out.

'You'll be back in profit on that fund by the end of the day,' Tom said, taking a sip of his cup of tea, and spearing a fried egg with his fork. 'The problem is already solved.'

I suppose, thought Sarah, when you walk to the gallows it feels something like this.

Right now, Semple had told her, the Chairman wanted to see her. Without delay. Slowly, she had pulled herself up from her desk, unsure if her legs would still be strong enough to support her. Semple stretched out a hand to help her as she stood. 'Right up the stairs,' he said. 'You can't miss it.'

Sarah could feel the eyes of the floor fixed upon her as she began walking towards the staircase that circled down towards the edge of the training floor. Sixty people were all looking in her direction as she moved across the black, tiled floor, the heels of her shoes clicking against the hard stone surface. For a moment, all the phone calls seemed to have stopped, the entire organization devoted just to staring at her. Towards the back of the hall she could hear two men laughing. They know, she thought to herself. They all know what I have just done and they all hate me.

Jean-Pierre Telmont was a legend in the financial markets, the founder and chairman of the Leopard Fund and one of the richest men in the world. Sarah knew plenty about him, but even when she was offered a job at the fund it had not occurred to her she might actually meet him. Not on the first day. And not in circumstances like these. But then it had never occurred to her that she might lose a hundred million dollars either.

She took a moment to try and control her breathing but realized it was useless. Her heart was stabbing against her chest and her head was swirling with a thousand different apologies and excuses. Above her she could see a tall, slim, immaculately-scented secretary rising from behind a frosted glass desk, who, standing silently in front of Sarah, pointed her towards the door. Sarah tried to steady herself, before stepping awkwardly inside, catching the edge of her jacket on the doorway as she did so. How could you excuse a hundred million dollars, she asked herself? How could you ever come up with an apology that big?

Telmont's desk was at the back of the room, almost thirty feet from the door. A sheer pane of glass rose up from behind him, looking out across the Thames and then on to the City beyond. Sarah walked towards the centre of the room, her feet moving swiftly over the stripped pine floorboards before she realized there was nowhere to sit down. Apart from the large black leather chair behind his desk, the room was entirely empty.

'Capital,' said Telmont, rising slowly from his desk, 'is the hardest thing in the world to accumulate, but the easiest thing in the world to destroy.'

He was no more than five-six, five-seven, with a slight droop to his shoulders, thick, tanned skin, and a voice that deepened every time he struck a vowel. 'I'm sorry,' Sarah replied, aware her tone was cracking.

'Sorry,' repeated Telmont, seeming to toss the word into the air and watch it tumble to the floor. 'I imagine you *are* sorry.' He paused, looking away from her, his eyes drifting towards the window. 'But not nearly as sorry, I suppose, as my investors. They are probably a hundred million times sorrier than you are.'

Sarah could feel the tears starting to streak her mascara; ten or twenty times sorrier, perhaps, she thought to herself, but not a hundred million times sorrier. Nobody could be that sorry. 'It just seemed to run away from me,' she said.

Telmont turned away from the window and, with a single motion of his index finger, beckoned her towards the desk. She walked slowly across the floor, resting her hands next to his computer. 'Most of the women cry,' he said. 'Sometimes even the men. But the women cry because they are sorry about the money, I think. The men cry because they are sorry for themselves.'

Sarah looked into his eyes, and saw that he was laughing at her. 'If I use this password,' Telmont continued, his hands running across the keyboard, 'Then I can change all the numbers coming up onto the Reuters and Bloomberg screens. I can even feed in dummy stories.'

It took a moment for Sarah to realize what he was saying; the words hung in the space between them, as though they were just there for decoration. Then it hit her; the last two hours had just been an elaborate joke, created by rigging the computers so it looked as if she had lost a fortune. She could feel the relief wash through her, yet at the same time she could feel a beat of anger drumming close to her chest. 'It was just a joke,' she said slowly. 'I didn't really lose any money.'

Telmont smiled. 'Fortunately so,' he answered.

'I suppose I should have realized,' Sarah said softly. 'Nobody gets that unlucky.'

Telmont shook his head. 'People get that unlucky all the time,' he said, standing away from the desk and walking across from the room. 'This is more than a little joke we like to play on our new recruits. It is a matter of teaching them what it is like to lose. Only then will they realize how little they would care to repeat the experience.'

Sarah turned her blue eyes up towards his. 'I think I've learnt that now,' she replied.

The good groove, thought Tom to himself. That just about captured it.

Later in the evening, he would find it hard to recall how those words slipped into his mind, and the mood that accompanied them. They were fragments, shreds of a memory, explicable only in the context of a very different world from the one he inhabited now. And yet, at the time, just a few hours ago, they had seemed to express everything he felt.

He had been riding home on the District Line, another day at the City offices of Samuelson and Company completed. An *Evening Standard* lay on his lap, but nothing in the news had engaged his interest for more than a few moments. A bunch of yellow roses was tucked beneath his arm, flowers he had bought from the stand outside Monument station, a place where the woman was familiar with his wife's taste for yellow. How he had slipped into the habit of buying her roses at the beginning of every week, he could no longer recollect, and yet it was now part of their routine: flowers, dinner, sex, all in the same order, every Monday evening. It was, he reflected, a pleasant and relaxing start to the week, even if he sometimes wondered if they were slipping into too much of a routine.

A few lines from a Van Morrison song were humming through his mind. *'You can't stop us on the road to freedom/You can't stop us, 'cos our hearts are free/She's as sweet as Tupelo Honey/Just like honey from the honey tree.'* The words looped through his mind, running on instant replay, locked into an aural backdrop that blacked out the sweaty mass of commuters hanging on to the railings of the tube train.

The good groove, Tom reflected to himself. Why the thought had come to him just then, he had no idea, but he remembered reading a Van Morrison interview once, where he was asked the only question that really mattered: how was it that all his records sounded exactly the same? With the sort of absolute wisdom, authority and finality that only a Celt can lend to a fundamentally ordinary thought, Morrison replied, 'When you find the good groove, there is no need to change it.'

The walk from Gloucester Road tube station to the small mews house they had shared for the three years they had been married took no more than ten minutes, but the words stayed with him for most of the journey. There was a simple, almost elemental, truth there, something that probably only a musician could capture. A good groove was what he and Tatyana had together. There was no need to change it.

Indeed, he reflected, there was no need to change anything very much. He had a job he enjoyed, one that combined his interests in economics with the politics and history of Eastern Europe. Since the stock markets in those countries had developed, the bank had valued him a lot more highly. True, he was not yet on the board, but then he was still only thirty-seven, and he was only a couple of promotions away. That could come in time, and, anyway, whether it did or not no longer worried him as much as it might have done when he was younger, or as much as it might worry his friends in the club. There was plenty of money coming in, more than enough to support the two of them, and to pay for a couple of children in due course. They had everything they needed.

He was surprised to find the door double-locked. A couple of evenings a week Tatyana might go out with some of the girlfriends she had made in London since moving here from Estonia four years ago. She had involved herself in a couple of charities to build up a network of acquaintances in her new city, and supported a group that raised money for charities in Estonia, though since few people in London could even locate the place on a map, the amounts were never huge. And she had been starting to do some work on translating one of the classics of Estonian folk history into English. All of those things kept her busy and interested in life, and sometimes took her away from home in the evenings. But not on Mondays. On Monday they were always together. That was part of the groove.

Tom turned the key in the lock, opening the door, and switched on the light. The entrance to the house opened straight onto the sitting room, a space they had furnished together, and which reflected both of their tastes. The room was painted a pale yellow, with a fireplace dominating one wall and three large pictures on each of the other walls, works they had chosen together on their travels through the frozen, northern hinterland of the old Soviet Union. On the mantelpiece was a small bronze bust of Stalin that Tatyana had bought as a joke. Tom checked his watch. It was just after seven-thirty, and, he supposed, if he started making supper she would no doubt be home soon.

He spotted the letter as soon as he walked into the kitchen; a simple, plain white envelope with his name written on it. He held it between his fingers for a moment, looking down at the familiar script. He took a knife from the drawer, slit the envelope open, and, sitting down on one of the wooden chairs around the table, started to read.

My dearest Tom,

This has been a painful letter for me to write, and only a very few of my emotions can be expressed in words. I have thought long and hard before making this choice, and have many times wondered what phrases or condolences I might choose, but now that I have finally put pen to paper, few of them seem to have any relevance. What can I say, other than that I am leaving and that I shall not return?

It is not something I have done lightly or casually. Were I a better woman, one more deserving of your love and affection, it is not something I would have done at all. That does not matter anymore. My path is chosen now, and I must make my own journey. It will take me away from you, and you from me. That is the way it must be. Do not try to question it.

Today I have left this house, never to return. I am with another man to whom my heart now belongs. Do not try to find me. It will only increase the pain this separation will cause for both of us. I can only say how grateful I am for all the love and kindness you have shown me over the past few years, and how guilty I feel at not having been

able to find a better currency with which to repay you. Do not seek
any more explanation than I have been able to offer in this letter. There
is none.

I hope you may soon find the happiness you deserve with another.

With my love and regrets,

Tatyana

From the movement of the single sheet of paper between his fingers,
Tom could tell that his hand was shaking, but he felt as if he had lost
all control of his senses. For that moment, he was convinced he could
neither see, sense, hear nor touch; all contact with the outside world
had suddenly shrivelled to nothing and only an inner, dark desolation
remained. Somewhere he could feel his pulse racing as he glanced
downwards once more, his eyes locking almost randomly on different
words as he scanned the page again and again. He tried putting the
words in a different order, rearranging them, turning them inside out,
breaking up the letters, hoping there might be some strange code there,
something he could decipher, something that could give him some hope,
but nothing made any difference. The meaning was always the same. She
was gone.

He could feel the stiffness in his knees as he stood from the chair,
placing the note carefully, face downwards, on the table. His shoulders
were hunched, and he could hear a long sigh escaping from his lips.
He glanced briefly around the kitchen, noting how everything, the pots
and pans, tables and chairs and machines, were all in their place.
Everything was as it should be. Except for the woman who inhabited
the place, the woman for whom it had been created. Everything was in
its familiar place. The sofa and two chairs were neatly arranged around
the coffee table. A couple of books were lying open: the latest Grisham,
and a nineteenth-century travel book that had recently been re-issued in
paperback. A coffee cup was sitting on the table, a smudge of lipstick
still visible on its rim. Tom picked it up and examined it, a couple of
lines from an old country song forcing their way into his mind. *'Your*

lip-print on a half-filled cup of coffee/That you bought and didn't drink/But at least you thought you wanted it/That's so much more than I can say for me.' The song disappeared, vanishing almost as quickly as it appeared, and his mind was empty again.

Who could this other man be? he thought to himself. There was no one Tatyana had spoken of, nor anyone among their mutual acquaintances who he could possibly imagine in the role. An image reared up in his mind, fierce and uncontrollable, of Tatyana lying beneath another man, her arms outstretched, her legs curled up in the air. He could see her clearly, the picture perfectly distinct, but the man he could not make out. It was impossible to put a face to him.

One day, that would have to be done, he decided. He would have to see the man, to find out who he was and what he looked like. Another day, another time, he reflected. After all, there would be plenty of empty hours to fill. Almost by accident, his hand brushed against the CD player, switching the machine to play. Noise, he thought. Any kind of noise would be better than this endless, empty silence.

The opening bars of a Julie London song started to hum through the room; a mellow, torched jazz, both sentimental and bitter at the same time. *'Take care of everything/I'm leaving my wedding ring/Don't look for me, I'll get ahead/Remember, darling, don't smoke in bed.'*

Tom listened, enjoying the lushness of the strings that soared on each successive upbeat, before a thought began to burrow forward in his mind. He started to scan the shelves, looking for the CD cover. Pulling the box from a pile, he glanced down at the listing. He was right: 'Don't Smoke in Bed' was track seven of the 1960 album 'Around Midnight'. If the disc just happened to be in the player, the last track already played, it would start again at track one. He looked down at the machine. It had been programmed; track seven selected to run in a continuous loop as soon as anyone pressed play. The song had been deliberately chosen, for his ears only, to fill the room after she had departed. Maybe she was worried I might start smoking again, thought Tom. Even though it is more than two years now since I gave up.

CHAPTER 2

Tuesday, 2 February

SARAH SCANNED HER EYES ALONG THE SEATING PLAN, SEARCHing for her own name. A Mr George Stockton, of Coopers & Lybrand, was seated to her left; to her right, a Mr Tom Bracewell of Samuelson & Co. An accountant and a banker, she thought to herself. How much fun can a girl pack into one evening?

Left to herself, she would probably not have come this evening. After a month of living in New York, preparing for her job at the fund's American office, this was her first trip back to London; they had flown her back for the induction week. There were plenty of friends she would have preferred to have been spending time with. But when you worked for the Leopard Fund, and when Jean-Pierre Telmont himself was speaking, it was not an invitation you could turn down. At least, not after her disastrous performance on the first day.

Her eyes wandered across the room, looking to see if there was anyone she recognized. A couple of guys from the office, she noted, but they were not among the people she had met yesterday, and Sarah was not in the mood for introducing herself. If she was being honest, her heart was still fluttering after the shock of yesterday morning. There were several people she recognized from her last job as a currency analyst with one of the big London banks, but not anybody she had been close to. Otherwise it was the usual City crowd: men in dinner jackets, and women in cocktail dresses and power suits, all making anxious conversation with one another. Heaven help me if I ever start enjoying this stuff, she decided to herself.

The sound of the bell summoning guests to dinner was a relief; at least now nobody would have a chance to strike up a conversation with her. Sarah walked through to table nineteen, noticing she had been placed close to the back of the hall. Not a very important person, she realized. But then, she had only just joined the firm, and her job consisted mainly of advising on currency positions. She was no more than cannon fodder, and for the moment happy to keep it that way.

Eight people were seated around the table, including two other women, one of whom worked for a law firm, and the other the wife of a guest. Sarah introduced herself to all of them in turn. As she sat down, she glanced through the menu: a halibut salad, followed by beef Wellington and then a cranberry mousse. There were also two good wines, Sarah noted, relieved to see there would be some entertainment. 'How can you work for this guy?' asked Tom.

Sarah held the fork she was about to place in her mouth, and pondered her reply. As an opening remark, it was surprisingly direct. Rude even. 'How can you eat his food?' she replied. As she spoke, she turned to face the man on her right, examining him more closely than she had done on their brief introduction ten minutes earlier. He was of average height, with black hair starting to grey slightly around the temples and a face that looked as if it had been chiselled from oak. Formal dinner dress did not suit him, she decided. He would look better in something more rugged: a Barbour jacket, perhaps, or a thick Aran sweater. Aside from that, he looked much like the rest of the City crowd. Except for the eyes, she noted. His eyes were shot to pieces, as if he had trouble sleeping.

'That's different,' he said. 'Supping with the devil is quite different from being on the payroll.'

'Okay, he's no saint, but then he's French,' said Sarah, looking across at Tom. 'They're Catholics. They leave morality to the priests. They don't expect it in their businessmen. Certainly not in their financiers.'

Something about the way Telmont's eyes swivelled around the room commanded silence, Tom decided, even though there must have been three hundred people present. A slim man, his black hair was swept back over his long, craggy face. His brown eyes were sunk deep into his skull, and his skin was heavily tanned, deep grooves running through it, like the cracks on the face of a cliff. A face, Tom decided, made from stone rather than flesh.

'The financial markets stand at a crossroads,' he began, addressing the room in a gentle soothing tone, 'Between opportunity and despair, between light and darkness, between the land and the sea, between the valley and the mountain. A time is fast approaching when we must choose. Do we want to rule the markets, or do we want the markets to rule us?'

Tom looked closely, but he could see no sign of a teleprompter, nor any notes on the table. Telmont spoke with a fluent ease, delivering each word with perfect weight, as if it had just occurred to him, and yet expressed as though he had been searching for years to find it. It was, he decided, an impressive performance.

Telmont drew his shoulders up, pausing for breath before continuing. 'There are those who would count the Leopard Fund among the forces of darkness within the financial community. There are those who would describe us as part of a culture of chaos. I remember reading such descriptions, in the main after we played a part, a very small part I might add, in the break-up of the European Monetary System back in 1992 and 1993, or in the collapse of the Asian currencies back in 1997. Hedge funds, of which ours is among the most prominent and the most successful, were accused of creating both those financial crises, of blowing away economic policies carefully created by national governments, of risking plunging the world into a new recession.'

Telmont hesitated, looking up to the ceiling of the large, heavily ornamented hotel ballroom where the dinner was being held, examining the paintwork as if he were searching for inspiration. 'And yet it is not funds such as our own that create the turbulence,' he continued. 'To blame those such as ourselves is to take a piece of driftwood floating on the top of a wave, and to blame that for the power of the tides.

The Leopard Fund moves with the great waves of economic history better than most of its rivals, and it understands the tidal forces of the markets at a deeper level than most, but it does not create those forces.' He hesitated, his eyes scanning the room. 'Governments still talk as if they controlled the markets, but the truth is the markets control them,' continued Telmont, the pitch of his voice starting to rise. 'And yet it is a mistake to believe that because of this the markets are out of control. Far from it. The markets are controlled by the people, not as a group, but as individuals. To those who say we should control the markets, make them safer, I would say only this. You should change the people, for they are the market.'

Telmont sat down as suddenly as he had risen, disappearing from view, leaving the audience momentarily confused, unsure whether he had finished speaking. A ripple of applause started to spread through the room, quiet at first, then louder. Telmont, a smile playing on his face, rose briefly to acknowledge the applause before sitting down again, a large glass of brandy lodged in his right hand.

'It's amazing how many people will just applaud money,' remarked Tom, looking across at Sarah.

'I don't see you sitting on your hands,' said Sarah.

'That's because he likes to be part of the world, and to be part of the world you must clap for the money.'

Tom glanced back over his shoulder. The man who had just spoken was leaning slightly, his hand resting on the back of Sarah's chair. What remained of his grey hair was combed in a fringe over his forehead, and his playful, amused expression suggested this was some kind of test. Tom got to his feet. 'How are you, Victor?' he asked.

'Fine, fine,' answered the man, looking across at Sarah. 'Your friend?'

'Sarah Turnbull of the Leopard Fund,' said Tom. 'This is Victor Radek. He taught me economics at business school.'

'You didn't like the speech?' said Radek.

'Not much,' replied Tom. 'It was pompous and self-important.'

Radek laughed. 'Those aren't Anglo-Saxon qualities, are they? But that doesn't mean he might not be right.' He turned towards Sarah, nodding curtly. 'No doubt we will meet properly some other time.'

Before she had a chance to reply, Radek had already turned to leave, moving through the tables towards the cloakroom. 'Notice the slight limp,' said Tom. 'A memento of the camps, I believe.'

'The camps?' said Sarah, the surprise evident in her voice.

'You have never heard of Radek?'

'Should I?'

'Not really, no, not unless you happened to know a lot about Eastern European economics,' answered Tom. 'He is Czech, and he used to be a prominent economist under the Communist Party there, a rising young star. Then in the 1968 revolution he turned on the regime and started criticizing it. Pointing out that central planning could never work, that sort of thing. After the Russian tanks moved in, they locked him up for a few years. Then I think he spent ten years or so working as a park warden in some provincial town. Eventually, some academics at the LSE managed to get him out to the West. He knows more about the economies of Eastern Europe than any other person alive.'

'That would be such a waste of a life,' said Sarah. 'To spend it fighting against a cause that was lost anyway.'

Tom looked across the table. 'There are lots of different ways to waste your life,' he said. 'You just have to choose one from the shelf.'

The cold night air blew fiercely into Henri Boissant's face. He drew the collar of his long leather coat up around his neck, and dug his hands deep into his pockets. He had always hated the cold. Even during his training for the French special forces, the Régiment des Parachutistes d'Infanterie de Marins, when he had spent whole nights sleeping out in the forests of Brittany, or the deserts of Algeria, he had loathed every minute. Sweltering, furnace-like heat he could march through all day. But the chilled ice of a frozen night had always disturbed him.

Tallinn in February, he decided, was not a place for a man who disliked the cold. The most northern of the three Baltic states, it was frozen solid through most of the winter months, temperatures seldom rising above zero, and daylight never appearing for more than a few brief, murky hours. Still, he reflected, work was work, and his mission was only just beginning.

The walk from the modern Palace Hotel to George Malone's bar on Harju Street took no more than ten minutes. Why there should be an Irish theme pub in a place like Tallinn, Boissant could not even begin to imagine. Ever since the Communists had been thrown out, the place had become so neat and tidy and efficient, it was now spiritually as close to Scandinavia as it was geographically. It was about as far from Ireland as you could get while remaining in Europe. And yet Irish bars seemed to be springing up all over the region. Why not a French bar, Boissant wondered? Somewhere you could get a cognac or a Pernod. Perhaps even something decent to eat.

A blast of Irish music hit him in the face as he stepped into the bar; Van Morrison or The Pogues, Boissant noted with distaste, or some other rubbish. He stepped up to the bar, ignoring the range of Irish stouts and bitters on offer, told the barman to bring him a bottled lager, and sat down at a table towards the back of the room. Lighting up a Gitanes, he took a deep drag on his cigarette and surveyed the bar. Empty for a Tuesday evening. There were a few locals, a couple of Germans who looked liked bankers, and two girls who might or might not be tourists. Not Irish, at least, thought Boissant. That was something.

Gregor Cepartinu noticed Boissant as soon as he walked into the bar. The Frenchman nodded in his direction, but he preferred to walk to the bar first, ordering a pint of Murphy's ale and sinking his lips into its smooth head. It was only after he could feel the beer in his stomach that he sat down opposite Boissant. 'I was told I had to see you,' he said.

Boissant dragged deeply on his cigarette, blowing a cloud of smoke into the air. 'It's time,' he said.

Cepartinu nodded. He had known this moment would come, and although part of him dreaded it, there was elation as well. It would be dangerous, but also exciting. And then there was the money. 'Is there any change in the instructions?' he said.

'No, just the timetable,' said Boissant firmly. 'We want it to start tomorrow.'

'Then I will need the money right away.'

From his inside jacket pocket, Boissant drew a small slip of paper, pushing it across the table. 'A million dollars has been deposited in this account in Luxembourg in your name. You use it as you see fit. Just make sure the job is done.'

Glancing down at the scrap of paper, noting the number of the account, and committing it instantly to memory, Cepartinu could feel a trace of sweat forming on his brow. 'You don't need a receipt,' he said with a thin smile.

Boissant shrugged, reaching for another Gitanes. 'We work on trust,' he said. 'We trust you know that if you fuck with us, we kill you. It's that simple.'

Cepartinu nodded nervously, aware the sweat on his brow was growing hotter and stickier. 'Just one question,' he asked. 'Why would a Frenchman come all the way to Tallinn and give me a million dollars to try and destroy confidence in the Estonian stock market?'

Boissant stood up, emptying his beer bottle with one swig. 'Work it out for yourself, Einstein,' he replied, stubbing out his cigarette. 'A million dollars buys me the right to remain silent.'

CHAPTER 3

T HE OFFICES OF SAMUELSON & CO WERE AT LEAST FAMILIAR, Tom reflected. He had been there for six years now, enough time in any City firm to be counted among the veterans. Encroaching middle age, Tom supposed to himself, but he found he quite liked the status of a survivor; it allowed him to adopt a tone of self-deprecating weariness around the office, as if he had seen it all before. Which in many cases I have, he realized. The markets only really had three states – panic, euphoria and boredom – and after a few years you had seen all three more times than you cared to remember.

He walked briskly through the trading floor towards his own cubicle in the research department. There was the usual ugly scent on the floor, he noted; a mixture of aftershave, electricity, and half-eaten McDonald's meals, the three commodities the dealers seemed to need to get through the day. Combined, they produced a pungent aroma that seeped into every crack of the building. I would recognize that smell anywhere, thought Tom to himself. And it would usually tell me which way the market was going.

This morning, there was a taste to it he could almost feel on his lips. The market was edgy and uncertain. It was a selling day, that was certain.

Tom sat down at his desk and looked straight into his photo of Tatyana, feeling his pulse start to race as he did so. Shit, he thought. For the next few moments he just stared at one of the photographs, lost in the mystery and beauty of the woman. Tatyana had long, dark hair, which curled down the back of her neck, and a fringe which just touched the edge of her deep, watery eyes. Her forehead was high, giving way to narrow, neatly-sculpted cheekbones, and around her lips there was an expression of beguiling innocence. Even though she was a woman of twenty-eight when this picture was taken – in a hiking lodge in northern Finland on their honeymoon, Tom recalled bitterly – she had the freshness and the immediacy of a girl at least a decade younger.

His fingers touched the edge of the frame. Do I keep it here, he wondered, because I hope to find her and to bring her back? Or do I throw it away because I want to forget about her, and start life afresh?

'What the fuck is happening in Estonia, Tom?'

He glanced over his shoulder, to see Mark Jones leaning over the partition that separated his cubicle from the rest of the office. Another economist, covering mainly Latin America, Jones was the only other member of the Breakfast Club who worked at KrippenBank. 'Has something happened?' asked Tom, aware he had been so preoccupied with the photograph he had not yet checked either his Reuters or Bloomberg screens.

'The currency has already fallen out of bed, and the index there is down about thirty points,' replied Jones, walking through into the cubicle, sitting on the edge of the desk and looking down at Tom. 'Are you all right? You look like crap.'

'A rough couple of days, that's all,' answered Tom. 'What do you think is happening?'

'No idea,' said Jones, clipping his thumbs into his bright blue braces. 'It's your area. There is an investment meeting at 10.30, so I guess it will be discussed then. The fund management people will need some idea of whether they should be getting out.'

'I'd better get my head around it,' said Tom.

'Nobody will be too worried, I don't suppose,' said Jones, getting up to leave. 'It's a Mickey Mouse little market. Nobody cares very much.'

I care, thought Tom, turning towards the screens on his desk and calling up the stories he could find on the Estonian market. Jones was right, of course. With a total value of eighteen billion pounds, the Estonian market was tiny by world standards; there were plenty of banks or fund managers, and even a few individuals, who could buy the whole place and pay cash. It could disappear from the face of the earth tomorrow and no serious money would have been lost. But that was to ignore the connections between all the different financial markets. Everything fitted together, likes pieces of a jigsaw.

The facts were plain enough to see. The Estonian currency had opened this morning thirty per cent down on its central rate against the euro. That in turn had led to speculation that the country's central bank would be forced to abandon its target rate, feeding anxieties into the stock market. The TALSE, the standard index for the country, had fallen heavily on widely circulating rumours of an imminent currency devaluation. Banks, in particular, had fallen hard, and stories were starting to gather momentum that at least two would fail because they would no longer be able to pay the interest on euro-denominated bonds they had issued.

Tom read through the reports on both news terminals, tracking the development of the crisis over the past two hours. What was impossible to see was any reason for the initial fall in the currency. The Estonian economy, according to most of the analysts who monitored its progress, was basically in good shape; industries had been privatized, inflation stabilized, and the budget deficit bought under control. There was absolutely no reason for the currency to collapse this morning. He looked up again at the picture of Tatyana, still sitting on the side of the desk where he had left it. What reason do you need for things to collapse suddenly? he thought to himself. And where do you start searching for an explanation?

A summons was the only way to describe it. When she had arrived at the London office this morning, still recovering from the amount she had drunk last night, the tickets and a note had been waiting on her desk. Telmont wished to speak to her, and since he happened to be in Germany this morning, he would see her there. The tickets were for the 9.30 flight to Munich. Luckily, her passport was in her handbag. That had been one of the sharpest instructions when she joined the fund. Always carry a passport: when the fund wants you to move, you move.

A car collected her at the airport, then turned eastwards from the city towards Augsburg. It was not a place she had ever visited before, and as the car started to draw through the tidy streets on the edges of the old city, she admired the intricate Gothic stonework that ornamented the houses. Unlike most German cities, it had survived the war with most of its history intact; the damaged buildings had long since been immaculately restored. The town, she observed, reeked of the kind of comfortable, arrogant Middle European prosperity that took generations to acquire.

The driver pulled up outside a church, opened the door for Sarah, and with a quiet smile indicated that she should go inside. She could feel the pit of her stomach starting to tense. A small church in Germany, she reflected, seemed an odd place to be holding a business meeting at close to lunchtime on a wintry day in February.

On the outside, the church of St Anna appeared a modest, medieval structure, of the sort that might be found in abundance in every ancient European town. By the doorway, she noticed David Sheldon, the smart young American she had met on Monday morning. He stepped briskly towards her, touching her lightly on the arm. 'Jean-Pierre is talking with someone else right now,' he said. 'We'll have to wait a moment.'

'Does he regularly hold business meetings in this church?' asked Sarah.

Sheldon smiled. 'Only occasionally, at least in the year I've been working for him,' he replied. 'He seems to like it. He's quite a religious man, you know.'

'Don't they mind?' asked Sarah. 'The priests, I mean. After all, mammon does not have many better representatives than the Leopard Fund.'

'That's sure true,' said Sheldon, chuckling. 'I think the Leopard

Foundation makes a reasonable contribution to the upkeep fund every year.' He looked towards the doorway, where a middle-aged man had just left. 'The last meeting is finished. I think it is your turn now.'

Sarah stepped carefully inside. At first glance the interior seemed as modest as the outside, but towards the edge of the nave she could see the glimmerings of a fabulous chapel. Telmont was sitting in one of the pews towards the altar, a grey overcoat slung over his shoulders, and with his head bowed slightly, a pose more of contemplation than prayer. Sarah was uncertain how you were supposed to introduce yourself to your boss in a church; not by crossing yourself, that much she was sure of. She approached the pew and sat down a few yards along the wooden bench. Telmont turned to look at her, his pale eyes locking onto her, alert with curiosity. 'You are not a Catholic, I suppose,' he said.

Sarah shook her head. 'Anglican,' she replied.

'It makes no difference,' he said softly, looking away from her and up towards the altar. 'Did you see the Estonian currency collapsed this morning? What should we make of that, I wonder?'

'An over-dramatic reaction to a persistent balance of payments problem, I suppose,' said Sarah, aware she was thinking on her feet. 'Or instability in the financial system. Those are the usual reasons for developing country currencies to collapse.'

Telmont nodded, looking towards her, and Sarah had to confess that, even though he was now nearing sixty, he was still an attractive man; there was a hard intelligence in his expression that endured even as his bones and skin started to weaken. 'You don't think it might be the start of a more general collapse of the Eastern European markets?'

Sarah hesitated before replying. 'I don't believe so,' she said. 'Those economies are now structurally sound. There is no reason for a general collapse.'

'I will be making a speech in a couple of days, when I would like to talk about this subject,' said Telmont. 'You should draft me something outlining that argument. I have been impressed by the intellectual vigour of some of your work before we hired you, and I would like you to contribute to the overall strategy of the fund.'

Sarah nodded. 'Of course.'

'Come with me,' said Telmont, standing up and walking towards the chapel to the side of the main altar. Sarah followed, both of them remaining silent. From a small notice at the side, she saw the chapel was called the Fuggerkapelle. The transformation once you stepped through from the nave was dazzling; where the church was consistently downbeat, the chapel was a lavish and ostentatious display of religious imagery. A rich, cold marble floor led up to an organ decorated with painted shutters, glimmering in the coloured light which beamed down from the stained glass windows. 'If the global financial markets have a shrine, which they probably don't deserve, then this would be the place,' said Telmont, looking up at a group of sculptures on the wall. 'Have you heard of the Fugger family?'

If this was a test, Sarah would have to admit she had failed. 'I'm afraid not,' she answered.

'This chapel was built by two brothers, Ulrich and Jacob Fugger, in 1509, as a private place of worship,' said Telmont. 'If you can imagine the City, Wall Street and Tokyo all rolled into one, then that was Augsburg at the time, the greatest financial centre in the world, and the first. Jacob was its master. The family had made money in the linen trade in the fourteenth century, but they soon realized moneylending was a more profitable activity. By the fifteenth century they were the greatest banking family in Europe, five times as wealthy as the Medici in Italy. They owned the banks, the mines and the spice trade, everything. There has been nothing like it since. And there is nothing that can happen in the markets that was not already known about here in Augsburg more than five hundred years ago.'

'And what did they do with the money?'

'Religion and power, those were their interests,' said Telmont, drawing closer to Sarah. 'The Hapsburg dynasty was paid for by the Fugger family; they filled the purses and pulled the strings. The Hapsburg dream of dominating Europe was really a plan to establish the Fuggers as the greatest power across the continent. But they were also men of some devotion. Luther was here in this very church, you know. He took refuge with the monks, in 1518 I think, and was still here when he was excommunicated by the Pope. The Fuggers stayed loyal to the true religion, of course, and lost many of their important German markets as a result. The Hapsburg connection remained, however, and the Fugger dynasty still has three separate branches that are among the richest in Europe.'

'Are they investors in the fund?' asked Sarah.

'Who knows?' answered Telmont, laughing. 'Probably. They are certainly rich enough. But Jacob would never have been an investor with me. He would have been my rival, and a worthy one at that.'

It was the way everything was precisely as he had left it that bothered Tom the most. He pushed open the door to the house and walked through to the kitchen to make some coffee. The milk, he noted, was where he had left it that morning. So too was the cereal box and the copy of yesterday's newspaper he had barely read. Usually when he came home, even if Tatyana was not there, there would be hundreds of small signs of her presence about the place. Now, everything was as he had left it, a crushing and sharp reminder that he was now alone in this place.

The phone rang twice before Tom answered it; he spent a fraction of a second wondering if it might be Tatyana before he recognized Sarah's voice from last night. 'I could use some advice,' she said, her tone quickening. 'You said you might be able to help.'

'Sure,' answered Tom.

'The Eastern European markets are wobbly, and suddenly Telmont expects me to know all about them. Isn't that your area?'

'I had a very busy day in the office,' said Tom. 'Everyone wanted to talk to me.'

'I could use a tutorial.'

'Over dinner, perhaps?'

'Why not?' said Sarah, hesitating just long enough to let him know she had thought about it. 'When I am back in London.'

'I'll see you then,' said Tom, putting the phone down. What, he wondered to himself, is that all about? Proving something to myself, I suppose. That I can still get a girl to have dinner with me.

CHAPTER 4

Thursday, 4 February

TOM FLICKED THROUGH THE POST, SAW THERE WAS NOTHING written in Tatyana's familiar slanted script, and was about to toss it aside when he noticed one of the letters was addressed to her. A bill, by the looks of it. From the credit card company.

Tatyana did not usually receive much post. In the years since they married, she had not worked; Tom's salary at Samuelson's was more than enough to keep two people comfortably in London. All the bills, bank statements and so on were addressed to him. Back in Estonia, she had no family, so her mail consisted of occasional postcards from her few girlfriends, and catalogues from some of her favourite shops. A bank account and credit card was all she held in her own name.

Tom sliced the envelope open. At first, he did no more than glance casually through the list of debits itemized on the account – the trip to her usual hairdresser in Chelsea, the stuff from the food hall at Harvey Nichols, a lunch with one of her friends at a place along the Fulham Road – they were all what he would have expected. Then he saw the evidence. There, in the neat lettering of the statement, were recorded four debits from her account in lek, the Estonian currency, one on 9 December, the other three on the 11th. None of the entries recorded where the money had been spent, but together it came to about five hundred pounds when converted back into sterling. Tom looked back up the list of debits; sure enough, a week earlier, there was a payment of £482 to Finnish Airways, presumably for her flight to Tallinn. How, Tom asked himself, could my wife go abroad for two days without my knowing about it? Surely that was impossible?

Swiftly, he recollected that he too had been away on those days; he had been summoned to the Frankfurt headquarters of the KrippenBank for a meeting of its economic forecasters throughout Europe. The conference lasted three days. If she stayed in Tallinn for just two nights, she could have made the trip and returned, and he need never have known. He had called, of course, as he always did when he was abroad, but it would have been easy for her to collect the messages from the machine and phone him from wherever. For that matter, there was nothing to stop her putting a call divert onto the home phone and taking the calls on her mobile. She could do that from anywhere, and he would never realize she was anywhere other than safely tucked up in Kensington.

For how long, Tom wondered to himself, had she been deceiving me before she left?

Sarah looked at David Sheldon across the floor of the small office the Leopard Fund operated in Augsburg. 'Is Telmont still here?' she asked.

Sheldon looked up from the laptop PC where his head had been buried for the last hour. 'He already left,' he replied.

'Where to?'

Sheldon shrugged, the look on his face suggesting the question was naive. 'I'm just an assistant,' he said. 'I don't ask and he doesn't tell me.'

Sarah glanced back down at the Reuters screen. The Latvian currency was down by forty per cent in the space of the last few hours, descending rapidly into the kind of chaos the small Baltic state had not seen since it won its independence from the Soviet Union in 1990. Already the bond market had started to move down sharply, and the tiny Latvian stock market was wobbling on the edge of a crash.

A few words from the brief conversation she had with Telmont earlier that morning ripped through her mind: 'You don't think Latvia will be the next domino?' It had been posed as a question, but, in reality, she supposed it was more like a prediction. Or a reprimand.

'So no one knows where he is at any time?' she said, looking back up at Sheldon.

'Only the Paris office,' he replied. 'You know, the keepers of the big secrets.'

'I wanted to contact him, to update the speech I prepared for him, to take account of what is happening in the Latvian market.'

Sheldon laughed, but the expression on his face was indulgent rather than mocking, as if he had found himself in this position countless times. 'Don't bother,' he said. 'Telmont won't use more than a few words of what you wrote.'

'Then why bother getting me to do it?' asked Sarah, aware she had failed to conceal the disappointment in her voice.

'Because he likes to have someone to bounce his ideas off,' replied Sheldon. 'For this week you are his sounding board. Enjoy it while it lasts.'

Tom was not sure why he had chosen to tell Radek so much about Tatyana. She had met Radek socially since they had married, but no more than twice, maybe three times. Perhaps, Tom reflected, because it was Radek who at business school had first inspired his fascination with the economies of Eastern Europe. And it had been that fascination which had led him to Tatyana.

They met in the back bar of the Waldorf Hotel, a cosy retreat with deep leather armchairs, wood-panelled walls, and waiters who were polite and discreet. When Radek asked him what he made of the Estonian crash, Tom had mentioned that he was going there tomorrow, and from there the story had tumbled out, a flow of unedited words, delivered with the speed of a man who has been holding something within himself for too long, the sentences leaping from his mouth like coiled springs.

'You don't think there might be some kind of connection, do you?' asked Radek.

'Good lord, no,' spluttered Tom. 'That thought hadn't even occurred to me.'

'A coincidence then, I suppose,' said Radek, his thick eyebrows narrowing as he spoke. 'And most unfortunate. You have my sympathy. I know something of what you feel. In 1968, after the revolution in my country failed, and I was sent to the camps, my wife was left in Prague. They would not even tell her if I was alive or dead. That was part of the process. She waited perhaps a year, perhaps eighteen months, but she was not a strong woman. To be alone takes real strength, a strength she did not possess. She met some other man, and by the time I was released she was lost to me.' He hesitated, half a smile playing on his lips. 'Not that I would have been much use to her once I had lost my status and position.'

'And you still miss her?' asked Tom.

Radek shook his head. 'I miss only the memory of how we once were,' he replied. 'I miss the way we began, not how we parted.' A silence fell between them, while they sipped on their beers, as if both men sensed that this conversation had been taken as far as they wanted it to go; they had revealed enough of themselves, it was time to move on. 'All the same, while you are in Tallinn, you should listen to what the people are saying about the market. There might be something for you to learn.'

'It baffles me, I must admit,' said Tom. 'The economy seems to be going fine, growing at four per cent a year, inflation subdued, unemployment tolerable, the government stable for that part of the world. Then suddenly, bang. The market collapses. I can't see any reason for it to happen.'

'There doesn't have to be a reason,' said Radek. 'Just a cause. Markets, almost by definition, don't have reasons. They are calculating but unthinking. They do have causes, however. Nothing happens absolutely by chance. There is always some kind of mechanism in place. It is just a matter of finding it.'

Tom shook his head. 'You are right, I am sure,' he replied, his mind already drifting back to Tatyana, to the strange, unknowable places to which she might have disappeared. 'But I can't imagine I'll find out very much just by dropping in for a day or two.'

'You shouldn't underestimate yourself,' said Radek slowly. 'Sometimes it can be the most unexpected and least qualified people who find out the most.'

CHAPTER 5

Friday, 5 February

THE PALACE HOTEL WAS ONE OF FOUR FIVE-STAR PLACES THAT
had opened in Tallinn since independence from Russia, and
the one Tom liked best. *Each time I stay here,* he noticed,
*the prices are higher and the service smarter. As good an indication
of economic progress as any,* he decided. *There is probably a perfect
mathematical relationship between the number of smart hotels, the
attractiveness of the local women, and the amount of foreign investment
into a country. Some day I must write a paper on it.*

In his room, he took a quick shower, changed into a pair of jeans, a thick
blue sweater and a long black leather jacket. He swigged back a coffee
while plugging his laptop into the phone socket, calling up a Bloomberg
screen. The news from the local markets was grim. The Latvian market
was still in free-fall, with rumours of bank closures pushing the currency
and stock markets down sharply; in sympathy, the Estonian market had
taken another hit. Elsewhere, it was as if nothing was happening. Wall
Street was touching new highs, Tokyo was still recovering, and all the
main European markets were moving upwards. *Nobody in the rest of the
world thinks what happens in the Baltics matters,* thought Tom. *But it
matters to me.*

Samuelson's German parent KrippenBank had opened a branch in
Tallinn four years ago. Few Estonians would bank there themselves –

there were still bitter memories of the Nazi occupation – but the vast number of German companies trading in the region provided plenty of business. Tom had met Boris Valdek, the local general manager, twice before; once here in Tallinn, and once in London. A skinny man, with nervous, twitchy eyes, and thinning black hair swept back over his long gaunt face, he appeared both tired and agitated when Tom walked into his office.

'A bad couple of days?' Tom said, aware it was as much a statement as a question.

Valdek looked up, his eyes bloodshot. 'The worst since I have been here,' he replied. 'A fifty per cent drop in the value of the lek against the euro in one day. People here just aren't prepared for that. They think capitalism is nothing but The Gap, Sony Playstations and new Volkswagens. Just the goodies. They don't realize it also means overnight collapses. Bankruptcy and ruin for no apparent reason. You and I might know that, but most ordinary people here thought capitalism meant you just got richer and richer for ever.'

'It has always been like that, wherever you go,' said Tom. 'Capitalism is like working on an oil rig. People only put up with the danger and discomfort because it pays so well.'

'Not here,' said Valdek.

'What happened?' asked Tom. 'The collapse came as a complete shock.'

Valdek shrugged, taking a sip from the mug of thick black coffee at the side of his desk. 'Nobody has had time for a forensic examination yet,' he replied. 'It started on Wednesday morning, with a wave of selling of the lek against the euro. After lunch, the selling spread to the bond market. All of our trade is in euros, so any kind of devaluation would hit bonds hard.'

'And the banks and companies have all taken euro-denominated loans, I suppose,' said Tom. 'So when you get a sell off in the currency and bond markets, it makes the repayments on those loans a lot more expensive. Pretty soon, people have to start questioning whether the banks are solvent.'

'In a developing economy, once the currency goes, the whole ball of wool starts to unravel,' said Valdek. 'That's what happened late on Wednesday night, and early yesterday morning. A twenty-five per cent drop in the stock market in just a few hours. On a smaller scale, as bad as the crash on Wall Street in 1987. Then, just when we thought things might start to stabilize, Latvia goes down.'

'Who started the crash?' asked Tom. 'The sell-off must have begun somewhere.'

Valdek shrugged. 'Who knows?' he replied, the tiredness evident in his voice. 'Some of the local speculators, I think. Then some of the hedge funds might have joined in.'

'Anyone in particular?' asked Tom.

Valdek thought for a minute. 'Some of our dealers were saying a man called Cepartinu was very active in the market on Wednesday morning.'

'Is that a familiar name?'

'He was involved in the government shortly after the liberation, but he never made it as a politician,' replied Valdek. 'Now he operates on the shadier fringes of the stock market.'

'And he might have started the selling?'

'Not by himself, I shouldn't think,' said Valdek. 'There is no way he would have enough money to make any impact. From what I hear, he has never been very successful with the markets.'

Tom sighed, looking across at Valdek. 'It looks like he is now.'

'We'll see,' answered Valdek. 'How's that lovely wife of yours?'

Tom froze for a second. 'Just fine,' he answered, faltering only slightly over the words.

'We can't lose too many beauties like that,' said Valdek. 'Soon there won't be any left here for the rest of us.'

From KrippenBank, Tom had turned sharply left, walking down the cobbled backstreets of the old town, towards the docks. Tallinn was a city he had come to know well in the past few years, and it was, if not somewhere he could love, a place he had come to respect. It had a sturdy resilience that appealed to him. Perched up on the far fringes of the Baltic Sea, freezing through most of the long winter, ever since it was founded in the twelfth century the ingenuity of its people had allowed it to make a far better living than could have been expected.

The building was as desolate as Tom had expected. A harsh, mono-chrome block constructed entirely from concrete breeze-blocks, it looked more like a barracks than an office. Lumps of concrete had flaked from its corners, throwing up thin films of dust that had settled into every crack on the stairway. Not somewhere you would choose to spend the day, thought Tom. Not unless you had to.

Jaak Terah had not been hard to find. Estonia, like most of the former Soviet republics, had plenty of men who made their living in the grey and uncertain world between organized crime and organized protection. Displaced soldiers, policemen, secret service men, the old regime had turned out security officials by the score, and most of them were still around, a little older and a little wearier, plying the same trade wherever they could find a demand. Terah had been recommended by Valdek. Whether he had been a policeman, or soldier, or whatever, he had no idea; all he knew was that he was a capable and discreet detective who could make enquiries around town.

'Two hundred lek a day, plus expenses of course,' said Terah, his tone dark yet unthreatening. 'Bribes to hotel clerks, that kind of thing. Basic. If it involves anything dangerous, I will need more money.'

A grey, metal-framed desk and two simple swivel chairs without arms were the only form of ornamentation in the small, second-floor room. The walls and floor were bare, and even the window, through which Tom could hear the lapping of the waves against the docks, had only a plain blind. Terah was a small man, but broad, and could have weighed almost two hundred pounds, more of it muscle than fat. He wore a thick black moustache, and was dressed in black jeans and a brown leather jacket. A local cigarette seemed attached permanently to the edge of his lip.

'Would you rather be paid in euros or lek?' asked Tom.

Terah looked across the desk and smiled. 'Right now, I think euros, don't you?' he replied. 'Tell me what you need.'

Tom had never visited a private detective before, nor, until this week, had he ever imagined that he might do so. They were people from another world, from television programmes, or newspaper stories – not the kind of person he would ever meet or consult himself. And yet, almost as soon as Tatyana had disappeared, one of the first things he had done had been to start flicking through the Yellow Pages, looking under D. In London, perhaps he could manage by himself. Here, he needed someone to ask questions for him.

'My wife has left me,' began Tom.

From the look in the eyes of the man on the other side of the desk, Tom could tell this was a line he had heard before; many times, no doubt, he reflected, and each time a man much like myself will be sitting here, on this side of the desk, looking for some kind of answer. Something that will make it all her fault, something that will absolve the other person. 'On Monday,' he continued. 'In London, where we live; but she had visited Tallinn a couple of months earlier.'

'Your wife comes from Estonia?'

'Originally, yes,' answered Tom. 'We met here five years ago.'

'And you think she has come back here?'

'I don't know,' answered Tom flatly.

He looked across the desk, wondering how much he wanted to confide. Sometimes he found it easier to talk to strangers. Perhaps that is because they have never met Tatyana, he reflected. They can only imagine her side of the story.

'But it is possible?'

'She came here in December,' answered Tom. 'I found that out from her credit card statement. I was away for a couple of days, so I didn't know about it.'

'Your wife often took trips without telling you?' asked Terah, his tone conveying neither disappointment nor surprise, for which Tom was grateful; having a wife who takes off without even telling you was not, he had started to realize, a detail of their life together he wanted to broadcast. Maybe that was why he preferred talking to strangers; he didn't have to worry about the shame.

'I didn't think so, but perhaps,' answered Tom. 'I don't know any more.'

'She has family here still?' Tom shook his head. 'Elsewhere, then?'

'They were all gone by the time I met her,' said Tom. 'She was an orphan. There was nobody else.'

'Did she come back here often?'

'We had been on holiday a couple of times, but otherwise, no, at least not as far as I knew.'

'And when you met her, what was she doing?'

'She was singing in a night-club a bit, jazz songs mostly, and waitressing,' answered Tom.

Terah looked at him closely, his eyes narrowing, sinking deep into his face. Trying to judge me, thought Tom. I suppose when you are a detective, clients lie to you all the time. Just like they lie to themselves. 'Forgive me for asking, Mr Bracewell,' he said carefully. 'But did she turn tricks?'

Tom knew the question was a fair one, but he minded all the same; it sent a bolt of pain jagging through his stomach, and for a moment he wondered if he was about to be sick. 'She was studying then,' he said firmly. 'Tatyana just served drinks for her wages and tips. And she sang. Beautifully.'

'Which bar?' asked Terah.

'The Double Bass, on Tatari street,' Tom replied. 'They might still know her there.'

'Those kinds of places have a pretty high staff turnover,' said Terah with a shrug. 'Give me a couple of days, and I'll see what I can find out.'

CHAPTER 6

Sunday, 7 February

THE SLUSH WAS THICK ON THE RAGGED PAVEMENT AS BOISSANT walked swiftly along the streets leading away from the centre of Minsk towards the plush residential district lying to the west of the city. He looked down at the mixture of snow and mud covering his thick leather boots, checking that he was not leaving footprints along the pavement. He had no great faith in the ability of the Belorussian police to check anything, but there was no point in taking chances.

'How much further?' he said, turning to his companion.

'Less than a hundred yards,' replied Valdis Sausne.

Boissant had hired Sausne in Riga. A tall, blond, light-skinned man, he had spent seven years in the Red Army before the liberation, and was now in his late thirties, working as a private security consultant for companies in Riga – a likely euphemism, Boissant had decided to himself, for a man who looked, acted and dressed like hired muscle. Still, he knew the region, its people and its dialects, and he knew how to pass unnoticed from one country to another. He also knew something about making bombs. For today's task, that was enough.

They had left Riga early on Saturday morning, driving through the border late that afternoon in a Renault Espace Boissant had bought in the city. As far as the border guards were concerned, they were a pair of French biologists on their way to survey the wildlife of the empty

Pripet marshes to the east of Minsk. The drive towards the capital took another eight hours, stopping along the way to collect the materials they would need.

Nothing too delicate nor intricate, Boissant had decided. Smooth professionalism was not the impression they were trying to create this evening. The work of dedicated amateurs, fired up by righteous indignation – that would be the desired effect; something that could, he estimated, be best achieved with a basic fertilizer bomb. The ingredients had all been collected from farm suppliers along the way, except for the detonators. These had been smuggled across the border from Latvia, straightforward explosive charges linked to simple Korean mechanical timers bought from a firm that supplied central heating boilers. Between them, they were carrying one hundred and fifty pounds of explosives in the two suitcases. Quite enough for my purposes, he reflected. A dramatic explosion going off like a massive firework in the centre of the city, that should shake things up. A couple of people killed perhaps, nothing more.

There was no point in going crazy, or turning this thing into a massacre, Boissant told himself. That would be barbaric.

Sausne pointed to the building up ahead. A large, late nineteenth-century villa, probably built by one of the prosperous merchants who dominated the city in the last century, it had been bought five years ago by the Lithuanian government and converted to an embassy. Briefly Boissant surveyed the scene. A small lane appeared to run down the back of the street, for deliveries to be made to the buildings along the main avenue. Boissant nodded to Sausne, and the two men walked briskly along the alley. When they reached the dump for rubbish, they scanned the lane, making sure nobody could see them. Boissant inspected the timers on both suitcases, then placed them beneath the rubbish, making sure both were well covered. He glanced down at his watch. Another eight hours before the detonation. By then, he should be safely across the border into Poland.

*   *   *

The coffee shop seemed crowded for a Sunday afternoon, filled with young local students, and families enjoying a lazy afternoon. Very different from the first time I came here, just after the revolution, Tom reflected. Then you couldn't even get a proper cup of coffee outside of a five-star hotel. There had been an atmosphere of drab, grey indifference then that appeared deeply ingrained in the soul of the place and yet, within a few years, had been replaced by a lighter, more colourful mood. It was as if the city had just been hibernating for a couple of generations, waiting for the spring to arrive.

Freedom, and relative prosperity, noted Tom. It does a lot for the look of a place.

He took a sip of his cappuccino, waiting for the caffeine to filter into his bloodstream, reviving his senses. It had been a late night, and he had drunk more than he should have. This morning he had woken with the low, dull throb of a hangover echoing through his tired and shattered mind. I am a decade past that kind of behaviour, he told himself. I can't keep up with the play any more.

Visiting Double Bass had been a mistake. He had known that even as he was walking down the street in the direction of the club, and yet he had felt drawn there all the same; some warped instinct was dragging him along, leaving him powerless to resist. You can't be that strong, he had told himself, not at a time like this. Sometimes you have to indulge your weaknesses.

The interior of the club was intensely familiar, although it was years now since he had last been there. There is something about the place where you meet the woman you love that sticks with you, he realized; the memories are always there, fresh and vivid in your mind, locked up forever. He could forget a hundred different bars he had visited since, but not this one.

It had gone downhill, but the scent of the place had not changed. A mixture of cheap local nicotine, flashy colognes and perfumes and potent hard spirits assaulted his nostrils as soon as he sat down at one of the simple black wooden tables. When Tatyana had worked here it had been one of the very few night-clubs in town, and one of the only places that was not overtly a brothel. In those days it was only visiting

businessmen who had any money to spend on night-life, and they only
wanted to go to places where there were girls available. At Double Bass
there was mostly just food, drink and music, and it was for those that
Tom had taken to visiting the place on his trips to Tallinn when the
country was establishing its first stock market.

He ordered a whisky and looked around. It was emptier now; there
were plenty of other bars and clubs around town, and there was nothing
in particular to recommend this one any more. Not unless you happened
to enjoy sad music and hard spirits. The stage where he had first seen
her was unchanged. A platform raised less than a foot from the ground,
and the basics of a jazz group: a drum kit, a piano, and, at the centre
of the stage, an upright double bass. There was nothing professional
about the club. Some of the local musicians would jam late at night,
and from time to time the waitresses might get up on stage and sing
whatever songs they could remember the words to. Tatyana that night
had been sitting on a stool at the edge of the band, her long dark hair
disappearing into the blackness of the stage; only the clear, pale, radiant
skin of her face visible at the table where Tom had been sitting. He had
been captivated by her almost at once, drawn immediately, he felt, into
her world and everything that filled it. Her lips, even at a distance, struck
him as alluringly sensual, and her voice seemed both sweet and tough at
the same time, like wild honey laced with whisky. Fragments of the song
she was singing then remained with him, the opening chords to the title
track of an early Sixties Sarah Vaughan album: 'When you must do without
him/But your dreams are still about him/You'll begin the lonely hours/When
your romance is ending/And your heart has stopped pretending/You are in
the lonely hours.'

Other girls sang that night, Tom remembered, and other girls waited
at the tables, but he was interested only in her. It turned out she knew
one of the local bankers who was drinking with Tom that night; one
of her girlfriends had been out with his brother, and that was how the
introduction had been made. When Tom complimented her on her singing,
and asked her where she learnt the tune, it sparked a conversation about
the classic torch songs. She had been impressed, she told him later, that

he knew it was a Sarah Vaughan track, and even owned the record it was taken from. Funny, he reflected, ordering another drink from the bar. If I had not walked into the club at that moment, and heard her singing those words, then none of this would have happened.

'How was your weekend?' asked Jaak Terah, sitting down in the chair opposite Tom and ordering coffee from a waitress.

'Too much to drink,' said Tom flatly.

Terah looked at him across the table. 'Let me give you some advice, my friend,' he said slowly. 'In this line of work, you meet a lot of abandoned lovers. Most of them are angry. All of them are confused. Try to stay away from the alcohol. And try to let go.'

'If I'd wanted a therapist, I would have hired one,' said Tom sourly. 'Did you manage to find anything?'

'Have you heard of a man called Henri Boissant?' asked Terah.

Tom shook his head. 'No,' he answered softly.

'He stayed with your wife the last night she was here, down at a small hotel just outside the old city.'

Tom could feel a tightening in his chest, and his breath seemed to be stabbing at the back of his throat. 'Together?' he asked.

'They booked two rooms, if that is what you mean,' said Terah with a shrug. 'Whether they stayed in them, I can't say.'

'A Frenchman?' said Tom, as much to himself as to the man opposite.

'Looks that way,' said Terah. 'According to the guest register, he checked in with an Italian passport under the name of Roberto Sanoli, but the receptionist says he spoke with a French accent. Your wife gave your address. He gave an address in Milan. I've already checked it out, and it doesn't exist. He paid his bill in cash, she put her room on her credit card. According to the lady at the desk, they checked in mid-afternoon, went out for the rest of the day, came back late and checked out early the next morning.'

'So how do you know he is called Boissant?'

'I don't, not for sure,' answered Terah. 'But the Italian identity is obviously a fake. He used a credit card to make a call from the hotel room. According to Visa, that card belongs to a Mr Boissant.'

'How did they act together?'

'The receptionist said they appeared quite friendly, but she could not say if they were lovers or not.'

'What else did she buy?' asked Tom. 'There were three things on the credit card.'

'A new ski coat, from one of the sports shops in town,' replied Terah. 'And she hired a car for the day.'

'Where was she going?'

Terah shook his head. 'I don't know,' he replied.

'Could you find out?' asked Tom.

'Perhaps, perhaps not,' replied Terah. 'Estonia is a small country, but people can still get lost.'

'Do your best,' said Tom. 'I don't mind paying for a couple of weeks' work.'

Terah knew he had no choice but to accept the offer. Foreign clients who could pay in euros rarely came his way, and he was not about to let this one pass. 'How well did you know your wife?' he asked.

Tom hesitated before replying. The question rattled through his mind. He had asked it of himself a thousand times in the past few days. 'How well does any man know his wife?'

'It varies, I think,' said Terah. 'Some better than others.'

'Like I said,' answered Tom. 'If I want a therapist, I'll hire one.'

'The point is this,' continued Terah, finishing his coffee and looking directly across the table at Tom. 'If you want to find out where someone has gone, the best way to start is to find out where they came from.'

CHAPTER 7

Monday, 8 February

T OM'S EYES FLICKED THROUGH THE NEAT BLACK LETTERING of the bank statement. There was, he reflected, something terrifying about how those tiny insignificant letters spat from a computer could convey so much information; ugly glimpses of another world – one which, just a few days ago, he could have barely imagined existed.

'Luxembourg and Berlin,' he repeated to himself, saying the words out loud. What in the name of Christ had she been doing there?

The flight back from Estonia last night had been heavy enough. Putting a name to his rival had at least given him some information to play with, yet did nothing to calm the riot of speculation running through his mind. For much of the journey he had been wondering about the pair of them, what they looked like together, where they went, and who they saw. Most of all, he had been wondering what they did to one another in bed.

He had arrived back to a flat as cold and empty and questioning as he had left it. As soon as he stepped through the door he checked the answering machine, but there had been nothing from her. One message was just a click; someone had called, and said nothing to the machine. Could that have been her? he wondered to himself. Probably not, he decided reluctantly.

His mind was still heavy with those thoughts this morning while he dressed, made coffee and collected the mail. On Friday, before leaving, Tom had contacted the credit card company, asking them to send him statements of Tatyana's account going back for the last year. It was her card, but the account was held jointly in his name, since she had had no credit record when she arrived in England. And yet, even though he was expecting to receive the statements this morning, nothing had prepared him for the money that was detailed on the account.

The craving for information had become so strong it was like a hunger. He ripped open the envelope the same way as a man who hadn't eaten for a day might tear into his food. Greedily, his eyes sank into the thin slips of computer print-out, scouring the words and symbols. Most were what he had expected: shopping, lunches, and so on, all at London addresses. Twice, however, in the last six months of statements, the card had been used abroad. In September, she had made a trip to Luxembourg. In November, a trip to Berlin. In neither case had he known she was anywhere but London.

Anxiously, Tom found his diary for last year, checking those days. In September, he had been in Hungary for three days, attending a conference on the creditworthiness of Eastern European governments. In November, he had been visiting Warsaw for two days to prepare a report on the progress of privatization. On neither occasion, he realized, would he have known if she had been out of the country for a couple of nights.

She must have been with *him*, he told himself. Doing whatever it is they do together.

A calculation started to run through Tom's mind as he stared down at the numbers on the statement; a rough reckoning of the amounts Tatyana had been spending in the past few months. About two, sometimes three grand, he figured, once the cost of all those trips abroad was taken into account. The precise figure didn't matter. It was something of that order. But he usually transferred a thousand a month to her account, enough to meet her day-to-day living expenses. All the bills, and any big items, he always paid for. So where, he asked himself, was the money coming from?

What was the question the detective asked him yesterday afternoon? How well do you know your wife? Tatyana had always worn her elusiveness like a rare piece of jewellery, as an ornament to make her more attractive, and that was part of her appeal. But now, he reflected, she was like a shadow that changed shape the closer you got to it. I wonder, he asked himself, if I knew who she was at all.

The story had not rated a mention on CNN or any of the other news broadcasts she had heard that morning; but it was there on the screen in front of her. Sarah knew at once her analysis for Telmont would have to be reworked.

According to the wire story, a bomb had exploded late last night outside the Lithuanian Embassy in the Belorussian capital. Two people had been severely injured in the blast, both now in intensive care. Nobody had been killed, and although the gardens and back wall had been destroyed, there was no major damage to the building. The explosion was thought to be the work of Belorussian nationalists, protesting about the treatment of the 350,000 ethnic Belorussians living in Lithuania, a long-standing issue between the two countries since both of them had left the Soviet Union. Hard-line nationalists, the report continued, wanted the Belorussian government to take a tougher stand against Lithuania. The bombing, said analysts in the region, would increase tension between the two countries.

Sarah knew she was far from expert in the delicate politics of the region – but even she could see that the reaction on the markets had been swift and brutal. By the time she arrived at her desk in New York, the European markets had already been open for four hours. Trading in Eastern European currencies had been frantic. The local crashes last week in Estonia and then Latvia had burned plenty of investors in the region, and most were just waiting for an excuse to start selling both the Lithuanian and Belorussian currencies. Falls of forty per cent against the euro had been recorded by lunchtime, taking both the Estonian and Latvian currencies down another twenty per cent each in sympathy. The stock market in Belorussia was too tiny for there to be any meaningful index to follow, but in Lithuania both stocks and bonds had been marked down sharply. Banking and financial stocks had been hit particularly hard, on fears that much of that sector could be wiped out by the sudden and precipitous falls in the currencies.

Sarah sat back in her chair, took a sip of her coffee, and watched the numbers in amazement. Telmont had been quite right, she reflected, to be taking such a close interest in Eastern European currencies. Through a period of turmoil like this, there was obviously a lot of money to be made, if the fund could make the right calls.

'Looks like you'll be plenty busy with that assignment,' said Sheldon, resting his chin against the edge of her office cubicle.

'I guess so,' replied Sarah. 'How much does the fund have invested in that part of the world anyway?'

Sheldon shrugged. 'Nothing, so far as I know.'

'Then why are we so interested in what is happening there?'

'Well now, I guess that question would have to be referred to the Paris office.'

'Paris?' said Sarah, unsure how she should take the remark.

'Like I said,' continued Sheldon. 'The keepers of the big secrets.'

'Right,' answered Sarah. 'I thought I had heard that somewhere before.'

'Not so much of a joke any more,' said Jones, peering into Tom's cubicle.

'I don't think so, no,' said Tom. 'This could be the crash.'

'That serious?' said Jones.

'It is usually a sequence,' replied Tom. 'First one country goes down, a small and insignificant place, just like Estonia. Then it spreads to a few other small places, just like Latvia and Lithuania and Belorussia.'

'Then perhaps it heads west,' added Jones.

'Who knows?' said Tom. 'I suppose any market collapse is like some new virus. No one really knows where it starts, or why, or how far it will spread. They certainly don't know how to stop it.'

'Not the clowns that run this bank, anyhow,' said Jones, his tone lightening. 'What's the view upstairs?'

'I told them I thought this could turn into a full-scale rout, the same line I was taking last week,' answered Tom. 'But all the Frankfurt people are so laid-back about the whole thing it's unbelievable. You know, "the fundamentals are sound", that kind of rubbish.'

'The ostrich strategy,' said Jones, turning back to his own desk. 'At least they're consistent.'

Leaning back in his chair, Tom wondered which call he should return next. It had been a frantic morning ever since he arrived at Samuelson's offices. His head had still been spinning from his discovery of Tatyana's trips abroad, and no sooner had he located his first coffee of the morning than he had been summoned to an investment committee meeting on the eighteenth floor.

KrippenBank employed plenty of economists around the world, but Tom was the resident expert on Eastern Europe, so as the crisis moved forward it was inevitable they would want his views. The investment committee of the bank met every Monday morning, bringing together, via satellite link-ups, its experts from Frankfurt, London, Singapore and New York to agree an overall global investment strategy for the bank. Tom only attended occasionally, when his area was under discussion. However, its deliberations on where to move a few billion of its clients' money always struck him as a fair representation of international capitalism at its most cold and cynical.

When his turn came to speak Tom began by outlining how the crisis had developed in the last few days, briefly describing the fear and panic he had witnessed in Estonia. 'My conclusion is that, for the time being, investors should steer well clear of the region,' he said, pronouncing the words clearly and loudly, mainly for the benefit of the Europeans. 'I suspect we are on the brink of a systematic meltdown in the region.'

Over the video screen that linked the London conference room with the bank's Frankfurt headquarters, Tom could judge his remarks had not gone down well. Jurgen Strich, the bank's chairman, and the person who always presided over investment committee meetings, was peering over his half-moon glasses with a look that hovered between boredom and disbelief. 'I think you probably are being melodramatic, Mr Bracewell,' he said, the words ground out in a slow German accent. 'The fundamentals are surely sound.'

'It's gone beyond that,' replied Tom. 'The markets are developing a story of their own, possibly manipulated by some of the big hedge funds. This has nothing to do with what is happening to the real economies of these countries. It is about financial systems, and they don't obey any kind of logic except their own.'

Looking back, Tom could tell Strich had not been impressed by that outburst, nor the tone of mild irritation with which it had been delivered. The committee, as he had expected, noted his views; its line remained that this was no more than a few small markets collapsing, and need not affect global strategy. That couldn't be helped, Tom decided. He had been under a lot of pressure in the last few days, and he was even wondering whether coming into work was the right thing to do. The fate of KrippenBank and the billions it controlled was the last thing on his mind right now.

Glancing through the collection of messages on his desk, from journalists, clients, and fund managers, only the request to call Radek grabbed his attention. Punching the digits into his phone, he found himself wondering what Tatyana might have made of events. I must kick that habit, he told himself. Not good for the soul.

'What was the view in Estonia?' asked Radek, on hearing Tom's voice.

'Gloomy,' replied Tom. 'The impact of a full-scale crash on that economy could be catastrophic.'

'I fear so,' said Radek. 'Any gossip on what might be causing it?'

'There was some talk about a local speculator doing a lot of selling last week, a man named Cepartinu, and that some of the hedge funds piled in on the back of that.'

'Certain it was Cepartinu?'

'No,' replied Tom. 'That was just the gossip. Why, have you heard of him?'

'An opportunist,' said Radek slowly. 'A Communist Party official under the old regime; then he tried to hitchhike a ride to power during the revolution. Now he crops up again as a financial speculator.'

'Not a pleasant character then.'

'The kind who sells himself to the highest bidder,' snorted Radek. 'Nothing would surprise me about that man. With the markets collapsing in Lithuania and Belorussia, this is getting more serious by the day.'

'I'm glad someone thinks so,' said Tom. 'No one much at KrippenBank thinks it matters at all.'

'Don't let that worry you,' said Radek. 'Don't take this personally, but if you study the archives you'll find the KrippenBank didn't think Hitler would amount to very much, and a few years later thought the Third Reich was invincible, then a decade or so after that was telling all its investors to keep out of Japan. Historically, it doesn't have much of a record of making the right calls. Like most big institutions. The point is to value your own judgement.'

'Which right now is that a pattern is starting to emerge,' said Tom. 'One market falling after another. Like a neat row of dominoes.'

'Any mention of the Leopard Fund among the sellers?'

'None, just some speculation about the hedge funds,' said Tom. 'I thought Telmont had said he didn't want to invest in Eastern Europe.'

'And you trust him?' asked Radek.

Tom laughed. 'About as far as I can throw him.'

'Don't even trust him that far,' said Radek. 'That man is bound to be involved somewhere.'

'But where?' asked Tom.

'That is what we need to find out,' answered Radek.

From the look on Telmont's face, Sarah wondered if she had said the wrong thing. The lines on his face had creased up, sinking his dark brown eyes into the far recesses of his skull, and his expression simmered with annoyance.

The summons had been as unexpected as all the others. One minute she had been sitting at her desk, battling with the basics of the Belorussian economy, next she was in the chairman's office. While the rest of the staff worked in a wide open-plan space, bathed by artificial lights, Telmont's suite of offices was separated from the rest of the building by secure, wood-panelled walls. They were used only one day a week, at most, but were staffed constantly by two of the most drop-dead gorgeous secretaries Sarah had ever seen, one of them American, the other French, each polished until they shone. Both, Sarah confessed to herself, made her feel nervous; they looked up at her with the kind of bored indifference that stupid yet beautiful women reserve for those sisters who are cleverer but not quite so stunning.

Telmont's private office looked out across Wall Street's seething mass of snarling and angry traffic, but the reinforced, tinted glass windows that stretched from the floor to the ceiling shielded it from even a whisper of noise. The room was decorated in chic, early Nineties minimalism, a style that always struck Sarah as saying more about a person's wallet than their taste: waxed floorboards, stripped and polished until they glimmered, white walls, and a desk that consisted only of a thin strip of black metal supported on two squares of large, thick glass. In one corner of the room, on a white stand, stood a Chinese porcelain vase, although of what date Sarah had no idea. As in London, there was just one chair, and that was behind Telmont's desk.

'You wanted to see me,' said Sarah, wondering already whether Monday morning would start with a confrontation with the chairman.

'Your work on Belorussia is interesting, yes,' said Telmont.

It was then she made the remark that seemed to anger him: 'I don't see why it is necessary to do all this work on Eastern Europe if the fund is not investing in that part of the world,' she said, the acidity in her tone painfully apparent.

Even before the words had been delivered, and certainly when she saw the shadows darkening on Telmont's face, Sarah regretted having spoken so sharply. Telmont, she had already learned, was a vain and egotistical man, someone easily seduced by flattery, and for whom staff mainly existed to provide applause and encouragement. He did not seem to be someone who appreciated having his opinions challenged. 'Who says we don't invest in the East?' he said, the look of anger on his face subsiding, replaced by one of playful amusement.

'It says so in the report to investors,' said Sarah. 'You said specifically, in the introductory essay, that you did not think hedge funds should operate in that part of world. You said there was already enough volatility in the region without the Leopard Fund making it worse.'

Telmont allowed his face to crease up into a grin. 'I seldom believe very much of what I tell the investors,' he said. 'They don't expect the truth, and neither should you.'

'So the fund does invest in the East?' asked Sarah, her tone cautious and suspicious.

'In currencies, yes,' answered Telmont. 'In some other financial instruments as well.'

'Even though everything has been collapsing over there?'

Telmont nodded, his eyes turning up towards the window. 'Of course,' he replied. 'It is at times such as this that a speculative fund can make its money. Indeed, we have been buying based on the analysis you provided. In fact, you might even find yourself named in the records as the person running the funds that have been operating in the market.'

'Me?' said Sarah, barely able to conceal her surprise. 'But I haven't made any decisions.'

'That is quite true, but not anything unexpected,' said Telmont softly. 'After all, I make the decisions around here.'

The sheets of fax paper from her bank lay curled on the side of Tom's desk in his study; he had asked this morning for statements going back for the last year. In the background, he could hear the same Julie London CD playing, the same soundtrack he had been listening to all week. '*Let our love take wings, some midnight, around midnight/Let the angels sing for your return/Let our love be safe and sound/When old midnight comes around,*' crooned the soft and sultry voice. 'Don't Smoke in Bed', he reflected, was a few tracks further along, but the song would come round soon enough, its simple refrain haunting and teasing him, a riddle still waiting to be unlocked.

Tom looked down at the bank statements, starting in January, and working his way steadily backwards. He punched the numbers into the calculator, and made some neat notes in the margin on the totals flowing through the account. Carefully, he double-checked his calculations. He would have imagined he knew the details of Tatyana's finances pretty well. The money he transferred to her account every month was for her to pay for the groceries, and a cleaner if she wanted one, although Tatyana always appeared to think there was something immoral about having someone else clean for them. He would have imagined it was all the money she had. Tatyana had no living relatives, nor friends close enough to give her money. There was no need for her to work, and she had not shown any inclination to do so. There were, so far as he was aware, no legacies upon which she could draw.

Tom stood up, and, cradling a cup of coffee in the palms of his hands, walked across to the window, watching the rain splattering through the night sky. He could feel a heaviness around his eyelids, a sensation that might have been tiredness, but could also have been despair. A single question was burning through his mind. How could she possibly have had fifty thousand pounds transferred into her account that month alone?

CHAPTER 8

Tuesday, 9 February

HER VOICE SOUNDED BREATHLESS AND URGENT ON THE phone. 'Meet me at eight on Wednesday,' said Sarah. 'We should both be out of work by then.'

'You okay?' asked Tom.

'Just worried by my work, that's all,' Sarah replied. 'I'll see you in Casey's Bar on Old Brompton Road.'

Tom put the phone down and glanced along the length of office. It had been a grey and dismal journey into work this morning, and the prospect of a day at the office had done nothing to lighten his mood. He was not sure he had the stomach for it. Getting to sleep last night had not been easy; he drank three neat whiskies in a row, and played two of Elvis Costello's bitterest albums, but neither alcohol nor loud music made him feel any better. It was a long time since he had last been dumped by a girl – more than a decade – and he had forgotten what it felt like: the helpless, pitiless rage, the endless questioning and recriminations, the futile investigations into the minute, forensic details of what might have gone wrong. I should let it drop, he told himself a hundred times. Walk away. Move on. The same advice he would give any of his friends; the same advice they too would refuse to act on.

'Have you seen what's happening in Poland?' said Jones, leaning into Tom's cubicle.

Tom looked up, relieved for a distraction from the overpowering melancholy descending over his small corner of the office. 'Nope,' he answered.

Leaning over the desk, Jones dragged up a display of the world's markets onto the Reuters screen. The Warsaw index was down by seventy points in the first half hour of trading this morning and showed no signs of having touched bottom. The zloty was in freefall against the euro, and the bond market was in turmoil. A click on the mouse brought up the news story.

Warsaw: 9/2: 8:49 GMT: The Polish market came under heavy selling pressure this morning, following rumours of a major banking collapse which could threaten the stability of the financial system. The chief executive of the Poznan Agricultural Bank, Janusz Slohan, was found dead last night at his home in the city. Market sources say Slohan committed suicide, leaving a note behind that said the bank was technically bankrupt. The note, according to police sources, said the bank had been heavily involved in loans to companies in the Baltic states of Estonia, Lithuania and Latvia, where there have been big falls in the value of stocks and currencies in the past few days. A failure of those loans could result in the collapse of the bank, prompting Slohan to take his own life. No comment on the rumours has yet been made by the Poznan Agricultural Bank, but local police sources have confirmed that Slohan has been found dead.

'Financial market contagion,' said Jones thoughtfully, glancing back down at the screen. 'So far it looks as if the DAX is dropping a bit in Germany, but the London market has hardly moved.'

'It will do, I'm sure,' said Tom. 'Before this thing is over.'

Jones stood up from the desk, walking away from the cubicle. 'By the way, Sally and I are having a party in a couple of Sundays' time,' he said. 'You and Tatyana must come.'

'Of course,' said Tom instantly, and without thinking.

Sooner or later I must start telling people what has happened, thought Tom, as soon as Jones had left. It is no use imagining she might be back by the end of the week and all this will be forgotten about. If I think that, I am just kidding myself.

'Account 912,' repeated Sheldon, his tone strained.

'Yes,' said Sarah firmly. 'Jean-Pierre said I could have access to that account. He just didn't give me the codes, that's all.'

'First name terms, I see,' said Sheldon, the lines on his shiny, immaculately-shaved face creasing up into a leer. 'Kind of cosy.'

'Standards at Harvard must definitely be dropping,' answered Sarah, affecting the most pleasant tone she could manage. 'Because you are the stupidest bastard I have ever met.'

'We're kind of feisty this morning.'

'Just give me the codes.'

They were standing by the water cooler, close to Telmont's private suite of offices. Sarah knew she did not have much time, and even with hours to kill, flirting with Sheldon was hardly her idea of a good time. Stepping into the offices of the Leopard Fund was, she had realized over the last couple of days, like walking into the locker room at school: the boys were excited by the presence of a woman, yet intimidated by the invasion of their space. Aside from the secretaries and receptionists, she was the only woman in the place. Why me, she asked herself?

Sheldon accompanied her back towards her desk, sat down heavily, and began punching a series of commands into the keyboard. 'It's quite simple really,' he started to explain. 'Different employees have access to different parts of the system. Junior staff can just see the PR blurb, really, the daily quote price and so on. Actually that covers most people. Only senior fund managers get much further, and they only see their own positions. Analysts get to see their sectors, of course, and the positions we have there. So I guess that applies to you. These settings will give you access to all the positions we have in currencies around the world.'

'Shouldn't I have access to any positions we have in Eastern Europe?' said Sarah.

Sheldon looked up, a playful grin on his face. 'I think we'd have to check that one with the Paris office,' he said. 'Anyway, the fund doesn't have any positions in Eastern Europe.'

'Check again,' said Sarah, her tone sharpening.

From the look on his face, Sarah could tell that Sheldon was hurt. They had reached a point where she might know more about what was happening within the fund than he did, and, in both their eyes, he was suddenly deflated. 'I'll do that,' said Sheldon, standing up to leave.

'Try the Paris office,' added Sarah. 'You know, the keepers of the big secrets.'

Sitting down at her desk, she wondered if she was being too hard on Sheldon. At heart he was a pompous, puffed-up toad, she reflected, but not actually a wicked person. He probably can't help taking himself that seriously. She glanced up towards the side of the office, where a large bank of monitors displayed the current price of the main Leopard Fund in bright red lettering; one hundred and twenty dollars per unit this morning, up twenty cents on the price yesterday. The display was there for a simple reason: to remind the staff of their sole function, which was to keep the red letters on the display ticking constantly upwards. Even in the short time she had worked there, Sarah had noticed the mood of the office was dictated by the digits on the wall. When the fund price was up, it seemed lighter; on days when it was down, the people around her seemed to retreat into the cubicles and offices, like rabbits burying themselves away at the smell of an approaching thunderstorm. Not pleasant, she reflected. But then she had not imagined working for a giant hedge fund would be fun.

The fund's positions in the currency markets were already displayed on the screen. Sarah started scrolling through the files, looking at the range of investments made in the past few days. She already knew the basic principles of a hedge fund well enough: to borrow as much money as possible to take huge positions in the market, usually using derivatives – complex financial instruments that allowed you to buy and sell stocks, bonds or currencies in the future – to increase its exposure, make big profits, then pay the money back and keep the difference. Even so, the scale of the fund's trades amazed her. In the last twenty-four hours, according to the spreadsheets displayed before her, the Leopard had switched twenty-five billion dollars from euros into yen, and another ten billion from Mexican pesos into Thai baht. That trade alone had been enough to mark the peso down a couple of points, and edge the baht up against the dollar, collecting a fat profit on the trade. Of the fifty billion dollars in the Leopard Fund, Sarah noted, three-quarters of the money had been traded already this week. Back in her last job, when she had been working for a traditional investment house mostly managing private pensions, the fund managers made about one investment a month, and then held it for years. This was a very different world.

She scrolled forward. Telmont had told her the fund had been investing in Eastern European currencies, and that she, nominally anyway, was in charge of its strategy in the region. He had laughed loudly when she insisted she had a right to know what trades had been made, but conceded she had a point, telling her to ask Sheldon for the codes. Who had made these trades, she had no idea, but the sums invested were starting to become huge in relation to the markets. In each of the three Baltic states, the fund had started buying heavily, but only after the currencies had started to tumble. In Belorussia, it had taken a position in advance of the collapse, and had added to it after the currency fell. In Poland, where the financial market was now more sophisticated, it had taken a series of futures contracts, all of which would start showing profits when the zloty fell against the euro, exactly as it had done this morning.

In each case, Sarah noted, the buying had been done by a nominee company; an anonymous, offshore bank account that held the position, but which would prevent anyone from discovering who was making the trade. Nobody, she realized, knew about the Leopard Fund's investments in the region, apart from Telmont or the local buyers. And now, of course, herself.

Radek held the fork in his hand, glancing thoughtfully at the food before speaking. 'Of course,' he said at length, 'I don't suppose that bank in Poznan is bankrupt at all.'

'Then why would the guy kill himself?' said Tom, the surprise evident in his voice.

'You are assuming he killed himself,' said Radek.

'That's what the local reports said,' answered Tom, finishing of the last of his steak. 'What else might have happened?'

The meeting for lunch had been Tom's suggestion; the old man seemed to have an endless patience for listening to Tom talk about Tatyana, and was a cool and lucid observer of events in Eastern Europe. They met in one of the basement bars off Cheapside, near Samuelson's offices, and had immediately begun discussing the crash in the Polish markets. By the time Tom had left the office at midday, the currency was down thirty per cent against the euro, the finance minister had put out a statement calling for stability, and nervousness was starting to spread to other Eastern European markets: Hungary, the Czech Republic, Slovakia and Romania were all sharply down.

'It is just too smooth for my liking,' said Radek. 'Take it as a whole. It starts out in Estonia, the very periphery of Europe. From there, it moves down through the Baltics and into Poland, one day after another.'

'From the periphery to the core,' said Tom. 'Isn't that a textbook example of a financial crash?'

'My point exactly,' said Radek. 'When you have been teaching eco-nomics as long as I have, you notice at least one thing. Nothing ever works the way it does in the textbooks. The real world is far too complex.'

'You think this is too neat to be real,' said Tom.

'Let me put it this way, if I was planning a crash, I might start something like this,' said Radek.

'Surely nobody would do that?'

'Don't be so certain,' said Radek. 'That man Cepartinu in Estonia. Apparently he turned into a large seller of both currency and stocks the day before that market crashed.'

'A lucky investor?' said Tom lightly.

'Or a catalyst, perhaps,' replied Radek.

'You think he started the crash?' said Tom. 'Estonia is a small place, but it still takes a lot of cash to put the skids under a whole market. You think he has that kind of money?'

'That's the curious thing,' said Radek. 'He doesn't. Or at least, he didn't. The man is, I'm told, a chancer, a spiv, a person who has tried and failed several different careers. And yet suddenly last week he was throwing money at the Estonia market like he couldn't wait to get rid of the stuff.'

'A front for someone else, perhaps,' said Tom.

'Quite possibly,' replied Radek carefully.

'But who?'

'Impossible to say, as yet,' said Radek. 'But it might be interesting to find out.'

Telmont stood with his back to her, his hands slipped inside his grey, charcoal trousers. 'May I give you some advice?' he said quietly, his eyes still peering down onto the street below.

'Please,' answered Sarah. 'I am here to learn, after all.'

'The old and the cunning,' Telmont said slowly, his eyes gradually turning away from the window, 'will always defeat the young and the clever.'

Sarah paused, unsure whether the remark was one of Telmont's endless riddles. 'I suppose that's true,' she said, wondering if the trace of nervousness was audible in her voice.

'Be very certain it is true,' said Telmont, moving away from the window, and walking towards her. 'Take your friend Mr Bracewell, for example. Quite young and quite clever, of that I have no doubt. But no match for me.'

'I wasn't aware that you knew him,' said Sarah. 'Or that either of you were in some kind of contest.'

'Aha, that is one of the differences between a man and a woman, Sarah, and one of the reasons why we will never understand each other,' said Telmont lightly, the glimmer of a smile playing on his face. 'Every man is in competition with every other man – that is the natural way of things. Women don't understand that, and so they naturally have trouble understanding how the markets work. The market is an arena in which everyone competes with everyone. By definition, it is a man's game.'

'I wouldn't have thought you had much to fear from Tom,' said Sarah, the puzzlement evident in her voice. 'He is just an economist at a London bank, whilst you control one of the biggest funds in the world.'

Telmont moved forward, standing close to Sarah, his eyes scrutinizing her; beneath his gaze, she felt like a specimen in an auction room, picked up, examined, then rejected. 'The enemy shifts all the time, that is what makes the game so fascinating,' said Telmont. 'This Bracewell, he is no more than a nuisance, but I have seen his research and it is unsympathetic to our cause. I don't think you should have been speaking to him.'

Sarah knew her mouth was hanging open, and she could feel her lower lip trembling, but for the moment she was too stunned to say anything. 'You knew I was speaking to him?' she said.

Telmont backed away, retreating several inches across the wooden floor, surprised by the severity of her reaction. 'Information is our business,' he said sourly.

'You listen to our calls,' said Sarah. 'The calls of all the staff, may I ask, or just mine?'

'All the staff,' said Telmont casually. 'It is good to know what our people are saying. It is naive of you to be surprised, and I cannot appreciate naivety in my staff. In the markets that can be a dangerous and expensive commodity.'

Her feet were starting to ache and Sarah would have liked to sit down, but there was no choice but to stand. Even though Telmont was an inch smaller than her, she could feel herself becoming minute in his presence. 'And nobody in the office minds that you listen to their conversations?' she said.

Telmont laughed. 'It is no concern of mine,' he replied, turning away from her and walking back towards his desk. 'In France, you know, we are far less concerned with these petit-bourgeois Anglo-Saxon notions of privacy. We piss in the street.'

And on your staff as well, thought Sarah. 'I suppose I should be more careful about who I talk to in future,' she said, trying to smile as she spoke.

'That would be wise,' said Telmont, his expression absent and distant, as if he had suddenly lost interest in the conversation. 'I don't want you to meet with him either.'

Sarah walked close to the window, looking down at the street below, glancing at the small figures walking through the street a hundred feet beneath her. 'It was planned as a purely social meeting,' she said carefully. 'Nothing to do with work. I wouldn't have thought the company presumed to tell me who I might and might not meet in my private life.'

Telmont stood up again, standing next to her by the window. 'You are far too young to remember 1968,' he said. 'The Marxists used to have a phrase then: the personal is political. Well, the personal is also commercial, I believe.' He paused, his hand sliding across the glass, touching the edge of the fringe hanging loose over Sarah's forehead. 'When you work for the fund, you must give it your entire soul. There can be no aspects of your life that are private from this organization. That is what success is all about.'

Sarah swallowed hard, looking down at the street, avoiding eye contact. 'I'll cancel,' she said, her voice sullen and empty of conviction.

Telmont allowed his hand to run softly down the back of her hair, and Sarah could feel herself recoiling inwardly from his touch. 'The fund will take care of you,' he said. 'The fund takes care of everything.'

The whisky felt good, cooling his nerves, and soothing the aching inside his head, but Tom could still feel a shot of nerves ripping through his guts as pressed the button on the answering machine. Terah had called, and told Tom to call straight back. Don't worry about the time, he had said. It's important.

'What is it?' asked Tom, speaking into the receiver. 'Have you found her?' He was aware that his breath was shortening and he was having trouble breathing, but the words still tumbled from his mouth.

'No, we have not found her, I'm afraid,' replied Terah sleepily.

'But I have found some information I thought you should be aware of.'

Tom wished he had poured himself another drink before making this call. His glass was drained, and he could hardly ask the man to wait. 'Tell me,' he said softly.

'Your wife was not an orphan,' said Terah, his voice empty of any emotion.

Tom remained silent. 'That's not possible,' he said flatly. 'She always said that her parents had died when she was tiny, that she had no memory of them.'

'Then your wife told you a lie, Mr Bracewell.'

Instinctively, Tom felt he should spring to her defence; that he should tell this man he could not speak that way of the woman he loved, but the moment of gallantry soon passed. After all, when your wife has left you for another man, you can hardly object to her being called a liar. 'How do you know?' he asked.

'One of the very few advantages of communism, Mr Bracewell, was its record-keeping,' said Terah. 'Bureaucracy. The Soviets couldn't get enough of it. Your wife was born in 1968, and so should have been registered at one of the state orphanages soon afterwards. That was the law. Her maiden name, you say, was Biemah. I have checked the records for all the state orphanages up until 1971. There was no Tatyana Biemah. Not in Estonia.'

'Her birth certificate,' said Tom. 'Would that say where she came from?'

'I checked,' answered Terah. 'She has no birth certificate.' The air around Tom seemed to freeze. He stood motionless, holding the phone in his hand, unsure how to respond. 'Would you like me to keep looking, to see if I can find out who she is and where she comes from?'

'Keep looking, yes,' said Tom, his tone hollow and empty.

He put the phone down, and walked silently across the room, picking up a framed picture from the mantelpiece. It showed the two of them together, in a cafe in St Mark's Square in Venice, looking into each other's eyes over a pair of frothy cappuccinos. That had been on a weekend away to celebrate their first anniversary. She looked so beautiful in that picture, Tom reflected briefly, as he held it in his hand. There was a sparkle to her smile, and an elegance to the way her black hair tumbled down the back of her neck that had held him in rapture, and she was still, he was sure, the most stunning woman he had ever seen. He walked through to the kitchen, holding the picture face down. To love someone, he told himself, is surely to know them completely. Anything else is merely infatuation. He glanced at the picture once more before putting it into a cupboard at the back of the room. I hardly knew her at all, he reflected to himself. Not even her real name.

CHAPTER 9

Wednesday, 10 February

'THANK GOD YOU'RE HERE,' SAID JONES, A LOOK OF EXAS-
peration illuminating his face. 'Everyone has been looking
for you.'

Tom glanced at his watch. It was past nine, and he should have been
here an hour ago, but somehow he had lacked the will to get up this
morning. He had stayed in bed for an hour or more, not sleeping, just
trying to re-assess things, wondering when his life with Tatyana
suddenly been bent out of shape. Something Radek had said to him
when they first spoke of her stuck in his mind, impossible to dislodge:
the challenge, he had observed, was not to discover where the relationship
had gone wrong, but where it might possibly have gone right. That was
just about it, Tom reflected. And the more he discovered, the less right
it seemed to have been from the beginning. It was not as if she had been
in love with him once, then started to lie after she met another man.
She had lied to him from the first evening they met, when they were
just casual acquaintances, a couple meeting in a bar. She had created
a whole past life for herself that had never existed. She had lied to him
when she didn't even need to. Presumably, just for the fun of it.

'Sorry,' answered Tom absently. 'I got a bit held up, that's all. What's
happening?'

'The Czech Republic,' said Jones. 'The next domino in the line.'

'Already?'

'The crown has just dropped by thirty per cent against the euro,' said Jones. 'The stock market is down by twenty per cent, and the bond market has been just about killed. This is getting so serious even the boys in Frankfurt have noticed. They are clamouring for some analysis.'

Momentarily, Tom could feel a shot of adrenaline running through his veins. If there was one thing to be said for the global capital markets, and right now he could think of much going for them, at least they took a man's mind off his personal problems. He sat down at his desk and looked up at the Reuters and Bloomberg screens. Jones was right. The Czech market was getting blown to pieces. 'Anything coming through on why this is happening?' he asked.

'A mystery,' said Jones. 'There has been some massive international selling of the currency, and rumours of political problems.'

Tom punched the stories up on the screen. Reuters reported heavy selling of the Czech currency, mainly by the big hedge funds, on fears the financial crisis sweeping through Eastern Europe would break the link between the Czech crown and the euro. That had depressed the stock and bond markets, and there was speculation among many of the fund managers that the turmoil could provoke a reaction against the free market reforms of the last decade.

'It is a volatile and dangerous situation,' said Tom, clearing his throat as he kicked off his opening remarks to the morning investment committee meeting. Inwardly, he was cursing himself for not having arrived earlier this morning; he needed more than a few minutes to check out the state of the market and compose his thoughts before addressing the conference.

'The countries of Eastern Europe have only a shallow understanding of market capitalism. We might understand that turbulence and disruption are inherent in the system, but people over there don't. If half their savings start to disappear overnight, nobody will see why that's happening, nor whether they will ever get their money back. Sooner or later, if this crisis gets much worse, it is bound to lead to a reaction against the reforms of the last decade. That is the real danger.'

Jurgen Strich, chairing the committee meeting from Frankfurt via the teleconferencing screen, looked across at Tom severely. 'The point is how we adjust our investment strategy in the light of these events,' he said.

'There are two ways we can go,' said Tom. 'Realistically, I think we have to recognize this crisis is not about to blow over. It is moving from country to country, for reasons we cannot yet quite understand. Looking after the bank's money, of course, has to be our first priority, and so we should definitely start closing down our positions in Eastern Europe. But we should be lobbying for the IMF to join up with the big European banks to shore up these markets. A collapse would be a disaster for the whole European economy, and so, of course, for this bank.'

'Your taste for melodrama is hardly diminished, I note, Mr Bracewell,' said Strich stiffly. 'The time for international intervention has not yet come, although I believe you should prepare a paper setting out the bank's position should that be necessary.'

'Okay, play it as you want, chairman,' replied Tom. 'At least the bank should start selling whatever positions it has in Hungary.'

'Why Hungary?' asked Strich.

'Because it's the next domino in the line.'

'Do you have the precise text?' asked Radek.

Tom cupped the receiver to his ear, and punched up the story on his Reuters screen. It was the longest in a series of articles about the crisis in the Czech Republic, describing the reaction in the Chamber of Deputies. He started reading it out over the phone to Radek. Karel Silva, the finance spokesman of the right-wing Republican Party of the Czech Republic, had, according to the reports, created the biggest impression with a hard-hitting speech calling for the immediate imposition of currency controls, for the nationalization of all foreign assets held within the Republic, and for a complete ban on any form of currency or financial speculation. The Republican Party was best known for its rabble-rousing invective against both Germans and gypsies, but its calls for action against speculators were, the Reuters report said, likely to prove popular. The possibility of foreign assets being confiscated had sent the markets into fresh turmoil, pushing the Czech crown down by another thirty per cent, breaking the link with the euro, and prompting another fourty per cent drop in the stock market.

'The foreigners are getting out of the market as quickly as they can,' said Tom.

'Frankly, who can blame them?' said Radek. 'If idiots like Silva are being taken seriously, why keep your money there?'

'Do you know much about him?'

'An opportunist and a scoundrel,' said Radek. 'I find it hard to believe anyone seriously wants a siege economy.'

'He does,' said Tom into the phone. 'At least, according to these reports. Should the Republicans be taken seriously?'

'Right-wing goons,' said Radek. 'They parade around in black shirts, as if my country had not seen enough of that type of person during the last war. But I suspect the markets are right to be worried. In a crisis, the centre will always trim to the right. If Silva and his cronies are calling for an economic blockade, then the government may feel obliged to make some compromises. Right now, I imagine currency controls would be very popular among the ordinary people. They thought their crowns were worth something, and now they find they aren't.'

Tom hesitated, allowing the thought to filter through his mind before speaking. 'His speech could almost have been calculated to inflame the crisis,' he said. 'In a falling market, the worst thing to do is to make any suggestion capital might be locked in. The only rational way for investors to respond is by getting out as quickly as possible. Surely a man like Silva would see that?'

'I imagine he does,' said Radek. 'He's a criminal, but not an idiot.'

'It sounds like a dumb speech then,' said Tom.

'If he was a trader in a futures market, you wouldn't say that,' said Radek. 'Politics is not a very different trade from the markets, except it deals in a different kind of currency. One man's crisis is another man's opportunity. When a price crashes, buyers start to move in. Same in politics. When a system crashes, people move into the empty space and start offering an alternative.'

'You don't think this has any connection to what is happening in the rest of Eastern Europe?' said Tom.

'On the contrary, there are connections all over the place,' said Radek carefully. 'We just haven't been able to see them yet.'

After Tom picked up the fax he was no longer sure he felt like meeting Sarah.

On the tube home, his mood had been lighter. For the first time since Tatyana had abandoned him, he could feel the blood moving through his veins again. His stomach was starting to rest, and the dark fury that clouded his mind for most of the day began to loosen the ferocity of its grip. I hardly know her, he told himself. She is a stranger to me. And yet, she was a woman, and an attractive one, and the mere fact of trying a date with someone suggested there was some hope, however faint, that his life might one day return to what it had been. Right now, he realized, it was hard to imagine himself with another woman. But then it was hard to imagine himself with Tatyana as well.

As he looked down at the fax waiting for him, his mood slumped again. At the top of the page ran the crisp logo of the Union Bank of Switzerland, and below, the reply to his letter amounted to just a few words.

'Dear Mr Bracewell,' it began. 'In accordance with your recent request, we can confirm that the transfer of £50,000 into the account at the Brompton Road, London, branch of Lloyds Bank held in the name of yourself and Mrs Tatyana Bracewell was made from this bank. In line with the policy of this bank, we are unable to give further information about which of your wife's accounts these funds were transferred from.'

Yesterday morning, while examining the entrails of Tatyana's bank statements, he had noticed the source code for the electronic transfer of £50,000 into her account. A quick check with one of his colleagues at the bank had confirmed that every financial institution can be identified from a row of five digits at the end of each electronic transfer instruction. That money, he was told, without a moment's hesitation, came from the Union Bank of Switzerland. He had sent a fax immediately, asking for details of which account the money had come from, using Samuelson's headed notepaper. It was an unwritten rule among all of the world's biggest banks that they always replied to each other's enquiries promptly. This reply had taken only a day.

He read the letter again, focusing in on the crucial words, making sure he had understood them correctly. '*Which of your wife's accounts* . . .' There could be no doubt that was what had been written. *Which*, he said to himself, out loud this time, listening to the word rattle through the empty flat.

I wasn't aware she had any bank accounts in Switzerland. And certainly not several.

Tom sat alone in the bar, staring at his glass of beer, wondering if he should order another. He glanced at his watch. It was now almost a quarter to nine. Already she was three quarters of an hour late. He would give it another fifteen minutes. If she hadn't shown by then, he would forget about it.

A sombre melancholy had sunk into him while he was sitting at the bar. It had been dark for several hours now, and a smattering of rain was falling onto the streets. For a few moments, every ten minutes or so, he would try to wrench his thoughts back to Sarah, remembering what she looked like when they met last week; but his mind kept wandering back to Tatyana, imagining what she might be doing now, where she might be, and who she could be with. Even her image was fading, he realized. He was losing her, and soon, he sensed, he would be left with just the memory. All contact with the real person would have vanished.

He knocked back the rest of his beer, looking around at the small groups of people in the bar, checking each face, making sure he hadn't somehow missed her coming in. Rude, he thought to himself, to be so late. Very rude. Of course, her flight from New York could have been delayed. Or perhaps she just thought better of meeting up. After all, I wasn't in the best of spirits on Tuesday morning.

Tom paid for the beer, wrapped his coat around himself, and stepped out into the street, turning down the Old Brompton Road in the direction of home. Several bank accounts, he thought to himself. In Switzerland. That meant there had to be money somewhere in her background, and since it now seemed unlikely she was an orphan, it probably involved her family. Terah was right. To find out where someone was going, you had to know where they came from. In time, perhaps, Tom reflected, that mystery will unlock itself. Then, just maybe, I might feel ready to think about other women.

A whistle at the side of the street swept into Tom's ear. 'Here,' said Sarah.

Tom turned around. She was sitting in a cafe, at the edge of the doorway, sheltered from the light rain, a large cappuccino on the table. It was a moment before he recognized her; at first she was just some strange blonde woman shouting from the side of the street, and he was unable to work out what she might want. 'Sarah,' he said out loud, as much to himself as to her.

'Sorry about this,' she said, pulling up a chair for him to sit down.

'Did I get the wrong bar?' asked Tom. 'I was waiting in Casey's for an hour.'

'It's more complicated than that,' said Sarah.

She stood up and walked towards the bar, looking back and asking Tom what he wanted. Cappuccino, he replied.

'It's Telmont,' she said. 'He didn't want us to meet.'

Tom shrugged, stirring some sugar into his coffee. 'So, just don't tell him,' he said.

'I didn't,' replied Sarah. 'He listens to my conversations.'

Tom hesitated, already aware the evening was not turning out anything like the way he had expected. 'You should go back to the beginning,' he said.

Sarah started to explain, her spoon playing in the froth of her coffee. 'I wasn't going to take any notice, of course,' she said quickly, the tone of her voice touched with anger. 'I'm not having anyone I work for tell me who I can meet and who I can't. He can go take a flying fuck as far as I'm concerned. But I had a strange feeling about it. I had told you where we should meet on the office phone, and I just figured he might have someone there to eavesdrop on us, so I waited here, just down the road, so I could catch you when you left the bar.'

'Surely he wouldn't do something like that?' said Tom.

'I don't know,' said Sarah hesitantly. 'He's a creepy guy. It's a creepy organization. The vibe there is not good.'

There was a hint of nervousness to her voice, a frailty, that Tom found instantly appealing, and though her fears about being followed might appear ridiculous, his world had been so transformed in the last few days he was no longer sure about anything; certainty, he reflected, had been the first casualty of last week. 'People are not always what they seem,' he said.

'Tell me about it,' said Sarah.

Tom was unsure how to respond, reluctant to involve anyone else in his private turmoil, and particularly a woman he might be attracted to. If there was one rule he could remember about dating, it was to never talk about your exes. 'It's personal, not important.'

'I'd like to know,' said Sarah, her hand moving across the table towards his.

He began to unravel the story, the words tumbling from his lips, and as he listened to his own story he realized how strange it must seem to an outsider, as if, immersed in the detail, he had lost sight of its complexities. 'So, you see, even the people you know best can turn out to be very different from what you expected.'

'She must have felt very lonely,' said Sarah. 'If she could not confide anything of what she was even with you. Perhaps with this Boissant man she is able to speak more openly.'

'Perhaps,' said Tom. 'Or perhaps she has told him a pack of lies as well.'

Sarah smiled. 'At least we can be sure that Telmont had nothing to do with her disappearance. Our stories aren't that similar.'

'True,' said Tom, his mood lightening for the first time that evening. 'We need something stronger than coffee. Let's get a drink.' Sarah nodded and, taking his coat, Tom stood up and started to guide her into the street. The rain was falling, and he pulled his collar up high around his neck. 'My house is not far from here,' he said, the words pausing in his mouth, unsure whether they should be spoken. 'We could get a drink there.'

Sean Jennings carefully attached the night vision lens to his Sony camcorder and turned it across the street, making sure the picture was accurately framed. The lens amplified the figures walking down the street, making them clearly visible. For identification, he decided, the quality was acceptable.

By the time the couple finally got up to leave, he had been sitting in his Vauxhall Vectra for almost two hours; nearly an hour while the girl waited by herself, another hour while they had been talking. Why they had not met in the bar where he had been told to watch out for them, he could not imagine, but it hardly mattered now. When he had followed her from the hotel, she had come to this cafe instead, and this had been as good a place to stake out as any.

As Tom turned the collar up around his neck, and put an arm protectively over Sarah's shoulder, the tape captured the moment. Jennings made sure he collected footage of them walking down the street together, checking their faces were clearly visible on the tape. As they began to disappear from view, he turned the ignition on the Vectra, pulled away from the kerb, and turned the car in the same direction. The camcorder was sitting on the passenger seat, ready for use. Even if I lose them, Jennings decided, Boissant should be happy enough with the evidence already on the tape. It was exactly what he had asked for.

CHAPTER 10

Thursday, 11 February

WHETHER SARAH GUESSED SHE WAS WEARING A DRESSING gown that had once belonged to Tatyana there was, Tom decided, no way of knowing. As he watched her emerge from the bathroom he realized nothing had changed; the wardrobes were still full of Tatyana's clothes, the kitchen still full of her food, the bathroom still full of her lotions and make-up. It was as if there had been little she wanted to take with her. Everything was to be left behind like an old skin she no longer needed.

'What would you like for breakfast?' asked Tom.

Sarah shrugged. 'Whatever,' she answered. 'Some cereal, coffee.'

The grinder, thought Tom. Tatyana had loved coffee, and always kept a selection of beans in the cupboard, selecting different ones each morning to match her mood. Left by himself, Tom was happy enough to stir up a cup of instant, but this seemed an occasion when he should make some effort. 'Real?'

'Sure,' she replied, leaning down into the fridge, taking out a carton of orange juice.

It was difficult, Tom decided, to know what to admire more: the shape of her thighs exposed by the gap in the robe, or the ease with which she seemed to settle into the flat. She moved from the bathroom to the kitchen, checking out the place, as if it was already hers. Even though they hadn't slept together yet. At least not properly.

It had, he reflected, been more of an evening than he was expecting. Whatever existed between them had developed far faster, and much further, than he would have thought possible. That she had accepted his invitation for a drink surprised him in itself; at most, he thought they might talk, kiss even. He had not thought she would stay the night.

But then she was on the rebound as well, a fact that had emerged during the third or fourth drink, after they had exhausted themselves talking about Tatyana, and Telmont, and the markets, and had started talking about her. It was, she explained, still only six months since she had broken up with Peter, a commercial lawyer five years older than herself, who she had been living with for the past four years. 'He was a nice guy, but he made too much money,' she had said. 'It made him think he was very special and very clever, and that made him insufferably smug.'

She had been with him throughout much of her twenties, and now she was turning thirty as a single woman. That, she supposed, had been one reason for taking the job with the Leopard Fund. She needed a change of scenery, something to help her get over the break-up of the relationship, something to bring some danger back into her life. They had kissed, and by the time Sarah suggested it was time she went home it was already past two in the morning. Tom mumbled his way through a sentence about how she could stay the night if she wanted to. Sarah, against his expectations, had said she would, so long as they didn't have to do anything more than kiss. She wasn't ready, she explained.

In truth, Tom was relieved. He was quite drunk, and not completely sure how he would perform with another woman after so many years. As she climbed into bed beside him, resting her head on the pillow and stretching an arm out across his back, he felt a flash of guilt, as if he were being unfaithful to Tatyana. And yet, after she had gone to sleep, and he lay awake in the dark, he realized he was feeling more relaxed than he had done at any time in the past ten days. It was better to be with someone, he reflected. Even if it might be the wrong person.

'Mind if I play a CD?' said Sarah, shouting from the sitting room.

'Help yourself,' replied Tom.

As he ground the coffee, he could hear the familiar strains of the opening track of David Bowie's 'Young Americans' album. Strangely at home, he thought to himself. As if she had been here a hundred times before.

'You think Telmont has been selling Eastern Europe?' said Tom, pouring the coffee.

'Like crazy,' said Sarah, tapping her fingers against the table top in time to the music. 'Sometimes he buys, sometimes he sells, but mostly he is selling.'

'Even though he has said publicly that he keeps out of those markets,' said Tom.

'He lies,' said Sarah.

'Of course, if the markets knew the Leopard Fund was selling, they would sink even lower,' said Tom. 'There is always a lot of money that likes to follow Telmont around the world. After all, the man has been proved right plenty of times before.'

'He isn't just selling himself,' said Sarah. 'He has this whole network of brokers around Eastern Europe who are on the payroll of the Leopard Fund. I stumbled across that by accident.'

'Could you get a copy of the list?' said Tom. 'That is, so long as it wouldn't be breaking any internal rules.'

'I'm breaking several rules just by being here,' said Sarah, pouring some bran flakes into a bowl. 'We should get ready for work. I've got to be at the office by ten.'

Bran flakes, Tom thought to himself, admiring the soft glow of her rumpled blonde hair as she began eating. Funny that she should like the same cereal as Tatyana.

There was an edginess to the trading floor this morning, Tom noticed, as he walked from the lift to his desk. It was not yet nine, and already the traders on the floor had their shirtsleeves rolled up. Orders were being barked out, and a stale smell of sweat and fear was hanging over the room.

By the time he sat down at his desk, he hardly needed to glance at his screen to know the news was going to be bad. The FTSE index on his Reuters screen was already a solid mass of red, down by a hundred and forty points at 6640, with no sign of buyers emerging. The Hungarian market had collapsed this morning, down forty per cent by nine o'clock, and the Hungarian currency had dived against both the euro and the dollar. Those falls had sent the rest of the Eastern European markets into a fresh tailspin, and the turmoil was hitting the Western European market hard. In Frankfurt, the DAX was down by eighty points, and in Paris the CAC by sixty. The futures market was indicating that this afternoon Wall Street would open heavily down.

Tom took a gulp of coffee, stirring in two sachets of sugar to help wake himself up. An image of Sarah in the dressing gown flashed through his mind, but he swiftly laid it to rest. Back to work, he told himself. He punched the mouse, bringing the Reuters story on the collapse of the Hungarian market up onto the screen.

Budapest: 11/2: 8:47 GMT: The Hungarian stock market came under severe selling pressure this morning after reports that one of the country's largest fund managers had disappeared, taking the bulk of the fund's money with him. Zoltan Kovaki ran the Prosperity Fund, one of the privatization vehicles designed by the Hungarian government. Most Hungarians had shares in Prosperity, but there are now fears the fund may prove to be worthless. Kovaki is reported by sources to have fled the country last night, having transferred the bulk of the assets of the fund into a series of offshore accounts. His whereabouts are not known, and, although some of the money may be recoverable, this will take some time. Fundholders have been selling this morning, driving the whole Hungarian market down sharply. After the collapse of other Eastern European markets, there are now fears that Hungary will also fall. 'This is exactly the kind of news the market did not need right now,' said one analyst. 'The market is already extremely fragile.'

Sarah checked over her shoulder. She could feel a shiver of excitement running through her spine, the same kind of visceral thrill she had felt as a child every time she stole a biscuit from the cupboard.

The Leopard offices had a ragged, tense feel to them this morning. There were men in corners with their shirtsleeves rolled up, their ties hanging loose around their collars, whispering to one another, their faces lined with nervous energy. Above her head, Sarah noted, the digital display showed units in the fund falling sharply for the morning. At least I don't have to trade, thought Sarah to herself. I can analyse, but at least I don't have to trade.

She had learnt in her last job how to examine payroll records. If there was one thing everyone in the City liked to know, it was how much everybody else earned, and the only place that was ever recorded was on the payroll system. Cheat codes – small programmes that allowed you to break through the firewalls surrounding most of the standard payroll systems – occasionally circulated on e-mails. Sarah had stored a few, and one of them was the programme for examining the Leopard Fund's files.

Her eyes flicked through the row of grey numbers displayed in front of her, her imagination briefly captured by the neatly tabulated display of greed and ambition.

Her plan had been to see if she could find out more about some of the brokers who were working with Telmont in some of the Eastern European markets. She was still shocked that the fund listened to her phone calls, and she wanted to know more about what it was doing while she decided whether to carry on working for them. Instinctively, she decided to call up her own files first. Human nature, she reflected. Like eavesdropping on a conversation about yourself – a girl could hardly be expected to resist.

The file downloaded onto her screen. Attached was a scanned copy of a memo. Sarah looked through it, the words piercing through her eyes. It instructed the headhunters the fund retained to approach Sarah Turnbull to join the company. 'Her father, I knew slightly,' it read. 'It would amuse me if she were to be a member of my staff. Make sure we offer her enough money to be certain that this is accomplished.'

Sarah could feel her heart sinking through her chest. Her spirit was suddenly deflated, as through the plug had just been pulled on all her senses. *He knew my father.* She repeated the words to herself, letting them echo through her mind, allowing the anger to ripple through her veins. That was why he hired me in the first place.

Telmont, she reflected to herself bitterly, was nothing but a sadist; someone who treated his employees as disposable toys, no more valuable than discarded pieces of brightly-coloured plastic. But I, she decided, have tired of being his victim.

The problem, Boissant thought, was always to find them alone.

He looked up and down the street, checking the address he had noted on a scrap of hotel paper. This was certainly the place. He glanced at his watch. Ten minutes to seven. According to his sources, Jurgen Strich should be along this way within the next five to ten minutes. That was about the only good thing you could say about the Germans, he decided. They were always punctual.

A cold wind was blowing through the suburbs of Frankfurt that evening, and the thick clouds meant there was no natural light. He could see the house about fifty yards up the wide road, and, even at this distance, he believed he could see two figures, both of them wearing thick woollen overcoats.

Boissant yanked the lead on the Labrador he had borrowed for the evening. It was over a decade since left-wing terrorists had posed any real threat to senior German bankers, but the assassinations of the late Eighties were still fresh enough for most of Frankfurt's senior financial figures to have protection around the clock. Boissant knew Strich certainly qualified for at least one bodyguard. Perhaps even two.

His knowledge of dogs was not great, but Boissant reckoned it was a spaniel that Strich was walking down the street. The man, so he had been told, always took a walk with his dog at this time in the evening, never varying his routine by more than a few minutes unless there was a crisis at the bank. His security would no doubt know this was a vulnerable moment of the day, and would be on their guard.

He began walking slowly towards Strich, the dog tugging on the lead; it was a high-spirited animal, that should play its part perfectly. Boissant checked the inside pocket of his overcoat. The materials he needed were all there, and inside the jacket he could feel the cold steel of the Hechler & Koch pistol.

The Labrador barked twice, and Boissant felt his muscles tense as it tried to rush forward to sniff the spaniel. He could see the guard in the background, walking about fifteen yards behind. Safe enough to be out of earshot, he decided. The barking of the dogs should help to drown out any conversation.

'He is too friendly,' said Boissant, speaking in the rough German he had learnt in the regiment. 'I try to control him, but he pays no attention to me.'

'It's okay,' said Strich, looking down at the two dogs, busy inspecting each other.

'It is a cold night,' said Boissant, turning and starting to walk alongside Strich, his arm holding the Labrador back.

'I prefer to walk alone, if you don't mind,' said the banker, coldly.

Boissant checked over his shoulder; the guard was still walking fifteen yards behind them, paying little attention, and across the road he could see another man sitting in a black Audi, also looking in their direction. Another guard, he decided. 'Most of us would prefer to walk alone,' said Boissant. 'But our past catches up with us all the same. Is that not true, comrade?'

Strich stopped, turning to look at Boissant, examining his face to see if he could recognize him. Although Boissant was still a relatively young man, the lines were etched into his face like grooves into a stone, and his eyes were empty and hard, like small pellets of rock. There was nothing Strich could see there. 'Keep walking,' said Boissant. 'Don't ask the guards to help you, don't turn around, you will only embarrass yourself.'

Strich continued walking down the street, the spaniel trying to run ahead of him. 'What do you want?' he asked.

Boissant pulled a sheaf of photocopied documents from the pocket of his coat, passing them across. Strich looked down, holding them briefly in his hands, his eyes scanning the words, then passing them back. He could see the guard in the car looking at him curiously, his eyes burning with suspicion, but he nodded to reassure him nothing was amiss.

'That was a long time ago,' he said.

'That is your judgement,' replied Boissant, with a shrug of studied indifference. 'It doesn't matter to me. I can send these to one of the newspapers tonight.'

There was silence as the two men paced slowly forward, the dogs still barking at each other. 'To prevent that, what would I need to do?' asked Strich.

Boissant handed across a single sheet of paper. 'Follow these instructions exactly,' he said. 'I may also call you over the next few days with other requests.'

'When does it end?' asked Strich. 'I refuse to be beholden to you forever. Nothing is worth that.'

'The end of this month,' answered Boissant. 'After then, you will not hear from us again. The files will be destroyed.'

'And I am supposed to trust you?' said Strich sourly.

'We all have to trust somebody in this world,' said Boissant. 'It might as well be me.'

Strich looked down at the paper Boissant had given him, glancing through the instructions. 'I will do as you ask,' he said. 'Now leave me in peace.'

Boissant yanked the dog's lead, turning away, walking back towards the subway station that would take him to the centre of town. To the guards, it would seem that nothing more had happened than two men out walking their dogs had chatted for a few minutes. There was nothing suspicious about that.

The follies of youth, he thought to himself, reflecting on how he had signed up for the regiment when he was eighteen, committing himself to a life of combat when he could have stayed on at school and found himself a far easier career. Still, I suppose we all make our choices, he decided.

And when Jurgen Strich had flirted with the Bader-Meinhof gang as a student in the late Sixties, then signed up to become an agent for the East German Stasi, he could never have imagined the consequences a couple of decades later. It was definitely not something he would want anyone to know about now he was a respected director of the KrippenBank. His cards had already been dealt, but his hand would now be played out by other people.

Tom could hardly drag his eyes away from the six crisp sheets of light blue paper. They had a mesmerizing hold on him, as if his eyes were tied to the numbers by a thread of invisible string.

How long British Telecom had been listing all the overseas numbers called in the last quarter when they sent a phone bill, he could not remember; several years, he was sure. He had never bothered to look closely at the bill before; he glanced at the total and wrote out a cheque.

Now, he scanned the pages intently, looking through the numbers listed for any that Tatyana might have called before she left.

Most of the numbers he recognized automatically: his office number, the numbers of a couple of her girlfriends, his mother's number, and a couple of his friends. All those were listed, plus a few other work calls he had made from home in the last couple of months: three to America, one to Germany, and one to the Czech Republic. It was the three other numbers listed under international calls that captured his attention: a number in Estonia, one in Latvia, and a number in Paris that had been called four times in the space of a single week at the end of January, each call lasting more than twenty minutes.

That was the week before she left, Tom thought to himself. And, as far as I knew, she didn't know anyone in Paris.

He walked through to the sitting room, pouring himself a glass of whisky. The alcohol felt good against his lips, and he slipped Bob Dylan's 'Blood on the Tracks' onto the CD, tapping his fingers to the opening bars of 'Tangled Up in Blue'. He stared down at the bill, examining the nine digits of the Paris number. It must be him, he told himself. The man she stayed with in Estonia was French. This number was in France. It must be him.

He took another sip of whisky, holding the sheet of paper in his hand. His fingers hovered two inches from the phone. Make the call, he told himself. You need to know where she is.

His breath was accelerating so fast he could feel it rushing through his lungs, swelling and deflating with the rapid beating of his heart. Perhaps you don't want to know what has happened to her? Perhaps you don't really care? Perhaps she knew that all along? Perhaps that was why she left?

Maybe Tatyana was right. It was wrong for them to be together.

He stretched his palms out along the coffee table, feeling his sweat stick to the glass. Putting the phone to his ear, he started keying the numbers into the machine. He stopped on the seventh number, put the phone down, stared at it, then picked it up and started dialling again.

It rang eight or nine times, without an answer. Tom glanced at his watch; it was seven-thirty now, making it eight-thirty in Paris. Late if this was an office number, but it might be someone's home. 'Bonsoir.' The woman's voice on the line sounded distracted and busy, as though she had better things to do than take phone calls.

Tom paused, squeezing the phone in his fist, trying to control the beating of his heart. 'I would like to speak to Monsieur Boissant,' he said sharply. 'Henri Boissant.'

What, he asked himself, do I say if he comes to the phone? What can one possibly say to the person who has stolen your wife? 'There is nobody here of that name,' said the woman.

'Are you sure?' asked Tom. 'Henri Boissant?'

'I am quite sure,' said the woman. 'I know all the names of the people who work here, and he is not among them.'

'Perhaps I have the wrong number,' said Tom. 'Where is this?'

'The offices of the Leopard Fund. Is there someone else you are wishing to speak with?'

'No, thanks,' said Tom. 'No one else. I'm sorry to have troubled you.'

He leant back on the sofa, letting the phone slip from his fingers. Why would Tatyana have been calling the Leopard Fund in Paris four times in the week before she left? And why did she not tell him?

He buried his face in his hands. If she never told me anything, not even who she was, could she have ever loved me? Even for the briefest moment?

CHAPTER 11

Friday, 12 February

TOM COULD FEEL HER BODY NEXT TO HIS, SENSING HER stomach rise and fall as she slept. He rolled next to her, holding her tight to his chest, resting his lips in the blonde hair that curled delicately around the back of her neck. The smell of her felt good. Different from the way he remembered Tatyana. Sarah was rougher, more natural; Tatyana was always so immaculately showered and scented that no trace of her lingered in the air. The smell of her came out of a bottle at fifty pounds a throw, reflected Tom. That should have told me something.

Out of modesty, Sarah had kept on a t-shirt she had borrowed, although Tom could tell she had nothing on underneath it. It was still too early, he sensed, for them to do anything other than sleep in the same bed. Thank Christ for that, he reflected to himself. In my current state I might not be up to much.

Pulling himself away from the bed, Tom walked down to the kitchen and started grinding some coffee. Almost out of beans, he noted; he had not been shopping since Tatyana left, and for the first time since her disappearance he noticed she had left the kitchen well stocked with food. There were plenty of ready-meals in the freezer, juices in the fridge, biscuits and chocolate and crisps in the cupboard. Tatyana loved to shop, and yet a trip to Sainsbury's was hardly the first priority of a woman about to leave her husband. Don't smoke in bed, he whistled to himself under his breath. She had left the house a certain way, as if she was trying to say something. Look after yourself, perhaps, Tom reflected. Or, maybe, try not to think of me as such a bad person. I did care for you in some ways. Just not enough to stay.

Tom left the kettle to boil and walked through to the sitting room, putting a CD of 'Fidelio' onto the hi-fi. I might as well choose something, he decided, rather than let Sarah take over. It was, after all, still his house. And Tatyana's too. He had, he pondered, as he walked back to the kitchen, levelled the score a little in the course of the night. If Tatyana could be unfaithful, so could he; they might not have had sex yet, but they were certainly moving down that track. And yet, here by himself, in a cold kitchen, watching the grey morning clouds drift past the window, he could not help but be aware of the sense of betrayal – a sickly, pale pang of conscience that started in the pit of his stomach, shivered along his spine and slammed into the back of his head like a hammer into a nail. It was a kind of fear, magnified and transformed into guilt. Tom poured the water into the pot, waiting for the coffee to settle. A point, he thought to himself, had just been crossed; Tatyana had betrayed him, now he had betrayed her. His way of taking revenge, perhaps, he wondered. Or his way of saying, okay, that is in the past, now it is time for me to move on.

From the sitting room, Tom could hear the opening chords of 'Dancing Queen', the first track on Abba's Gold Collection, the volume turned up louder than he would have liked. She's changed the CD, he noted. Clearly a woman who likes bouncy music in the morning. 'Hi,' said Sarah brightly, looking around the kitchen. 'Let's get something to eat. I'm starving.'

Her blonde hair, Tom noticed, was wrapped up behind her head, held in place by a black hairband. When the light caught her skin, she radiated a soft and gentle charm, and he realized that it was only in her presence that he could forget about Tatyana for a few moments. A trick for which I could forgive anything, he reflected.

'What do you think you'll do about your wife, then?' asked Sarah, pouring two bowls of bran flakes, and taking a carton of long-life milk from the cupboard. 'Do you think you'll divorce her?'

'I haven't really decided yet,' answered Tom, the tone of his voice distant and non-committal. 'It's far too early to say.'

'It's easy isn't it?' said Sarah lightly. 'So long as one of you admits to adultery, then it is just automatic. Bang, and it's all over.'

'I'm hardly an expert,' said Tom cautiously. 'Although I suppose I might have to become one.'

'My friend Rosie got divorced. It only took two or three months,' continued Sarah. 'You'll have to meet her.'

'Perhaps,' said Tom, his tone flat and empty. He looked up at her, his expression hardening. 'Can you think who Tatyana might have spoken to at the Leopard Fund?'

Sarah shook her head. 'I haven't been to the Paris office yet,' she answered. 'Apparently it's tiny. London and New York is where all the work gets done.'

'Could you find out if a Henri Boissant works there, or if anyone knows a Tatyana Bracewell?' asked Tom.

'I'll ask around,' said Sarah. 'But, you know, they don't like me asking questions that much.'

'I wouldn't want you to get yourself in trouble,' said Tom.

'It's my decision,' said Sarah. 'I'm a big girl.'

Tom cleared away the bowls, waiting while Sarah took a shower and got dressed; it was almost eight and they would both need to leave for work soon. She had, he reflected, an energy and vitality about her that he found enthralling, and for a moment he found himself wondering if Tatyana's departure had not been a blessing. Perhaps he was meant to be with a woman more like Sarah, someone who came from his own world. 'Where are you spending the weekend?' he asked, taking her bag and carrying it out into the street.

'Here would be best, I think,' Sarah replied, her tone suggesting she was thinking about something else. 'I'm not scheduled to go back to New York until early next week, and there is no point in my staying in a hotel, not now.' She paused for a moment, searching for something in her bag, before looking back up at Tom, a huge smile opening up on her lips. 'If that's okay, of course.'

'There's nothing I'd like more,' Tom replied, wondering, even as the words moved off his lips, whether that might be true. He put an arm around her waist, and together they started walking towards South Ken tube.

Across the road, Sean Jennings wound up the window of the Ford Transit van he had rented for the day. It had been a long and cold night, and he had not allowed himself a moment's sleep; by now he was sure he knew all the insomniacs who called the phone-ins at three in the morning. Still, he decided, the Frenchman was paying well, and for that kind of money he didn't mind missing a night at home. He had the tape of the couple going into the house, and coming out again. That was what he was being paid for, and anything else would be unnecessary. He would drop the tape off, grab a good fry-up breakfast, then catch up on his sleep.

Tom looked up again at the e-mail resting on his computer screen, and rested his face in his hands. A completely different person from the one I thought I married, he said to himself. Everything about her had been a sham.

Finding the details of her bank account had been easier than he imagined. Even though Tom had spent the last fifteen years of his career working within financial institutions, it had always been as an economist; he had never picked up much idea of how they dealt with their customers. He imagined bank accounts were confidential, and Swiss accounts totally secret.

On mentioning this to Danny Berstein, the head of security at the London office, two days ago, he had discovered differently. The subject was raised as casually as possible; he spun a line about how a friend was trying to check the credentials of a potential business partner, who claimed to have a lot of money hidden in Switzerland. Whether Berstein saw through that story didn't, he decided, matter very much.

The information was what counted. Swiss banks, Berstein explained, don't allow the tax authorities or the police access to their accounts, nor will they ever hand over evidence for use in court. But if you wanted to know how much money was in an account, that should be easy. Just use an employee.

It was the same at all banks, Berstein explained, and so few customers were aware of it that it was not really worth the expense of trying to prevent it. Plenty of internal staff had access to accounts, just to process transactions. Some of them had contacts with private detectives, and would, for a fee, access any information you wanted. There was almost no chance of getting caught, and it was a profitable sideline. It was the same in any banking centre in the world. About two hundred and fifty pounds was the going rate in London, Berstein reckoned. 'In Switzerland, probably more,' he had added. 'Expensive place.'

In fact it had cost £500. Berstein had helpfully suggested a couple of names he might call, and the first man he rung, Leopold Baltan, a Frenchman operating out of Geneva, had quoted that price; Tom had been in no mood to quibble, and had taken the deal on the spot. Less than forty-eight hours later the information was sitting here on his screen.

'Our investigations have so far come up with the following information,' the e-mail began. 'The three accounts operated at the bank in the name of Mrs Tatyana Bracewell currently contain the following balances. Account 612345 contains twenty-eight million, four hundred thousand, two hundred and twenty-eight pounds in British sterling. Account 612346 contains sixty-one million, seven hundred thousand, two hundred and twenty US dollars. And Account 612347 contains forty-one million, one hundred thousand, six hundred and four euros. There appear to be linkages between these three and several other accounts, as well as several nominee accounts at different locations for holding stocks and bonds. Please advise if you would like this firm to investigate further.'

Tom wiped his brow and took a sip of the coffee resting at the side of his computer. Three or four times he had read through the same information now, and yet he was still not sure he could either comprehend or believe what it was saying. Millions upon millions stacked away in secret Swiss bank accounts; there were many different ways he had pictured Tatyana during the years he had loved her, but millionairess had never been among them. Briefly, his thoughts started to drift back to the first few weeks he had known her. People, he had always thought, were at their most open when you had just met them, and when the relationship was still being invented. She had not seemed rich then. Far from it. Singing and waitressing in the bar at night, she was only just surviving from the tips she earned, just enough to keep her while she studied during the day. Her room was no more than a bed, a desk, and a few pictures; the most valuable thing she appeared to own was a long-wave radio to pick up foreign broadcasts. He remembered how, soon after they met, he took her to dinner at the Palace, one of the grandest hotels in Tallinn. The look of innocent, playful pleasure on her face as she sipped the wines, ate the fine food and absorbed the elegant splendour of the dining hall, was not that of a girl who had been raised to expect such luxury. It was, he felt sure, entirely new to her. And yet, and yet, Tom fretted to himself, looking back up at the e-mail. There could be no doubt she was, by now at least, a woman of substantial wealth, and presumably always had been. It was, he reasoned to himself, surely impossible for her to have made tens of millions without him having suspected anything.

'Please check the details, it is vital that a mistake has not been made,' tapped Tom, replying to the e-mail. 'And please investigate any further accounts, or stock holdings, as urgently as possible.'

'Apparently it has started,' said Jones, leaning against the partition.

For a moment, Tom was confused, too wrapped up in his own thoughts to be aware of anything that was happening around him. Anxiously, he closed the widow on his computer, reluctant to let anyone see the message he was sending. 'Just like Strich said they would, the traders have been told to liquidate any long positions they've taken in Eastern European currencies or stocks,' Jones continued, walking into Tom's cubicle and resting against the edge of the desk. 'The bankers have been told to start calling in their loans, and the fund managers to start unloading their shares, if they can find any buyers, which I doubt right now. It's madness.'

'I thought it might be some kind of awful joke this morning,' said Tom glumly.

'No joke, old boy,' said Jones. 'Strich was quite serious.'

'But even he must realize this is the worst thing anyone can do,' said Tom, the irritation evident in his voice. 'The market is going to be wiped out.'

Jones shrugged. 'We said our piece this morning,' he said. 'I don't suppose there is much more we can do.'

'There must be,' said Tom, tapping his fingers against the desk. 'There must be something.'

'Well, nobody is bigger than the bank,' said Jones. 'We've talked about that before.'

'But the bank has never been this stupid before,' said Tom.

'Which is quite saying something for the boys in Frankfurt,' said Jones, laughing at his own joke. 'Are you and Tatyana coming on Sunday or not?'

Tom paused for a moment, looking across at his screen. 'I can't,' he said finally. 'We've split up.' He hesitated, catching the lump in his throat and swallowing hard. 'It's okay, really,' he continued. 'I'm fine, really I am. Fine.'

Sarah looked behind her, making sure no one was walking past who might be able to read her computer. She checked that she could immediately switch to a different display if anyone approached. Sure she could not be spotted, she slipped a floppy into the computer and started to download.

Like any big financial institution, everything the fund did was recorded on computers. The access codes Sheldon had given her earlier in the week took her into the currency trading database, a program that stored and analysed all the currency positions taken by the fund. Currency trading was one of the fund's main activities, and it often bought and sold two or three billion of currencies a day; even those sums were a small part of the one hundred and twenty billion dollars of foreign exchange traded every day in

London alone. About half of the fund's trades were computer-controlled; programs had been set to buy and sell when the market hit certain targets. Often the computers were buying from other machines, running different programs. Currencies might only be held for a few minutes, waiting for the price to change by a fraction, then sold on. The other trades were ordered by the dealers here in London, and in Paris and New York, who played with blocks of a few million on which they tried to make profits by pitting their judgement against the market. The winners received big bonuses, the losers were shown the door. Those, however, were the small bets. When the Leopard Fund bet big, the orders always came from Telmont, and the traders were there to buy or sell billions of a single currency, orders that they executed with ruthless and fanatical efficiency.

On average, the Leopard Fund made five thousand currency trades a day and all of them were stored on the database; details included the quantity, the price, the seller, and the trader who completed the deal. In the course of a single week, that amounted to over one hundred thousand bits of information, more than she could possibly hope to sort through. On the database, she managed to exclude all the Far Eastern and Latin American trades, restricting her list to the trades between the dollar, the euro, and the main Eastern European currencies. That took her down to about two thousand trades a day. Then she narrowed the list down to futures and options trades. Next she sorted the deals by size. Telmont, she knew, never gave an instruction in amounts of less than a hundred million dollars; it was a rule around the office that when he said, 'Buy me five yen', what he meant was five hundred million dollars of yen. By restricting the database to futures trades above one hundred million dollars, she should be able to look directly at the moves made by Telmont personally over the past two weeks. That, she decided, should tell her what he really thought was going to happen to the markets over the next few weeks. After she had downloaded it, she could study it at home.

If he knew about my father and hired me because of that, Sarah reflected, any revenge I can take on the man is surely justified.

*   *   *

Tom glanced at the documents again, scanning each of the five pages before placing them flat down on the fax machine. He pressed nine for an outside line, keyed in the eight digits of the fax number, then, taking a deep breath, pressed the 'send' button. On the display, he could see the number being dialled, the connection made, and the first sheet start to slide into the machine.

He stood next to the fax machine, keeping a watchful eye on the people walking through the open-plan office. The fax machine was shared with about a dozen different people, including two secretaries, and he didn't want anyone to discover the documents in the out-tray. That, he realized, could prove very embarrassing.

A deliberate leak was, he knew, a provocative act, and yet, at this moment, Tom felt as if he had no choice. He was just responding to other forces in the only way he could. The decision by the investment committee to sell all the bank's holdings in Eastern Europe was turning into a fiasco. Prices had been tumbling across the region, and even in Western Europe the markets had taken a heavy knock. In Frankfurt, the DAX had closed one hundered and eighty points lower on fears that the banking system could be left with huge losses in the East, and KrippenBank shares had fallen by four euros, a drop of almost seven per cent. If the markets could be made to realize the turmoil was largely the work of a few big speculators, led by the Leopard Fund, then there was a chance the chaos might be tamed. A slim chance, Tom admitted to himself. But one that he felt he had to take.

Bank economists always have good contacts with the financial press. They are always useful for a quote, and on a slow news day can usually rustle up some kind of prediction that can be turned into a story. Tom had known Charles Barker, the economics correspondent at the *Sunday Telegraph*, for some years, and felt he could trust him. When Tom called, suggesting he might like a copy of his report, Barker sounded relieved. His editor was hassling him for a fresh angle on the Eastern European story for Sunday, and Telmont always made a good headline; the Leopard Fund was one of the very few financial institutions the editor had actually heard of. 'Put it on the fax,' Barker had told him. 'I'll make sure it goes in on Sunday.'

Tom collected the report from the fax and walked back to his desk. A risk, he reflected to himself. Things leaked from the London office all the time, and he knew it irritated the Germans over in Frankfurt intensely. In Germany, nothing ever leaked to the press, and they could never understand why it was always happening in England. There would be the usual enquiries, all carried out with great solemnity, but with little real hope of proving anyone guilty. After all, lots of people internally would have seen the report. Anyone could have passed it across to the paper. And anyway, he thought to himself as he sat back down at his desk, it doesn't matter that much. A job I can take or leave; there is always another one around the corner. It's not as if I have a wife and kid to support.

The smell in the air was unmistakable. The scent, Boissant reflected to himself, of philosophy, art, literature, of the finest food and wine, and the most elegant, desirable women; the scent, in short, of civilization. After almost two weeks of travelling through the pits of Central and Eastern Europe, it was good to be home. Another week, he thought to himself, and this work will be done.

The offices of the Organization for Economic Co-operation and Development were located at 2, Rue André Pascal, in the sixteenth arrondissement of Paris. Ever since the world's richest nations had set up their own club just after the Second World War, it had always been headquartered in Paris, and had always occupied a lavish and opulent building. It would, many of its employees had reflected over the years, hardly have been appropriate for an institution dedicated to advising and protecting wealth not to have allowed its staff some idea of what it tasted like.

Parked almost a block away, from the back seat of his Renault Espace Boissant could see the entrance to the building clearly, neatly dressed office workers filing in and out of its revolving glass doors in an unending, grey flow. He leant forward to the driver. 'Start the engine, Michel,' said Boissant softly. 'Our prey will be out in a moment.'

To discover that Julian Frinton left the office between five-ten and five-fifteen most evenings had not been difficult; a matter of paying a detective to follow him for a few days to unlock the pattern of his day. An Englishman, educated at Cambridge and the London School of Economics, Frinton had moved to the OECD six years ago after his French wife had been offered a senior job at Credit Lyonnais. Since she was the person in the family who earned the most money, they lived where her work in the bank took her, and he fitted in around her plans. For the same reason, it was Julian who left the office early each day to collect Edward from his playgroup, while she worked late in the office. It was not, Frinton had reflected many times, an arrangement he had any trouble with. Many men, he knew, might have seen it as a threat to their masculinity, but, in truth, he had never much enjoyed being in the office, and was glad of the excuse to leave early every day. Eastern European economies interested him, but he hardly needed to be at his desk to ponder the region's economic future.

Darkness had already fallen on the city by late afternoon, but the lights from the office buildings, shops and cafes, seeped across the pavement and onto the road. The night vision scope was hardly necessary, Boissant realized, but he kept it pressed to his eye anyway. 'It's him,' he barked to Michel. 'Drive.'

Julian Frinton failed to notice the Espace drawing up alongside him as he strolled towards the Metro. It was only when he saw Boissant standing at his side, his hand reaching out across his shoulders, steering him towards its open door, that he began to pay any attention. 'Get in,' said Boissant firmly.

'Let go!' said Frinton, trying to brush the man aside. The one thing he hated about Paris was the number of madmen hassling you on the streets. It was even worse than London.

From his inside pocket Boissant pulled the picture Michel had taken across the park yesterday morning. 'If you want to see him alive again, you will do as I say.'

Frinton glanced down, his breath catching in his throat. 'Where did you get that picture of Edward?' he asked.

'Get in the car,' Boissant repeated, grinding the words through his teeth in a flat, relentless monotone.

The sliding door of the Espace shut firmly behind them, and Frinton could feel the power of the engine as Michel pulled away from the kerb and out into the early evening traffic. He could feel his knees start to tremble, and sweat forming on his back, soaking into his shirt. His stomach was heaving and he felt he might be sick at any moment. 'Where is Edward?' he said, the words sagging on his lips, as if he were already on the brink of despair.

'You will see,' said Boissant, leaning back in the seat, a placid smile playing on his lips. Terror, he thought to himself. It was all a matter of acting, really. So long as you played the part the right way, they would believe you were capable of any atrocity. 'There is no point in asking now.'

The drive took almost twenty minutes, a journey completed in an icy, cold silence, interrupted for Frinton only by the rapid beating of his heart. The Espace drew up alongside the playgroup building, and he could see the familiar faces of the other parents, almost all of them women with whom he enjoyed flirting when he picked up Edward. The French mothers were all very amused by the thought of a father collecting his child every day while the mother went to work, and the fact he was English made it twice as funny. 'Ask if your son is there,' instructed Boissant. 'But don't even think about asking for the police. They can't help you.'

Frinton walked mechanically towards the entrance. He could see several children with their mothers, but no sign of Edward. 'Is he here?' he said to Marie, one of the young girls who looked after the playgroup.

'His uncle collected him,' she said casually. 'About half an hour ago.' She looked up nervously towards Frinton. 'He had a letter from your wife saying it was okay.'

Instinctively, Frinton knew what had happened. He walked back towards the Espace, climbing into the back seat. 'What is it you want?' he asked, looking directly at Boissant.

'You co-operation, that is all,' Boissant replied. 'That should not be so hard. You work for an organization that promotes co-operation, after all, and so do I. We just have our different methods.'

Frinton cupped his face in his hands. 'Is Edward all right?' he asked.

'Do as I say, and nothing will happen to him,' Boissant replied. 'But disobey me, and . . .' He hesitated, pausing for effect, and pulled a picture from his pocket, handing it across the back seat of the car. The churning of Frinton's stomach grew suddenly worse as he looked at the image of a small white boy being buggered over a rough wooden table by a large, fat Arab, whilst in the background two other men, one Arab, one black, looked on, their hands stuck down into their flies. 'This little boy in the picture was raped by all three men, then they cut his throat to stop him from telling anyone,' said Boissant slowly. 'I know these men. They are always looking for fresh victims. Trust me, it will not be pleasant for him.'

The words drilled into Frinton's ears like a nail being hammered into rock, while his eyes remained glued to the picture. 'What do you want me to do?' he asked.

'The OECD report on the economic prospects for Eastern Europe, it will be published this week, will it not?'

Frinton nodded, looking up towards Boissant, trying to read the man's eyes.

'You have control of what it says,' continued Boissant.

Frinton nodded again, but remained silent. From a case, Boissant produced a sheaf of papers and two computer disks, handing them across. 'This is the report you will produce,' he said softly. 'You may make changes for house style. Otherwise this must be exactly what appears. Is that understood?'

Frinton took the papers in his hands, glancing at them, but not bothering to read the words. 'It is a small thing, surely?' continued Boissant. 'After all, who cares what some economic report says? It is unimportant compared with the life of your son.'

CHAPTER 12

Saturday, 13 February

TOM WATCHED THE SUPPLE CURVE OF HER THIGH, THE RIPPLE of flesh against robe, as Sarah knelt in front of the six shelves of compact discs choosing something to play. She immediately scanned past the rows of classical recordings, glanced only briefly at the jazz, then studied the pop records carefully, before eventually choosing a Diana Ross collection of love songs. Her possession and self-control were, Tom reflected, as he watched her moving gracefully from the CD shelves back towards the kitchen, immaculate. She took control as if control were the most natural thing in the world to take, not something to be resisted and fought. I would have hesitated to put that album on without asking, he realized, and it happens to be my house. That is the difference between us.

'Did she like to cook?' asked Sarah, looking at the rows of spices along the side of the kitchen.

Tom nodded. 'Not obsessively,' he replied, the evasion apparent in his voice. 'Maybe a couple of times a week she would make something herself,' he continued. 'The rest of the time it was M&S or Covent Garden soup or whatever.'

'I wish I could cook,' said Sarah, pouring the water into the coffee pot. 'Perhaps that is what we should do today – go to the supermarket and then cook something.'

Sarah took a copy of the *River Cafe Cookbook* and started leafing through as she sipped her coffee. Tom noted the way her eyes rested on the pictures rather than the words, and after a few minutes she pushed it aside, her interest already exhausted. 'Do you have a computer?' she asked.

'Sure,' answered Tom with a smile.

'I wanted to check some information I downloaded from the Leopard Fund records,' she said. 'I have the disks in my bag.'

Tom leant forward on the table, cradling the coffee cup in his hands. 'I'm puzzled,' he said.

'About what?' said Sarah, a hint of anxiety drifting across her face.

'About you,' answered Tom. 'I don't think I know what makes you tick.'

Across the table, Tom could tell she was buttoning up; there was a tensing of her shoulders and in her eyes he could see invisible shutters being drawn down. 'Usual things,' she said softly. 'Nothing special.'

Tom sighed, suspecting she was not about to tell him much more, not this morning anyway. For now, she would remain an invaluable but mysterious presence in his life, just one of the many riddles that surrounded him. 'What's on the disk?' he said.

'The trading records.'

'Of the fund?'

Sarah nodded. 'I downloaded it all yesterday,' she said. 'I think I just captured all the trades in Eastern Europe. I wanted to take them home and analyse them.'

A grin spread across Tom's face. 'So we could know precisely what Telmont has been doing in the region for the last two weeks?'

'Cool, don't you think?' said Sarah. 'I mean, he might be the greatest liar ever born, but the truth should all be there in the trades.'

Tom leant across the table, kissing her on the lips, and feeling a shudder running down his spine as her left hand started to inch its way across his chest. 'Why did you marry someone you hardly knew?' she asked.

Tom drew away. 'I thought I knew her,' he replied. 'And I thought I loved her. That was all that seemed to matter.'

'You never worried that you didn't know who her parents might have been, who her friends were?'

'I don't know,' answered Tom. 'Tatyana had this quality about her that demanded you take things on trust.'

The barman poured two shots of brandy into the glass and pushed it across the bar. Boissant took it, sinking the alcohol into the back of his throat before asking for a refill. God, I hate the cold, he thought to himself.

Fighting in the jungle or the desert had been the best part of his military service. The regiment had been involved in special operations in three different parts of Africa during the 1980s, and Boissant had never minded the flies or the stench or the sweat; far better than the chilled waters off New Zealand during operations against Greenpeace activists. The heat, he liked to think, had a kind of life about it, whereas the cold seemed like a first draft of death; an early premonition, he reflected, of the freezing earth where we would all eventually be buried.

The hotel bar was almost empty. Two travelling businessmen in one corner, Boissant noted, probably wondering where they could meet some women; a Russian who appeared to be by himself – mafia, most likely, Boissant decided to himself, but not on duty this evening; and a barman who couldn't have been more than eighteen and was still unsure how to work the till. Still, Boissant decided, it was better than that dreadful Irish place they had met last time. At least they served a decent cognac.

Boissant glanced at his watch as he saw Gregor Cepartinu walk through the doors of the lobby and turn towards the bar. It was 8.27, which made him seven minutes late; unpunctuality was yet another sign of the weakness of the civilian character. Cepartinu seemed to have grown in stature since the last time they met. If it were possible for a man of his age to add a foot to his height, Boissant imagined he might have done so. His manner was more confident, his clothes more expensive, his watch fatter, and the look on his face spelled substance and position. The effect of money, Boissant reflected; it had an instant ability to make a man appear bigger and sleeker, at least in his own estimation. It suits him, Boissant decided. It is just a shame the money isn't his.

'Surely all men of your age were drafted by the Red Army?' said Boissant, looking up at Cepartinu as he sat down next to him. 'Military service was compulsory, was it not?'

The Estonian smiled, and looked towards the barman, asking him for a large shot of rum. He looked back at Boissant, scrutinizing the man carefully. 'Problems with my liver,' he said, his smile revealing his discoloured, gappy teeth. 'It was always possible to find something wrong if you knew the right people. Of my class at school, twenty boys were drafted by the Russians. Two of them died in training, one of them beaten to death by his squadron, the other in some kind of accident. Three died in Afghanistan. One in four casualties, and that's without there even being a proper war on. Not good odds.'

'But it might have meant you were a man, instead of vermin,' said Boissant, the tone of his voice deepening as he completed the sentence.

The look of smug self-satisfaction on Cepartinu's face was wiped completely away, like spray from a windscreen, replaced by anxiety mixed with fear. His eyes loomed out from the rolls of flesh on his face, scanning the room, as if checking the possible means of escape.

'You are not pleased with me,' he said hurriedly, trying to remain calm. 'Surely I have done all that you asked?'

Boissant surveyed the man coldly, allowing his eyes to move slowly across his face – a technique, he had been taught in the regiment, that crocodiles used to rattle their prey. If a man could hold his nerve under that sort of examination, he might be worth something – but Cepartinu was not in that league. The fear was sweating out of the pores of his skin. 'You have not used your brain,' said Boissant slowly.

'The money you gave me, it has all been used exactly as you asked,' said Cepartinu. 'It has been used to destabilize the local market, in accordance with your instructions. What else should I do, other than follow my orders?'

'Follow orders discreetly,' snapped Boissant. 'You have been noticed spending money around town. People are suspicious.'

Cepartinu shrugged. 'I must speculate to have any impact on the market,' he said.

'But not like a fool,' said Boissant. 'Use a series of brokers. It must be impossible to trace your actions back to a single firm.'

'You wish me to continue?' asked Cepartinu.

'For one more week,' said Boissant. 'Until next Friday. You will receive precise instructions later, but by Friday you must have the pieces in line for the market to crash spectacularly.'

'As you wish,' said Cepartinu.

'One more thing,' said Boissant. 'How well do you know the forests?'

Cepartinu looked at him closely. 'As a place to spend the weekend, nothing more.'

'I will be bringing a woman to the Estonian forests next week,' said Boissant. 'I will need some protection.'

'A captive?'

Boissant shook his head. 'No,' he replied. 'She will come willingly. But for two days it will be important that it is impossible for anyone else to reach us.'

'I can find men who will take care of that,' said Cepartinu. 'The forests are a good place for a person to hide.'

'She already knows that,' said Boissant. 'She comes from here.'

Sitting behind the computer, her hair tied up in a band, Sarah appeared lost in a world of numbers. Her eyes were attached to the screen and her fingers moved over the keyboard with a precision and determination Tom could only admire. He stood at her side, placing another cup of coffee on the desk, her third of the morning. 'Thanks,' she muttered, the word barely escaping from her lips.

Sarah seemed oblivious to everything, but Tom noticed the shabbiness of their surroundings. The study was the one room in the house that had not been decorated; the paintwork had started to grey with age. Both he and Tatyana had known that it should have been the nursery. There was no point in decorating that room until she became pregnant, but the pregnancy never arrived. Why, Tom had never been sure. Now, he could only presume it was because she didn't want to have his child. She wanted someone else's.

'The bastard,' muttered Sarah, her eyes still captivated by the rows of black numbers lining across the screen. 'The evil, lying bastard.'

'What have you discovered?' asked Tom, leaning forward, his chin close to her cheek.

Sarah jabbed the keyboard, scrolling the pages back to the beginning. 'He has been selling all along, right from the start,' she began. 'Here we have a record of all the Leopard Fund's dealings in Eastern Europe since the middle of January, during which time Telmont has been going around telling everyone he is a great supporter of that part of the world, and he would never try to speculate there. Complete lies. The fund has been trading all of those countries furiously, mainly in the currency market, but also in stocks and bonds.'

'Buying or selling?'

'Both, of course, but mainly selling,' said Sarah firmly. 'On the surface, this looks like a series of arbitrage trades, trading one market against another to take advantage of price differentials, the sort of thing hedge funds do all the time.'

'But that's just a smoke-screen,' said Tom.

'Absolutely,' replied Sarah. 'The objective is to confuse the market about what he is really up to. The fund buys a hundred and one, and sells a hundred, then everyone in the market thinks it is just trading, but really it is buying.'

'I thought you said he was selling,' said Tom.

Sarah nodded firmly, scrolling the screen downwards. 'He is,' she said. 'On a massive scale. Telmont has been buying sell options everywhere he can find them. That means he is positioning all the fund's money so that the markets will be at one precise point at a precise time in the future.'

'For Eastern Europe?' asked Tom.

'Every market in that region, as well as most of the main markets in Western Europe and North America,' said Sarah. 'This looks like one of the greatest bear gambles of all time.'

Tom leant forward, looking into the screen, his eyes scanning through the numbers displayed there. 'He's betting on a crash.'

'Looks that way,' said Sarah. 'If the markets collapse, the Leopard Fund makes a fortune, while everyone else will be wiped out. That's the way he's positioned himself. If the markets don't collapse, then he wipes himself out. The Leopard Fund will be finished. It's all or nothing. One throw of the dice.'

'By when?' asked Tom. 'When are the sell contracts set for?'

'Friday,' answered Sarah. 'Next Friday at noon. That is when the sell contracts all expire. The markets have to crash by then.'

CHAPTER 13

Sunday, 14 February

'YOU DON'T THINK TATYANA WILL COME BACK TO YOU?' ASKED Radek, the tone of his voice low, almost conspiratorial.

The question struck home. For the past few days, Tom realized, he had begun to think less and less about the possibility of her returning; the prospect had departed his thoughts like a swift and brutal but quickly forgotten argument. 'It doesn't look very likely, does it?' he said. 'It's two weeks now, and not so much as a whisper from her.'

'That might mean many things.'

'Like she is so busy with that French guy, she doesn't have time to call her husband.'

Radek shrugged. 'Or that she is frightened.'

Tom shook his head. 'Tatyana was never frightened of anything,' he said.

Sarah was carrying a tray with a coffee pot and three cups, and it was clear from the silence when she walked into the room they had been discussing a subject from which she was excluded; the silence was shifty and uneasy and unnatural, not just a lull in the conversation. She looked down at Tom, and for the first time he imagined he could detect a hint of irritation in her eyes. 'I bought you this,' said Radek, standing up and handing a book to Sarah. 'I thought it might interest you.'

Sarah glanced at the cover. *The Dialectic of the Markets*, read the title, written in clear bold type above the name of its author, Jean-Pierre Telmont. He was pictured on the jacket, in profile, his hair looking darker than it was now, and the lines on his face less deeply grooved into his skin. 'It was published in America, but only in a small edition subsidized by the author, I think. It is quite hard to get hold of.'

'Is it any good?' asked Sarah.

Radek laughed. 'Of its genre, perhaps it is not so bad,' he said.

Sarah scanned the blurb on the back jacket. 'A unique exploration by one of the world's leading money managers of his own startling philosophy of how the markets operate,' it read. 'Jean-Pierre Telmont, Chairman and Chief Investment Officer of the Leopard Fund, argues the markets are subject to the same historical laws as the rest of human history, and that it is only through an appreciation of the wider social and economic forces in play within society that the movement of asset prices can be understood.' She paused, looking back up at Radek. 'Actually, I've already read it, but thanks all the same.' She poured the coffee, handing cups to both Tom and Radek. 'That stuff is too old to help us with what is happening right now.'

'Sarah has found out some sensational information about Telmont,' said Tom. 'That's what we wanted to talk to you about.'

'Telmont is not just dealing massively in Eastern Europe. There have been thousands of trades back and forth in the last couple of months, but when you study them, when you look at the whole picture, the fund is positioned to make a fortune after the markets in Eastern Europe, and then the West as well, collapse. By next Friday,' she said. 'He is preparing for a crash.'

Radek leant forward. 'Preparing – or planning?' he asked.

Sarah looked closely at Radek, deciding if she knew what to make of him. There was, she realized, no way of judging his angle on anything, and that disturbed her. 'Does it make a difference?' she asked.

'In the final analysis, no,' said Radek. 'Markets are paradoxical, self-fulfilling beasts, and about as easy to find your way around as a dark room full of mirrors. If enough people think there will be a crash, and sell to avoid any losses, then the crash will duly arrive. So the preparation becomes the thing itself, which in turn becomes a signal to buy, and so it goes on. A paradox that endlessly reinvents itself. That is the beauty of a market. Before then, there is a big difference. Preparing for a crash is when you sit back and wait for it to happen. Planning is when you actively make it happen.'

'How could you plan a crash?' asked Sarah, the words fading from her lips.

Radek looked up at her, peering into her eyes above his glasses, shaking his head slowly. 'Not how, but why?' he said. 'That is always the real question.'

'Okay, why?' said Sarah, a trace of impatience infecting her voice. 'We need to know why.'

'In my country, we have a saying, that to find how high a tree will grow, you must study its roots,' said Radek, his voice slowing as he moved through the sentence. 'The answer must be in the past. In Paris somewhere, I suspect.'

The Cafe Michel in the eighteenth arrondissement had always been a favourite of Boissant's. Although he had grown up in a village ten miles to the south of Bordeaux, and it was of there that he had his fondest memories, it was here that he had formed his first impression of Paris, and it was to here that he most liked to return. The regiment had its Paris headquarters just over a mile away, and it was there he received his first training in the skills and tactics of the French special forces, a breed of men who regarded themselves the toughest in the world. On the few hours a week they were allowed out, most of the men drifted towards the night-clubs and brothels of Pigalle, but Boissant had always preferred to walk here, towards this cafe, enjoy the food, drink a good bottle of wine, and soak up the atmosphere. Sometimes he would flirt with the waitresses, but more often he would just swap stories with some of the regulars, and discuss battles with the owner, Michel, a veteran of the Algerian war who knew more than most men about how wars were fought.

Michel was dead now, and, Boissant noted as he sipped on his coffee, the place was not quite the same without him. Still, he remained loyal to the old place, even stripped of much of its character. There were good memories. And, after all, it was here he had first been recruited to the cause.

Telmont hesitated for a moment in the street outside the cafe, his eyes running first left, then right. He could see nothing except for a single car, and an elderly man out walking his dog. Nodding towards the waiter, he ordered a coffee and sat down next to Boissant. 'You are ageing,' he said, resting his arm on Boissant's shoulder.

'The world is ageing,' said Boissant. 'I can feel the tiredness in the air. An exhaustion of the spirit, I believe.'

'The task is almost complete,' said Telmont.

'By Friday, still?' asked Boissant.

Telmont nodded curtly, stirring two lumps of sugar into his coffee. 'Everything has been put in place,' he said softly. 'The Leopard Fund has been prepared, and nobody in the market is aware of what we are doing.'

Boissant reached down at his side and pulled a newspaper from a pile on the floor. He pushed it across the table. 'Telmont Sells Eastern Europe Claims Secret Report: Fears Grow of a Market Collapse' ran the headline about halfway down the front page of the business section of the *Sunday Telegraph*. 'Only a few people in Paris read the London papers, but they are here first thing every morning,' he said, looking across at Telmont.

A look of anger flashed across Telmont's face as he read the story; a darkening of his eyes, and a deepening of the lines on his forehead.

'A KrippenBank report blaming the economic crisis sweeping through Eastern Europe on the activities of a small group of massive hedge funds, led by Jean-Pierre Telmont's Leopard Fund, has been suppressed by the bank,' ran the introduction to the story. 'The report was prepared last week by the bank's senior economist specializing in the region, Tom Bracewell. Telmont is known for taking huge positions in the market, and was one of a small group of fund managers who forced the pound out of the ERM in 1993. The report concluded that the KrippenBank and its investors should ride out the storm, but the bank refused to publish. The KrippenBank is rumoured in the market to have started selling all its assets in Eastern Europe last week, a move that was highly criticized within the region.'

'Tell me something,' said Boissant, looking up at Telmont. 'Have we identified who called the fund asking for me?'

Telmont looked up coldly. 'As you suspected, Bracewell,' he said, his voice calm and level.

'Everywhere, I am hearing this name, Tom Bracewell,' said Boissant, the words freezing on his lips. 'When a man calls the Leopard Fund asking for me, it is Bracewell. When a report is written identifying the fund as a factor in the Eastern collapse, again it is Bracewell. Your currency specialist, Sarah, she dates a new man and his name is Bracewell. And then there is Tatyana. If either of us is to speak to Tatyana, well then, we may as well just use her formal title. We may as well call her Madame Bracewell and have done with it.'

Telmont leant back in his chair, rocking slightly, his eyes running along the empty, quiet street. 'I don't believe he need trouble us,' he said. 'The Englishman is a nuisance, nothing more.'

Boissant squeezed his palm against the rough surface of the table top. 'I don't like it,' he said. 'He is everywhere. You know what the English are like. Dogged, persistent people, not very intelligent, but they can keep scratching away at things. They can cause trouble.'

'He should not have written that report, it is true,' said Telmont, looking down again at the newspaper story. 'It was not helpful. I think you should call your new friend at the KrippenBank, and make sure he is dismissed.'

'And make a hero of him?' said Boissant.

Telmont shook his head. 'Tell the German he is to be dealt with, but on terms that ensure his silence,' he said. 'He will not want to risk his pay-off. All the English care about is money these days. They have no principles any more.'

Boissant waved to the waiter for another coffee. 'That will be done,' he said. 'Our man will keep a watch on him as well, at least for the next week. We need to make sure he doesn't come any closer.'

Telmont nodded. 'And Tatyana is safe?' he asked.

'Quite safe,' said Boissant. 'The arrangements for her transfer have been taken care of.'

'And she will co-operate?'

Boissant allowed a thick smile to spread across his lips. 'After what she has been through,' he said. 'I don't believe there is any question about that.'

What made Tom decide to examine the history window on his copy of Microsoft Internet Explorer, he would later be unable to recollect. An insatiable sense of curiosity, he supposed. A fanatical desire to know everything it was possible to know about her, to peer into every private moment she had spent alone in the house.

It was, he reflected, a kind of emotional archaeology: searching for clues in the most unlikely places, and trying to reconstruct some kind of version of the truth from the broken fragments she had left behind. I am, in truth, he confessed to himself, while staring blankly at the computer screen, far more interested in Tatyana now than I ever was when she was still around.

While Sarah was busy taking a bath – her second of the day, Tom noted – he had logged onto the Web, checking his e-mail to see if there was anything from Tatyana. After calling up the Yahoo search engine, he had typed in 'Jean-Pierre Telmont' just to see what might come up. A long list of sites sprang onto the screen, most of them either financial or from press cuttings. Tom glanced at a couple, but soon lost interest. Like most things on the Web, it was just a slow and frustrating way of finding something you could have found in a decent library. Except, he realized, that when you browsed in a library you did not leave any kind of a trail.

That Tatyana used the Net, he already knew. He had got the connection at home about three years ago, around the time when everyone was getting Internet access, and at first she had treated it with the indifference she reserved for all technology; cashpoint machines were the only computers she showed any interest in. Maybe two years ago, he had shown her how to use it, and she had played with the system sporadically since then. Last summer she had used it to book the hotel they stayed at in Corsica. Perhaps once a fortnight she would send him an e-mail at work, usually about something she had bought during the day. That she used it more than occasionally, he had not imagined.

Tom clicked on the edit icon, then clicked again on the history window, bringing onto the screen a long list of files, a record of every site that had been visited over the last few months. A surge of excitement started to roll through him, a sensation with which he was now familiar; he felt it every time there was the prospect of fresh information about her. Most of the sites were predictable – travel reports, and lists of ticket prices to different destinations; pages detailing jazz and classical concerts coming up; a home page devoted to Julie London, the 1950s torch singer who was among her favourites; and so on. Nothing you might not find on millions of web browsers all over the world. Only one word stood out amongst the many listed: *Metsavennad*. Tom clicked on the browser, taking him to that page, but when it came up he could see it was written entirely in Estonian. He had memorized a smattering of words on his trips to Tallinn, and Tatyana had shared a few phrases with him, but this he could not read. A couple of words seemed familiar: 'memory' was there in the introduction, and so was 'struggle'. But the rest meant nothing.

He shut the browser down, walking across to the bookshelf. Most of the books were his. Tatyana, as he recalled it now, had never been a great reader, usually restricting herself to biographies of iconic beauties, women such as Jackie Onassis, Grace Kelly or Princess Diana. A book on Napoleon and Josephine was the only piece of history he had ever seen her read, apart from a few serious works in her native language. *Metsavennad*, he wondered to himself, flicking through an English-Estonian dictionary. 'The woodsmen, a slang expression,' it said simply.

Woodsmen, pondered Tom. Even as Tatyana became gradually more distant, slipping more and more into the realm of remembered things, her capacity for surprise was endless. What, Tom asked himself, could have been her interest in the remote Estonian woods?

CHAPTER 14

TOM FELT THE GLACIAL CHILL DESCENDING OVER THE OFFICE as soon as he stepped through the doors. The security guards greeted him with the same morose indifference they reserved for all the staff, but everyone else watched him walk through the corridor with a mixture of awe and paranoia. He could sense their eyes watching him from a distance, moving away as he drew closer. That's what you get for working for a German bank, Tom reflected. Step an inch out of line here, and you become a marked man. Individuality was not a quality KrippenBank prized.

He had known leaking the report to the Sunday papers would be dangerous. The papers were desperate for an angle on the crisis in Eastern Europe, and it had been followed up in both *The Times* and the *Telegraph* this morning. There would be an investigation, and inevitably he would be the most likely culprit; it was his report and he had made a fuss at the meeting about it being scrapped. Still, plenty of other people might have leaked it, Tom decided. The bank was a big place.

'Was it you?' asked Jones, standing at the side of the desk.

Tom glanced through the office, checking whether anyone might be able to hear him. 'What does Bart Simpson always say?' he replied. 'I didn't do it, nobody saw me, you can't prove anything.'

Jones grinned. 'The shit is really hitting the fan.'

'I thought it would.'

'Not like this you didn't,' said Jones. 'Apparently, the boys in Frankfurt have gone ballistic about leaks. We are all getting memos warning us that if we want to talk to any journalist about anything, it has to be through the press office. Disobey, and we are out faster than you can say redundancy.'

'Pretty tough,' said Tom.

'They're even threatening not to pay bonuses to anyone who steps out of line.'

'Ouch,' said Tom. 'They are serious.'

Jones checked over his shoulder, smiling at one of the trainees, but waiting until she had passed by before continuing. 'Why did you do it?'

Tom shrugged, glancing down at his desk. There were two messages marked urgent, he noticed, one from Radek, the other from Sam Houseman, the bank's in-house lawyer. 'It had to be done,' he said. 'Anyway, I think I have put up with enough crap for one month.'

Jones patted him on the shoulder and started to walk away. 'I hope it was worth it.'

Telmont sat back in his chair, watching Sheldon shift nervously from one foot to another, struggling with the decision of where to rest his weight. Designing an office without chairs for your visitors was a trick he had learned while a young man, from the mayor of Lyon, a petty, malevolent tyrant of a man who had collaborated with the Nazis before joining the Free French in the closing days of the war. The man's politics he had always detested, and yet his ability to humiliate and control people had been a lesson in the raw exercise of power.

'I will need all the staff to be particularly alert this week,' said Telmont casually. 'Put out a memo saying every holiday is cancelled. Nobody is to take lunch away from their desk, not even for working lunches, and nobody is to see much of their wives or husbands or even go on a date. Everybody this week must devote their entire being to the common purpose.'

Sheldon looked composed, his face solid and immobile, like a slab of rock. 'Is that really necessary, sir?' he said. 'The markets look pretty quiet right now, after the last couple of weeks.'

Shifting slowly in their sockets, Telmont's eyes moved across Sheldon's face, scanning each perfectly-shaven pore on his skin. Americans, he muttered to himself; in the financial markets they could not be ignored, but they were so completely immune to subtlety or nuance it could bring tears to the eyes of a statue. Even worse than the English. 'Are you familiar with Napoleon?'

'Of course,' answered Sheldon crisply.

'In his report after the great victory at Austerlitz, he wrote, "There is a moment in engagements when the least manoeuvre is decisive and gives a victory: it is the one drop of water that makes the vessel run over . . ."'

'I wasn't familiar with that quotation, sir,' said Sheldon.

'Check it, and make sure it goes in the memo,' said Telmont sharply. 'This week, I suspect, will see many such moments, and several such drops of water.' He paused, looking out of the window. 'And as great a victory, of course.'

'Perhaps you should be more careful with your women friends,' said Radek, the words slowing, as if he were reluctant to complete the sentence. 'Or at least familiarize yourself with their backgrounds.'

Tom hesitated, unsure how to respond. 'What do you mean?' he asked.

'Forgive me if I am intruding on your private affairs,' Radek continued stiffly. 'There may be things of which we should not speak.'

'Go on,' said Tom. 'I'm tired of secrets.'

'Since you have been kind enough to enquire after my advice, I thought it would not be too unreasonable to check something.'

'About who?' said Tom, his voice quickening. 'About Sarah?'

'She intrigues me,' said Radek. 'Nobody has read that book by Telmont.'

Over the phone, Tom could picture Radek smiling mischievously to himself. 'Not even you?'

'I tried, but I couldn't get much beyond the first few pages,' he continued. 'It's impenetrable rubbish, the worst sort of pseudo-Sixties Marxist babble. Only somebody with an obsessive interest in Telmont could possibly have read it.'

'She does work for the man.'

'Even though she now seems to loathe him,' said Radek.

Tom paused, wondering if he had missed something during the few days of their relationship. His confidence that he could know anything about women had crumbled in the last two weeks, and not much remained except a certain passive acceptance of the unexpected. 'What have you found out?' he asked.

'I just made a few phone calls around some of my old contacts in the markets,' said Radek. 'I don't suppose you have ever heard of a firm called Proby, Finer & Turnbull, have you?'

Tom shook his head slowly into the phone. 'Sarah Turnbull,' he said. 'Some connection, right?'

'It was part-owned by her father,' said Radek. 'And by his father before that.'

'What happened?'

'They were metal traders,' said Radek. 'This was before the Big Bang, when commodity trading was still done in the old way, in the pits on the floor of the exchange. It was a more gentlemanly trade, I suppose. The firm specialized in tin and copper mostly, buying and selling futures contracts. In 1983, Telmont started taking massive positions in the tin market, buying everything in sight. Some people thought he was trying to do something similar to what the Hunt brothers tried in the silver market in the late Seventies, corner the market and drive the price up. It turned out he was playing a different and more subtle game. He made it look as if he was trying to corner the market, while actually dumping all the stocks he had quietly accumulated in the few months previously. James Goldsmith did the same thing in gold in the mid-Nineties. It caused chaos in the market.'

'What happened to Proby, Finer and Turnbull?'

Even before the words had escaped his lips, Tom sensed he knew the answer. After all, if the firm was still around, he would have heard of them. 'Bankrupt,' answered Radek.

'And the old man?'

'David Turnbull was ruined by the episode, but he was a City man of the old school, and he knew that if you lived by the markets, you had to be prepared to die by them as well,' said Radek, the pace of his voice quickening. 'Of course, he never worked again, and he died five years later, in 1987, when he would have been sixty. A broken man.'

'She would have been thirteen when it happened,' said Tom. 'It's a difficult age.'

'She hasn't talked to you about her parents?'

'Never mentioned them,' said Tom. 'Do you think Telmont knows?'

'Of course,' said Radek. 'He's French. It is routine for the French banks and finance houses to get detectives to check people's families before they hire them.'

'And he still hired her,' said Tom. 'It's crazy. Why take on somebody you know hates you?' He paused, looking around the office, noting the eyes of his colleagues moving away from his desk. 'It's madness.'

'Not madness, no,' said Radek. 'Telmont, in truth, is more of a spider than a leopard. He likes to lure his prey into his web.'

The list of names scrolled down the screen, each one marked out in neat black lettering against a white background. Against each name was recorded an address, all of them located in a different Eastern European city, and next to the address a sum of money to be paid by the Leopard Fund every month. All the accounts listed to receive the payments were located in one or other of the Caribbean islands.

Glancing through the list, Sarah made a quick mental calculation; the fund was spending in the region of $250,000 a month to keep these men on the payroll. Yet none of them, as far as she could tell, had any official role within the organization.

Finding the list had taken all her nerve. First thing that morning, she had walked through to Telmont's office. Both secretaries looked at her coldly as she stepped through the door, but she ignored the disdainful curl of their lips as they surveyed her appearance. I need to check my holiday entitlement, she told Marie-Claire curtly, whether it is four weeks or five weeks. The secretary suggested she might check with the personnel office in New York, but Sarah insisted she had to know right away. Standing next to her shoulder, she prepared herself for two seconds of total concentration. While the delicate pair of manicured fingers tapped up the personnel files, she looked to see where her fingers went on the keyboard when she tapped in the password for that part of the system. 'Allumettes', she decided, although the fingers moved so fast it was hard to be certain that was the word being typed. Five weeks, Marie-Claire had told her, looking back from the files flashing onto her screen. Thanks, Sarah replied curtly. For more than you can imagine, she added silently to herself as she strode back in the direction of her desk.

'Allumettes', typed Sarah as soon as she got back to her desk. The password worked perfectly. On her screen, she was taken straight through to the personnel files. Moving her fingers across the keyboard, she created a spare file and stored the details onto her hard disk. Next she started searching through the files, looking not among the staff but among the agents. The fund, she knew, employed a range of experts in different countries, all of whom would feed back information on local market conditions that would help the fund decide its trading strategies. It also employed a series of local freelance brokers, usually wealthy businessmen who would place orders using the fund's money. Telmont's profile was so high, he often bought secretly, since just a rumour in the market the fund was buying a stock or a commodity was guaranteed to drive the price upwards. Sarah stored the names and moved on. After rooting through the files for several minutes, she found the list of Eastern European agents, stored under the heading: 'Miscellaneous Operatives'. There were names in all of the Eastern European countries, ranging from Estonia in the far north right down to Macedonia and Croatia in the South. 'MOs', read a note at the bottom of the file, 'report directly to, and are controlled by, Henri Boissant.'

Sarah stared at the screen, wondering if she had read the words correctly, or if she might have made a mistake herself. Boissant was the man Tom had been asking about, the man who he was convinced Tatyana had left him for, the man she had probably been ringing at the fund's Paris office. The man, also, whose very existence they had denied to Tom just last week.

'I think we should speak.'

Sarah turned, startled, unsure how to react. The arch of Telmont's back was exaggerated as he knelt forwards, leaning into her face, brushing his hand softly against the padded shoulders of her jacket. He was so close the dry smell of the coffee on his breath drifted towards her nostrils. 'In my office,' he continued.

Tom could only recollect talking with Sam Houseman twice before. Once when a legal action had been threatened over a piece of analysis he had prepared for the bank. And once when he and Tatyana had been trapped at the Christmas cocktail party by the bank's senior lawyer and his wife, who spent a half hour telling them about the private schools their children were going to. About as interesting as the lessons in Stalinism back at the orphanage, he could remember Tatyana joking when he finally managed to steer them away. An enjoyable joke at the time, Tom reflected, but one that acquired a sour taste when processed by memory. Tatyana never went to an orphanage, at least not in Estonia, and he could not help but be amazed how even in the smallest moments of their marriage she had managed to lie to him with perfect poise, style and grace. She must have laughed herself to sleep at night at what an idiot I was, he reflected bitterly to himself.

'You saw the weekend papers?' said Houseman, looking up from his desk.

Tom sat down opposite the sturdy wooden desk. Houseman was about forty-seven, forty-eight, and ageing badly. His hair was grey and thinning, swept across his brow, and he was running rapidly to fat around his stomach and his jowls. The lines on his face were turning into deep grooves, and his eyes were sinking back into his face, as though they were trying to retreat from the daily grind of his life. Not a man, Tom reflected, who took much pleasure in his work – but then, when you mostly dealt with the employment contracts of vain and overpaid City bankers, it was hard to imagine how you could take any satisfaction from it. 'I glanced at them,' said Tom, his tone casual and unhurried.

'They have proved very embarrassing for this bank,' said Houseman hesitantly.

'I know that,' said Tom. 'Believe me, Sam, if I knew who had leaked that thing to the press I'd knock the guy's block off myself. It's me that's most embarrassed.'

Houseman looked at him closely, watching the ease with which his lips ground out the words. A good liar, he decided to himself; one of those people, probably, who had such a tenuous grasp on reality they no longer knew the difference; it was all just stories, true or untrue. Or maybe he was telling the truth; that would explain the look of injured innocence that was playing on the man's face. Either way, it mattered little, Houseman realized. This was not a courtroom, and he was not a judge. Merely the executioner. 'We're going to have to let you go, Tom,' said Houseman. 'I'm sorry.'

Houseman waited anxiously, aware it would take several seconds for the words to sink in. It always did. How exactly the bank's lawyer had become the person responsible for telling people they were fired, he could not imagine; he would have thought it was something the chief executive, or one of the other directors, might do. Each sacking was different, of course, but they all had one thing in common. They left Houseman feeling cheapened, as if he were nothing more than an office cleaner, paid to sweep away the bank's debris.

'You can't fire me for a leaked report,' said Tom. 'You can't. It just isn't done.'

He had a point, decided Houseman. It was unheard of for anyone to be sacked in the City for talking to a journalist, and they didn't even know if Tom was guilty or not. The call from Frankfurt this morning had shocked him, but there had been no measure of doubt in the instructions. Tom Bracewell had to be out of the bank by lunchtime. It doesn't matter what we have to pay him, Strich had insisted, just get him out of there immediately. 'We can and we are,' said Houseman firmly, looking back up at Tom. 'Your contract of employment states clearly that allowing any unauthorized information to be passed from the bank is a breach of that contract.'

Whether he had actually read the contract when he joined the bank seven years ago, Tom could no longer remember; he didn't usually bother with the fine print of documents. He certainly couldn't recall now what it might have said, but he was sure Houseman would have read it ten minutes ago. 'Who says I leaked any information?' he answered, fixing his eyes directly on the man on the other side of the desk.

'Be serious, Tom,' said Houseman, attempting a smile. 'We all know it was you.'

'Prove it!' snapped Tom angrily.

Houseman hesitated, looking down at papers on his desk. 'You can fight this if you want, Tom, but you must know there isn't any point,' he continued, slipping into a tone he hoped was sympathetic. 'Even if you did manage to hold on to your job, would you really want to be here now that this has happened?' He waited, hoping for some response, but could see only the dark, remorseless anger in Tom's eyes. 'Our terms will be most generous.'

'Fuck your terms,' said Tom. 'Just tell me one thing. Did Telmont put you up to this?'

'Telmont?' repeated Houseman stiffly. 'I don't understand.'

'He wants me out because I was too close to the bloody truth,' said Tom. 'Can't you see that?'

'I don't believe that one of the largest banks in Europe would be influenced by the views of a hedge fund manager,' said Houseman stiffly.

'Then you are a complete bloody idiot, like all the other bastards running this bank,' said Tom, rising to his feet, and moving away from the desk. 'Right now, Telmont is pulling all the strings. You just can't see it.'

'As I was saying,' continued Houseman, struggling to find the right words. 'The terms will be most generous, but much more generous if there is no fuss. I'm sure that gorgeous wife of yours will want to make sure you are looked after.'

Houseman could see Tom's expression darkening as he leant over the desk, peering directly into his eyes. 'The terms don't fucking matter. Can't you see that?' he said, the words hardening on his tongue. 'All that matters is finding out what Telmont is doing, and stopping him. The bank can either help, or it can get the fuck out of my way.'

Houseman watched despondently as Tom turned, stalking away from the desk, shutting the door softly behind him. He hated it when they cracked, and could never rid himself of the sense of guilt, as if he might in some small way be responsible for what had happened. Security should be notified, I suppose, he thought with a sigh; there was just an outside chance he might decide to take too much with him. Under the heading 'Employee's reaction' on the dismissal record lying on his desk, Houseman wrote in neat lettering, 'Paranoid, verging on psychotic.'

A glimmer of sunshine flicked through the dark clouds gathering over the river, bathing a strip of the bleached, stripped floorboards in a fierce and unrelenting light. Sarah neatly side-stepped the area; she already felt exposed enough, without standing in the spotlight. 'Why were you looking at those files?'

Sarah could feel her cheeks reddening, and cursed herself for blushing. 'What files?' she asked defensively.

'I imagine you thought you were quite clever stealing the password.' Telmont turned, walking away from her. 'If you are planning a career as a computer hacker, I suggest you go back to kindergarten,' he continued, his tone relaxed and calm. 'Our system automatically records and displays who is using which files. That is a common feature of even the most basic corporate networks. Once you were inside that part of the system, you were identified immediately.'

He walked closer to the window, looking down at the river below. 'Why, Sarah?' he said. 'Most people we hire here don't spend most of their time spying on the fund. Some of them are even quite grateful we have given them a job, that we pay their wages every month.' He looked up, his brown eyes fixed on her. 'I am not the enemy, Sarah.'

'If not you, then who?' asked Sarah, the words rising smoothly from the back of her throat.

'The past,' said Telmont firmly. 'The past is your enemy.' He turned, looking away from her. 'That is where we differ, you and I. For me, the future is the enemy.'

'I am not sure I understand,' said Sarah, her tone fractured and distant.

'I believe you do,' said Telmont, his expression becoming more sombre. 'The past, as I said, is your enemy.' He looked at her across the room, peering darkly into her. 'Do not take me for a fool, young lady.'

'I have never done that,' she said.

'But you already have,' replied Telmont. 'Do you not imagine that we check who our staff spend the weekends with? Do you not imagine that we check whether they have the degrees that they claim, that they have worked for the companies they say they have worked for? That we check that they are who they say they are?' He paused, leaving the words floating across the room, then lowered his tone to nothing more than a whisper. 'That we check whether their families have any connection with the fund?'

'But you knew all along,' said Sarah, struggling to suppress the anger in her voice. 'You knew about my father, yet hired me anyway. Deliberately.'

'You interested me,' answered Telmont. 'I like to know my enemies, get them up close, where I can keep my eye on them.'

'Did you know my father?'

'I met him once or twice, perhaps,' said Telmont. 'But no, I hardly knew him.'

'And yet you took his life.'

Telmont walked back towards the window, looking down at the City below. 'An exaggeration, surely?' he replied. 'The markets took his life.'

'I don't see the difference,' said Sarah, struggling to control the emotion in her voice. 'The fund was behind the chaos in the tin markets. That bankrupted him. Afterwards he was never the same man, never. He had lost all of his strength, and all of his will-power.'

'Why do you think we called it the Leopard, Sarah?' said Telmont. 'Has that never occurred to you?'

'Because it is quick.'

'Not just for speed, but because the leopard is both the quickest and deadliest carnivore on the planet,' said Telmont, the words resting lightly on his lips. 'It consumes flesh, preferably raw and bloody. The fund is the highest expression of capitalism, its greatest and purest achievement, just as the leopard is the greatest predator the natural world has ever created. It is no use asking a giant cat why it hunts its prey. It does it because that was what it was built for. And so for ourselves. It is no use asking why the fund destroys its opponents in the market. It does it because that was what it was built for.'

'Suppose it is immoral?' said Sarah.

Telmont laughed softly. 'The system may be immoral, that is a debate we might have another day. But the fund, no. Destruction is what capitalism is about. Our role is to make that plain, so even the fools can see it.'

'I can't live with that,' said Sarah. 'I won't be part of it.'

Telmont turned from the window, looking at her across the room. 'But that is just because you are squeamish, because you don't have the stomach to look at reality as it is,' he said, his tone taut, the words coiled like a spring. 'I hired you because I wanted to examine your potential as an opponent, to see whether you were someone I needed to fear. But I can see now that you are weak, you are nothing. We need waste no more of each other's time.'

Sarah could feel the muscles in her neck tightening, squeezing the breath from her throat. 'I am not just a victim, I am a person,' she said.

Telmont shrugged, a laugh escaping from his lips. 'Then be out of here by the end of today. I don't wish to see you again.' Telmont walked closer towards her, a thin smile creasing his lips. 'Like your father, you will have to live with the humiliation of being beaten.'

CHAPTER 15

Monday, 15 February

J ONES HELD THE PICTURE IN HIS HAND, GLANCED AT IT BRIEFLY, then handed it back to Tom. A fine-looking girl, he thought to himself; one that any man would find it painful to lose. 'It isn't a lot to show for all that time,' he said.

'You mean the marriage or the job?' asked Tom.

'Both, I suppose,' said Jones, wondering where he should look. 'I still can't believe they did that to you.'

Tom shrugged. 'Maybe I had it coming,' he said. 'Perhaps I shouldn't have leaked that report.'

'People do it all the time,' said Jones, shaking his head. 'If they are going to start firing people for it, they could at least let us know in advance. I can't think of much good to be said about working for a German bank, but you do at least expect the bastards to play by the rules.'

'The rules just changed, I suppose,' said Tom. 'My guess is that somebody somewhere is playing a very different game. I'm caught up in it somehow.'

'What are you going to do?'

Tom sighed, looking down at the picture of Tatyana. He could remember the bright sunny day in Finland when that photo was taken, and how proud he had been to display it on his desk; everybody who came into his cubicle always told him how sensational she looked. Paris

had been the first place they had gone away together after she had moved
to London, and it was there, on that day, he had proposed to her. Funny
how the picture stays the same even as the memory sours and fades, he
reflected, as he placed her image in his briefcase. 'Find out what the
game is,' said Tom, looking back up at Jones. 'And find out how I start
playing.'

'My guess is your report was just about the money,' said Jones. 'I haven't
worked in banking for fifteen years without learning nobody gets upset
when you're wrong. If Telmont *is* organizing the chaos in Eastern Europe
then he is probably behind your sacking as well. It sounds crazy, I know,
but even the KrippenBank can be leant on.'

'Not crazy at all,' said Tom quickly. 'I've already assumed it was
Telmont who wanted me out of here. My question is whether he is
behind Tatyana's disappearance as well.'

From the look in Jones's eye, Tom could tell he was being examined
for signs of madness; there were times, he knew, when suspicions were
better left unspoken. 'That's going a bit far isn't it?' he said. 'You've had a
rough few weeks. You should take that new girl off to the Canary Islands
for a week or something. Put your feet up and think things over.'

Tom shook his head. 'I'm going to find out what's happening,' he said
firmly. 'I may need a few good men to help me, though. If I call you later
in the week, can I rely on your support?'

'Of course,' said Jones, without hesitation. 'Breakfast Club rules. Be
loyal to your friends, because nobody ever heard of a bank buying you
a drink in the bar.'

Tom grinned. 'Thanks,' he said. 'I might need to remind you of that
before the end of the week.'

Sarah turned towards her computer, switching on the Internet connection
and taking herself through to the Yahoo home page. Clicking onto the
file for creating a new e-mail account, she tapped in a new address for
herself: Zaretsky@yahoo.com, then tapped in a six-letter password for
the new account. Methodically, she began sorting through the files she

had stored on her hard disk, starting with the list of agents throughout Eastern Europe she had filed this morning. Posting each file onto an e-mail, she then sent each one to her new address, checking that it was safely dispatched before moving onto the next. Two hours were all Telmont had given her to clear out of the building. There was no time to waste.

'I'll be sorry to see you go,' said Sheldon, leaning over her desk, his white teeth gleaming into a grin. 'Jean-Pierre was just saying it is always kind of sad when a good-looking lady leaves the Leopard, and I must say I agree with him.'

'I'm sure you'll get over it.'

Sheldon nodded. 'Uh-huh, I guess so,' he said. 'Still, if there is anything I can do to help, like if you need any of your stuff or anything, be sure to let me know. I'd be happy to help out.'

Sarah looked up into Sheldon's eyes, wondering if he meant it or whether he had just been sent to spy. 'You could do one thing,' she said.

'Be glad to,' said Sheldon.

'Find out for me who Henri Boissant is, and what he does for this company.'

Sheldon rubbed his head. 'I'm not sure that would be allowed.'

Sarah looked up at him, her eyes mixing pity with anger. 'You really have no idea what is going on here, do you?' she said.

Tom glanced around the office, aware this would probably be the last time he set eyes on this building or these people. KrippenBank was not like an Oxbridge college, he reflected; they don't ask you back for a reunion every ten years. When you were gone, you were gone. And you were usually swiftly forgotten.

Radek answered the phone on the third ring. Tom glanced at his screen, noting the DAX was down another eighty points this afternoon, on fears the growing crisis in Eastern Europe would damage the German banking system. Madness, he thought to himself. They are not just destroying themselves, but the European economy as well. 'They sacked me,' said Tom bluntly.

'It was always a possibility,' answered Radek. 'Nobody behaves the way you have behaved if they mind losing their job. I think you wanted this.'

Tom remained briefly silent. 'I suppose I needed a change,' he said eventually, his voice touched with sadness. 'This might be more change than I can cope with right now. Now I have to worry about why I lost my job as well as why I lost my wife.'

'Don't be ridiculous,' said Radek sharply. 'You're an economist, you should know better than to say things like that.'

'You'll have to unpack that one for me,' said Tom, attempting a smile.

'If there is one thing economics teaches us, and it may well be the only worthwhile lesson the subject has, it is that everything is linked,' he said. 'Your job is gone for the same reason Tatyana is gone. That is what you must focus on.'

Tom hesitated, allowing himself time to digest what he had been told. 'Perhaps,' he answered at length. 'Just now I can't seem to make the connection.'

'That doesn't mean it isn't there,' said Radek. 'It just means you aren't looking hard enough.'

'Okay,' said Tom. 'Then tell me, have you ever heard the word *metsavennad*?' he asked.

'*Metsavennad*,' repeated Radek, his pronunciation different from Tom's, emphasizing the middle syllable. 'Where did you hear that phrase?'

'I found it on the Web,' said Tom. 'Tatyana had been looking at a website about it, before she left. I found the translation of the word; it means woodsmen. I couldn't understand the rest of the site.'

'Some people of my generation have heard of them,' said Radek. 'Not many of yours, I would imagine. I am surprised Tatyana should have been interested.'

'Who are they?'

'They were an Estonian liberation army,' said Radek. 'As you probably know, Estonia was taken by the Germans during the Second World War. They conscripted most of the local young men into makeshift units. After the war, as the Germans retreated, most of them deserted and started fighting the Red Army instead. They wanted their independence, as the Baltic states always have done. Of course, they didn't have a hope. After a couple of bad defeats, they took to the woods and started a guerrilla campaign against the Russians. Hence the name, *metsavennad*, the woodsmen. The amazing thing is how long they lasted. August Sabe was the last of them. He was killed trying to swim across a lake while escaping from KGB officers. That was in 1978, thirty-four years after they took to the forests.'

'They knew something about survival,' said Tom.

'More than any group in the world, including probably the Vietcong,' said Radek. 'But forgotten now, of course. I haven't heard their name mentioned in years.'

'Still, you know something about them.'

'In Prague, when I was young, they were heroes of ours,' said Radek. 'We idolized them because they had the guts to take the Russians on, to fight them with guns, not just words. I suppose it was similar to the way many western students back then idolized the Vietcong for standing up to the Americans. Russia was our imperial power, and its enemies were our friends. A few idealistic young men even went off to join them.'

'What happened to them?'

'No one knows,' answered Radek. 'They were never heard of again. Presumably they died. I don't think anyone could survive a winter in the Estonian forests unless they had been born to those kind of conditions. All that changed after the tanks came in sixty-eight, of course. In Prague, everything changed. But there was always the *metsavennad*. For some of us, they were always the last and best hope of Central European civilization. No matter what happened, they never surrendered. They always fought to the last man.'

'Why, I wonder, would Tatyana be interested?'

'That is something else you need to figure out,' said Radek.

'It could just be a coincidence, I suppose,' said Tom. 'She might just have been researching her country's history.'

'Did she ever mention it to you?'

'No,' said Tom, closing the lid on his mobile Bloomberg Traveller, and tucking it into his briefcase.

'Then it is not a coincidence,' said Radek firmly. 'Those things that people fail to mention are invariably the most important. Everything is linked to everything else. That is the only lesson our trade teaches us. You should have learnt it by now.'

Tatyana sat in the back of the grey Mercedes, remaining completely silent, watching the harsh cold streets of Berlin slip away from view. It was the first time she had been out for several days, and although she was tiring of the sight of the small two-roomed apartment they had placed her in, the cold, grey streets did little to lift her spirits. Berlin, she reflected, had always been a hard, unrelenting city, a place she had always avoided. It was somewhere she could leave without regrets.

'Where are we going?' she asked.

Boissant turned around to face her, a grimace hardening the taut features of his face. He glanced at the cool elegance of her closed lips, admiring the delicate poise of her expression. A shame she was born a woman, he reflected to himself. She would have made a good soldier, although for whose army it was hard to say. 'Lichtenberg station,' he replied softly.

'What time are we leaving?'

'Two minutes past eleven.'

'The St Petersburg train?'

Boissant nodded. 'The express, via Warsaw,' he said. 'But we are not going to the end of the line.'

'Then where?'

Boissant looked out the car window, keeping his eyes fixed on the road ahead. 'Right now, I cannot tell you,' he said. 'You will know soon enough.'

'I am not a captive,' said Tatyana. 'We agreed that.'

'True, you are not a captive,' said Boissant. 'But you are not exactly a free woman either.'

Tatyana leant back in the seat, brushing her black hair away from her face, resting her chin in her hand. Boissant could feel her eyes focusing on the back of his neck, and shifted in his seat; he could feel the fierce glare of her eyes drilling into his skin, mentally ripping away the folds of flesh and severing the arteries below. He looked towards the driver, muttering to him to speed up. 'You were wrong,' said Tatyana.

Boissant lit up a cigarette, letting the smoke curl around his lungs. 'About what?' he asked.

'The train,' she continued, keeping her eyes fixed on the road passing beneath her. 'I am sure we are going to the end of the line.'

Glancing at his watch, Tom noted it was just before six; he had not expected to find her at home so early. Strange how quickly you adapt to new circumstances, he reflected. Only two weeks ago, he expected every night to find Tatyana waiting for him. Now he expected to be alone.

A U2 record was blasting from the speakers. 'With or Without You', Tom realized, not a record he had in his collection. Perhaps she had been out CD shopping. Or perhaps she had started moving her stuff into his house. Why not? he decided. I am too old to be chasing girls any more, and I don't suppose they'll be queuing around the block for an unemployed 38-year-old economist waiting for his divorce to come through. I should be grateful for her company. 'You're home early,' said Tom.

Sarah stood up, turning down the music. 'Telmont sacked me,' she said.

The words were delivered bluntly, the sentence emptied of any emotional content, as though it no longer meant anything. Tom put his arms around her, and she rested her head on his shoulder, her mouth so close to his ear he could hear the breath escaping from her lips. 'The same thing happened to me,' he whispered.

He could sense her fingers first tightening around his chest, then slipping away, as she stood back a pace. Tom could feel himself being scrutinized, as though he were someone she had just met. 'Both of us on the same day,' Tom continued. 'Some kind of coincidence.'

'You think so?' asked Sarah.

'No,' answered Tom, shaking his head. 'I don't believe in coincidences any more.'

Walking through to the kitchen, he took a bottle of Chilean wine from the rack. Tatyana, he remembered, had developed a passion for Chilean wines last autumn, and had bought at least two cases of the stuff. I don't suppose she will miss it now, he decided, tasting the wine and pouring a glass for Sarah. 'Tell me what happened,' he said.

By the time both of them had finished recounting the events of the day, the bottle was almost finished. Tom could feel Sarah's hand stroking his brow, and he marvelled at the warmth of her touch. 'They said they would give me six months' salary,' she said, when she had finished the story of her day. 'And a reference if I needed it, so I guess it could be worse. I didn't like the job.'

She had said nothing about her father, Tom noted. 'Tell me what happened to you?' she asked.

He could hear the concern in her voice and found it reassuring. 'Not so different,' replied Tom, the words languid on his lips. It took several minutes to run though a brief summary of the day, the pace of his narrative quickening as he reached the decisive moment. As he completed the story, he could feel his mind hardening. With just a few hours of hindsight, it seemed painfully obvious what had happened. Obvious, too, what he should do about it.

'You think Telmont was behind it?' asked Sarah.

'Of course,' answered Tom. 'It's too convenient. I leak a report to the press blaming him for the collapse in Eastern European markets; next thing I know I have been fired. Nobody ever got fired for talking to the press at KrippenBank before. Never. It is unheard of.'

'But to have that kind of power,' said Sarah, her voice drifting. 'It is the largest bank in Europe. Would they care so much what Telmont thinks?'

'More than they care about me, that's for sure,' said Tom. 'Money is the only language banks understand, and Telmont has a lot more of it than I do. If he wants them to do something, they do it.'

'So what do you want to do now?' asked Sarah.

Tom hesitated for a moment, thinking not about the answer to the question – of that he was already certain – but of the words to express it. A tumbling lexicon was falling before his eyes, but he felt unable to reach out and take any of the material he needed. 'The same as you, Sarah,' he said, the words delivered slowly, as if he were thinking aloud. 'I suspect you knew that all along. Perhaps that is what attracted you to me in the first place.'

Sarah drew closer to him, cradling her arms around his back, and nestling the edge of her cheek into his chest. 'What do you mean?' she asked.

'Revenge,' said Tom quickly. 'Isn't that what we are both looking for here? Out there, for sure. But perhaps in each other as well.'

CHAPTER 16

Tuesday, 16 February

I T WAS YEARS, TOM REALIZED, SINCE HE HAD STAYED IN SUCH A tacky hotel. Travelling for the bank had spoiled him, and even when he and Tatyana took a holiday she refused to stay anywhere cheap; anything less than four stars put her in a horrible mood. Strange, he reflected, that a woman who grew up in an orphanage should slip so easily into a life of comfort and affluence. One of the many clues I should have detected that she was not whom she claimed to be.

'So where do we start?' asked Tom.

'Right here, and right now,' said Sarah sharply.

The Eurostar had arrived in Paris at eight minutes before twelve, local time, and the walk to their hotel had taken just twenty minutes. The decision, Tom reflected, was spur-of-the-moment, something you could do when you no longer had an office you needed to go to. At the back of his mind was an idea Terah had planted; if you want to know where someone is going, find out where they have come from. He was speaking of Tatyana, but it applied to Telmont with equal force. 'We know he is trying to crash the markets in Eastern Europe,' he had said to Sarah as they lay in each other's arms. 'We just don't know why. We know one of his people is mixed up with Tatyana. We don't know why. Until we have a reason, I don't think we know anything.'

'We need to find out,' she replied.

'But how?' asked Tom.

He had felt her shrug against his shoulder. 'In Paris,' she said. 'That is where the Leopard Fund comes from. I remember his sidekick Sheldon saying once that Paris was where all the big secrets were kept. I thought he was just joking at the time, but now I am not so sure. If there are any secrets, then that is probably where we will find them.'

The decision had been made drowsily, with little thought for the consequences, and by the time Tom had collapsed into sleep he was no longer sure if they meant it or not. 'Let's go to Paris in the morning' was what he imagined lovers might say to one another late into the first few nights of their relationship. By morning, Sarah had seemed more determined than ever. He awoke to find her collecting a few of her belongings into a travel bag, and, at first, he thought she might be leaving him. Twice in the same month, he thought sharply to himself. Surely that is not possible? 'There is a train at eight,' Sarah had told him. 'I've ordered a taxi for seven-fifteen, so we should make it.'

Tom had not felt minded to argue; he had made enough decisions recently and sometimes it felt good to pass the buck down the line. By the time he had showered, Sarah had packed a few of his clothes and the taxi was already waiting. On the journey they had discussed how much they knew about Telmont. On his laptop computer, Tom had pulled up most of the press cuttings on the man, but although there was plenty in the file, it was nearly all concentrated on the last two decades of his life: a series of financial coups on the market, growing wealth and power, and in the last five years a chain of ponderous statements on world affairs, usually delivered at academic bodies generously endowed by the Leopard Fund. Little was said of his background: the information that was available was sketchy and impersonal. He was born in 1945 in Saulieu, a small town fifty miles to the east of Dijon. His father had been a butcher and his mother a hairdresser, and Jean-Pierre, according to the records, was their only son; there was a sister, but the cuttings made no reference to what had become of her. A brilliant mathematician, he had taken his first degree in maths in Dijon, graduating at the age of just nineteen. From there, he had moved to postgraduate work at the

Sorbonne in Paris, and then to the ENA, the finishing school for the French elite. Afterwards, he had worked in banking in Paris, London and New York, before starting the Leopard Fund. 'That,' remarked Tom on the train, 'is about what we know.'

'So what did he do between 1969 and 1972?' said Sarah.

'There is nothing on his biog?' said Tom.

'No, look,' said Sarah, pointing to the screen. 'He completed his studies at the ENA in 1969, when he was already twenty-four. That makes sense. Then in 1972, he gets a job with Credit Lyonnais.'

'Travelling and private studies,' said Tom, scrolling down the display on the computer. 'That's what it says here.'

'But what if he is lying?' snorted Sarah. 'Nobody graduates from the ENA and then bums around for three years. The ENA produces the most fiercely ambitious people on earth, and Telmont certainly falls into that category. I know him. Smoking dope on the hippie trail is the last thing he would be doing.'

'We should find out,' said Tom. 'It might be our best lead.'

Stepping out of the Comfort Inn into the ramshackle collection of streets close to the Gare du Nord, Sarah reminded him of those words on the train. 'Three years is a big slice of a man's life to go missing, particularly in their early twenties.'

'I know,' Tom replied. 'But nobody disappears without leaving any traces.'

Tatyana looked up at the dark, stained lettering, out across the grey, frosted rooftops, and felt a sliver of ice shiver through her spine. It was five years now since she had looked out on any scene so morosely calculated to crush the spirit. A long time, she pondered to herself. Almost long enough to forget.

The train had travelled overnight from Berlin to Riga, hauling its way first through the eastern stretch of Germany, then through Poland, cutting through Belarus, and stopping in Kaunus in Lithuania before turning up into Latvia. Boissant had insisted on sharing a cabin. She had protested at first, telling him she had no intention of trying to escape, and she had no intention of ending her life by attempting to leap from a moving train, but his reply was hard and unyielding. 'I trust you about as much as I trust myself,' he told her with a rough laugh. 'We stay together.'

She remained awake all night, listening to the slow grinding of the wheels against the track. She could remember making this journey as a small girl in the company of her father, and the stops they made each hour had a strange, distant familiarity, summoning up images of herself from other times. As a girl, she could recall imagining herself making this journey as a woman, wearing the finest clothes and jewels, but, in her girlish fantasies, it was in the company of a handsome prince, not a French gangster. On the bunk below, Boissant snored and farted, the noise stopping only when the train halted for another set of border guards to come aboard and inspect their passports. Neither his French nor her British documents aroused much interest; it was Belorussians or Ukrainians or Russians they were looking for, not Westerners. Sometimes the soldiers stared at her for a few moments as they examined her passport, but that was only in hope of catching sight of some naked flesh.

For most of the night she lay still, half an eye watching the countryside roll past her, thinking occasionally of Tom, wondering how he might be surviving without her.

By the time the train pulled into Riga, dawn had already seeped over the horizon. Tatyana had adjusted her watch forward one hour for Eastern European time, setting it at twelve minutes past seven. Her limbs were tired from the hard surface of the couchette, and her eyes felt as if she had been punched. She washed in the small basin in the train toilet, and played with a layer of make-up. By the time she emerged onto the platform, she already felt as if she was ready for a hot bath, some breakfast and then bed. 'Where are we going?' she asked, looking across the platform at Boissant as he cupped his hands to light his cigarette.

'The Metropole,' he replied, blowing out a long stream of smoke with a grunt. He took her bag and lifted it over his shoulder. 'We'll get a cab downstairs.'

Tatyana started to walk behind him, her shoes crisp on the thin film of iced frost that covered the paving stones. 'It is only five minutes on foot,' she said.

'You know it?'

Tatyana looked up, glancing into the harsh, rugged lines of the man's face. 'Of course I know it,' she replied. 'What do you think I have done all my life?'

'It was a closed city, was it not?' said Boissant. 'In the days before independence.'

Tatyana wrapped a scarf up around her neck. 'Not closed to me,' she answered.

The ash lingered on the tip of the professor's cigarette, ready to collapse over the green cord jacket that rested limply on his shoulders. Why doesn't he find an ashtray, Sarah wondered to herself? Waiting for the ash to fall was grating on her nerves. 'He was a fine student, you know,' said the professor, speaking in English but through a thick French accent. 'He could have done many different things. Why he devoted his life just to the markets, I cannot imagine? A waste.'

'He made a lot of money, I suppose,' said Sarah.

'Money, pah, nothing,' said the professor, raising his right hand. 'Keynes made a lot of money on the markets, yet if that were all he had done, his name would not be remembered for five minutes.'

Tom had been surprised how easy it had been to see Patrick Doden. Radek suggested they visit the professor of economic philosophy at the Sorbonne, pointing out that he had been at the school for forty years, so he must once have taught Telmont. 'Mention my name, and tell them you are researching a magazine article or something,' he had told Tom on the phone. When they arrived at the university building, after taking ten minutes to find the economics department, Doden had been sitting in his office reading. He seemed grateful for the interruption, Tom noted, putting down his book, and asking both of them to sit down in the small book-lined office. Tom removed some papers from a chair while the professor lit a cigarette, blowing the smoke high into the air.

'Some men are driven by money, I suppose,' said Tom. 'Even when they are students.'

The professor rubbed his brow. 'Not Telmont, you know,' he answered. 'I suppose he equips himself with some of the things that money might buy – the cars, the houses, the women – but those are no more than decoration, I think. There are only two things that money can buy that might interest a man such as this: respect and influence. But, really, you know, for him, I think the game is quite different. For him the Leopard Fund, I believe, is really an intellectual process.'

'A process?' asked Sarah, a bemused smile starting to play on her lips. 'I would have thought it was a commercial enterprise.'

The professor cast a playful look in her direction. 'Of course, in the Anglo-Saxon world, capitalism is viewed as a static, given entity. A monolith. Here in France, we view it more as a process. For Telmont, this is true, I think. The Leopard Fund is an idea, in truth, an idea designed to test the system to destruction.'

'A dialectic, you might almost say,' ventured Tom.

'But of course,' answered the professor. 'What else?'

'Which would make him a sort of Marxist,' said Sarah.

The professor laughed, his hand trembling as he did so, prompting the cigarette ash to fall onto his jacket. He brushed it to the floor with his hands, took a drag on the cigarette and stubbed it out. 'I do not imagine you would be conducting this research without looking up when Telmont was born?' he said.

'1945,' said Tom.

'Precisely,' said the professor. 'Which means that he came here in 1965, and he was a student in Paris for the next five years.'

'And that he was here in 1968,' said Tom.

The professor lit up another cigarette, again blowing the smoke high into the air. 'You know enough of the events of that year, I suppose, to know something of the atmosphere of the times. We were all communists. Certainly the students.'

'I would have thought of him as an arch-capitalist,' said Sarah.

'An irony, yes, I suppose,' answered the professor. 'But then the world is full of ironies. That is one of the things that makes it interesting.'

'Lots of people are very left-wing when they are students,' said Tom. 'It isn't usually serious.'

The professor took a drag on his cigarette. 'Telmont was always a serious young man.'

'He was involved in student politics?' asked Sarah.

'But of course,' replied the Professor. 'They all were, you know. It was natural. But Telmont took it with the same seriousness he took everything.'

'An organizer?' asked Tom.

The professor laughed, shaking more ash onto his jacket, then sweeping it to the floor. 'There was not much organization around in those days, but so far as there was, then Telmont was an organizer.' He looked across at Sarah, a smile on his lips. 'If it is not impolite to make such an enquiry of so beautiful a young woman, when were you born?'

'In 1970,' answered Sarah, her tone amused.

The professor nodded. 'It may be hard for someone of your age to imagine how 1968 was,' he said. 'Amongst many people here in Paris, and elsewhere in the world as well, I think, there was this belief there would be a revolution one day. It was not speculation, you know. Just a matter of timing. And young students, although they don't realize it themselves, they are drawn naturally to power. Of Telmont, this is true. Like many of us, he thought that power would lie with the revolution, so he was drawn to the revolutionaries. Later, of course, he changed. When it seemed that power lay with the capital markets, he switched his allegiance to that cause.' The professor sighed. 'My students today all want to be bankers and traders, because, as they perceive it, that is where power lies. For myself, I think it was more fun when they wanted to be revolutionaries.'

Sarah leant forward in her chair. 'Do you know what happened to him after he left university?'

'To Telmont?' asked the professor, a note of surprise creeping into his voice. 'He became a banker, I believe.'

'Not straight after, no,' said Sarah swiftly. 'He spent three years just travelling and studying. What was he doing then?'

The professor shrugged. 'I don't know,' he said. 'Perhaps you should ask the party.'

'What party?' said Sarah.

'The Communist Party, of course,' answered the professor.

Telmont looked down at both the Bloomberg and Reuters screens, his eyes moving with the changing colours of the pixels on the screen; he had flashed the FTSE onto one display, the German DAX on another. 'You know what a young man such as yourself should do?' he remarked, looking up at Sheldon.

'What is that, sir?' asked Sheldon, walking closer to Telmont's desk.

'Take a year out, go somewhere remote, like a Tibetan hillside perhaps, or a Patagonian ranch, and then when you get there you should plug in one of these machines, and spend a year in complete silence just watching the markets unfold, minute by minute, hour by hour.'

He looked up, checking that Sheldon was paying attention. 'There is, you see, a rhythm to the way prices change, a beat, but you have to absorb it over time, as a musician absorbs the nuances of his instrument.'

'I'm sure that's good advice, sir,' said Sheldon, his tone stiff and formal.

'For this week, however, you are too busy dealing with my affairs,' said Telmont, his lips creasing into a dry smile. He looked back down at his screen. Although the day's trading was not yet half finished, he noticed that the Czech index was down eight per cent, Hungary by nine per cent, and Poland by twelve per cent, each of them crashing down by the hour. The DAX was off two hundred points, the FTSE one-fifty and the CAC in Paris down ninety. The markets, he judged, were developing a momentum of their own, lurching each morning towards a fresh abyss. Soon they would not need much more encouragement from him. 'Where is Sarah this morning?'

'I thought you sacked her, sir,' said Sheldon.

Telmont looked up darkly. 'For this week, I should like to know where Sarah is, every minute of every day,' he said. 'If you can't organize that, then I will have to find someone who can.'

Perched on the edge of the small desk that furnished one corner of the room at the Comfort Inn, Tom flipped open his laptop, calling onto the screen a brief snapshot of the European markets: all of Eastern Europe had fallen sharply, the West was coming down, and it looked as if Wall Street would have a nervous opening in the next few hours. He clicked onto a market report.

> *London: 14:21 GMT. Eastern European markets remained volatile in early trading today,* it opened. *There were sharp falls in fragile Eastern European markets after rumours that KrippenBank, one of the largest investors in the region, was having trouble liquidating its portfolio of stocks and bonds. There is also speculation that other Western banks may soon be forced to follow KrippenBank's lead in pulling out of the Central and Eastern European markets. 'If the German banks pull out, then there won't be much point in the rest of the world being there either,' said George Pointer, a London analyst with Morgan Stanley.*

'Tuesday afternoon,' said Tom, glancing up from his screen towards Sarah. 'If your numbers were right, the fund should be building up to a crash this week. The markets are already looking nervous.'

Sarah curled a hand around the back of his neck. 'I wonder what difference it makes that he was a communist when he was young?'

'Hard to imagine,' answered Tom. 'Except that he never mentions it on his CV.'

'Who would?' answered Sarah. 'Not many people own up to being a communist any more.'

'In France it is okay,' said Tom. 'They still get ten per cent of the vote in every election. No, I don't think you would lie about it, not unless it meant something.'

'Like what?' asked Sarah.

'I don't know,' said Tom. 'But as Radek keeps reminding me, everything is connected to everything else. I am starting to believe that might well be true.'

The rows of elderly women wrapped in thick woollen coats, their heads tightly bound with scarves, selling lighters, cigarettes and lucky charms in a long, dismal line stretching from the train station, reminded Tatyana of her childhood. So too did the thick, brutal architecture of the station, a slab of steel and concrete wrenched from the ground, its platforms dark and smelling of rodents and vagrants. In the distance she could see the vast Soviet Statue of Liberty, a monumental sabre, stretching high into the air, looking down with kitsch cynicism on the citizens below. That, too, was familiar.

But otherwise, Riga looked very different. She had last visited the city in 1981, when she was eleven, travelling with her father, and had not been back since. Until a few months ago, it would not have occurred to her ever to return. Its colours, shades and temperament had changed violently since 1981. Advertizing hoardings now lined the grand, wide boulevards strung through the centre of the city. The shops were fiercely lit. The women were brightly decorated with smart new clothes, handbags and perfumes, and the men, with their long overcoats and thick scarves, moved about the town centre with a sense of purpose, as if they were going somewhere. That's different, Tatyana reflected. Nobody in this town used to be going anywhere, a truth written into the slow movement of their feet across the pavement. There hadn't been anywhere to go.

Boissant insisted on a taxi; he was not a man, Tatyana had observed, who liked to walk. He remained half a pace behind her at all times, following her as they walked into the lobby and up to the desk. It was different from the way Tatyana remembered it, smaller, less grand, but also fresher and cleaner; the chandelier hanging from the ceiling of the lobby had lost its thin film of dust. 'We have booked two rooms,' said Boissant curtly to the receptionist. 'Both in the name of Roberto Sanoli. One night.'

The receptionist nodded, and handed over two keys, signalling them towards the lift. 'An Italian couple in Riga,' said Tatyana. 'A rarity, I suspect.'

'I prefer not to use my real name,' said Boissant.

Tatyana smiled. 'If it comes to that, who says any of us use our real names?'

Downstairs, the receptionist glanced down at the list of names kept by her and her colleagues underneath the desk; a list of names supplied and updated by a local private detective every few days. Most of the names were Russian, some Latvian, a few Ukrainians, some from as far away as Georgia and Azerbaijan. Apart from Sanoli, Boissant and Bracewell, none of the names on the list was Western. A detective in Tallinn was prepared to pay a hundred dollars for a sighting of them, either individually or together. Enough for several new outfits, thought the receptionist to herself, as she picked up the phone.

CHAPTER 17

N AIVETY, TOM REFLECTED, AS HE LOOKED INTO THE FEAR IN her face. Over the next few days that will be our greatest enemy.

He had been sitting in a cafe whilst she went inside. Her French was far superior to his, and this, she argued, was still a country where a woman was treated more sympathetically than a man. He watched and waited, playing with his black coffee, but when she emerged he could guess it had not gone well. 'What happened?' he asked.

'They threw me out,' she replied, her tone fractured.

Act confident, Sarah had told herself as she approached the headquarters of the French Communist Party, a grim, austere building occupying a whole block of a square in the twelfth arrondissement. Act as if you have a right to be here. The doorman merely nodded when she explained she was here to ask about membership, and passed her on to the enquiries office. Second on the left, down the corridor, he said.

One person was ahead of her in the queue when she arrived, an elderly man involved in a deep discussion with the woman at the desk, who took several minutes before turning to Sarah. She would like to check membership records from the early 1970s, Sarah had explained. To see if someone was a member. 'From the look on her face, I might have asked to see Lenin's boxer shorts,' Sarah explained to Tom. 'Her lips froze, and for a few moments she said nothing. Then this incredibly dark look came over her face, and she told me membership records were confidential. I explained I was doing some research for a magazine, and she just said I would have to try the press office, but they would tell me the same thing. Then I asked her if she happened to know whether Jean-Pierre Telmont happened to be a member. Or had a been a member back then. She stared at me again, as if she was trying to decide whether I was dangerous or just mad. Then she told me I had to leave. I protested for a few seconds, insisting there must be some way I could check, when this large security guard appeared, as if from nowhere, and told me I had no permission to be on the premises. He looked like he might turn heavy if I didn't get out.'

Tom gripped her hand, signalling to the waiter to bring them some more coffee. 'It wasn't very likely they would give us the information,' he said. 'The French Communist Party was always the most strictly Stalinist in Western Europe. Openness was never part of the creed.'

'There was something about the look on that woman's face,' said Sarah. 'As though I had touched some kind of nerve when I asked if Telmont had been a party member.'

'He's obviously hiding that,' said Tom. 'Otherwise he would mention it somewhere, in his book, or in one of his press articles.'

'But how do we find out for sure?'

Tom shook his head slowly, a frown creasing up his brow. 'That isn't the real question,' he said, his eyes looking into hers. 'We know that for sure, I think. The real question is what he did for them.'

Boissant knocked on her door, listening for any sign of movement. He knew she could leave if she wanted to – that was part of their arrangement – and that knowledge made him nervous. She was, he knew, the one person with the power to destroy all their plans. Tatyana was covered only by a long white dressing robe when she answered his knock, and Boissant could not resist admiring the slender curve of her hips. 'Yes?' she said sharply.

'I will be gone for some hours,' he said.

'It matters nothing to me where you are,' said Tatyana. 'If you never returned, I wouldn't care in the slightest.'

He stepped past her, walking into the room, noticing the unpacked clothes on the floor and the collection of make-up jars already gathered on the desk. This was, he reasoned, a woman who liked to look her best, even when she was the captive of a man she despised. 'We will leave early in the morning,' he said.

'Where to?'

'You will find out,' Boissant replied. 'We will breakfast at seven and depart immediately afterwards. I would prefer it that you stayed in your room until then.'

'I may come and go as I please.'

'That is perhaps true, for today at any rate,' replied Boissant. 'Even so, you have heard what I have said.'

He stepped past her, nodding curtly as he did so, and walked from the room. Behind, he could hear her shutting the door firmly. He dug his hands into the pockets of his long grey overcoat and walked through the lobby into the street outside. Though it was not yet four, darkness had already descended on the city, and a few flakes of snow were drifting through the night air. Boissant curled his collar up around his neck, protecting himself from the biting winds blowing in from the Baltic Sea, and started walking alone through the streets.

His destination was perhaps two miles away, on the modern northern edges of the town, but he decided against getting a taxi. He had been trapped long enough within the train, and the next three days held only the uncomfortable promise of more confinement. I could use the exercise, he reflected to himself.

The buildings here in the residential district of Riga had been built during the Russian occupation: big, ugly, poorly-built Soviet apartment blocks, where the damp stained the concrete surfaces and the snow collected on the stark communal staircases. Lukas Bodin had already been waiting for ten minutes by the time Boissant slipped into the chair next to him in the small cafe. 'A coffee,' said Boissant, speaking in English. He might have learned the Latvian word once, but he could not be bothered to remember it.

'It was as you wanted it, no?' said Bodin.

Boissant looked at the man carefully, peering into his brown eyes, calculating the fear. Afraid, yes, that much he could tell. But *how* afraid it was impossible, as yet, to judge. 'The money has been spent?' he asked. 'All twenty million of it?'

Bodin nodded. 'Every dollar has been used to destabilize the lat,' he said. 'The results are as you wanted them, surely. It has halved in value. The stock market has slumped to a new low. The economy is in crisis.'

Boissant nodded. 'That is satisfactory,' he said. 'You have not disappointed me.' He hesitated, smiling up at the waitress as she put the coffee in front of him, and stirring some sugar into the cup. 'But there is more you must do.' He could see Bodin recoil as the words escaped his lips. Even traitors have some limits to the damage they wish to inflict on their own people, reflected Boissant to himself. 'Your contacts with the leaders of the Russian population here are good, yes?' he said.

'I know those people, yes.'

'Then this is what I want you to do,' said Boissant. He pushed a single sheet of paper across the table, taking a sip of his coffee as he did so, recoiling from its bitter taste. Next week I will be back in France, he thought to himself.

'It will be expensive,' said Bodin.

Boissant shrugged. 'So long as you make it happen, I don't care how much it costs.'

The notes were written clearly on Jaak Terah's notepad. A man with a French accent using an Italian passport in the name of Sanoli checked in this morning at the Metropole Hotel in Riga, accompanied by a black-haired woman. So far, she hadn't gone anywhere, nor had she been seen with anyone. That was all they knew.

Terah glanced down at the photograph Tom had given him. He was struck, as he had been the first time he looked at it, by the sculpted delicacy of her features, the darkness of her hair, the shallowness of her cheekbones, and the evident ease with which she tanned. Quite different, he reflected, from a typical Estonian woman; often blonde, usually large-boned, the Estonians were a Nordic people, their features designed to protect them from the cold. So far as he could tell, Tatyana had not told her husband the truth about anything. Why should she not lie about her nationality? he reflected.

Until today, his investigations had turned up nothing of any importance, except that it was almost impossible she was an orphan. He had traced the bar where she used to work, but the turnover in those places was high, and no one was left from four years ago. It was not a place to keep detailed employment records. It was true she had been a student, but in Tartu, Estonia's main university town, about eighty miles inland from Tallinn. She had studied English and French there in 1993 and 1994, but none of the students still there could remember very much. One girl, now a postgraduate, had remembered a few things: that she was secretive and kept herself to herself, which stuck Terah as unsurprising; that she liked to sing, particularly karaoke, which also fitted with what he knew; and that, unlike any of the other students, she didn't appear to worry about money. There was no sign she had any – no car, or big apartment, or designer clothes – but no debts either. Money just didn't trouble her.

As an orphan, reflected Terah, you would expect her to have even less money than the rest of them. One more puzzle to crack. Glancing back at his notes, he dialled the number Tom had given him. 'This is Jaak Terah,' he began. 'From Tallinn. I have a trace on your wife.'

For several seconds, Tom remained silent. The words seemed to descend upon him with a suddenness and ferocity he could not have imagined. He could feel his pulse quickening, and his fingers start to tremble. In the last few days – he could not remember when – he had started to become used to life without her, had begun imagining a future without her, mentally rearranging the furniture of his dreams. 'Where is she?'

'In Riga,' answered Terah. Though the words had been simple, he could hear the emotion in the man's voice, and thought it best to deliver the information cleanly. 'She checked into the Metropole Hotel this morning.'

'Was he with her?'

'The Frenchman?' said Terah. 'Yes, they checked in together.'

'Is she there now?' asked Tom, his voice fractured and breaking.

'I don't know,' said Terah. 'That is all the information I have. There are some leads on where she lived as a student in Tartu – I am checking those – otherwise nothing. That is all I know.'

Tom wondered whether he knew the Metropole Hotel. He had been to Riga several times on business and, though he had not stayed there, he was sure he had walked past it several times. For the first time since she left, he could picture her somewhere, and her image was suddenly so strong in his mind he could almost reach out for her. He closed his eyes for a moment. Tatyana's cheek was next to his, her skin resting against his. 'Chase everything,' he said crisply. 'Hunt down every lead.'

He looked up towards Sarah, but she was now different. No longer his new girlfriend, she had flipped back to being the woman he was having an affair with, a vacation from his marriage, not its replacement. 'Who was that?' she asked.

Tom could hear the suspicion in her tone. 'The detective I hired in Tallinn,' he said. 'I told you about him. The one who was looking for Tatyana. He found her in Riga.'

Sarah looked in his eyes, and could tell she had started to fade from his presence. 'Is she with that Boissant man?'

Tom nodded, but remained silent.

'Are you going to call her?'

Tom shook his head, his eyes rooted to the ground. 'I think I should go there,' he replied, not looking up. 'I need to see her.'

Telmont looked down at the river flowing past his office window; a grey, featureless mass of water heading for the sea, illuminated only by the lights of the buildings opposite. The Thames was not his choice of view this afternoon, he reflected. The Seine would have been more to his liking. And yet, in truth, it was London and New York that were the centres of the financial world, and for the next few days it would have to be here that he would make his base. A few more days were all that was needed.

The call from France had left his nerves briefly rattled. No name had been given by the woman who asked after him at the headquarters of the Party in Paris, but the description given by the head of security there was too close for a mistake to have been made: an English woman, late twenties, medium-length blonde hair, blue eyes, a crisp upper-middle class accent. There were, of course, thousands of women just like that in London. But there was only one he had just sacked, and who showed an insatiable interest in his past.

Perhaps I underestimated her spirit, Telmont pondered. Maybe she was not as weak as her father? Still, if there was fight in the woman, then she would have to be crushed.

Boissant answered the call on the third ring. He was walking back towards the hotel and reckoned he should be there in another five minutes. 'Why is that girl in Paris?' growled Telmont.

Boissant shrugged, looking down at the snow gathering on his black leather shoes.

'And why is she asking questions about me at the party's head-quarters?'

Boissant stopped, moving into a shop doorway and fishing a packet of Gitanes from his pocket. He crouched from the wind, lighting his cigarette, feeling the warm smoke curl through his lungs as he took his first drag. 'Are we sure?'

'A blonde Englishwoman, making enquiries about whether I was a member?' said Telmont. 'There can be no question, it was her.'

'And Bracewell?'

'We know nothing of his whereabouts.'

Boissant sucked on his cigarette. There were times, he reflected, when it was unfortunate he could be in only one place at once. 'The party will have told them nothing.'

'That may be true,' said Telmont. 'But this of all weeks! My past must be my affair and my affair alone.'

'I will call Jennings,' he said. 'I think we need a trail on both of them.'

Telmont snapped shut his phone and looked up towards his screen. The markets had closed now across Europe, all of them down sharply. He flashed through a series of brokers' forecasts, noting that all the big houses were now desperately trying to talk the market back up again. The IMF had started talks with both the Latvian and Lithuanian governments about emergency loans, and the Ukraine had decided its currency would no longer be convertible into dollars or euros. They are retreating, thought Telmont. The markets have beaten them.

On a second screen, Telmont retrieved a draft of the talk he was due to deliver tomorrow morning, adjusting the numbers to take account of the movements in the market during the past twenty-four hours. He glanced out towards the river, enjoying the silence of the early evening. There would, he reflected, be few people with whom he could share the unfolding triumph of the week ahead. Associates in an enterprise such as this were never likely to be much in evidence. That was something he had learnt at least two decades ago. Money may not buy you much in the way of happiness, he reflected to himself. But it can buy you all the chaos you want.

The lights stretching out along the platform of the Gare de L'Est struggled to shatter the fierce darkness of the night. A strip of pale light beamed down from each bulb, but was soon defeated, its illumination fading quickly. Tom kept his eyes on the pavestones as he walked, watching Sarah's black leather shoes pacing at his side, not wanting to look up at her directly. In truth, he realized, he knew that he should look into her eyes, but he was unsure what he might find there.

It had been a fragile and tense evening. Why they had made love for the first time just after he told her he was going to look for Tatyana was a mystery he was as yet unable to unlock. Perhaps they both sensed there might not be another chance. They had tumbled on top of each other, clinging desperately to each other's bodies. The sex was angry and urgent, not soft and gentle, yet when they were finished Tom found himself close to tears.

'What will you say when you find her?' asked Sarah, her tone fragile.

Tom had shrugged, looking into her eyes. He could tell she was searching for something. 'I will ask her how she could have despaired of me so completely as to have done this,' he answered.

'And will you go back to her?'

Tom had seen the question coming, a fuse just waiting to be ignited. 'It's hardly likely to be an option, is it?' he said, unable to disguise the bitterness in his voice. 'A woman does not disappear to Riga with another man because she really wants to be with her husband.'

Sarah smiled, slipping her hand into the pocket of Tom's overcoat, resting her fingers against his. 'Women are hard to understand sometimes.'

Tom nodded. 'So why are you racing around Europe chasing down obscure facts about a French financier with a man you just met?' he asked. 'It won't bring him back, you know.'

Sarah shook her head. 'No, but I suppose it is like an autopsy. It isn't meant to bring anyone back. Just to provide some sort of explanation for those of us who are left behind.' She hesitated, looking up towards the dark metal of the train carriage, slipping her hands around Tom's waist. 'I'll be here for you when you get back,' she said.

CHAPTER 18

Wednesday, 17 February

T ELMONT CHECKED HIMSELF IN THE MIRROR, COMBED HIS hair and straightened his tie, then strode purposefully into the room. Immediately he felt the warm, almost sensuous heat of the television lights, and heard the bursting of the camera flashes. No matter how many times you gave a big press conference, he reflected, the adrenaline burst was always the same. He could feel the chemical surging through his veins, stimulating and cajoling him. It was at moments such as this, he reflected, that a man could truly feel the master of his surroundings.

He looked through the audience gathered in the basement conference centre of the Leopard Fund's London headquarters, smelling the air and judging its temper. The press office had done well in gathering all the major news organizations, he decided, but it was his own name that drew them. In a world where information was the most valuable commodity of all, he had long since realized that the ability to make news was the most powerful weapon a man could possess. They would listen to him this morning because he had already spent a decade commanding their attention. Everything had led up to this moment.

'I don't suppose many of you have ever heard of *Confusion de Confusiones*?' he began, casting his eyes around the room. From the expressions of blank indifference on the faces of the reporters, he could tell that none of them was likely to respond to the question. 'Not many people have,' he continued. 'It is a book written in 1688 by Joseph de la Vega, a Portuguese gentleman who happened to live in Amsterdam during the great tulip speculation of that century. It is perhaps the first book every written about financial speculation, and still one of the finest. Allow me to read you a few words.' Telmont glanced down at his notes, drawing his breath inwards before starting the passage he had chosen. 'This enigmatic business that is at once the fairest and most deceitful in Europe, the noblest and the most infamous in the world, the finest and the most vulgar on earth. It is the quintessence of academic learning and a paragon of fraudulence; it is a touchstone for the intelligent and a tombstone for the audacious.'

Telmont cast his eyes upon the assembled reporters, grinding out the last few words with immaculate slowness. 'I think when Vega said the markets could be a tombstone for the audacious, he was absolutely right,' he continued. 'There will, I may suggest, be very many tombstones in evidence before the week is out. I have called this press conference this morning to announce that the Leopard Fund is about to unwind all its equity holdings around the world. Our dealers have been instructed, as of this morning, to move into cash, and then into physical assets – gold, property, oil, commodities. The reason? You may well ask. As far as I am concerned, the game is over. For the last twenty years, capital has had everything its own way. It has moved through the world unimpeded; all the controls and restrictions upon it have been removed piece by piece; it has been allowed absolute freedom. I believe we are coming to the end of that period in our affairs. In the next few days, the markets are going to fall so far and so fast that that kind of freedom will not be tolerated any more. We have already seen the collapse of the markets in the Far East and Russia. My belief is that Eastern Europe is now about to crash totally, and that the main European and American markets will not be far behind. A cloud of deflation will spread across the world, destroying economies like a plague of locusts destroys a crop. Very little will be safe. But it is the markets of Eastern Europe that will be worst hit. They do not have, I fear, the strength to survive a crash such as we are about to witness. It is there the selling should begin.'

Telmont peered out into the room, inviting questions. 'Why would the Leopard Fund tell people it is liquidating its portfolio?' asked a woman from Reuters. 'Why drive the price down before you sell?'

'These are unusual times, no?' replied Telmont. 'Normally you would be right. But in a catastrophe of this magnitude, nothing this fund can do can make any difference. It would be like spitting into a hurricane.'

The expression on his face suggested there might be more he wanted to say, but had thought better of it. 'Does the fund not have a duty to try to prevent a panic?' asked a reporter from the *Telegraph*. 'Surely your decision, announced so publicly, can only make matters worse?'

Telmont hesitated, looking into the television lights before replying. 'Panic is what the fund feeds upon,' he said. 'To say we have a duty to prevent it is like saying a leopard in the jungle has a duty to prevent panic among the wildebeest that are its prey.'

'What are the total holdings of the Leopard Fund right now?' asked a reporter from *Institutional Investor* magazine.

Telmont smiled. 'I cannot give a precise figure right now,' he replied. 'But you may be assured it is above one trillion dollars.' He paused, allowing the figure to rest in the air, and enjoying the numbed silence it generated. 'I use, of course, the American, not the French, usage of the word. By one trillion, I mean one thousand billion. All of it is to be sold in the next few days.'

He looked down at the stand, collected his few cards, and glanced out across the room. A clamour of questions was starting to rise to the floor, but he merely nodded to the press girls at the back to start distributing his statement, smiled at his audience, and walked slowly towards the door. The secret of handling any sort of audience, he reflected, was always to leave as soon as possible.

Tom first checked that his mobile was working properly, then plugged the portable modem into the side of his Bloomberg Traveller. He flicked through the list of countries, choosing the number for CompuServe Germany to open up an Internet connection. Switching on the machine, he looked straight for what was happening on the main markets, then at the key news stories. The decision by the Leopard Fund to ditch its entire holdings of stocks and bonds was leading the market reports.

He glanced up once at the bustle of people surging through the station, pushing aside some of the rubbish that had collected on the coffee shop stand. Looking back down at the machine, Tom clicked onto the details of the statement.

London: 17/2: 9:21 GMT: European stock markets reeled this morning following a dramatic announcement by hedge fund manager Jean-Pierre Telmont that his giant Leopard Fund would be selling its entire holdings of stocks. After the announcement, the FTSE fell 150 points, the CAC-40 by 90 points, and DAX by 113 points. 'Confidence is looking very fragile,' said one trader. 'People are starting to worry that it would not take much to turn this into a full-scale crash.'

It's started, thought Tom, as he sipped his coffee, drawing strength from the caffeine surging through him. The night had been rough and harsh, the noise of the train making it hard to sleep, and the images running through his mind making it impossible. As he lay on his bunk watching the dim lights of the German countryside flash past, the questions looped through his mind, stuck on permanent replay: What do I say when I find her? What possible words can I summon up to meet the situation?

Ever since she left, a thousand imaginary conversations had played out in his mind. Most involved Tatyana returning to the house in Kensington, her manner meek and abject, declaring her love and seeking his forgiveness; he might be yielding or harsh, depending on the temperature of the moment. Others pictured him passing her in the street, or seeing her across the room in a restaurant, where he would make some casual and cutting remark, a barb so perfectly slung it would leave her speechless and humiliated. Those, I suppose, are dreams, he told himself a hundred times during the night. The reality will be very different.

It had felt strange to be waking up alone.

Sarah had felt his absence as soon as she had climbed from her bed this morning; a kind of emptiness that was both physical and emotional. She might have known him for just a few days, but already it seemed like a lifetime. She had already adjusted to his presence at her side. As if his skin were her skin, his disappearance made her feel naked and alone. Breakfast had been served in a small corner of the hotel, and she lingered over the coffee, bread and jam, thinking through her options. She could hardly resent Tom for setting out for Riga to see Tatyana; she had not, she realized, known him long enough to claim any sort of ownership of his emotions. And the disappearance of his wife might well be connected in some way to Telmont's attack on the markets. How, she could not imagine, and yet she felt sure the answer was here in Paris. If only she could start finding some answers, then suddenly everything might change.

By the time she returned to her hotel room it was already approaching ten. Radek answered the phone on the third ring. 'It doesn't surprise me in the slightest,' he remarked, after Sarah explained how the professor had described Telmont as a communist during his student days.

'Why not?' she asked, her tone lightening. 'I wouldn't have thought one of the world's fiercest capitalists would turn out to have been a communist.'

'Well, Engels was a successful factory owner, as you probably know,' Radek replied. 'And Telmont's endless pronouncements on the future of global capitalism, and his taste for predictions of its imminent demise, always had a Marxist ring to them. It is always the same mindset, and it always leads to the same conclusions.'

'I asked at the headquarters of the French Communist Party whether he had been a member,' said Sarah. 'They threw me out.'

Radek chuckled. 'Openness was never part of that party's creed,' he said.

'I'm not sure where we go next,' said Sarah. 'I don't think we have any leads.'

'On the contrary, you have plenty of leads,' said Radek.

Sarah was starting to feel teased, a sensation she was not sure she enjoyed. 'I don't see them.'

Radek paused. 'The French party was always the most strictly Stalinist of the western communist parties,' he said. 'There is no way it would ever give you any information. But I know someone who may be able to help you.'

'Who?' asked Sarah, her tone quickening.

'Someone I knew in Prague before I left,' said Radek. 'Karel Vereden. He used to work with the Czech intelligence service, but switched allegiance after sixty-eight and helped to smuggle people out. He fled himself in the early Eighties, and I think he lives in Paris now.' There was a silence on the line while Radek searched through his address book, then read out a number. 'He may have the contacts to help you.'

'Can this really take us anywhere?' asked Sarah. 'None of it seems very relevant to what is happening at the moment. I'm not sure it really matters whether Telmont might have been a communist when he was a student.'

'But it matters where he got the money from to start the Leopard Fund.'

'Yes,' answered Sarah. 'That matters.'

'Then that is what we are finding out,' said Radek.

The house was cold and empty, its heating turned down and all the appliances switched off. They have already fled, Jennings decided. Probably yesterday, judging by how cold it was.

Getting into the small Kensington house had not been a problem. A quick survey of the site had established nobody was at home, and the back door leading out onto a tiny patio was overlooked only by a pair of bedroom windows in the house behind. The chances of anyone seeing him were too small to be worth worrying about. The door was held by a standard Chubb deadlock. Jennings took an electric toothbrush from his pocket, inserting a thin steel needle into the head where the brush fitted. Turning the machine on, he stuck it into the keyhole; the vibrations of the toothbrush were enough to unpick the lock in fifteen seconds. Jennings smiled to himself as he swung open the door; if people knew how easy burglary was, they wouldn't bother with locks.

Boissant had told him they were probably in Paris, but he wanted the house checked anyway. There might be some evidence of where in Paris they were staying, and what they might be doing there. Examine the place, he had said. Tell me about everything you find. Jennings picked his way through the kitchen. It looked as if they had left in a hurry: there was a stack of plates in the dishwasher, and some clothes left in the washing machine. He walked through to the sitting room, examining it carefully. A couple of CDs were lying open by the machine – John Coltrane and *Madame Butterfly* – and some newspapers on the sofa. They definitely left in a hurry, he decided. And they weren't planning to go away for too long. Anyone making a long trip always clears up first.

He walked slowly upstairs, taking care not to disturb anything. The bed was unmade, and there were some clothes on the floor. He went through the pockets, but found nothing except some tube tickets and taxi receipts. There was nothing here, he decided, apart from the usual debris of an ordinary middle-class life. A photograph on the dressing table had been turned to face the wall. The man he had been paid to videotape earlier, the owner of the house presumably, together with a dark-haired woman. Not the blonde. Jennings looked carefully at the picture. There was a distance to the woman, he judged, as if she were holding something back. He replaced the picture. Whoever she was, she was obviously gone by now. The blonde seemed to have moved in.

He walked back downstairs, collecting the mail from the doormat. It looked like bills and junk mail, but Boissant had said to take it. A message was flashing on the machine. 'This is Victor. Call me,' it said. Jennings pressed 1471 and noted down the digits read out by the mechanized voice, then punched a number into his mobile and waited for Boissant to reply. 'There's nothing here,' he said. 'Apart from some old mail and a phone message. They must still be in Paris.'

'Then find them,' said Boissant quickly. 'I want to know where they are. If you need more men, just say so. That can be organized.'

If he wanted them followed, he should have paid me to keep tabs on them twenty-four hours a day, Jennings reflected. Once you lost track of a person in a city the size of Paris, it could be hard to track them down again. 'Have you any idea where they are staying?' he asked.

'None,' answered Boissant. 'But put some pressure on the man who left the message. He must know.'

There was a petulance to her expression this morning that Boissant did not much care for: a curl to her lip and a tired suspicion in her eyes, as if she were becoming bored by the game they were playing. 'Where to now?' she asked.

'Further north,' Boissant replied.

Eastern European women, he decided, never held much attraction for him. French, Italian or Spanish girls, even North Africans, they were more to his taste. The Latin temperament, I suppose, he reflected to himself. From the Rhine northwards, the women were as cold as the climate and about as appealing. Maybe I have done that Englishman a favour by relieving him of this piece of baggage.

'How far?' asked Tatyana.

'A few hours' drive, no more,' answered Boissant.

The car met them in the street outside the Metropole hotel. A black Volvo saloon, about three years old, its driver was dressed simply in jeans and a long thick waterproof coat with a woolly cap pulled down over his ears. A discreet enough car, Boissant decided. They did not want to look like local gangsters, nor did they want to draw any attention to themselves. He held the door open for Tatyana, unable to help himself from admiring the smooth outline of her legs as she stepped into the car. He placed her bag in the boot alongside his own, and climbed into the seat next to her. He nodded to the driver, remaining silent while the car pulled away from the kerb, turning out across the street and driving into the dark, bleak suburbs of the town. 'Much snow on the road?' he asked the driver.

'Some,' he replied with a shrug. 'We will be able to pass, I think.'

'We are crossing the border, then?' asked Tatyana.

The driver looked across at Boissant, unsure whether he was allowed to talk to the woman. 'Into Estonia, yes,' he replied.

'It is the lady's homeland,' said Boissant.

The driver turned to look at her, a grin creasing up the rough features of his face. 'You will be pleased to see it again, then,' he said.

Tatyana allowed a thin laugh to emerge from her throat. 'If it were to disappear from the map, I shouldn't mind in the slightest,' she said. She looked towards Boissant. 'We are going towards the base, I suppose.'

'That was the plan,' he said. 'You will do as you agreed?'

Tatyana nodded. 'It will be as you wish,' she said. 'Nothing has happened to make me change my mind.'

The one thing Tom liked about voicemail was that you could dial into it from anywhere in the world. Apart from that, he reflected, it was a waste of time. Back in the office, he had often longed for the days when you had secretaries who left Post-it notes on your desk. There was only so much automation he could stand.

He pressed '4' on his mobile to make sure he had heard correctly. 'Mr Bracewell,' it said, repeating the last message. 'This is Leopold Baltan calling from Switzerland. I may have some more information on your wife's accounts. Please call me.'

Tom let his eyes drift out of the window of the bus onto the frosted countryside. No snow seemed to have fallen yet, but the fields rolling past were dusted with white powder, and every stretch of water shimmered with ice. He was three hours out of Berlin, and the bus was almost full this morning. They had been held up for almost an hour at the Polish border while the guards scrutinized the passengers' passports, although why anyone should break out of Germany into Poland Tom could not imagine. 'The most hostile border crossing in Europe,' one of his fellow passengers, a Latvian on his way back from an engineering course in Hamburg, had remarked in broken English, and as he stood stretching his legs in the chilly morning air Tom saw no reason to disagree. A more miserable stretch of land, guarded by so many men, it was hard to imagine.

'You asked me to call,' said Tom when Baltan picked up the phone. 'What have you discovered?'

Tom imagined he could hear a pause on the other end of the line, and tried to picture the man who might be sitting there. Bald, probably, wearing slacks and slip-ons and a checked blazer, possibly with gold buttons, and a face that was tanned every winter in a tropical resort. Strange, he reflected, that my fate should at times hinge on a person with whom I have so little in common. 'Your wife, Mr Bracewell,' answered Baltan, the words delivered in a tone that was both slow and breathless, 'was a mysterious woman.'

Over the past two and a half weeks, Tom had learnt to brace himself for news of Tatyana. His muscles would tense, and within his gut he would feel his nerves start to shield themselves from the inevitable blow; it was the only form of immunization he could imagine. 'Tell me about it,' he said.

'I have been tracing the accounts, as you asked me to,' said Baltan. 'Let me tell you, in Switzerland this is not easy. Banking secrecy is not what it was, but it is still strong. As I told you last time, there were three different accounts, all of them registered in her name, each with many millions of dollars in them. One of those accounts had regularly been transferring money into and out of another set of accounts in the name of Tatyana Stokhoil. Does that name mean anything to you?'

'It was her maiden name.'

'I thought so,' answered Baltan. 'There is more money located in those three accounts. About one hundred million dollars. I could get you a precise number if you need it.'

'It doesn't matter. Where does the money come from? That's what I need to know.'

'I have been searching for that,' said Baltan. 'The first point is that most of these accounts were opened between 1968 and 1970, a long time ago.'

'That was when she was born, 1968,' said Tom. 'I am surprised Tatyana could set up a Swiss bank account now, never mind when she was just a few months old.'

'Then a parent, I suppose,' said Baltan. 'Or a relative or a guardian of some sort.'

'She had none, she was a . . .' Tom started saying, the words tumbling from his lips before he had time to think. 'Actually she wasn't an orphan at all. She only said she was.'

Why do I defend her still, he wondered to himself. Surely the moment for that has long since evaporated? 'That doesn't help much,' said Baltan, his voice flat, empty of any kind of judgement. 'I traced back those accounts, and though they had been active since sixty-eight or seventy, it was only in the Eighties that big money started to flow through them. All of them were linked to another set of eight accounts, all of them corporate. Most of them, judging by the names, are French companies.'

'They are the source?'

'I think so,' said Baltan. He read out a list of names, spelling out each letter so Tom could write it down. 'The money she has in these accounts, most of it as far as I can tell, was originally paid in from these French companies.'

Tom sighed. 'I didn't even know she had been to France,' he said, his voice distant and empty.

'A mysterious woman, Mrs Bracewell,' said Baltan. 'Why would she have all this money at her disposal, yet choose to live like an itinerant orphan?'

'If you have any answers, let me know,' said Tom. 'I'm fresh out of them.'

Baltan paused before he answered, turning different possibilities over in his mind. 'Maybe she was frightened of the money.'

*   *   *

Telmont was always reluctant to walk through the dealing floor. He preferred to remain an aloof and distant presence from his staff, brooding alone in his office, issuing terse commands by e-mail or phone, sometimes summoning victims to his sanctuary, but rarely meeting them on their own territory. It is better to remain apart, he would sometimes remark, both to your employees and to the markets. Things that are familiar may command respect, but it is only the distant and mysterious that can command awe.

Today, he resolved to himself, was different. Like a military commander, he told himself, it was sometimes necessary to show yourself on the field of battle.

The London office contained the main dealing hub for Europe and Asia: about fifty traders, nearly all of them men, who spent the day working the phone, buying and selling from their peers at other banks and brokers and funds throughout the city. Their orders came either from the computer programmes that ran many of the Leopard's arbitrage funds or from the strategists in different regions or financial instruments. All of them were ultimately directed by Telmont himself, but he was well aware that a skilful trader could have a big impact on the profits of the fund, and on whether a particular strategy made or lost money. They were his front line.

'Do you know what Tolstoy once wrote of Napoleon?' asked Telmont, stopping by the desk of Terry Semple.

'Of course not, boss, you know that,' said Semple, slamming down the phone and entering a row of numbers into his computer.

Telmont looked up at the thin strips of bright neon shining down from the ceiling, a frown creasing his forehead. 'Napoleon kept on winning his battles not because he was a genius but because he was more stupid than his enemies and never got bogged down in planning or strategy. He only bothered about seeing that his soldiers were well-fed, embittered and as numerous as possible.' Telmont shrugged. 'That, anyway, was Tolstoy's view.'

'Sounds okay to me, boss,' said Semple, his expression already turning bored.

Telmont looked down at the three screens on the desk, concentrating on the display of world markets. 'How is it going?' he said.

'You've caused a few ripples, boss,' said Semple.

Telmont smiled. 'That was my intention.'

'Not everyone believes you, of course,' Semple continued. 'Lots of the traders think you're about as straight as a corkscrew. They reckon that if you are saying sell, it might just be the time to buy.'

'Like most traders, they are trying to be too clever,' said Telmont. 'Sometimes it is better to be stupid. That was the point of the quote.'

'It is making it a lot easier for us to sell,' said Semple. 'It means there are some buyers out there. The prices we are getting aren't great though.'

Telmont lent closer. 'The prices don't need to be good,' he said. 'Make sure everyone on the floor understands that. The whole point of the next couple of days is to drive the prices in the markets downwards.'

'Even when we are selling?' asked Semple. 'We're going to lose a lot of money.'

'It doesn't matter,' said Telmont. 'This is about more than just money.'

'It's way too deep for me, boss.'

Telmont smiled. 'It's too deep for most people,' he said. 'But that is only because they look for complexity where there is none.'

CHAPTER 19

Wednesday, 17 February

T HROUGHOUT EASTERN EUROPE, TOM REFLECTED, THE MO-
biles were one of the few things that could be relied upon to
work properly. The land lines were usually so bad that everyone
used cellular connections instead. Looking out from the bus at the shabby
roads and desolate Soviet factory towns of Lithuania, as they approached
the Latvian border, he was relieved to find he was close enough to a base
station for his phone to work.

He glanced through the wire story displayed on the screen of his
laptop.

*Riga: 17/2: 12.42 GMT: The Latvian capital of Riga was rocked
today by a large demonstration by Russian nationals calling for the
independent Baltic state to be reunited with Russia. Trouble flared
between demonstrators and police, who fired tear gas and plastic bullets
into an angry crowd. Latvia broke away from the old Soviet Union in
1992, but with nearly half of its population of Russian rather than
Latvian origin, there has always been a significant minority unhappy
with independence. The unrest in the capital hit the country's finance
markets, prompting a dramatic decline in the local bourse, and in the
currency, the lat. A spokesman for the IMF said this morning it was
keeping close tabs on the situation in Latvia, while in London the*

European Bank for Reconstruction and Development said the Latvian Government had requested an emergency loan.

Tom switched screens, checking the state of the other markets across Europe. Germany, France and Britain were all down marginally, but it was Eastern Europe that was taking the beating: all of its markets were slipping into freefall, its currencies tumbling. Exactly, Tom decided, the result Telmont would have been looking for when he made his statement yesterday about liquidating the Leopard Fund's portfolio. He glanced out of the window, looking at the flat, barren, frozen fields. He has to be stopped, Tom told himself. A man who remained idle when he knew what was going to happen would not be able to live with himself.

The phone was answered on the third ring. 'You have to help me,' he said, his tone flat and edgy.

'Christ, Tom! Where are you?' said Jones.

Tom looked towards the road, but recognized nothing. 'In Lithuania,' he replied. 'Somewhere close to the Latvian border. I'm on a bus heading for Riga.'

'Should I ask why, or would it not be worth it?' said Jones.

'Tatyana,' said Tom. 'She's in Riga. At least she was this morning.'

There was a silence on the line, and Tom could imagine Jones sweating over the words he should choose next. He was a rock of a man, with a heart of pure oak, and they had been both colleagues and friends for years, but he was reserved and silent, uncomfortable in the presence of any kind of emotion. 'Tell her I think she's crazy,' he said finally. 'Tell her Sally thinks she's crazy as well. She said so just the other night.'

'Thanks,' said Tom. 'But that wasn't what I was calling about.'

'What kind of help do you need?'

'The markets.'

'The markets need all the help they can get, right now,' said Jones. 'But you have better things to deal with.'

'It's linked,' replied Tom. 'For sure. Telmont is preparing a crash, and we have to stop him.' He could hear a silence on the other end of the phone, and imagined he might be moving too fast. 'You remember what we always used to say when we were preparing forecasts?' he continued, his tone relaxing, slowing down. 'You can think everything through, crunch all the numbers, do all the analysis, but in the end you have to go on gut instinct.'

'Sure,' said Jones. 'In the end, our instinct is what we can trust.'

'That's exactly what's happening,' said Tom. 'I'm trusting my instinct.'

'I'll run with that,' said Jones. 'Just tell me what you want me to do.'

Jennings put an extra pound into the meter, taking it up to the full two-hour limit. This should only take a few minutes, he said to himself with a smile, but I wouldn't want to come back and find the car clamped. Not when I might need to escape in a hurry.

He dug his hands into his pockets and turned the corner sharply. He had been careful not to park on the same street, just in case there might be any CCTV cameras in the area. Neighbourhood watch schemes and street surveillance, he was sometimes forced to admit to himself, had added a lot of unnecessary detail to his life.

Number 18 was an ordinary Victorian Highgate house, divided into two flats. Tracing the phone number, he had discovered Victor Radek lived in the ground-floor flat. He pressed the buzzer. 'Gas meter reading,' he said as the door slid ajar. Not original, he reflected. But as good as anything to distract their attention for a few seconds.

Jennings jammed his foot into the door, using the muscles in his ankle to hold it open while he clenched his fist around the frame. Radek resisted, using his weight to try to slam the door shut. At least sixty, perhaps sixty-five, thought Jennings as he looked at the frail figure pushing against him. This shouldn't take long. Leaning his shoulder into the door, he pressed his weight against it, forcing Radek down to the floor. The door flung open and Jennings stepped inside, shutting it firmly behind him. He knelt down on the floor, creasing his coat, looking down into the man's eyes. He could see the fear widening the pupils of his eyes and shortening his breath. 'Trying not to pay your gas bill, grand-dad?' he said roughly. 'Not very civic minded of you, is it, like? We all have to pay our bills.'

'What do you want?' asked Radek.

Jennings hooked Radek by the arm, lifting him from the floor with one swift movement, pulling him to his feet. The old guy could get up by himself, he thought, but it was always worth letting them know how strong you were. 'Information,' he said.

Radek looked at the door, but his way was blocked. 'Where are you from?'

'It doesn't matter,' said Jennings, shaking his head. 'It's not you I'm interested in, so you can get out of this without getting hurt. Just co-operate, like, that's all. I'm looking for two friends of yours, Tom Bracewell and Sarah Turnbull.'

Radek looked closely at the man. His shoulders and neck were thick, as if he might once have been a boxer, and his face was dull and cruel and stupid: the kind of face that belonged to professional criminals. 'You work for Telmont,' he said.

'It's none of your business,' spat Jennings, his tone rising and turning angry. Never engage them in conversation, he told himself. Always a mistake. 'Just tell me where they are.'

'How much is he paying you?' said Radek.

The blow swept lazily across his face. Jennings had not put much force into the first strike; it was no more than a warning, but it was enough to take Radek to the ground. He lay on the floor, sweat pouring off his brow, nursing the pain he could already feel searing through his cheekbones. Jennings leant over, peering at the man on the floor, his expression brutal and unforgiving. 'Listen, grand-dad,' he yelled, 'I'm on a fucking meter, so don't waste my fucking time with a lot of half-arsed fucking questions. It don't make no difference to me whether I kill you or not, so just tell me where they are.'

'You have no idea what you are doing,' said Radek, his breath short, and the words unclear. 'How can you do this when you don't even know what you are working for?'

The heel of Jennings's boot stamped down hard on Radek's hand, crushing the bones in two fingers. Radek could hear them snap, and turned his fist inwards, tried to fight the pain that was searing up his arm. 'I said like no fucking questions.'

Jennings stepped quickly over him and into the sitting room. His eyes moved across the furniture until he spotted the message pad next to the phone. Picking it up, he scanned though the list. One French number was written down. 'Is this where they are?' he asked, waving the piece of paper in front of Radek.

'Don't do this,' muttered the old man.

Jennings grabbed the phone and dialled. 'I'd like to speak to Mr Bracewell or a Miss Turnbull,' he said. He listened for a moment, then said: 'No, no message, I'll try later.' He walked back towards Radek, picking him up off the floor, pinning his chest against the wall. 'Don't even think about telling them I know where they are,' he spluttered. Radek tried to shake his head, but it was too late. Jennings had already thrown him to the floor, and he could feel himself starting to lose consciousness. A boot slammed into the side of his chest, and a fist struck the side of his head.

Kneeling, Jennings checked his pulse. Still alive, he thought to himself; he looked like a tough old geezer, could probably get through worse than this. But he won't be talking to anyone for a day or two. He checked his watch. Another hour and a half on the meter. A terrible waste of a quid, he told himself.

The man reeked of cigarette smoke, and his skin was creased and lined, indented and grooved like a piece of old stone. His hands, Sarah noticed, trembled slightly as he spoke, the bones and veins becoming visible as he did so. 'Victor Radek said you might be able to help us,' said Sarah.

Karel Vereden nodded, the skin on his neck creasing up, and pulled another cigarette from his coat pocket, stabbing it into his mouth, leaving it hanging unlit from his lips. 'For an old comrade, there are still favours,' he said.

Sarah looked around the dingy cafe, located just past the Bastille opera house, and ordered a coffee. 'You knew him in Prague?' she asked.

'You have been there?'

Sarah nodded. 'It is a small place,' he continued, with a shrug. 'We all knew each other.'

'I need some information,' explained Sarah.

Vereden smiled, revealing a thin set of stained and broken teeth, saliva sticking to his gums. 'Are you familiar with the trade in that commodity?'

Sarah looked away. 'I've worked in the financial markets,' she said. 'A lot of information is traded there.'

'But not secret information,' said Vereden, nodding to himself. 'That is a rougher trade. I will spare you the details. Tell me what it is you need.'

Sarah slugged back a hit of coffee. 'Jean-Pierre Telmont, the financier,' she said. 'I have been told he was a communist in his youth, but I want to confirm that.'

Vereden took a metal lighter from the pocket of his coat, reeking of fuel, and clicked it open, releasing a high flame, torching the cigarette still hanging from his lips. 'Telmont,' he said cautiously. 'In France, he is considered a great man, but then the French admire power above everything, and I suppose they think he is powerful. A communist, you say?'

'Are you surprised?' asked Sarah, turning her nose away from the huge gust of cigarette smoke blowing across the table.

'Not much surprises a man of my age,' answered Vereden. 'Just confirmation of membership. That is all you need?'

Sarah looked into his eyes, trying to judge the kind of man she was dealing with. A cynic, certainly, with few scruples, and fewer ideals, but perhaps some remnants of loyalty to an old friend. 'It would be good to know what he did for the party as well,' she added. 'If that is possible. There are about three years in his life when nobody knows what he was doing, between being a university radical and re-emerging as a financier.'

Vereden shrugged, his eyes seeming to retreat into the hollow pits in which they were sunk. 'You know much about the French Communist Party?' he asked.

'Why should I?' said Sarah flatly.

'True, it is a very specialist subject these days,' said Vereden. 'I used to work for the party also, back in Prague, this was before sixty-eight. I am ashamed of it now, but there it is. By the time you get to my age, many of us are ashamed of many things. We all took our orders from Moscow, of course, but there was a network as well. The Czechs co-operated with the Poles and the Hungarians, and so on. We also worked with the parties in Western Europe, sometimes, on some projects. Why not? We paid all their bills. But there were only some people you could rely on. The Italian Communist Party, no. The Spanish, no. The British and the Greeks, to some extent. The Germans occasionally. The Portuguese, more often than not. But there was one party in Europe that was one hundred per cent loyal, one hundred per cent of the time.' He stopped, coughing, and thumping his chest with his fist while reaching for another cigarette. 'Only one party could be relied upon, and could be used as a bridge between east and west. They were our closest friends, and that was the French Communist Party.'

'What are you suggesting?'

Vereden waved a hand through the cloud of smoke that had started to form around his head. 'Only that the French party was not just a few middle-class kids handing out leaflets and selling newspapers on street corners. Even in Prague we thought they were unnecessarily loyal to Moscow.'

'You can find out what he did for them?'

Vereden stubbed out his cigarette and looked up into her eyes, surveying her, before looking out at the rain falling into the street. 'I sometimes still mix with the old crowd,' he said. 'I'll see what I can do.'

Boissant answered the mobile phone on the third ring; he already knew who was calling, and he always took a moment to relax himself before speaking to Telmont. 'How's it going in the markets?' he asked.

Telmont looked up at the rows of red numerals displayed on his Reuters

and Bloomberg screens. 'Bad,' he said. 'Very bad. Everything is starting to
ratchet downwards, just as we planned.'

'The demonstration in Riga went as ordered?'

'According to the wire reports, yes,' said Telmont. 'Enough of the
economists and analysts here seem to have picked up on it as another
reason for selling the Eastern European markets. It might be best, I think,
if there can be another demonstration tomorrow morning.'

'Those people are desperate for euros and dollars,' said Boissant. 'I'm
sure they will be happy to make a few more. It can be arranged.'

Telmont glanced from his window, down to the river: a brutal and
ugly stretch of water, he reflected to himself, without any refinement or
elegance. 'The report will be out tomorrow, I trust?' he said, the tone of
his voice rising. 'And the woman will co-operate with us? Those are the
two most important elements.'

'Don't worry,' said Boissant. 'Both of them are taken care of.'

'Is she with you now?' asked Telmont.

Boissant looked to his right. Tatyana was sitting next to him, her eyes
fixed sullenly on the ground, as they had been ever since they left Riga.
'Right here,' he said.

'I should like to meet her one day,' said Telmont. 'She sounds like
a remarkable woman. And after all, the Leopard Fund owes her quite
a debt of gratitude. A still greater one, perhaps, over the next couple
of days.'

Boissant laughed. 'May I give you some advice?' he said. 'Never mix
with the enemy, not if you can help it. It makes it harder to deal with
them later.'

Telmont hesitated before replying. 'I worked that kind of sentiment
out of my system a long time ago,' he said. 'In my world, there has been
no room for weakness. You know that.'

The sheaf of microfiches weighed no more than an ounce, and felt light,
flimsy and insubstantial in Sarah's hand. Surely I won't find the answer
in here, she thought to herself. The documents, so fresh it appeared they

had never been examined before, seemed to have little form or substance, as though they could not hold anything of consequence; the burden of any kind of historical truth would surely break these thin sheets of plastic.

A long row of desks stretched out before her, beneath a high, vaulted glass ceiling. Each desk was occupied by a microfiche reader, and a researcher, almost all of whom seemed to be elderly white-haired men. It was so quiet she could almost hear the breath escaping from her lips. A message had been waiting on her mobile when she finished her coffee with Vereden, and she had called Tom back right away, surprised he was still on the bus heading towards Riga. How long can it take, she had asked? It doesn't look so far on the map. Forever, he had told her, when you have to travel along pot-holed Soviet roads, held up by backfiring Ladas that struggle to do more than fifty miles an hour. Find some details of a group of French companies, he had told her. When they were set up, who they belong to, and so on. Why, she had asked, aware of the hesitation in his voice before he replied. Because these were the companies through which the money was paid into Tatyana's Swiss bank accounts. The money he knew nothing about, and which demanded an explanation.

The smell of fresh plastic escaped from the envelope, hitting the back of her nostrils hard; like glue, it made her feel slightly giddy. Her knowledge of company accounts was sketchy. Since leaving university, Sarah's work in the City had been in the currency markets, never in equities, and she knew little about corporate structure. Even if these had been English companies, she would not have been sure where to start. Tom had given her a list of five companies, all of which at different stages had been paying money into accounts controlled by Tatyana. She took the record for each one from the envelope, placing it into the reading machine, magnifying the microfiche twenty times. Words and numbers appeared on the screen, and she carefully noted down the information. The first three companies were all described as general trading businesses. 'Involved in the import and export of general commercial items' was the phrase used in the articles of association, words that could mean almost anything. The next two companies

were investment businesses; the articles described their purpose as
'the procurement of general investments in property and other areas'.
That tells me a lot, thought Sarah to herself.

The turnover of each company ran to tens of millions. Sarah noted
down the figures in her pad, then examined the shareholdings in each
business. Each time, the shares were owned by another company. She
noted down the name of each parent company, then went back to the
desk, this time asking for another set of five microfiche records, one for
each of the parents. She also asked for a full set of the accounts of the
Leopard Fund, stretching back to when it was founded in 1973. 'Wait
here,' said the lady at the desk. 'It will take a few minutes.'

Sarah grabbed a coffee from the machine in the corridor and walked
outside. Breathing deeply, she filled her lungs with crisp, fresh air. A
group of researchers were standing on the steps, dragging on cigarettes
in the furtive huddle smokers naturally form outside any building. Dusk
had already begun to descend upon the city, sending shadows crawling
out across the streets, changing its mood from light to dark. She took a
mouthful of the strong, dark espresso, waiting for the caffeine to seep into
her veins, draining the flimsy paper cup, chucking it into the bin. I can
do this, she said to herself. So long as I am determined. And strong.

The darkness Tatyana could remember well. A melancholy, sombre night-
time that would descend upon the country in October and last until the
next spring, turning the days into little more than brief flashes of light, as
if the sun were a torch constantly switched off to preserve its power. It
was a darkness she recognized as soon as they crossed the border between
Latvia and Estonia, a desolate, frozen checkpoint, guarded on both sides
by teenagers huddled in wooden shacks, loaded with machine guns. As
the car pitched its way along the twisting single-lane road, its headlamps
could hardly dent the depth of the night.

Nothing could be seen through the windows, but then, Tatyana
reflected during the drive, there never was anything much to see
anyway. They were now driving through the endless plains that stretched

from here to the Urals, a flat, pastoral landscape rolling forward for hundreds of miles, broken only by the lakes and pine forests. Edging the window down, Tatyana breathed deeply, collecting the smell of the pine needles in her nostrils. Since she left, there had been little she had missed about Estonia, but the fragrance of pine had always stayed close to her heart. In the supermarket, she realized, she had always been buying pine-scented cleaners, subconsciously, she supposed, because it reminded her of home.

The drive from the border to Tartu took just over two hours, and they arrived at the Barclay Hotel after six in the evening. A four-storey grey building, it lay between the main Victorian square next to the Emajogi river and the modern concrete bus station and shopping centre. 'You know this building, I suppose?' said Boissant, as they stepped into the lobby.

'Of course,' answered Tatyana.

'It was different when you were last here, I suppose?'

Tatyana glanced through the spruced, polished lobby, then looked across at the Finnish and Estonian businessmen drinking in the bar. 'Last time I was here, all the men were in uniforms,' she replied. 'But since it was the headquarters of the Red Army, that, I suppose, is what you would expect.'

'I thought it might be an appropriate place to stay,' said Boissant, a thin smile starting to spread across his lips.

'How long will we be here?' asked Tatyana.

'One night.'

'And then?'

Boissant collected her bag from the floor and pointed towards the lift. 'We leave for the base in the morning.'

Lucky to have the hotel so close to the station, thought Jennings to himself as he stepped out of the Eurostar terminal at the Gare du Nord. Saves the trouble of queuing up for a taxi. On his map, the walk to the Comfort Inn shouldn't take more than seven or eight minutes, he decided, but he would take it slowly. Get to know the area. Find his way around.

The hotel sign glared out at him from the end of the road. Jennings walked slowly down the street, rehearsing his moves in his mind. If they were there, it was his job to take them, any way he could; if they were out, he would have to wait for their return. The entrance was plain and functional, standardized to the model of a thousand other hotels around the world. Jennings stood still for a moment, pretending to read some tourist leaflets, before approaching the girl at the desk. 'A Mr Bracewell and a Miss Turnbull,' he said in fractured French. 'Are they staying at the hotel?'

He could hear the girl's red fingernails running across the keyboard of her computer. 'Miss Turnbull is still here,' she explained. 'Mr Bracewell checked out yesterday.'

Jennings nodded. 'Can you tell her I am here?' he asked.

The woman punched three digits into the phone on her desk, while Jennings watched carefully, making a mental note of the number: two-nine-seven. 'She's out,' she said, looking back at Jennings. 'Can I give her a message?'

Jennings shook his head. 'I'll try later,' he replied.

He stepped away from the desk and walked out to the street, pulling his collar up around his neck to protect himself from the chill blowing through the night air. Crossing the road, he walked into the cafe opposite, ordered a beer from the bar, and sat down at a table by the window, checking the view of the hotel entrance was clear enough for him to be able to see everybody going in and out. He pulled the mobile from his coat pocket, and punched eleven digits into it. 'Bracewell has left town,' he said into the phone.

'Are you sure?' asked Boissant.

'I've just been to the hotel,' he said. 'He checked out yesterday.'

'And the girl?'

'She's still there, but out,' said Jennings. 'I have the place covered right now.'

Boissant paused. 'Then get her instead,' he said. 'She will be able to tell you where he is.'

Jennings clicked off, and folded the phone back into his coat pocket.

He took a sip of beer and asked for a packet of cigarettes. His eyes remained peeled on the entrance to the hotel. This, he reflected, has the makings of a long and boring evening.

Tom could feel the cramp in his legs as he looked out at the bus station in Riga. It was so long since he had stood up, his muscles had started to ache with stiffness. He climbed from the seat, stretched, and stepped down onto the frozen concrete, the soles of his shoes struggling to find a grip on the icy surface. Around him, he could hear the sound of mothers greeting their sons, and wives their husbands, most of them returning from work on the building sites of Berlin, and found himself glancing into their faces before retrieving his bag from the boot of the bus. Reunions should be joyous moments, he reflected; sometimes, but not always.

According to his map, the hotel was no more than a ten-minute walk from the station. Tom slung his bag over his shoulder, walking through the bus station. At a cashpoint, he stopped, withdrawing a hundred lat on his Visa card. Enough to get me through tonight, he thought to himself. At the single snack bar in the corner of the bus depot, he ordered a coffee, ignoring the scowl of the waitress as he handed over a twenty-lat note. The coffee scalded the back of his throat. All around him there was a thick cloud of cigarette smoke, and Tom breathed deeply, tasting the nicotine in his nostrils. If I can get through the next few hours, I really will have given up smoking, he reflected.

He glanced down at his watch. It was a quarter past nine, Central European Time, an hour later than it was in Paris or London. Taking his bag, Tom threw back the last of the coffee and stepped out into the cold night air. On earlier visits to Riga, he had always arrived by plane from London; finding his bearings took a moment. Ahead of him, he could see the train station, and beyond that the long, curved arch of the Statue of Liberty. He began walking, his feet treading into the snow scattered across the pavements, oblivious to everything around him. What do I say, he asked himself, when I see her? The moment had been rehearsed a thousand times in the last three weeks, reeling around his mind like a tape caught in a loop, yet, now it approached, the words abandoned him. In truth, he reflected, I don't even know if I want to see her again.

The doors to the Metropole Hotel swung aside. Tom walked calmly up to the desk, trying to mask the anxiety on his face. He looked briefly into the clear green eyes of the girl at reception, and for a brief moment thought perhaps he should abandon the idea, go stay in another hotel, get out of here in the morning. 'I'd like to speak to Mr or Mrs Sanoli,' he said, his tone calm and strong. 'I believe they are guests here.'

His pulse quickened as he watched the girl's eyes sweep through the guestbook on her desk, then across to the computer, her hands skimming over the keyboard. She looked back up towards Tom, smiling up at him, her red lipstick smudging on her teeth. 'I am afraid they checked out this morning,' she said.

Tom sighed and nodded. 'I don't suppose you might know where they have gone?' he asked.

She looked at him suspiciously, then shook her head. Tom dug his hand into his pocket and pulled out three twenty-lat notes, pushing them across the desk: about two weeks' average salary, if he remembered his statistics on the Latvian economy. 'I would very much like to know,' he said quietly. 'Just the general direction.'

The girl looked at the money, then back at Tom. In her eyes, he could see the calculations she was making. Reaching down, she collected the three notes in her fingers and folded them into her purse. 'They hired a car,' she said. 'I could ask the driver. It might take a few minutes to find out.'

'I'd be grateful,' answered Tom. 'In the meantime, I'd like a room.'

She pushed across a registration form. So close, thought Tom to himself as he filled in the details. I missed her by less then twelve hours. The receptionist looked down at the form, then at his credit card and passport. 'She's my wife,' he said, looking up at the girl.

She handed across the room key. 'I'm sorry,' she said, her face falling downwards. 'I'll call you when I have the information.'

*   *   *

The packet of cigarettes on the cafe table was half empty, a pile of butts starting to tumble from the ashtray. Jennings's beer glass had been joined by two empty cups of coffee. He had been contemplating a third, when he noticed her climbing from a taxi. A night such as this, you need a lot of coffee, he reflected. It pays to stay alert.

The view was not perfect. Her coat was wrapped around her, and a scarf was tied tightly around her neck, but he could see the blonde hair pinned back behind her head, held in place by a clip, and Jennings felt certain only English girls wore their hair that way. A blonde Englishwomen staying at this hotel. It had to be her.

He stubbed out his cigarette, chucked the packet into his coat pocket, placed a note on the table and walked briskly from the cafe. Rain was still falling, and visibility in the street was not good. He walked past the hotel twice, each time glancing through the glass doors. Stepping inside, he walked up to the desk, nodded in the direction of the receptionist, smiled, then walked through to the staircase. The best thing about cheap hotels, he reflected, is they never check who is going in or out.

Tom threw his bag onto the bed and walked into the bathroom, splashing water onto his face. He could feel his breath coming in gasps, escaping from his lungs in bursts, and his pulse was beating furiously.

He could hear his mobile ringing, but for a few seconds he decided not to answer. He stood in front of the mirror, looking at the lines around his eyes, and wondering how much he might have aged in the last three weeks. 'Something weird is happening,' said Sarah, when he answered the phone.

'Tell me,' said Tom sharply.

'A man has been here asking for me,' said Sarah, her voice cracking. 'The receptionist told me. He didn't leave a name, but he was looking for me.'

'Get out of there,' said Tom. 'Get out of there right away.'

'You think there might be some danger?' asked Sarah.

'Don't even stop to think,' interrupted Tom sharply. 'Just get out of there right away!'

He could hear her breathing sharply, and the sound of her mobile phone being snapped shut. Tom sat down on the edge of the bed, sipped some water, wiping away the sweat on his forehead. He looked down on the square, its neon lights glancing up towards the hotel window. Christ, he thought to himself. This doesn't get any easier.

CHAPTER 20

Thursday, 18 February

I COULD LEAVE RIGHT NOW, THOUGHT TATYANA. IF I WANTED TO. She adjusted the two rings on her fingers, glancing out of the glass lobby of the hotel at the people making their way to work and the students on their way to lectures. Most of them appeared smartly, if cheaply, dressed, and they looked warm and well-fed. It has changed so much since I was last here, she reflected to herself. Foreigners were not even allowed into the city.

She sipped her coffee and took a bite of the sticky Danish pastry on her plate, trying to force the food down her throat; her appetite had vanished, but she was worried her figure might be starting to lose its shape. Her eyes scanned the faces passing the window, looking to see if anyone she might recognize passed by. It would be comforting, she reflected, to see the face of someone she knew. Even though it would be impossible to speak to them.

'We will not want to linger over breakfast,' said Boissant. He sat down heavily opposite her, an aroma of soap and aftershave drifting over the table.

'I am not delaying anyone,' said Tatyana.

She watched as his pudgy fingers pierced the pastry he had taken from the buffet, cramming the food into his mouth. 'That's just as well,' he said. 'There is much that needs to be done.'

'You have arranged transport?' Boissant nodded. 'And clothes?' Tatyana added. 'We will need the right clothes.'

'They will be here with the jeep,' said Boissant. 'In just a few minutes.'

Tatyana took a sip of her orange juice, allowing the taste of the fruit to linger on her tongue. 'How long do we need to be there?' she asked.

Boissant shrugged, lighting a cigarette and blowing the smoke across the table. 'I can't say,' he replied. 'Two nights, perhaps more. Long enough.'

'And after that I am free?'

'That was the bargain,' answered Boissant. 'I wouldn't break my word.' He stubbed out his cigarette, and jabbed another piece of pastry into his mouth. 'On one condition, of course,' he added. 'That you don't break your word either.'

The five members of the Breakfast Club attracted no attention from the regulars at the Bankside Grill, even though it was rare for them to gather there on a Thursday. The traders from Liffe were still sitting around the tables, as they were every morning, along with the workers from some of the nearby building sites. A thick smell of lard and eggs filtered through the air, sticking to the clothes and hair of everyone who sat down. A last outpost of proper bloke food, thought Jones, amongst the rows of cappuccino bars. 'Five full English,' he said to the waitress. 'And coffees all round.'

Both Andrew Taylor and Ian Fletcher were looking dog-tired, complaining about how their new babies had kept them up for half the night; John Dundee was looking sleeker, and slightly plumper, his shine the result of his most recent promotion at Mercury Asset Management; and Alan Gibson looked frazzled by the late nights in the office trying to keep up with the wild swings in the equity markets. But it was good to see all of the gang, Jones reflected. Just odd that Tom was not here among them. Of all the regulars at Breakfast Club meetings, Tom was always the most emphatic that the tradition had to be upheld.

'I still can't believe he didn't tell any of us,' said Fletcher. 'I mean it isn't every day your wife leaves you. Unfortunately.'

'You know how secretive Tom could be about women. Always has been,' said Jones. 'Ages ago, he was knocking off that girl from institutional sales for about six months before anyone knew.'

'None of us knew about Tatyana until they were married,' added Dundee. 'Mary isn't going to believe it when I tell her they've split up. She's always saying they seem like such a perfect couple. Why can't we be more like Tom and Tatyana, she says every few weeks.'

'Not any more,' said Jones. He hesitated while the breakfast arrived: five sizzling plates of bacon, eggs, sausages, mushroom, fried bread and beans. Taking some ketchup and squeezing it over his beans, he looked up at the men around him. 'The question is, are we going to help him?'

Dundee looked back at him across the table. 'It's not really a question, is it?' he replied firmly. 'Of course we'll help him.'

The rest all nodded. 'The only question,' Dundee continued, 'is what do we have to do? And what the hell is he doing in Riga anyway?'

Tom poured some coffee from the percolator, took a gulp of the hot steaming liquid, and looked at the buffet spread out across the table. Although he could no longer quite remember when he last ate a proper meal, he could feel his stomach churning at the sight of the hot food. I must try to eat, he told himself. During the next thirty hours I will need all my strength.

He took a table in the centre of the dining hall, glancing out across the room. Where would they have sat, he wondered to himself, when they were having breakfast here yesterday? Not here in the middle of the room, surely. This was not the place for a couple eloping together. He looked into the corners. Over there, perhaps, he reflected. In the darkness. Perhaps I should ask one of the waitresses. Maybe they could tell me what they looked like together, whether they acted like a couple, whether they held hands, and looked into each other's eyes. Maybe then I would understand why she left me.

He answered the mobile on the first ring, taking another swig of coffee. 'Jaak Terah here.'

Tom nodded into the phone. 'She's gone to Tartu,' he said. 'The Barclay Hotel. The firm the driver works for told me that was where he took them.'

'Have you ever been there?' asked Terah.

'No,' answered Tom.

'Do you know much about it?'

'University town, that kind of stuff,' said Tom. 'Maybe Tatyana was a student there.'

'I don't think that's her connection with the place,' said Terah.

'What then?' asked Tom. 'Tell me your theory.'

'Are you going to go after her?' asked Terah.

'Of course,' said Tom, the words delivered without a moment of hesitation. 'I haven't come this far to let it rest. Of course I'm going to Tartu. I need to speak to her.'

'I'll meet you there,' said Terah. 'I can tell you then. If you get a car, it won't take you more than four hours. I'll see you at the fountain outside the town hall at two.'

Julian Frinton lingered outside the door of the office, hesitating before he stepped inside. Perhaps if I were a braver man I would just go home right now, he reflected to himself. I could collect Edward from his school, go to the police, tell them what has happened, then deal with whatever the consequences might be. He could feel his heart sinking. The trouble, I suppose, is that I am just not that brave.

The door swung open and Frinton stepped inside, riding the elevator alone, and settling down at his desk. The usual pile of papers was lying there, but this morning he was in no mood for looking through his post. A copy of the report was ready, waiting only for his approval. And the screen of his computer was telling him a message was waiting to be read. 'Don't forget our trip last week,' ran the message. 'The report this morning must be exactly the same as I instructed last week.'

Frinton glanced at the source. The message, he could see, had been sent via a fake hotmail address, making it impossible to trace. On his desk the phone was ringing. 'You got the e-mail?' said Boissant.

'I just read it,' said Frinton.

'The report will be issued this morning?' asked Boissant.

'As usual,' replied Frinton. 'The OECD report on the progress of the Eastern European economies is issued on the third Thursday of the month, every third month.'

'And it will be as I instructed?'

Frinton hesitated, reluctant to let the words escape from his lips. 'The market is already very fragile,' he said uneasily. 'A report like this, from the OECD in particular, could trigger the entire region into a full-scale collapse.'

'That is of no concern to me, nor should it be to you,' said Boissant. 'All I ask is that you do as you are told. Of course, it is not you that will suffer if you don't. Just the boy.'

'It will be done,' said Frinton, a sigh escaping his lips as he put the phone down. He glanced at the report on his desk, flicking through its pages, despairing at each dire warning of total economic collapse throughout Eastern Europe, and at every graph and chart predicting its descent into ruin and chaos. Picking up the phone, he put a call through to the publishing department. The report, he told them, was ready to be released.

A surge of excitement started to run through his veins, Telmont noticed, as he strode through the trading floor towards his office; the familiar thrill of overwhelming victory. Nobody ever spoke to him as he walked across the floor, and Telmont rarely stopped to speak to any of the dealers or fund managers. The Imperial Chinese court, he had always maintained, had been absolutely right in believing that authority had to be remote and cruel to be effective. Yet a tour of the battlefield occasionally did no harm. Particularly when you were winning. It reminded the troops of how much they owed to him.

Sheldon was already waiting at the entrance to his office. Telmont glanced briefly at him, a frown playing on his forehead, then walked through, Sheldon following meekly at his rear. 'There are a lot of calls from the press, sir,' he said, his voice nervous.

'That is how I expected it to be,' said Telmont, a smile starting to play upon his lips. He took the neatly typed list of names, scanning through those he recognized. Each of them had asked for a comment on the OECD report this morning predicting economic collapse throughout Eastern Europe. 'Call back Reuters, Bloomberg, the *Financial Times*, the *Journal* and *Les Echoes*,' he said. 'Tell them this. The OECD report this morning vindicates my decision earlier this week, on behalf of the Leopard Fund and its investors, to unwind our equity holdings around the world and particularly in Eastern Europe. As the world's most respected economic forecaster and administrator has accurately pointed out, the region has been unable, and will continue to be unable, to sustain a transition to a stable market economy. Therefore, it should not receive any investment from the developed world. Other banks and funds, if they are to behave responsibly towards their investors, should also be selling the region immediately.'

He looked up towards Sheldon, a command written into his expression, listening quietly while the quote was read back to him. 'There is some speculation we might have had a leak of what the OECD would say, sir,' said Sheldon. 'Because of the announcement we made yesterday.'

Telmont's laugh briefly filled the empty, hollow room. 'Nobody ever gets a leak of an OECD report, it is unheard of,' he said. 'Just tell them, a leopard is a creature with a unique ability to anticipate movement. That is what this fund is all about.'

Sheldon nodded, noticing that Telmont was looking towards the door, and Sheldon began edging from the room, unsure if he should turn his back. Punching a series of numbers into the phone, Telmont looked down at the screens on his desk. The reaction to the report this morning had been as he had anticipated: a bloodbath throughout the markets. In London, the FTSE was down two hundred and ten points, in Frankfurt the DAX was down two hundred and seventy points, and in Paris the CAC was down by one hundred and fifty-four points. All the Eastern European stock markets were showing falls ranging from ten to fifteen per cent, and on Reuters a story was running, speculating that Hungary, the Czech Republic and Poland had already asked both the IMF and the European Union for emergency loans to support their currencies. All three countries had raised their interest rates this morning to fifteen per cent, while in Estonia, Latvia and Lithuania, interest rates had now been set at thirty per cent, with talk they might have to rise further. In the Ukraine and Belarus, interest rates were now over one hundred per cent and rising, and all trading in their currencies against the euro and the dollar had now ground to a halt. A story on Bloomberg, Telmont noted, reported that the IMF chairman Michel Analotev was this morning contacting leaders of the Group of Eight industrial powers to put together a package to help Eastern Europe. 'Where is the girl?' said Telmont into the phone.

'She slipped past us,' said Boissant, his tone firm and unyielding. 'My man was waiting for her at the hotel, but when he went up to the room, she had left.'

'We don't know where she is?' asked Telmont, his pitch rising.

'A search is being organized,' said Boissant. 'Jennings is a good man, he will not let us down.'

'And Bracewell, do we know where he is?'

Boissant hesitated before replying. 'I am told that he spent last night in a hotel in Riga,' he said quietly. 'I think he is following us, so my guess is that he will come to Tartu next.'

'In Tartu?' said Telmont cautiously. 'How is that possible?'

'It's a free country. He can go anywhere he likes,' said Boissant. 'Of course, he will never find us. It's impossible.'

'Are you sure?'

'It is quite certain,' said Boissant. 'Nobody can find the base unless they know where it is. And if he should find it, what of that? We will just kill him.'

Sarah edged her way across the street, her coat wrapped up around her neck, her scarf worn high, not to protect her face from the cold, but to conceal it from anybody who might be looking for her. She walked nervously into the bar, checked the faces of the few people having breakfast, decided none of them was showing any interest in her, and sat down in the corner, ordering a coffee, juice and croissant.

Looking down at her hand, she could see she was trembling, her veins vibrating beneath her skin. From her reflection in the window, she could see the tiredness written into the lines in her face. Not surprising, she reflected to herself. I have hardly slept more than a few hours a night for several days. She took the large cup of café au lait between her fingers, breathing in its milky aroma, resting it on her lips. The hotel, she decided, might be small and shabby, populated mostly by Algerians and cockroaches, but, Sarah reflected, it had one thing to be said for it: they didn't ask for a passport, they didn't ask for a credit card imprint, and they took cash.

When Tom had told her to leave last night, she had not hesitated. At first she had felt lost, baffled as to why anyone should be looking for her in an obscure hotel in Paris when she hadn't told anyone where she was going. He had seen it sooner than she had; if anyone knew where she was, it was because they were tracking her. From the bed she had collected a few of her things, stuffed them into her bag, left her toothbrush and make-up in the bathroom, and swept down stairs and out the door. She hadn't bothered to pay; they could collect the money from her credit card all the same. Walking quickly down the street, she hopped into the first taxi she saw, told it to take her to Les Halles. After walking for ten minutes through the side streets, she had checked into the hotel, spending the night in a fitful, uncomfortable and restless sleep, her mind crowded with images of her own demise.

'Are you okay?' she said into her mobile.

'Of course,' said Tom. 'It's you I'm worried about.'

'I'm all right,' said Sarah. 'A bit freaked, that's all.'

'Where are you?' he asked. 'Is it safe?'

'I think so,' answered Sarah, her lips stumbling over the words. 'I'm in a cafe. I don't think anyone could have followed me when I left the hotel.'

'They will still be looking for you,' he said. 'You can't afford to relax.'

'Paris is a big city,' said Sarah. 'One English girl will be hard to find.'

'We have that on our side,' said Tom. 'When you see Vereden again, ask him for his advice. He must know something about disappearing.'

'You don't think I should go to the police?'

'And tell them what, exactly?' said Tom. 'That you are scared one of France's most respected financiers is trying to kill you, the same guy who sacked you earlier in the week? I don't think they'd take you very seriously.'

'I suppose not,' replied Sarah, her voice drifting from the phone. She glanced down the street, trying to focus on some of the people. 'Do you really think they might be trying to kill us?'

'I don't know,' said Tom. 'But I don't see why they should send someone after you. And I wouldn't wait around to find out what they do want.'

'But why?'

'My guess is that we have pissed them off, and they are looking to strike back,' said Tom.

Sarah wiped the edge of a tear away from her eye. 'I didn't think anything like this was going to happen,' she said. 'If I had, I don't think I would have ever started.'

Tom hesitated, looking down at his watch to see how much time he had before his rental car arrived at the hotel. 'I don't suppose either of us wanted things to be like this,' he said. 'But that's the way they are, and we have to deal with them.'

'I wish you were here with me,' said Sarah.

The car can wait a couple of minutes, thought Tom to himself. 'I wish you were here as well,' he said. 'But the next twenty-four hours are something we both have to do by ourselves. Once it is all over, then we can be together.'

CHAPTER 21

Thursday, 18 February

I WILL ONLY HAVE TO WORK WITH THE FRENCHMEN FOR A COUPLE of days, decided Jennings. For the money they are paying, I should be able to stand it.

The unit consisted of five men, gathered on Boissant's order. Their leader introduced himself as Alain Comtes, and since he was the only one who spoke English, it was through him Jennings was forced to communicate. A tall man, with thick dark hair, and rugged weather-beaten skin, Comtes carried himself with the kind of bearing that suggested he might have been a soldier once. Not any more, though, Jennings reflected. Now he was just muscle for hire. 'She was last seen at a hotel here,' he said, pointing at the map spread out on the table. 'Last night.'

'Does she know anyone in Paris?' asked Comtes.

Jennings shook his head. 'I don't believe so.'

Comtes spread his hand over the map, his palm covering most of the city centre. 'My guess is she will be somewhere beneath my hand,' he said. 'If you are a stranger in a city, the instinct is to move to somewhere you recognize. In London that might mean Trafalgar Square or Westminster Abbey. In Paris it means Place de la Concorde, the Opera, Les Halles – somewhere like that.'

'It's still a big piece of turf,' said Jennings. 'Even if you count me in, there are only six of us.'

Comtes shrugged. 'Six men are enough if they are the right six men,' he said. 'The streets of this city, any city I suppose, have their own network. Tramps, beggars, pickpockets, prostitutes, runaway kids: there are plenty of people who make their living on the streets. All of them need money, and all of them have eyes. My men know them.' He paused. 'You have the picture?'

Jennings fished into his case, placing a stack of photographs on the table. He had taken them from the video he had shot for Telmont last week, and the image was neither crisp nor flattering. But for identification, it would do. 'This is her,' he said.

Comtes took the top picture from the pile, holding it between his fingers, examining the contours of her face as if she were a model in a magazine. 'Blonde hair, red lips, quite the English rose, no?' he said.

'We just want to find her, that's all,' said Jennings.

Comtes took the pictures, handing a dozen copies to each man, and counting out ten thousand francs each in one-hundred franc notes; they looked a rough crew to Jennings, and he didn't have much confidence they wouldn't just take the money and drink it. 'And when we find her, what then?' asked Comtes, turning back to Jennings.

'Take her prisoner, hold her securely, then deliver her to me,' he replied calmly.

Comtes turned back to the small unit, barking a fresh set of instructions in French. One by one they filed out of the room. 'Come with me,' said Comtes to Jennings. 'Let me introduce you to the streets of Paris.'

One pine tree looks much like another, reflected Tatyana. After the first few thousand, they all merge into one.

The drive from Tartu had been slowed by the snow blocking the road, and even the Jeep Boissant had supplied had trouble holding its grip against the icy surface of the road. They had driven due east from the city, in the direction of Lake Peipus and Lake Pskov, the two massive waterways that marked the border between Estonia and Russia, keeping to the main road for the first twenty miles, then turning south in the direction of Polva, a desolate and bleak factory town constructed entirely of concrete and tangled corrugated iron. Tartu might have acquired a veneer of prosperity, Tatyana decided, but out here the country seems to have regressed. Carts were pulled by oxen, stoves were lit by wood, and from the barns she could see the old wooden ploughs had been polished up and brought back to life. Past Polva, the road narrowed, turning into mud, frozen so hard the Jeep skidded across its surface like a stone sliding across a sheet of ice. Twice it got stuck in craters in the road, forcing her out of the vehicle while the driver tried to wrench the machine back onto the track. 'It feels good to be home, perhaps,' said Boissant, looking across at her as they stood on the side of the dirt road.

'This was never my home,' said Tatyana.

'And yet the places where we have spent time as a child, we feel some affection for them always, do we not?' said Boissant, blowing the smoke from his cigarette high into the air. 'That is the nature of the human spirit.'

'I find it hard to believe you have any knowledge of the spirit,' said Tatyana, wrapping the collar of her coat around her neck. 'Maybe the kind that comes in a bottle. Nothing else.'

'You judge me too harshly, Mrs Bracewell,' answered Boissant, tossing his cigarette into the snow, watching as it melted into the ground. 'The path I have chosen is not so different from yours. You too are a mercenary, I think. A different coin, that's all.'

From here, Tatyana calculated as she climbed back on board, the drive was another twenty minutes or so. How many years is it now since I have seen this place? Twenty, I suppose. For it still to be there, and for it to be intact, was a miracle. But then, I suppose it was built to withstand just about anything short of nuclear assault.

Eight miles down the dirt track, the Jeep turned again, this time into a clearing in the forest. A river ran northwards, drifting away into the valley, its surface now frozen solid. Tatyana gripped the door handle as the Jeep started to turn down the bank of river, descending into the incline, tracking the thin strip of land where the river met the trees. One wheel slid along the ice, the other gripped the hardened moss and bracken, the driver edging the machine slowly forwards. At her side, Boissant lit another cigarette. 'Don't worry,' he said. 'This driver knows the terrain. We will get you there all right.'

'It makes no difference to me,' said Tatyana sharply, her tone harsh and unforgiving.

She turned away, looking down at the contours of the river as it ran down the hillside. The path was no more than three yards wide, its track overgrown with weeds, saplings of pine trees already sprouting uneasily from the ground; from their height, Tatyana judged it was at least five years since this route had been driven regularly. The Jeep lurched violently, swaying between the ice and the craters pitting the ground, its heavy wheels crunching the saplings as it drove forward. Tatyana looked up at the steeply rising mountain, its surface covered in pine trees and snow, her nostrils breathing in the fresh scented air. She remembered how much she had enjoyed coming here as a child. The adventure and mystery of the forest had captivated her, and she recalled how she could sit for hours as a little girl looking out at the trees, imagining herself a princess pursued by an evil knight, waiting for her prince to come and save her. Childish dreams, she reminded herself. This is real life.

Two miles down the hillside, the Jeep turned sharply east, following the track of a small stream into a valley. The clearing between the trees was no more than three yards, the path guarded by trees, blocking the light of the sun. Tatyana could feel the darkness surrounding them, and she could hear the sound of the wheels crushing the snow and wood as it drove forward. The trees live for hundreds of years, she reflected; they will have hardly changed since the last time I was here.

The clearing was bathed in sunlight. Forty yards by forty yards, the opening spread out in a wide circle. A split in the clouds allowed the sun to shine through and Tatyana could feel her pulse quickening as she looked out at the base – a grey dome of steel rising from the ground, its bolts browned with rust, its surface scarred by the weather, and its roof covered in a thick layer of snow. Ice had frozen into the doorways, hanging in long, thin tubes like glass, catching the sunlight and sending out shafts of brightly-coloured light. The Jeep swung round from the track, its wheels skidding to a stop on the strip of frozen concrete stretching out from the doorway. 'Familiar?' said Boissant, breathing smoke into her face.

'Of course,' said Tatyana.

He climbed from the Jeep, walking around the vehicle, holding her door open, offering her his hand to guide her to the ground. 'You are pleased to be back?' he said.

'Back?' she replied, allowing her eyes to linger on him for a fraction of a second. 'It isn't the sort of place you ever really leave.'

The cough was instantly recognizable; a low, throaty growl that seemed to start somewhere in his gut, hurtled through his throat, then spluttered onto his lips, rattling through the thin, smoky air of the cafe. Sarah looked at Vereden from the doorway, motioning him to join her. He waved a cigarette in her direction. 'Can we go somewhere else?' she asked, walking across to his table.

'What's wrong with here?' he asked.

'There might be someone following me.'

Vereden nodded curtly, swiftly emptied thirty francs onto the table, tucked the cigarette between his lips, and put the packet in his pocket. Remaining silent, he walked from the cafe, holding her by the arm, and steered her out into the street. He walked quickly for someone of his age and condition, she noted, his step springy, and his grip on her arm delicate. They walked through the street, turned left twice, then walked right down a side street, stood for a minute gazing silently into a shop window, then walked back up the side street, turning left this time, then taking the next right. Vereden pointed to a cafe, pulling her inside, drawing up a table for two, and asking the waitress for two coffees and a jug of water. 'No one is following,' he said. 'But that doesn't mean they aren't looking for you.'

'How can you tell?' asked Sarah, struggling to catch her breath.

Vereden opened up his lighter, releasing a sharp smell of petrol into the air. 'The route,' he replied, fishing a cigarette from his pocket and lowering it into the flame. 'We would have seen if someone had tailed us through that trip. Who are they?'

'I don't know for sure,' said Sarah. 'A man was looking for me at the hotel yesterday. I didn't wait to see him. I left and spent the night somewhere else. I might be paranoid, I don't know.'

'You did the right thing,' said Vereden. 'Had either you or your boyfriend told anyone which hotel you were staying at?'

'Only Radek,' said Sarah. 'I left him my number.'

Vereden sighed, dragging deeply on his cigarette. 'Then they've got to him,' he said, his tone heavy and cold. 'I'll check they haven't killed him.'

Sarah found herself numbed into silence, the words frozen on her lips. She looked up as the waitress placed a coffee on the table, clasping her fingers around the cup, feeling its warmth but unable to drink anything. 'They wouldn't do that, would they?' she said eventually.

'What do you think this is, the thousand-acre wood?' said Vereden. He snapped his fingers together. 'They'd break people like matchsticks if they needed to.'

'You found something out?' asked Sarah.

Vereden smiled. 'Of course I found something out,' he said. 'Although, right now, I think I'd rather not know.'

Sarah lifted the cup to her lips, taking a sip of the rich, sweet coffee, letting it linger on her tongue, calming her nerves. 'Tell me,' she said firmly.

Vereden pushed his packet of cigarettes across the table. 'Smoke?'

'I don't,' she replied. 'I don't like them.'

Vereden took one himself, dragged deeply on it, blowing the smoke into the air. 'You might want to soon,' he said.

Sarah looked down, avoiding his gaze, examining the rough surface of the cafe table. 'Telmont was a party member, right?'

'Sure, sure,' said Vereden. 'Of course he was. That wasn't hard to find out. I had a friend who checked their records. Did it a bit more subtly than you could have. His name was there all right. But so what? Lots of kids joined the communist party in the late Sixties. Lots of kids went on demos. It meant nothing.'

Sarah looked up, wondering if she could ever count the lines etched into the contours of his skin. 'There was something else, though,' she said. 'With Telmont it went further.'

Vereden nodded. 'I don't suppose you know much about how the communist party worked?'

Sarah shook her head. 'Kids today don't,' continued Vereden. 'It was organized the same way in Prague, here in Paris, everywhere. The same fundamental Leninist structure. It was arranged in circles. On the outside, the sympathizers and liberals, sentimental well-wishers, who liked some of the ideals. Then there were the casual members, the activists, the organizers and so on. Eventually you came to the core, the inner circle.'

'Telmont was part of that?'

'There were two inner circles, the soft and hard cores,' said Vereden, squinting and rubbing his eyes as he lit another cigarette. 'The Politburo was the public face of the party. Then there was the leader's bureau, divisional chieftains who took charge of different aspects of the party's organization. Telmont was extraordinarily young to be admitted to that kind of group. He was still in his early twenties then. But he had one skill the party valued.'

'What was that?' asked Sarah.

'You know already,' replied Vereden quickly.

'He knew how to handle money?'

'Of course,' wheezed Vereden. 'It is the one thing he does better than anyone else.'

Jaak Terah blended naturally into the background, as inconspicuous as one of the stones in the buildings. Tom could see him as he walked through the town square, leaning on the edge of the fountain, still dressed in the black jeans and brown leather jacket he had worn the last time they met. His back was resting against the fountain that stood in front of the town hall, a cigarette hanging from his lips, his expression dulled and vacant, as if leaning against this fountain was all he did most days.

Tom walked close to the fountain, leaning against the cold granite, a thin spray of water blowing into his face. 'You're early,' said Terah.

'It's not such a long journey,' answered Tom.

The drive had taken under four hours. He had collected the car from the hotel, taken a close look at the map, then started driving towards the Estonian border. At the border, the guards had delayed him for almost an hour; English tourists driving rental cars by themselves were a rarity at any time of the year, but particularly in February. Eventually they had accepted his explanation that he was visiting his wife's family. In a way, he reflected, it had even been true.

He crossed the border near Moniste, a small rural village, then drove due north, up past Voru towards Tartu, a journey that took him nearly halfway across Estonia. Along the way he reflected how little he had come to know his wife's country in the three years he had been married to Tatyana. Their time here together, brief enough, had been restricted to Tallinn, and the strip of coast alongside the Baltic Sea opposite Finland. They had never ventured into the interior of the country, nor had Tatyana ever suggested they should do so. Another way of shrouding herself in mystery, Tom decided; she didn't want me as a witness to any aspect of her past. History, so far as Tatyana had been concerned, was something you found in books. It was not something people had themselves.

The harsh, unrelenting cold of the journey obscured the land through which he passed. The snow lay across the fields like a veil over a bride's face, concealing and erasing everything that lay beneath. The villages were sparse and lightly populated, consisting of blocks of flats constructed from concrete and iron, smoke belching from the chimneys. Nearly all the old farms, Tom realized, must have been destroyed during collectivization, and only the apartment blocks remained. Only the roll of the forest, never more than a few miles distant, lent any kind of grandeur to the scenery. 'You see much?' asked Terah.

'What's to see?' answered Tom. 'Fields and snow and trees.'

'The interesting things are all buried,' said Terah, tossing his cigarette into the fountain. 'That is the way in the countries of the north. The snow covers up everything.'

'I'm starting to learn that,' said Tom.

The square was dominated by a huge, pink, classical town hall built, Tom guessed, when Estonia was still a province of the Russian Empire. A stretch of classical buildings ran down towards the river, then turned into dense concrete blocks, standing close to one another like commuters on a train. Around the fountain, the older men of the town seemed to gather to smoke and talk, paying little attention to the students walking past on their way up to the university. 'Tatyana never brought you here?' said Terah.

'It's my first visit,' replied Tom. 'We never spent much time together in Estonia – just a few trips – then she came to England soon after that. She wanted to leave it all behind.'

'I can understand that,' said Terah. 'Someone might have recognized her.'

Tom took a sharp intake of breath, and he could feel the freezing air hitting his lungs, lowering the temperature in his veins. 'You found out who she is?'

Terah shrugged. 'I don't really expect to find out who she is, but I have some better clues,' he said. 'Let's get a drink.'

They walked through the square in silence, Tom glancing into the faces of the women they passed, wondering if, behind the headscarfs and hats they all wore to protect themselves from the cold, he might catch a glimpse of her. At moments, he felt he recognized her features, a nose here, a cheekbone there, lips or ears on someone else – and yet he could never assemble a whole face. Not in the same person, anyway.

Terah ordered two coffees and slipped his leather jacket over the back of his chair, resting his face in his hands. 'Tartu is not a big place,' he said. 'Know much about it?'

Tom shook his head. 'University town, founded in the early eighteenth century by the Swedes, I think,' he replied. 'A place Estonians consider their spiritual and cultural capital. A big military base as well, during the Soviet period.'

'Peter the Great first took the city for Russia in 1704,' said Terah. 'They haven't been far away ever since. We Estonians remember these things.'

'And Tatyana,' he asked. 'She spent time here?'

'Of course, we have established that,' Terah answered, lighting a cigarette, letting the smoke drift over his face. 'As you say, Tartu was a military base. It was one of the largest air-force bases in the whole Soviet Union. I can remember it myself, the times I visited the city back in the old days. The fighters and bombers would fly over all day. The buildings would shake every time one of those giant Antonovs rolled through the clouds belching fire and smoke. Anyway, I think we can be pretty certain she wasn't really an orphan. She had parents, and she grew up somewhere pretty much like any normal kid. That place might as well be here as anywhere. In those days, there was just one local paper published in Tartu, the *People's Sentinel*. It came out five days a week, in both Russian and Estonian editions, although the Russian one was on better paper and had a couple more pages. They still keep copies at the library in Tallinn.'

Terah took a long sip on his coffee, his eyes foraging through the nearly empty bar, making sure nobody was looking at them. 'A local paper is a great place to start when tracking people,' he continued. 'The one thing local papers love to do is print pictures of kids. Their mum buys ten copies, their gran and aunt another ten. Print a picture of five kids and you've sold an extra two hundred copies.' He paused, taking his wallet from his jacket. Carefully unfolding an A4 strip of photocopy paper, he pushed it across the table. 'Do you recognize her?' he asked.

Tom could feel his fingers shake as he lifted the paper – as if he had just been given a mild electric shock. His eyes locked onto the picture, peering into the shades of black ink. There were five girls, all of them in neat white blouses, black bootlace ties, and pleated black skirts. She was standing second on the left. Her hair was shorter then, stopping half an inch above her shoulder, and her skin was looser, less tightly drawn across her jaw. But her eyes and her lips looked out at him with perfect clarity, as vivid and as memorable as his own face looking out at him from the mirror. It might have been taken many years ago, but there could be no question in Tom's mind. 'It's Tatyana,' he said, looking across at Terah, the thump in his heart almost audible as he pronounced the words. 'When was it taken?'

'Fourteen years ago, during Soviet times,' he replied. 'She would have been eighteen then, still at school. This group of girls won an award for the finest choral singing in the whole south-east Estonia region.'

'She sang beautifully,' said Tom.

'I remembered,' said Terah. 'That's one reason I started looking in the local paper. Schools love to give out singing prizes, and papers love to print a picture of the winners. I thought I'd find her somewhere.'

Tom held the picture up to the light. 'She photographed beautifully as well,' he said. 'I remember asking her once if she had any pictures of herself as a kid. She told me no, they didn't take pictures in the orphanage.'

'Once you tell one lie, you have to tell a lot more,' said Terah. 'That is always the way. There are probably plenty of pictures of her somewhere.'

Tom put the picture back down on the table. 'Did the paper give her name?'

'Tatyana Draka,' answered Terah. 'Of the Tartu High School for Girls. She was a student there between 1981 and 1986. That was before she went to university.'

Tom leant forward, his elbows resting on the table, the smoke from Terah's cigarette hitting the back of his throat. 'From the name, could you trace who her parents were?'

'I didn't really need to,' Terah replied. 'I knew the name already. One had to check, of course, to make sure, but I was pretty certain as soon as I saw her name in the paper.'

'Who was her father?'

'Leonid Draka,' replied Terah, his eyes scanning the bar. 'The senior commander of the Red Army forces for the Baltic States.'

*   *   *

Sarah could hear Vereden coughing at her side as he sat down, the sound echoing through his hollow lungs and spluttering from his throat. Across the wooden bay, four of the white-haired elderly researchers looked up, disapproval playing upon their faces. Within their tribe, coughing in the library was not allowed. 'Are you okay?' she whispered, leaning over his desk.

'Fine, fine, the cigarettes, I suppose,' said Vereden quickly, the veins prominent in his cheekbones reddening slightly as he spoke. 'I have been cutting down, you know.'

'We're close, don't you think?' said Sarah, wondering if it was possible for any person to smoke more than Vereden.

'Almost there,' he replied.

They had been in the library for almost four hours now. Sarah had taken the financial records of the Leopard Fund, from when it was first incorporated in 1974. It had begun its existence as a French-domiciled investment firm, and had not moved offshore until 1982. Its initial capital was a modest five million francs, and the fund was controlled by three directors: Telmont himself, who was described as the chief investment officer, plus Pierre Novat and Daniel Favere, two men who described themselves simply as businessmen. In its first full year, it recorded a loss of two hundred thousand francs. The next year, 1975, was worse; it made a loss of four hundred thousand francs. 1976, was better; it turned a profit of one hundred thousand francs. By 1977 it had been recapitalized, with further investments totalling eighteen million francs, and a profit of one million francs was recorded in the accounts. From there, the graphs pointed straight upwards. Between 1978 and 1982, Sarah calculated the fund drew in capital of almost four billion francs, even though the returns on the fund remained relatively low. The bulk of that came from a series of investment companies, some of them registered in France, others in Switzerland and Luxembourg. Slowly, Sarah began to compile a list of the companies that had invested in the Leopard, noting down their line of business, and their directors. Many seemed to be little more than shadow companies, conduits through which money was flowing, but with no purpose of their own. Ultimately, all the companies seemed to be controlled by one investment vehicle, Société d'Investissements Chambéry SA, a trading company registered in the French town close to the Alps, and of which Daniel Favere was also a director.

While Sarah was studying the accounts of the Leopard Fund, Vereden was checking back on the companies that had been directing money into Tatyana's bank accounts in Switzerland. Sarah had already traced the money back through one layer of shadow companies. Over the course of the afternoon, between slipping outside to refill his lungs with nicotine, Vereden had taken it back through another five layers of trading and investment companies. By the time the investigation was complete, the answer was obvious: ultimately the money flowing into Tatyana's accounts had come from Société d'Investissements Chambéry. 'Curious, don't you think?' said Vereden, resting the two charts next to each other on Sarah's desk. 'This one company is the source of millions poured into the Leopard Fund, and of millions poured into the account of a young woman living in England.'

'I don't get it,' said Sarah, the tone of her voice rising high enough to attract stares from the researchers on the desk opposite.

'Favere is the key,' whispered Vereden. 'Along with Telmont, he is the most important part of the jigsaw.'

'Who is he?' asked Sarah.

'Who was he, you mean,' answered Vereden.

'He's dead?'

'Some years ago, I believe,' said Vereden. 'Though I don't suppose anyone mourned his passing very much.'

'But you've heard of him.'

'The name has a familiar ring to it, yes,' said Vereden. He plucked a microfiche from her desk, slipping it under the electric reader, his thumbprint sweaty on the plate-glass. Pointing to the list of shareholders registered at Chambéry, his fingernail rested on the two largest holders of stock, both of them companies registered in Moscow. As well as the two corporate shareholders, two individuals were also listed among the stockholders: Daniel Favere and Leonid Draka. 'Those are the two names you want to concentrate on,' said Vereden.

His slipped his jacket from the back of his chair, and began walking towards the door, nodding at Sarah to follow. Time for him to fill up on nicotine, she decided, pulling on a sweater, and scuttling towards the door. He moves quickly, she noted, when there is a cigarette waiting for him at the end of the corridor. When she stepped onto the street, Vereden was already leaning into a post, cupping his hands to protect his lighter from the wind. A look of contemplation rested on his face as he dragged on the cigarette. 'Favere and Draka,' he said, pausing to blow smoke into the freezing night air. 'Who would have imagined it?'

'Tell me about them,' said Sarah.

'Favere was what in England I think you call a champagne socialist,' said Vereden. 'In the Fifties and Sixties he made his money in the steel industry in France, largely because he was the only person who could deal with the unions, who were, of course, controlled by the French Communist Party. Officially, I think, he was a sympathizer with the party, not an actual member. He was a fixer, though, a go-between, a broker of deals. In Prague, in the secret police, if hard currency was needed for a mission in the West, or for creating a dummy company as a front for a covert operation, then Favere was the man we used. He could get things done. Of course, I'm sure all the Western intelligence agencies knew exactly who he was and what he was up to, but he was still useful. He was one of the channels through which money flowed from east to west during the Cold War.'

Sarah shivered, the cold evening air freezing the skin on her face. She pulled her collar up around her neck, almost grateful for the warm smoke drifting across from Vereden's cigarette. 'And Draka?' she asked. 'Who was Leonid Draka?'

'The General,' said Vereden, holding his fist to his mouth while he cleared his lungs, wiping the residue away with his handkerchief. 'A fine soldier, by reputation. He had the respect of his men, at any rate. In the mid-Sixties, he was commander of the Eighteenth Tank Battalion of the Red Army. I don't suppose you've heard of it?'

Sarah shook her head. 'Sorry,' she replied, wondering if she should feel guilty. 'I don't know much about tank divisions.'

Vereden looked at her and smiled. 'Why should you?' he said, a smile on his lips. 'You have better things to think about. The Eighteenth always took the Red Army's best soldiers. It was the first tank division to drive into Berlin in 1944. It was also the first tank division into Prague in 1968, and Draka was in charge of that. Maybe that is why the name has stuck in my mind. He was an honourable man, I believe. He had his job to do, and he did it with ruthless efficiency, but without unnecessary cruelty. Under a weaker man, I suppose those tanks could have flattened half the city. That's who Draka was.'

'What happened to him?' asked Sarah.

'He became senior commander of the Red Army in the Baltic States, I think, one of the most important positions they have,' he said. 'The Baltics, if you remember, were only captured after the war, and had to be ruled by force. Always. There was a constant risk of rebellion. But Draka was more than just a divisional commander. He was also the controller of the Red Army finances. I forget the precise dates. But certainly from the early Seventies to the mid-Eighties.'

Sarah hesitated, letting the words hang momentarily in the air, grasping for her own reply. 'Let me get this straight,' she said eventually. 'Chambéry was controlled by Soviet money? That financed the Leopard Fund?'

'Looks that way,' said Vereden, his shoulders slumped against the wall. 'We shouldn't be so surprised, you know. The Red Army was the most important component of the Soviet State, and it controlled the arms industry and the labour camps, which were the only two export industries the Soviet Union had. Guns and raw materials. That was what they dealt in, and the Army ran both of them. That they would work it through France, and through the French Communist Party, does not surprise me. The French were always very close to the Russians. I guess this was one way of laundering some cash into hard currencies.'

'It makes a certain sense, I suppose,' said Sarah, the excitement evident in her voice. 'The fund deals in a huge number of currencies all the time. It is a great front for laundering money. It explains where Telmont got all his money from. When this gets out, he'll be finished. Completely destroyed.'

'You'd like that, wouldn't you?' said Vereden, looking down at her.

Sarah ignored the question. 'The rest of it still puzzles me, though,' she said. 'Why would they be pouring money into Tatyana's accounts? What was the point of that?'

'Still a mystery, I'm afraid,' said Vereden. 'But I think you'd like to know that as well.' He tossed his cigarette, the third he had smoked in a row, onto the ground, coughed into his hand, and nodded towards the door. 'We should get on.'

In the doorway of the library, the tramp who had been sitting on the edge of the step, his tin can held out, rattled it in front of them. Sarah glanced down, briefly catching his eye. A man of almost fifty, with deep, shallow eyes and high cheekbones, the grime of the street was painted onto his face, and the blanket wrapped over his shoulders and torso did nothing to stop the shivering. Fishing a ten-franc coin from her pocket, Sarah dropped it into his hand. 'Merci, Madame,' he muttered, looking up into her eyes, watching as she walked though the door.

After Sarah had walked away, the tramp reached inside his pocket, pulling out a slip of photocopied paper, half a sheet of crumpled A4, with a picture printed on one side. He looked down at the blonde face on the paper, then glanced back at the door. Had to be, he thought to himself. She was even speaking English, just as the man who had given him the picture this morning had said she would. Slowly, the tramp struggled to his feet, shivering as he did so, and wrapping the blanket tightly over his shoulders. Already he was thinking about the hot meals and the nights in the hostel that the ten thousand francs reward would buy him.

Telmont watched the tug drag a rusting barge towards Tower Bridge, concentrating on how the swell from the ship's bow moved through the water with the same precision and force a skilled trader moved through the market. Turning away from the window, he looked across at Sheldon, his eyes resting on his, peering darkly into him. 'How much money did we lose today?' he asked, his tone distant and cold.

Beads of sweat had already formed on Sheldon's forehead, and there were traces of dampness on his shirt. 'A lot, sir,' he answered, the words catching on his lips, as if he was stammering.

Telmont walked closer towards him, the sound of his heels hitting the wooden floor echoing through the long, empty office. 'I know we lost a lot,' he said sharply. 'I am not so stupid as to imagine we made money today. I want to know how much.'

Sheldon glanced down at the sheaf of papers in his hand. 'The Polish market fell twelve per cent, so we lost six hundred million dollars there; Hungary by nine per cent, so we lost eight hundred; and the Czech Republic fifteen per cent, so we're down one point two billion there,' he said, the words tumbling from his mouth. 'All of the Baltic States were down another twenty per cent. Ukraine and Belarus have just about ceased to trade. You can buy the whole of both countries for loose change. Do you want me to go on?'

Telmont sat at his desk, resting his face in his hands. 'You know, of course, there is no sound I like more than a description of the Leopard Fund's movements in the market place. But give me the total.'

'In Eastern Europe, so far, we are down twelve point eight billion dollars,' said Sheldon, surprising himself with the calmness with which he delivered the words. 'But, of course, the real damage is in the West, in Western Europe, since those markets are now falling heavily as well, and that is where most of the fund's money is tied up. Right now, our total losses look to be in the order of sixty billion dollars.'

Telmont paused, letting the number hang silently in the air. 'It's an incredible number, don't you think?' he said. 'All the rulers of the world build monuments to themselves, you know. The Egyptians had their pyramids, the Romans their amphitheatres, the Christian church its cathedrals. Now the markets rule the world, what do we build? Huge great numbers, towers of dollars reaching up into the heavens, piles of money so immense we feel dwarfed in front of them. That is what power is all about – making the rest of the world feel small.'

'It's a lot of money, sir,' said Sheldon.

Telmont stood up, walking back towards the window. 'That's the trouble with you, Sheldon, you have no feeling in your bones. Brittle, like a piece of dried-out concrete. I will speak to you only of the facts; everything else is just so much wasted breath. How much longer can the fund endure these losses?'

'Another day, sir,' he answered. 'The Leopard Fund has total assets of thirty billion dollars, and borrowings of seventy billion, making a total of one hundred billion dollars. Most of our positions are in derivatives, though, so our total exposure to the market has to be multiplied by a factor of ten. Call it a thousand billion, or a round trillion dollars. A bit less than the one point two trillion dollars Long Term Capital Management had under its control when it went bust, but not by much. If we carry on losing capital at the current rate, the fund will be technically insolvent by this time tomorrow.'

Telmont smiled, a long thin smile that crawled out over his creased, tanned cheekbones. 'A lot of people would enjoy that, would they not, Sheldon?' he said.

'I guess so, sir,' Sheldon replied. 'But not us, sir. Not the people working here, nor our investors.'

Telmont's dry laugh echoed around the room. 'It won't happen,' he said. 'By tomorrow this fund will have more money at its disposal than every other financial institution in the world. It is the markets that will be broken, not the Leopard Fund.'

'How's that, sir? We've been losing heavily.'

Telmont walked closer to Sheldon, resting a hand on his shoulder, his left thumb briefly playing with his blue braces. 'You obviously haven't seen what our real position in the markets is,' he said. 'In the futures market, we have been planning for this crash all along.'

CHAPTER 22

Thursday, 18 February

SARAH STOOD IN THE DOORWAY, CUPPING THE PHONE TO HER ear, straining to catch the words. Her coat was wrapped up around her neck, but the chill of the evening was still starting to freeze into her bones. 'Are you keeping warm?' she said into the phone, only realizing as the words slipped through her lips that she was starting to sound like his grandmother.

'Warm, enough,' said Tom. 'It's about fifteen below zero here, colder out in the countryside.'

'We've found the link,' said Sarah, the words leaping from her throat. 'We've found out where Telmont gets his money from. It looks as if Tatyana got her money from the same place as well. You were right, it all fits together.'

Tom took a deep breath. The revelations of the day had already been so intense, he could feel his brain wading through a swap of different connections. 'Tell me,' he said, struggling to keep his voice calm.

Her tone fluid and excited, overflowing with exhilaration, Sarah raced through the research they had completed; how the funds traced back through layer upon layer of shell and dummy companies until eventually they had tracked down the true source. 'It came from the Red Army,' she said finally. 'Basically, the Leopard Fund was a mechanism for laundering profits made by the Soviet Army all through the Seventies and Eighties.

That is where Telmont got all the cash from, through this guy Leonid Draka, who apparently was controller of the Red Army finances for almost two decades. His name is even listed as a director of one of the French companies.'

'Run that name past me again,' said Tom, his voice quickening.

'Draka,' repeated Sarah. 'Controller of Finance, Red Army; also, so Vereden says, Commander of the Red Army in the Baltic States.'

'And the final piece in the jigsaw,' said Tom.

'Meaning what?' asked Sarah.

'He was also Tatyana's father.'

Sarah fell silent, listening, the mobile squeezed tight into her ear while Tom ran through everything Terah had told him. 'Of course, I think we knew that Tatyana had to be linked to the Leopard Fund in some way,' said Tom. 'And I suppose it makes sense that Draka should channel money into Western Europe via accounts set up in his daughter's name. And I suppose it might well be the sort of thing you would want to keep secret, at least if you were planning to hide in London for a few years until you decided to reclaim the money.'

Sarah could detect the bitterness creeping into his voice. 'Are you okay?' she said.

'I think so,' said Tom. 'The main thing is to find Tatyana, and to stop Telmont. Then we can put this whole thing behind us. Can you e-mail me all the research you have?'

'Sure,' answered Sarah, her voice growing distant. 'I'll do it now.'

'Can this Vereden guy look after you, make sure no one is on your trail?'

Sarah nodded into the phone. 'I think I'll be okay.'

'I love you,' said Tom. 'Take care.'

'I love you too,' said Sarah, listening as the mobile fifteen hundred miles away clicked shut. She slipped her own phone back into her pocket, glanced out over the crowded street, and turned back inside the library. Behind her, Vereden scanned the street, tossed the end of his cigarette into the gutter, and followed her inside.

'It's her all right,' said Jennings, lowering the telephoto lens he had

been training on the entrance to the library from a van parked across the
street for the last half hour. 'No question.'

'I will instruct my men to hand over the reward to the tramp,' said
Comtes.

'I'm impressed,' said Jennings. 'It didn't take long to find her.'

'The streets of Paris have eyes everywhere,' said Comtes, a smile sliding
over his face.

'And you have never been to this place?' said Tom hesitantly.

'Never,' said Terah, shaking his head.

'But you think you know where it is?'

'I have a fair idea.'

'Go over it once more.'

Terah took a swig of his beer. His eyes lowered, sliding away from
Tom's face, looking down at the table. 'One clue we have overlooked so
far, the one about how Tatyana had been studying a website dedicated
to the *metsavennad*.'

'The forest brothers, right,' said Tom. 'Estonia's freedom fighters.'

Terah looked back up from his beer, meeting Tom's eyes directly.
'Draka was in charge of the campaign against them. The movement, as
you may know, started just after the war, mainly among the demobilized
Estonian army units. It controlled the countryside around here until
the early Fifties, then it went into decline, but there was always a
group of partisans in the forests. It picked up some support after
sixty-eight, largely because people saw some chinks in the regime. A
few students, some idealists, particularly from the Czech Republic. But
deserters mostly. Young boys who didn't like being conscripted into
the Russian army. Came home to the farms, only to realize they were
heading straight for Siberia as soon as they got caught.' Terah shrugged,
taking another sip on his beer. 'If you are going to die, it might as well
be for yourself.'

'And Draka fought them,' said Tom.

'Right,' answered Terah. 'Took him until 1978. That was when they caught the last of them, called August Sabe. But there is a lot of forest around here, and the forest has always been a good place for a man to hide. Remember Robin Hood. Every country had similar stories. Draka did what was necessary to defeat them. He moved his men out into the woods as well. Here in Tartu, this was nominally the Red Army headquarters, but the operational base was out in the forests, out where the *metsavennad* were.'

'Is it far from here?' said Tom.

'About thirty, maybe thirty-five miles,' replied Terah.

'You think she might be there?'

'She's not at the hotel. Checked out this morning,' said Terah. 'She is not just passing through Tartu. Nobody does, it's not on the way to anywhere. She has to be going somewhere. My bet is she is going back to the base where her father used to run his operations. She must have been there as a child.'

Tom clenched his fists together, squeezing the muscles tightly into each other. 'But why?' he said. 'I don't understand why.'

'Who knows?' said Terah, his voice calm and even. 'Maybe she left something behind.'

Sarah keyed the last of the information into her laptop, attached the file to an e-mail and pressed 'send'. She folded the computer up, placed it back in its case, and looked up towards Vereden and nodded. 'Time to go?' she asked.

He stood up uneasily, slipped on his coat and started walking from the library, Sarah walking at his side. 'Shall I stay at the same hotel tonight?' asked Sarah. 'Will it be safe?'

As they approached the doorway, Vereden was already fishing out a cigarette, holding onto his lighter, ready to strike the moment they hit fresh air. 'Move around,' he said, with a curt shake of his head. 'The first principle of evasion. It is much harder to hit a moving target.'

'I could go to another hotel,' said Sarah.

'I know an apartment where you should be okay,' said Vereden, lighting up as soon as they stepped outside, the nicotine hitting his throat quicker than the cool night air. 'We'll just collect your things.'

On the other side of the street, Jennings nodded to Comtes, who looked across at the two men sitting at the end of the van. 'Go,' he said softly.

The two men, dressed in identical black jeans with black leather jackets, and with black woollen hats pulled down over their skulls, jumped onto the road, crossed swiftly and started walking down the street. Behind them, the van had swung away from the road, completed a U-turn, and was inching its way along the kerb. Ahead of them, the targets were walking slowly, held up by the delicate pace at which the old man was walking.

Sensing the van was no more than inches away from them, the first man quickened his pace, brushing past the couple, moving two paces in front of them, hesitating for a second to check the van was in place, then suddenly stopping in the middle of the street. Sarah collided into him, bouncing off his muscled shoulders, recoiling away from him. 'Sorry,' she said, speaking instinctively in English. 'I mean, *pardon*,' she added quickly.

The hand from behind reached up around her neck, pulling her head back, a gloved fist digging into her mouth, stifling the scream about to escape from her lips. Her eyes moved desperately to the right, in time to see Vereden's legs being kicked from beneath him, the old man falling to the slippery pavement, the cigarette still hanging between his lips. She could feel, but not see, her ankles being gripped firmly in two strong hands, then yanked from the pavement, taking her up into the air, twisting the muscles in her hips. A hand was still pressing into her mouth, tightening her breath, and her arms were being held tightly together. Lying almost horizontal in the air, held up by the two men, she could see the puzzled looks on the faces of the people in their cars passing along the road, but none of them stopped, and none of them looked for more than a second. Across the road, a man was shouting something in French, but she could not focus on the words. She glanced down at Vereden, catching his eyes, watching the movement of his lips. 'You have to out-think them,' he seemed to be saying.

With a sharp spin, Sarah could only watch helpless as the men turned her, pushing her towards the open doors of the van. Another man gripped her by the legs, pulling her inside the moving vehicle. Behind her, the two men clambered aboard, slamming the doors behind them, encasing the interior of the machine in darkness. Sarah could hear the engine start to roar as it accelerated away from the kerb.

An eight-year-old Volkswagen Golf was the best they could find this late in the day. Tom looked down at the machine, his eye drawn to the sagging, rusted metal hanging from its frame. The Golf was a rugged car, no question, he reflected to himself: well-built, reliable, good handling. Even so, it wasn't the machine you would choose to drive deep into the Estonian forests late at night in the middle of winter.

Terah had asked around, but the Golf was the best they could do. The hotel rented out a few cars, but its only four-wheel drive had been taken this morning by the Frenchman, and it had nothing else left. This machine came from a local car dealer, who rented out the ancient Volkswagens that were now ubiquitous throughout all the Baltic states. 'Ready?' said Terah, looking up towards Tom.

'About as ready as I'll ever be,' Tom replied, trying to suppress the anxiety in his voice.

The last two hours had been spent preparing themselves for what could prove to be a tough day ahead; probably the toughest day I'll ever spend in my life, Tom thought to himself. They started in Tartu's main computer shop, where Tom had bought two spare batteries for his laptop, making sure both of them were fully charged before they left. He had also equipped himself with a mobile field satellite system, consisting of a portable dish twenty inches across attached to a longlife battery, and a box of complex electronics. The dish would bounce mobile phone signals directly off an orbiting satellite, making sure he could still make calls even when they moved out of range of a cellular base station. Following Terah's instructions, they stopped next at a clothing store. If they were to be sure of surviving the night, they would need the right equipment, Terah explained.

The shop was warm enough, and Tom didn't mind when the salesman told him to strip in the changing room. Three layers of clothing would be necessary, Terah explained. Tom started with a set of full-body under-wear, manufactured from the heaviest possible acrylic, and designed to withstand temperatures of twenty degrees below centigrade. The fabric clung to his body, leaving only his head, hands and feet exposed. On top of that, Tom pulled a fleece sweater, and then a pair of thick, nylon jogging trousers, both of them loose fitting to allow plenty of room for air to move between the two layers of clothing. Next, Tom was given a blue Gore-Tex coat and hood, and a pair of Gore-Tex leggings, both of them designed to keep out moisture, while allowing room for his skin to breathe. Making sure his feet were absolutely dry, he pulled on a pair of nylon socks, followed by another pair of woollen socks, making sure not a single piece of skin would be exposed to the elements. A thick pair of black walking boots completed the outfit.

'We'll go then,' said Terah, opening the door to the car, and climbing behind the wheel.

Tom glanced out over the town, taking in the bright lights from the bars and shopfronts. My last sight of civilization for a while, he thought to himself. After this, it is just the woods.

The Golf started on the third turn of the ignition, its wheels struggling to get a grip on the frozen surface as it slipped away from the kerb. The drive through the outskirts of Tartu, a dismal collection of rotting concrete blocks, took little more than ten minutes. After that, they were into the countryside, the darkness descending upon them with an absolute suddenness. Occasionally, the moon would break through the cloud, sending a weak shaft of light earthwards. But once it slipped away, Tom could see nothing beyond the reach of the headlamps. 'How long do you think this will take?' he asked.

Terah shrugged, leaning away from the steering wheel. 'About an hour, no more,' he said. 'Then we may have to ditch the car and complete our search on foot.'

*   *   *

The hand removed itself swiftly from Sarah's mouth, but even though her lips were now free, she had lost the desire to scream. Her eyes moved carefully over the van, as if any kind of sudden movement might be threatening. She could see the driver, with two men sitting next to him on the front seat. Four men sat inside the van, two of them smoking, their expressions bored, two others leaning over her, looking down at her with leers in their grins and lust in their eyes. She moved her eyes away from them hurriedly, looking intently at the roof of the machine, listening as it twisted its way through the streets.

Sarah could feel the sweat trickling down her back, and the beating of her pulse drummed in her ears like a dance record with the volume turned up too high. Stupid, she thought to herself, stupid, stupid, stupid. I should have organized a car to take me to the next destination. When you were on the streets, you were always vulnerable. What can they want from me? she thought to herself. Her mind began racing through the possibilities, each darker and more dreadful than the last. Then it came to her, a moment of realization that was as clear and still as ice. Their secrets were meant to remain secrets. What they want from me is silence.

Her arms lay by her side, motionless. Sarah was too nervous to lift her wrist to look at the time, but it was a little after eight when they left the library, and they must have been driving for six or seven minutes. Glancing around the van, she saw Vereden was not there. They must have left him behind on the street where they knocked him to the ground, she reasoned. Though she knew she was probably summoning up nothing other than phantoms, Sarah briefly comforted herself with the thought that Vereden might find some way of rescuing her.

He could at least get some word to Tom. So long as you stay alive, she struggled to tell herself, through the rising fear and tension, there is always some hope left.

The van pulled to a gentle stop. Sarah preferred not to look up, but she could hear the ignition being killed, and the doors opening. At her side, the men rose, climbing from the back of the van, ignoring her. 'Get up,' said Jennings sharply, poking his head into the van.

Sarah lifted herself from the cold floor, aware of an ache in her hip where a muscle had been strained. She looked into the face of the man staring down at her; a thick nose, once broken, thick hair, dark, large eyes and a rough layer of stubble over his chin, he looked at her as if she were a piece of loose furniture lying broken at the back of a truck. She wiped the edge of a tear from her eyes, coughed on the cigarette smoke collected in the van, choked back the urge to vomit, and edged herself forward. 'I said get up,' repeated Jennings, reaching out and grabbing her hand, pulling her roughly.

Her feet landed on a cold slab of concrete. Looking up, Sarah could tell she was in some kind of garage; alongside the van, there was a silver-grey Mercedes, and a Renault Clio. Jennings took hold of her arm, leading her through a metal doorway and up a narrow flight of stairs. Another man followed closely behind, blocking her exit. Through another door, Sarah peered around at the room: a square box, with some old furniture at one side, and a pile of ageing toys in another corner. She guessed she must be in the storeroom of a private house. 'Over there,' said Jennings, pointing to an armchair, its fabric faded, the stuffing starting to spring out of the tears in its covering. 'Sit down,' he continued.

'I prefer to stand, I think,' answered Sarah, her voice fractured and broken, the words almost a croak.

Jennings leant close to her, and she could smell the food on his breath. In his hand, she could see he had picked up a length of orange nylon rope, running it slowly between his fingers, wrapping it over his fists. 'I don't give a fuck what you think,' he said. 'Now sit the fuck down and shut the fuck up.'

The car had been skidding violently ever since it turned off the main road and onto a dirt track. Along the pits in the road, water had gathered, freezing over, creating thin pools of ice that caught and spun the wheels. Beneath him, Tom could feel the suspension shuddering as the metal strained under the knocks it was receiving. They were sliding rather than driving.

Two miles down the track, they hit a fork in the road. Terah brought the car to a reluctant stop, climbed out and started examining the road with a torch. 'Broken ice,' he said when Tom joined him. 'A vehicle has passed this way, some time in the last twelve to fifteen hours. That's how long it takes for the ice on the road to re-form after it has been crushed by a car. The trail should be clear enough from here on.'

Tom looked up at the trees rising at the side of the road, their trunks reaching imperiously up to the sky. He could feel the brooding stillness of the forest starting to bear down on his shoulders, a weight he was no longer sure he could carry. The cold scent of pine filled his nostrils, and as he breathed the air, he wondered if he could smell Tatyana yet. 'You think she is out there?' he said, glancing across at Terah.

'I guess,' Terah replied. 'There aren't many other places to go round here.'

'You know this forest pretty well,' said Tom.

Terah climbed back into the car, strapping on his belt, and turning the lamps up to full beam. 'My father was in the *metsavennad*,' he replied, shutting the car door and steering the Golf down the track. 'Spent half his life out in these forests.'

For a moment Tom remained silent, reflecting that no matter how great your troubles, the world had space for an immensity of sorrow, and your own difficulties could never hope to occupy more than the most insignificant fraction of its disappointments. 'What happened to him?'

'Died in 1972,' replied Terah. 'Shot by Russian soldiers while ambushing a routine patrol for weapons and ammunition. He'd been out here since 1960, a year after I was born. Some kind of disagreement with the secret police back in Tallinn meant it was Siberia or the forests. Made quite a life for himself.'

'But you never saw him.'

Terah shook his head, looking across at Tom, his lips starting to crease up into a half-smile. 'Used to see him most Sunday afternoons. So did my mum. There used to be a small group of us kids from the city. We'd come out to the forests at the weekend for a picnic, go camping. Our fathers would suddenly drop out of the trees and there we'd all be, happy families once again. My father would sometimes take me off for a few days at a time. We'd go hunting and trekking. Great fun, at least for a small boy. That's where I learnt about the forests.'

'It must be painful to return,' said Tom.

'Not really,' replied Terah. 'Sometimes it's good to revisit places. In this country, everything always returns to the forests. That is where we come from. It is where we go back to.'

Cepartinu took the flask from his hip pocket, breathing deeply, enjoying the scent of the trees and the taste of brandy on his lips. In the stillness of the night, he could hear the slow movement of the breeze through the forest, but apart from that, nothing. He turned towards Boissant, offering him the bottle. Putting it to his lips, Boissant drank, handing it back to him with a smile. 'I thought you only drank vodka up here,' he said.

'Not when we can afford something better,' said Cepartinu. 'Brandy is not cheap, but in a place such as this a man needs something other than his blood to keep him warm.'

'The guards have their instructions?' said Boissant, squinting through the darkness.

'Four men, just as you asked,' he replied. 'One on each corner. All of them are armed, and I have told them to shoot on sight. I don't think we should be disturbed.'

'What kind of men are they?' asked Boissant. 'Red Army?'

Cepartinu nodded. 'They all did their military service, two of them in Afghanistan,' he answered. 'They know what they are doing.'

Boissant walked closer to Cepartinu, treading the night snow beneath his feet. He took the flask from the man's fist, pressing it to his lips, wetting his tongue with the brandy, rolling the hot liquid inside his cheek. 'A cold night,' he said, nodding towards the bank of trees rising up twenty yards from the doorway they were standing in. 'I wouldn't want to be out there.'

'Do you think he'll come?' asked Cepartinu.

Boissant shrugged, taking a cigarette from his pocket and cupping his lighter in his hand to protect it from the breeze. 'He has come all the way to Tartu,' he said slowly. 'If he can find us, I suppose he will come here as well. But he will not find us, I think. Few people ever knew about this place. And those that did are, I believe, now dead.'

'She is a fine-looking woman,' said Cepartinu. 'A man might come a long way to reclaim her.'

'Tatyana? No,' answered Boissant slowly, breathing smoke from his lips. 'An arrogant slut like that, I think you would be pleased to be rid of her.'

'How did you find me?' asked Radek, feeling his elbow ache as he held the phone to his ear.

'Asked around the hospitals in your part of London,' answered Vereden. 'It wasn't hard. If you weren't in one of those, I'd have started checking the mortuaries.'

Radek nodded to himself, a thin smile hurting his jaw. 'I'm alive, just,' he answered. 'How'd you know something happened?'

'Sarah,' said Vereden, wheezing on his cigarette. 'If they've found her, it had to be through you.'

Radek froze, leaning forward in his hospital bed. The plaster encasing his leg and his ribs strained, and he could feel it softening. 'They found Sarah?' he whispered.

'Took her this evening,' answered Vereden bluntly. 'Had her hotel last night, but she slipped them. They took us coming out of the library, bundled her into a van. Don't think they knew who I was, just thought I was some old man out for a stroll, so they pushed me to the ground, and took off.' He paused, coughing into his hand. 'I'm sorry,' he added. 'I should have seen them coming. I've been out of the game too long.'

'They must be Telmont's people,' said Radek, a slice of pain searing up through the nerves of his face as he spoke. 'She must have been getting closer to the truth.'

'We'd already got there,' said Vereden.

'You found out where the money comes from?' asked Radek.

'As you always suspected, the party,' said Vereden. 'Telmont was the Red Army's money manager, receiving hundreds of millions in investments via Draka. You remember that name, I imagine.'

'Neither of us will forget,' said Radek. 'Nobody in Prague in those years ever would. But those are our memories, nobody else's. Nothing to do with the girl. We must find her.'

'How?' asked Vereden. 'She might be anywhere in Paris by now. Anywhere in France.'

Radek paused, allowing the electrical static of the phone connection to fill up the space between them. 'You know how to find her,' he said. 'It doesn't matter how long you've been out of the game, you never forget.'

'We're old men, Victor, our day is done,' said Vereden, the click of his lighter audible down the phone line.

'Not yet,' said Radek. 'It doesn't matter how many years have passed. A debt is a debt. It always falls due one day.'

Sarah could feel the sweat trickling down her back. Her clothes were damp with fear and tension, her stomach shot and her mind a mess of conflicting terrors. The chair they had tied her to was next to a metal electric radiator, its heat turned up far too high. A smell of stale oil drifted from the garage, and the single uncovered bulb in the centre of the room shone with a harsh light that clouded her vision. How long she might have been here now, she was uncertain; an hour, maybe two, she decided. A parched dryness had started to affect her throat, and she could feel her vocal chords swelling.

Jennings shut the door quietly behind him, turning the lock in the key as he did so. A length of rope was hanging between his fists. He remained silent as he walked towards her, his eyes sliding over her body, examining her with an air of studied detachment, his expression becoming more relaxed the longer he looked down at her. He leant forward, leaning into her, close enough for her to smell his breath. Sarah rolled her eyes up towards his. 'What do you want?' she hissed.

Jennings shrugged, drawing back. 'Co-operation that's all,' he said. 'For now. Beyond that, I can't say. Don't make the decisions around here, you see. Just follow my orders.'

The end of the rope was dangling from his hands, its tip brushing gently against Sarah's belly. She watched it closely. 'Co-operation with what?'

'Where your boyfriend is, for starters,' replied Jennings, collecting up the rope, twisting it over his knuckles. 'We have you, now we'd like him as well.' He paused momentarily, his expression thoughtful. 'Reunite you, like.'

'I don't know where he is,' said Sarah, her voice tired and strained, the words breaking on her lips.

'Left you, has he?' said Jennings. 'Not your day, is it?'

'I didn't say he had left me,' said Sarah. 'I just said I don't know where he is right now.'

Jennings moved closer, leaning into her face, his eyes vivid before her. The orange rope tightened as he pulled it between his two fists, bringing it down to her neck. She could feel the nylon chord brushing her skin. 'I thought I said I wanted you to co-operate,' said Jennings, his tone harsh and unyielding. 'Make it easier for yourself, like.'

'He's gone,' said Sarah quickly. 'Out of Paris. You won't find him here.'

'Looking for his wife, is he?' said Jennings. 'Don't see why you're protecting him, like, not when he isn't here protecting you, but out there somewhere, looking for another woman.' He leant forward, close enough for Sarah to measure the stubble on his chin. 'Not much of a deal, like. He's out there looking for her, but nobody's looking for you.'

'I'm not protecting anybody,' said Sarah, summoning all the strength she could find. 'I just don't know.'

Jennings drew back, the rope still hanging from his knuckles. 'We'll soon see about that,' he said.

*   *   *

The car drew to a nervous halt, its tyres skidding over the frosted mud surface of the tracks. It stopped with a fierce jolt as the bumper collided with a tree. Terah killed the engine, its noise echoing off the trees before the silence of the forest surrounded them. 'Far enough,' he said, taking the keys from the ignition.

'How close are we?' asked Tom.

'Can't say, exactly,' replied Terah. 'About five miles due north, I think.'

Tom lifted himself from the car, climbing out, his feet sinking into eight or nine inches of snow. He could feel the cold of the night air wrapping around him, chilling the skin on his face. 'The rest is on foot?' he asked.

'Only way,' replied Terah. 'A car in these woods can be heard two, perhaps three miles away. If we want to be that visible, we might as well call them up in advance and book ourselves an appointment. We should make camp here for tonight and complete the journey in the morning.' He looked across at Tom. 'Do you know much about cold weather camping?'

'My room at Oxford was pretty cold,' he replied. 'But no, I don't even know much about ordinary camping.'

'The main thing to remember is that it isn't as bad as it feels,' said Terah. 'So long as you stay dry, you should be okay. Any kind of wetness will give you frostbite in less than a minute.' He looked around him. 'We'll need a shelter.'

From the back of the Golf, Terah retrieved two shovels, handing one to Tom. He pointed to a gap between the trees, seven yards from the car. 'That should do,' he said. 'We need a pile of snow, about six feet high and six feet across. It's called a quinchie.'

The work, Tom found, was warming, and helped to distract his mind from what might lie ahead over the next twelve hours. He gripped the shovel firmly between his hands, piling the snow in large loads, packing it down with the back of his spade. Terah had filled a bucket with snow, gradually melting it on the bonnet of the car, advising Tom to drink as much as he could. In this cold, he warned him, he would dehydrate much faster than he would in normal weather.

Building the pile of snow took no more than twenty minutes; a firm block, it looked like a giant ice cube, standing by itself next to the trees. 'Give that about half an hour to settle,' said Terah. 'Then we can get some rest.'

From the car, Tom retrieved the mobile telecoms equipment he had bought in Tartu. Fixing the box to the car battery, he unfolded the tiny satellite dish, no more than twelve inches in diameter, pointed it upwards, then plugged it into his mobile. He switched the machine on. Two messages were waiting for him. One was from Radek, the other from Sarah. He glanced at his watch. It was now just after midnight local time, making it just after ten in Paris and London. Checking Sarah's message, he saw that it was an e-mail, and made a note to download it to his computer. He tried Sarah's number, letting the phone ring for what seemed like several minutes, but there was no reply. Worried, he punched Radek's number into the machine. 'It's so long since I heard from you, I thought you'd vanished,' he said when he caught a voice on the line.

'I almost did,' said Radek, briefly explaining the injuries he had received.

'My God!' said Tom. 'Are you all right?'

'I'll live,' answered Radek. 'I've suffered worse, and at the hands of the same people as well. But they've captured Sarah.'

Tom fell to his knees, feeling the frozen ground against his clothes. He dug his gloved hand into the snow, taking a handful and squeezing it between his fist. 'What can we do?' he asked.

'Vereden is looking for her in Paris,' said Radek. 'He will do his best.'

'Has he gone to the police?'

'No point,' said Radek. 'The Paris police won't mount a huge operation to track down one English girl who's been missing for a couple of hours. No, if we are going to rescue her, we will have to do it ourselves. You concentrate on Draka. That is the key to everything.'

'You knew about Draka?' asked Tom.

Radek paused. 'I suspected,' he answered. 'That is very different from knowing. Money used to flow out of the old Soviet Union, and we know Telmont had to be collecting his money from somewhere. As I might have said before, everything is connected.'

'Even Tatyana,' said Tom, the sadness evident in his voice. 'She too is connected. It looks as if she has been working with Telmont all along.'

'You'll have to ask her that,' said Radek. 'The important thing is to bring Telmont down. Have you made your plans?'

Tom gripped the phone tighter; at times it felt as if the words were trapped within his chest, unable to find any way to escape. 'I am doing what I can,' he answered. 'Based on the figures Sarah discovered at the Leopard Fund, Telmont is taking a huge gamble that the FTSE will be below 7250, the CAC-40 in Paris will be below 4300 and the DAX in Germany below 6100. If those markets are above those figures, then he's finished, wiped-out. His bet is the collapse of Eastern Europe will trigger a huge sell-off in Western Europe as well.'

'Then we have to make sure the market goes up,' said Radek. 'While I suppose we have to assume Telmont will be doing everything he can to push the market down.'

'He's done plenty already,' said Tom. 'Confidence is completely shot to pieces and all those markets are below those figures already. I'm doing what I can, but I don't think one man can single-handedly push up all the stock markets across Western Europe.'

'Don't be defeatist,' cautioned Radek. 'If one man can bring down the markets, then one man can bring them back up again.'

'He has several hundred billion dollars at his disposal,' said Tom. 'It's hardly a contest.'

'You have something more important than money,' said Radek. 'You have your wits. Ultimately, a market is not a battle over money, it is a war of nerve and intelligence. You should know that.'

'Any advice?'

'Get some sleep,' said Radek. 'And stay warm.'

The mobile phone felt dead and limp in Tom's hand; disconnected from the satellite, it turned back into a dead pound of silicon and plastic. He slipped it back into his pocket, looking towards Terah. Standing wearily to his feet, he took a cupful of melted snow from the bucket, holding the freezing liquid to his lips. 'Anything stronger?' he asked.

Terah shook his head. 'It's bad to drink in this kind of weather,' he replied. 'When I was with my father, the woodsmen would build a big fire some nights and get blindingly drunk, but the rest of the time they stayed sober. Alcohol dehydrates you, and lowers your resistance to the cold.'

'I'm cold enough already,' said Tom wearily, wrapping his arms around his coat. He took his spade from where it was resting next to the car. Together the two men started digging through the mound of snow they had constructed, hollowing it out like a cave. They remained silent as they worked, Tom enjoying the sweat forming on his brow, and the mindless vigour of the task. After fifteen minutes, the mound had been hollowed out, creating a tube of snow six feet long and five feet wide. 'Good enough,' said Terah inspecting their work. 'We should make it through to the morning.'

From the car, he retrieved a blanket, and a roll of plastic. He placed the plastic on the hardened ice, with the blanket on top, and crawled inside, lying himself out at full stretch. 'We need to sleep,' he said. 'All our strength should be saved for the morning.'

Tom looked up at the night sky, admiring the darkness of the clouds gathered above the forest. Checking he was dry, he knelt down next to the quinchie, crawling inside, lying down on the blanket. At the entrance, Terah had placed a single candle, spreading a pale light and gentle warmth through the cave. Putting his head down on the ground, Tom could feel the hardness of the ice beneath the hood of his coat. In his mind, a picture of Tatyana briefly flared, and he wondered if she knew how close he might now be to her, and what she would say if she knew; whether she might think of him differently if she knew how far he had travelled to find her. An image of Sarah swiftly replaced it, a picture of suffering he was not sure he could endure for long. No matter how determined to investigate Telmont she might have been, she did not deserve to be led into this kind of danger. Tom shivered as the pale warmth of the single candle started to fade away, and the cold seeped into him. Could it be, he wondered to himself, that the woman who left me could be responsible for destroying the woman I now love? In his chest, he could feel his anger against Tatyana growing. A wave of resentment swept through him, quickening his pulse, and tearing into his guts. So far, he realized, I have not been much use to either of them. Tomorrow has to be different.

CHAPTER 23

Friday, 19 February

SARAH TURNED HER ANKLES, FLEXING HER MUSCLES TO LOOSEN the rope against her skin. The binding was loose enough to allow her to move, but tight enough to keep her legs strapped to the chair. Her eyes had started to ache with tiredness, and her limbs were numb from remaining still for so long. *Perhaps I have slept*, she thought to herself; although that was an unlikely description of her brief moments of rest. *Spasms of unconsciousness*, she decided to herself. *A movement from one nightmare to another.*

Jennings shambled into the room, his hair matted and tangled, his face drawn. 'Coffee, like,' he said, his eyes moving across her body.

Sarah looked at him closely. This was the first time since she had been captured he had shown any interest in whether she might be hungry or thirsty. 'Thanks,' she answered cautiously. 'I need the loo.'

'Okay,' said Jennings. He knelt down, unwrapping the rope from the chair, but leaving her feet bound. Extending a hand, he helped lift her from the chair, holding onto her hand as she moved towards the door. Jennings led her up a small flight of stairs, pointing her towards the lavatory. 'Just a couple of minutes, like,' he said. 'I'll be waiting.'

'I'll need my hands free,' she said, pushing her bound wrists forward. 'Otherwise, I can't undo my trousers.'

Jennings grinned, looking embarrassed, but unwrapped the rope from her hand. 'It goes straight back on,' he said, turning away from her.

Sarah sat down, taking advantage of a brief few seconds of privacy to compose and calm herself. She looked through the tiny, windowless room. No hope of escape, she told herself. It is me in this house, against four or five fit, strong men, who may well be armed. She leant over the sink, splashing cold water into her face. Briefly she could feel it reviving her, revitalizing the veins on her skin, tuning up her senses. Looking into the mirror, she could see the strain staring back at her: a mixture of fear and exhaustion, her complexion had turned grey, and the blood in her eyes had turned red and swollen. Discover their weaknesses, she told herself.

Jennings took her up another half flight of stairs, leading her into a small kitchen. Four men were sitting around the table, coffee and rolls in front of them, two of them smoking, the other two reading the back page of the newspapers. On the radio, she could hear the rapid beat of a pop station; Simply Red's 'Stars' was playing. 'Bind her,' said Comtes, looking across at Jennings.

He took a rope from the pocket of his leather jacket, slipped it over her wrists, and tied a loose knot that allowed for an inch or so of movement. Over the table, Comtes pushed across a large white mug of coffee, and pointed to a pile of croissants. Seven-fifteen, she heard the disc jockey saying on the radio. She looked towards Jennings, taking a sip of the coffee and feeling the hot, milky liquid start to fill her veins. 'You rise early in the kidnapping trade.'

'We have work to do, like,' said Jennings.

'Who for?' asked Sarah.

'That would be telling.'

'I think we both know you work for Jean-Pierre Telmont.' Sarah took another slug of coffee, glancing from Jennings towards Comtes. Although Jennings's eyes remained dull and empty, she could see a flash of interest in Comtes's eyes when she mentioned Telmont's name. Jennings certainly knows who he is working for, she decided, but the French guys are just hired local thugs. They have no idea who they are working for. Or why.

'We aren't here to discuss that,' said Jennings, his tone turning bitter. 'Not with you, like, not with anyone.' He slid a mobile phone over the table. 'Call him,' he said.

'Call who?' said Sarah, some strength returning to her voice. 'My father? Tell him I'll be late home for the weekend?'

Jennings leant close into her face. 'Your boyfriend.'

'Like I said, I don't know where he is.'

Jennings grinned. 'Then call him on his fucking mobile and ask him,' he said quickly. 'That's the point about mobiles, like, you don't need to know where someone is.'

Sarah looked up, smiling into the line of stubble that was so close it almost touched her face. 'I don't know the number.' She looked across at Comtes, but could read nothing on his face except a stony indifference to her conversation. 'How long do you plan to keep me?'

'As long as it takes,' replied Jennings. He turned away, leaving the phone lying in front of her. 'We already have his number,' he continued. 'Your mobile stores all the numbers you call. We just read it off the handset.' He looked down the table towards her, staring at her. 'Now, give him a call.'

Sarah picked up the phone and switched it on, glancing down at the illuminated set of keys in front of her. A number tells you nothing, she reflected. He could still be anywhere.

Tom stirred himself uneasily, unsure whether his limbs ached from tiredness, he had torn a ligament, or the blood had just started to freeze in his veins. On the other side of the quinchie, seven or eight inches from him, he could hear Terah snoring, and could see his cold breath rising. The ground under Tom's back felt as hard as granite, and he shifted stiffly to his side, shivering inside his clothes.

Whether he had slept at all, Tom was not sure. The night seemed to have passed in a fitful, broken series of dreams, each one worse than the last. The image that lingered in his mind the longest was of a giant boulder smashing into him, leaving his body crushed like an insect. No point in subjecting that to deep Freudian analysis, he reflected. I can already guess what it means. Over the edge of the horizon, he could distinguish the first glimmer of the dawn. A burning orange circle of light was rising over the cusp of the horizon, its pale beams winding their way through the trees, catching the tips of the pine needles. Reaching forward, Tom lifted himself free of the ground, sliding into the open. A blast of chilled air struck his face, freezing his lips; it might have been cold inside the quinchie, he thought, but it's even colder out here.

Looking around, he could see a fresh layer of snow had fallen during the night. Their tracks had disappeared, and the surface of the ground appeared unblemished, as if no one had walked here for weeks on end. The Golf was covered in snow, its position marked only by a mound. Terah was right not to have spent the night in the car, Tom reflected; we would have been buried in a heavy snowstorm and suffocated inside the machine. Retrieving the shovel from the side of the quinchie, Tom started digging the car free. The work warmed him, pushing the blood back into his veins, and into his cheeks. There is a cleanliness to snow, he thought to himself, that is unmatched by anything else in nature, a purity so entirely self-contained it is immediately sullied and spoiled the moment it comes into contact with any other element. Looking out at the morning light streaming through the white frosted trees, Tom allowed himself a moment to be captured by the raw, elemental beauty of the place. I can see why Tatyana wanted to come back, he decided. It is not the kind of place you could ever leave completely.

Terah arrived at his side, pushing away the snow, pulling the car door free. He leant inside the Golf, struggling to break the ice that had frozen up over his pocket. Retrieving the keys, he stuck them firmly into the ignition, looking back at Tom and grinning. 'Let's hope she still works.' Tom listened to the turning of the key. The sound of metal waking itself up cracked through the morning air, a heaving moaning of steel and iron, shaking loose the rust and frost, smashing into itself. The car shook violently, rocking Tom back on his heels, then fell silent. 'The oil freezes up, that's the main problem,' said Terah.

He turned the ignition again, replaying the same shudder of reluctant iron. 'Won't that crack the engine?' asked Tom.

Terah nodded. 'If it doesn't start soon, yes,' he replied.

Tom stood back, watching while Terah turned the key once more, this time sparking the car to life. The engine erupted with a huge roar, spinning furiously, smoke rising from the exhaust as the engine revved noisily, its bark bouncing from the trees and rising into the air. Looking around, Tom wondered how far away it might be heard. 'We're in luck,' said Terah. 'I spent a lot of Sunday mornings with my dad, struggling with engines that wouldn't start.' From the boot he collected a small electric ring, plugging it into the car's cigarette lighter and filling a pan with fresh snow. 'Grab some pine needles,' he said, looking across at Tom. 'As many as you can.'

Tom looked back at him and grinned. 'We can't be that hungry.'

'Pine needle tea,' said Terah. 'Best thing for you in this weather.'

No chance of running out, anyway, thought Tom to himself. Taking a small bag from his pocket, he shook a branch, unleashing a small rainstorm of pine needles. Most of them ended up in the snow. Handing the bag back to Terah, Tom watched as he poured the needles into the water, removing his gloves and wrapping his hands in the steam starting to rise from the pot. 'It's an acquired taste, I'll grant you that,' he said, looking across at Tom. 'But it has all the vitamins and nutrients you need to survive in the snow.'

The Leopard Fund kept an apartment permanently booked at the Savoy Hotel on the Strand for Telmont to use on the nights he spent in London. If he could, he usually returned to Paris for the evening. I prefer to sleep on French sheets, with French ground beneath me, he sometimes told people, should they enquire why he would regularly go back to Paris at night, spend the evening alone in his apartment there, then come back to London early the next morning. A man draws his life and his inspiration from the soil, he would explain. And my life comes from the soil of France.

This morning, he had decided, it would be better to stay in London. In theory, he reflected, the markets could be ruled from anywhere: from a swamp in Kenya, from the Argentinian pampas or from a Greek island in the Aegean Sea. Yet, in reality, a man had to be in the middle of it all, he had to feel the markets surging, swirling around him, taste their forces, and only then could he judge their temper. For this morning, he decided, the centre of the markets was the City of London. It was there that he needed to be.

The silver-grey Mercedes 500 drove him through the morning traffic, along the Embankment, towards the fund's riverside offices. He had dressed carefully this morning: a heavy, thick, grey suit, cut loose to flatter his figure, a pink-striped shirt with a patterned Chanel tie, and personalized cufflinks, struck from twenty-two carat gold and embossed with the letters JPT. When a man means to win, he must look the part, he told himself.

A hush greeted his arrival in the office of the Leopard Fund. For Telmont to arrive before eight in the morning was unheard of, and yet this morning he had taken a long route through the trading floor and back offices, making sure his presence was visible everywhere. Eyes turned, looking at him as he walked past. Officially, work at the fund started at eight, but most people started at seven-thirty, and by ten minutes to eight the office was already humming. Telmont stopped at Terry Semple's desk, resting his hand on his shoulder, smiling out over the rest of the floor. 'How is it looking?' he said.

Semple shrugged, taking a swift bite from the Breakfast McMuffin in the McDonald's carton on his desk. 'Hong Kong took a bit of a hit last night,' he said. 'So did Singapore and Bangkok, all of them down about five per cent. Taipei and Seoul held up better. All of the markets are watching Europe. That's where the action is expected.'

'Then we should give them a show,' answered Telmont, his voice softening. Semple nodded. 'Still down?' he asked.

Telmont leant forwards, his lips close to Semple's ear. 'You and I go back a long way, Terry,' he said. 'We have seen a few dramatic days together, no? The time we forced the pound off the ERM, that was quite something. The trades we took against Barings in the Japanese futures market. The damage we inflicted on the Malaysian ringitt in the summer of ninety-seven. The day we destroyed the rouble in ninety-eight. But this, Terry, this, I assure you, will be our finest day in the markets. Eastern Europe has already just about collapsed. This morning, we finish it. And as it crashes, the West will go with it.'

Semple swivelled in his chair, taking another bite of his McMuffin, chewing slowly on the roll, looking directly at Telmont as he swallowed. 'How far should we be pushing the markets down?' he asked.

'As low as you can. I'll tell you when to stop,' Telmont said. Semple could feel Telmont's hands resting on his shoulder blades, his fingers tapping against the cotton of his shirt. 'Don't let me down,' he said quietly. 'I'm relying on you.'

Telmont looked out across the rest of the floor, making sure everyone could see he was watching them, turned away from Semple's desk, and walked briskly towards his own office. He nodded curtly towards the two secretaries, pausing only briefly to smell the faint traces in the air of the Dior perfume he had instructed them both to wear this morning, then strode into the office, positioning himself behind his desk. Looking up towards the Reuters and Bloomberg screens, he checked the news from Eastern Europe. A report from Riga predicted another large demonstration by the ethnic Russian population of that city, calling for Latvia to be reunited with their motherland. The report went on to speculate that the prospect of its relatively successful economy being submerged back into Russia was creating a massive capital flight from the country, and was expected to provoke another devaluation of its currency, the lat, possibly within hours. Telmont smiled to himself as he read through the report. Another piece of wire copy reported that, in an interview with *Die Welt* this morning, Jurgen Strich at KrippenBank had explained its policies of dumping all its holdings in Eastern Europe, and refusing fresh loans in the region; too much money was being lost in an area damned to instability, he said. The report went on to say that other banks in Germany, the biggest single group of investors in Eastern Europe, were now under pressure to start selling their holdings. Some already were. In Poland, there were reports of more banking collapses in the wake of the downfall of the Poznan Bank. In the Czech Republic, Karel Silka was calling for the imposition of a siege economy, while in Hungary the disappearance of the country's main fund manager was still fuelling panic. And investors were still withdrawing money following the OECD report forecasting a total collapse of the region.

Like clockwork, thought Telmont to himself as he scanned the words on the screen. The most delicate, carefully engineered Swiss watch could not run more smoothly, nor keep time more perfectly. He took a sip from the glass of Evian water resting on the desk, cradling the phone into his neck. Pausing only to check the view from his window, he started punching Boissant's mobile number into the phone. Everything must be prepared, he told himself. Nothing, this morning, can be left to chance. As Napoleon always observed, to win any battle, a commander must have overwhelming forces at his disposal.

Tatyana rose carefully from the simple metal cot. Whether it was a military or hospital bed, she was uncertain; it consisted of no more than a simple steel frame, with a thin mattress thrown over it. Rust had started to claw away at the base, releasing a pungent aroma of rotting, decaying metal into the room. The smell had kept her awake for half the night. That and the nightmares.

Outside, she could hear Boissant's fist hammering on the door. Glancing down at her watch, she saw it was just after seven-thirty local time. The room was a small cubicle, ten feet long, eight wide, its walls constructed of grey steel, the floor made of bare concrete that froze beneath her feet. Boissant had placed an electric heater in the room after his men had managed to get the generator working, but it had done no more than blunt the teeth of the cold. The chill was still biting. Tatyana had slept in her clothes, and they now clung to her body, held in place by grime and sweat. 'I shall be with you shortly,' Tatyana said, looking across at the door.

In the corner of the room there was a single tap above a rusting steel basin, green mould starting to grow around the plug. The pipes started to shudder and groan as she turned the tap. The water, when it spluttered through, was brown and murky. Snow mixed with rust, Tatyana decided, as she splashed it onto her face, feeling the nerves in her skin start to prickle and freeze. She washed vigorously before taking some mascara and lipstick from her bag, applying a simple layer of make-up to her face. Without a proper mirror, she reflected, it was impossible to do her eyes properly. Beyond a couple of pencil strokes, there was no point in bothering.

Boissant looks no better, Tatyana thought, after she opened the door. He had shaved, but not well, and there were still stray stubble marks around his mouth; his hair was matted to his head, and the cold seemed to have deepened the lines on his face. 'Good morning,' she said quietly.

'This is not a time for oversleeping,' said Boissant, a grin spreading over his face.

'In this place?' said Tatyana. 'Little chance of that, I think.'

He led her through a dark corridor, their path illuminated by the torch Boissant was holding in his right hand. Every ten yards there was a light bulb in the wall, but all of them had been broken long ago, and it was years since anyone had thought to replace them. It looks much smaller than I remembered it, thought Tatyana to herself. But then everything looks big to an eight-year-old girl, and that is the way you remember it.

A working light had been found for the kitchen, and the wood-fired stove had been brought back to life with some swiftly chopped pine logs, its warm glow burning through the room and filling it with a rich, fierce warmth. Two packets of Gitanes lay open on the table. Cepartinu had already lit one, handing it to Boissant. 'Coffee?' he said, looking up at Tatyana, his eyes scouring her body.

'Black,' she replied. 'With one sugar, if you have any.'

Cepartinu took the pot from the stove, pouring the heavy liquid into a metal cup. It tasted harsh and bitter on Tatyana's lips, but she could feel it waking her, alerting her senses. The man, she noticed, was staring at her, his eyes roving across her skin as though she hardly existed. Looking back, she allowed her lips to crease into a slow half-smile. 'It's good, thank you,' she said.

'Check your men,' said Boissant. 'Give them some coffee as well. I want to make sure they all stay awake.'

'There are guards?' asked Tatyana.

'Of course,' said Boissant, the smoke from his cigarette trapped by the low ceiling and drifting back down towards his face. 'This morning you are a valuable commodity. Too valuable to be left unprotected.'

'I am flattered by your concern,' said Tatyana.

'And so you should be,' replied Boissant. 'Just now, this is more trouble than anyone else is taking over you. That includes your husband.'

Tatyana took another sip of her coffee, wishing it were hotter; throwing it into his face, she reflected, might wipe the malicious grin from it. 'You know something about Tom?' she asked, careful to keep her voice calm and even.

'We are keeping tabs on him, of course,' said Boissant. 'That is only natural, you'll agree.' He leant closer towards her, his heavy forearms resting on the table, the fat around his eyes folding up. 'Already he is with another woman, you know,' he said. 'Probably lying in her arms right now, even as we speak.'

Tatyana paused for only a second before replying, her eyes recapturing their composure before turning on Boissant. 'I have parted from my husband. He is no longer of concern to me.'

'The heart does not abandon people so easily,' said Boissant. 'Even yours.'

'You know nothing of my heart.'

Boissant shrugged, a fresh cigarette jabbed between his lips. 'Perhaps no man ever will,' he said sharply. 'For this morning, that hardly matters. So long as you do as you are told, all shall be well between us.'

'I have agreed,' said Tatyana, her eyes resting on Boissant. 'That should be enough.'

Boissant nodded. 'Finish your breakfast,' he said carefully. 'We have a long morning ahead of us.'

*   *   *

The last plate of sausages, eggs, bacon and fried bread arrived at the table of the Bankside Grill just as John Dundee sat down. The team was now assembled, thought Jones, looking up at the four tired faces around the table.

'Any word from Tom?' asked Alan Gibson.

'I spoke to him last night,' said Jones. Reaching inside his pocket, he took out four sheets of photocopied paper, handing one to each man. Glancing down, each could see a series of three numbers, the levels that any two of the FTSE, the DAX and the CAC-40 had to reach by noon today if their friend was to be saved. 'It's that simple,' continued Jones. 'If two markets meet those numbers, Tom thinks it will be all right.'

Dundee shook his head. 'The FTSE above 7250,' he said, his tone lowering to almost a whisper. 'It's at only 7015 this morning, and it's heading down. The CAC is almost two hundred points short of our target of 5300, and the DAX is at 5920, meaning we have to get it up by nearly two hundred points as well. On a morning when everyone in his right mind is going to be selling German equities, this is going to be tough.'

'Particularly with Telmont selling in the market against us,' added Taylor. 'As well as the KrippenBank, and just about every other major financial institution in the world.'

Fletcher looked up from his breakfast. 'But it only needs to be for a few minutes – that's our one strength. The futures contracts Telmont has taken out across the market all stipulate the markets have to be below those levels at noon GMT. That's the time they cut out. What happens before or afterwards doesn't count. So long as we can get the markets to those levels at twelve, we win.'

'That's right,' said Jones, his eyes suddenly lighting up. 'We all know our roles. If we all do exactly as we agreed, then there's a chance.'

Dundee lifted his mug of tea from the table. 'It's us against the Leopard Fund then,' he said, raising the cup into the air. 'If you don't know what it's like to be a snowball in hell, you're about to find out.'

CHAPTER 24

Friday, 19 February

'WHATEVER HAPPENED TO TOM BRACEWELL?' ONE OF THE secretaries asked Jones while he was getting a coffee from the machine. Terrible thing, she continued, getting rid of him just like that; made everyone feel insecure. 'No idea,' answered Jones quickly. 'Haven't heard from him. Seems to have disappeared from the face of the earth.'

He took the coffee quickly back to his desk, settling into his chair behind his screen, his eyes moving hastily around the office, checking no one was watching him too closely. Logging on to his computer, he snapped through the state of the markets – still falling heavily right across Europe – then checked KrippenBank's own trading. It had been selling heavily all week; with the market tumbling, heavy losses were being recorded on each trade.

Jones took a slug of his coffee, logged out of his computer, took a deep breath, then logged back into the machine, this time using a password assigned to the Systems Department. The break-in would be detected easily, but since everyone had this password it should be impossible to track down who had made the intrusion. Once inside the system, he opened up the files marked 'computerized trading'. One advantage of working for a German company, Jones reflected; they took the systems very seriously, and everything was always filed away exactly where you expected.

Like most big banks, KrippenBank had installed what the management referred to reverentially as 'black boxes'. Jones had never actually seen a black box, and he was certain they weren't black; they would, inevitably, be the same off-beige colour as all the other computers. The term was shorthand for all the computerized trading systems, slabs of software programmed to play the markets. In the mid-Nineties, following the fashion on Wall Street, the bank had drafted in teams of young scientists, mostly lecturers in physics and mathematics, quadrupled the salaries they were earning, then set them to work designing complex mathematical trading models. By some estimates, more than half the trading in the City, at least in the currency and bond markets, was now black boxes dealing with one another. Since most of the computers' positions were only held for a few seconds, they were never checked; the performance of the boxes was simply reviewed at the end of the day to see if they had made or lost money.

Jones had sat on the committee that installed the boxes, and he knew their capabilities. To drive the market up, the way they wanted it to move this morning, the boxes were the perfect instrument. The machines had a rugged, persistent doggedness Jones could not help but admire; they stuck to their program, no matter how overwhelming the evidence against them might be. Nobody had ever heard of a black box getting stressed and quitting the game. Traders did that all the time. Nor had anyone ever heard of a black box deciding its instructions were ridiculous and ignoring them. Traders did that as well.

On idle afternoons, when the office and the markets were stone dead, Jones and Tom would sometimes discuss ways they could sabotage the bank. The boxes, they agreed, were the key. Dumb and brutal creatures that could be manipulated at will, they were the perfect foot soldiers for an assault on the markets. The trouble, as Jones would point out towards the end of their discussions, was that the designers of the boxes had seen that possibility. The boxes were so obviously the perfect material for fraud and manipulation, they had more security built into them than a Pentagon computer. Any attempt to alter the parameters of a program, to change a trading strategy, or to alter its instructions in any way, meant the computer would just stop functioning. It would freeze completely, the software would be junked, and the programmers would have to start again from scratch. It was expensive, but it made the boxes hacker-proof.

Except for one possibility. Tom had noticed it just after the long weekend at the start of 1999, when the entire City had been working on the introduction of the euro. KrippenBank, like every other bank in Europe, had switched its systems to euros, but the London operation still accounted in sterling. That meant the black boxes were still working in sterling, but had been designed to convert to euros once Britain joined the single currency. What, Tom had speculated that weekend, if you flicked the switch now, told the boxes Britain had signed up for the euro, and sterling had now vanished? The boxes would think they were trading euros. But, of course, each euro was worth only sixty-five pence. Suddenly, to the black boxes, every price in the market would look incredibly cheap. The boxes, following their programs, but in the wrong currency, would start buying every bond, stock and currency they could. It would be the mother of all buying sprees. And it wouldn't stop until someone noticed what the boxes were doing. Or until the boxes had driven the market up by more than thirty per cent.

So long as it works, thought Jones to himself. He scanned the list on his screen, noting that KrippenBank currently had sixty-seven black box programs, between them controlling thirty-seven billion euros. A fair slug of money, he reflected. Enough to give the markets a jolt if it started changing direction.

He had watched as the software engineers had switched the computers from trading in francs, deutschmarks and lire to euros; so far as he could tell, it involved little more than turning on the conversion program. Jones clicked on the icon displayed on his screen. 'Which currency do you wish to convert?' asked the program. 'Sterling,' he typed. 'On which date?' the machine asked impassively. '19 February,' Jones typed. 'At what time?' flashed the message on the screen. Jones thought for a moment. It would take a little time for the machines to start buying in the market, yet to leave it too long risked someone within the bank noticing what the black boxes were doing. '11.45,' he typed.

The words disappeared into the innards of the machine, and for a moment there was nothing on the screen apart from a cartoon of a pair of dolphins swimming; one of the dumber KrippenBank screensavers, Jones decided, wondering nervously if any authorization was needed for the program. 'Conversion accepted,' flashed a message on the screen. 'All sterling values will be converted to euros at 11.45 today at a rate of 1.412 euros to the pound. Please press enter to confirm these details are correct.' Jones could hear a sigh of relief escaping from his lips. I've done what I can, old boy, he said to himself. Let's hope the rest of us can deliver.

Telmont looked up at Sheldon, his eyes narrowing, and the lines on his forehead creasing into a frown. 'I thought I told you I was not to be disturbed.'

Sheldon shifted from his left foot to his right, his eyes glancing towards the door. 'It's Peter Davenport, sir,' he said. 'Nobody refuses to take a call from the Governor of the Bank of England.'

A thin smile started to spread over Telmont's lips. 'Put him through,' he said. 'Fools also have a right to be listened to, I suppose.' He turned, looking down towards the river, adjusting the cufflinks on his shirt. 'Peter,' he began, cupping the phone into his chin. 'It is so good to hear from you.'

'Likewise, Jean-Pierre,' said Davenport. 'Enjoyed your speech the other night.' The delivery was crisp and matter-of-fact, delivered with a rasp from the back of the throat. 'You've made quite a stir with your decision to liquidate the Leopard's entire portfolio.'

Telmont laughed. 'In this market, cash is everything,' he said. 'Surely you would not disagree.'

'You can have too much cash,' shot back Davenport. 'I'll be blunt, Jean-Pierre. This has the makings of a full-scale crash. If the markets keep falling, several banks are going to collapse. If that happens, then it can't be guaranteed that the Bank of England, the Federal Reserve or the ECB can keep the system propped up. Systematic failure. You'd be wiped out along with everyone else.'

Telmont hesitated before replying, calculating the odds. 'And what
would you like the Leopard Fund to do precisely?' he asked.

'Start buying again,' said Davenport. 'We have no jurisdiction here –
your money is your own to do what you like with. But the market needs
something to bolster its confidence.'

'Consider it done,' answered Telmont. He looked towards the screen;
the FTSE, the CAC-40 and the DAX were each a swamp of red, prices
tumbling by the minute. 'After all, we have no interest in seeing the
financial system collapse.' He put the phone down, turning towards
his desk, smiling to himself. A good general, Telmont reflected, always
spreads disinformation amongst the enemy.

Andrew Taylor looked at the view from his office on the eighteenth
floor of the IM Pei Tower in Canary Wharf; the elegant curve of the
river from this height always soothed his nerves, and he could feel some
of the tension ebbing from his shoulders. He turned back towards his
screen. The bond markets had been taking a pounding all morning;
the carnage had started in the German corporate sector, on fears that
collapsing markets in the East would hurt their profitability and so their
ability to pay back their debts. That had spread through all the markets
in European corporate bonds, and was now dragging down prices in
Government bonds. The market was already starting to calculate the
chances of a recession, and was savagely marking down the prices of
Treasury notes in every European market. Stories were running on the
wires about riots in Minsk and Riga, about the government collapsing
in Tallinn, about rumours of a coup in Slovakia, and whispers of a
run on the banks in Budapest. The region was descending into chaos,
reflected Taylor.

He punched up a fresh page on his screen, scrolling through a series of
numbers. The market in Eastern European government bonds, he began
to write, had never been lower; prices were so low, they assumed some
kind of return to communism, and that all debts in the West would be
abandoned. That, he concluded, was unlikely. Now, he argued, was the

time for the bank to be buying as much Eastern Europe debt as it could find in the market place.

Taylor leant back in his chair, glancing out of the window once more. It was a dangerous prediction; the market was crashing through the floor, and it might well prove far too early to call the bottom. Still, he decided, he had been in this job long enough to survive a couple of mistakes. Leaning into his screen, he saved the note, then marked it for distribution to the bank's dealing rooms around the world. Not everybody would act on the advice, he decided. But if enough dealers should start persuading the bank's clients to move into Eastern European bonds, it would be enough to give the market a jolt.

An equity strategist, Gibson reflected, was like an army chaplain; you were there to give encouragement and heart to the men, but you shouldn't expect anything you said or did to have much influence on how events unfolded. You tried to explain how the markets were behaving, and to predict where they might go next, but everyone knew the markets were unknowable. You might as well try to predict the shape of the next snowflake to fall. In essence, he was in the reassurance business.

There was, he concluded glumly, nothing reassuring about this morning. Even as he walked through the dealing floor, he could feel the sweat dripping off the traders. The markets were plunging all around them, and they no longer had any idea whether they should be buying or selling. A stillness descended upon the office, Gibson noticed. The men had lost all sense of direction, and were so confused some of them were already refusing to trade. The financial equivalent of shell shock, he decided.

Standing next to David Markham, the bank's chief equity dealer, Gibson leant forward. 'I hear we're in big trouble,' he said, his voice barely above a whisper. 'Heavy losses in Singapore overnight. Could be curtains for the lot of us.'

Markham looked up at him, his brown eyes already red and strained by tiredness. 'The whole market's fucked,' he said. 'Wouldn't surprise me if several banks went down.'

'Apparently we can still trade our way out of trouble,' said Gibson. He slipped a single sheet of paper onto Markham's desk. 'Apparently if the European markets can make these numbers by midday, some derivative positions in Japan will come good. Should be enough to tide the bank over to the end of the day.'

Markham scrutinized the figures, then looked back up at Gibson, a question playing in his eyes. 'You on the level?'

Gibson shrugged. 'You ever known an equity strategist be this gloomy?' he said, his tone edged with metal. 'We're normally just here to cheer you boys up.'

Markham stirred from his seat, his back straightening in his chair. 'For real,' he said. 'The bank needs these numbers to survive.'

'Of course,' answered Gibson. 'The directors just can't tell you themselves. Against the rules, old boy. We're supposed to be making a market independently of the bank's own positions. Chinese walls, and so on.'

'Hence the whispers.'

'That's right,' replied Gibson, his tone hardening. 'All our jobs and bonuses for this year might well depend on hitting those targets. Personally, if the FTSE, the DAX and the CAC-40 don't hit those numbers, I can't even pay the school fees.'

Moving closer to his computer, his fingers already poised on the keyboard, Markham looked upwards, the lustre returning to his eyes. 'The market can't recover that much by noon,' he said. 'We're all fucked anyway.'

Gibson leant forward, his arms perched on the top of Markham's desk. 'In which case we might as well give it our best shot, and sod the rules.'

'Meaning what precisely?'

Gibson beckoned Markham to move closer, leaning into the man's ear, his voice lowering to a whisper. What he was about to suggest, he explained, was not something he wanted the rest of the trading floor to overhear.

*   *   *

There were moments when Ian Fletcher wondered what had made him accept the job of head of derivatives trading. His plan had been to make enough money in the City in his twenties to finance spending the rest of his life as a pitifully badly-paid mathematics researcher at whatever university would leave him in peace to solve some of the advanced equations in chaos theory that had fascinated him since he was a student. The bonus, I suppose, he thought to himself, as he wended his way from Monument tube station to the bank's Cannon Street headquarters. The bonus and, just occasionally, the thrill of the job. Whether a bank that was ultimately owned by the French Government made or lost money could hardly have bothered him less. But there were not many roles in life where the ability to calculate differential regression analysis in your head while talking on the phone and issuing a dozen different instructions at the same time was considered anything other than an eccentricity. The derivatives market had made mathematicians employable and wealthy. Other than that, he couldn't think of much they had contributed to the world.

It was just after nine-fifteen when Fletcher arrived at his desk. He had made it a condition of taking the job that he didn't have to be at the office before nine-thirty. I can't control what time I leave the office, but I can at least control the time I come in, he had pointed out to them. The traders on the floor were already busy. From the long rows of Styrofoam coffee cups, and from the crowds gathering in the tiny smoking room, Fletcher could tell it was a bad morning. I don't need to look at a screen to see if the markets are still collapsing, he thought to himself. The numbers are written in their faces.

Secure in his own office, Fletcher took a Diet Coke from the fridge, then switched on his computer. For the last two months he had been playing a game of chess against Deep Blue, the IBM programme that had managed to beat Gary Kasparov. He usually spent the first half hour of the day playing against the machine; it was a way of limbering up his mind, he explained when anyone asked him about it, the same way you see footballers exercising on the side of the pitch. You never wanted to go into the markets cold. So far, Deep Blue had beaten him eight times in a row, and their current game was moving the same way.

One advantage of the derivatives market, he reflected, was that the instruments they traded were so fiendishly complex almost nobody could understand them. The dealers understood their own trades, but they usually had no idea what the person standing next to them was trading. The bank's management had completely lost track of the division. Only I have the complete picture, thought Fletcher to himself. And for a couple of hours at least, that could make me a person to be reckoned with.

A girl he dated once asked Fletcher to define what he did exactly, and the best answer he could summon up was: I buy and sell different versions of the future. It is like an auction. The version of the future that commands the highest price wins. She dumped him after the third date, but it was a definition he had stuck with ever since. This morning, Fletcher thought, I can try feeding a different storyline into the system.

As he did every morning, Fletcher called onto his computer screen a spreadsheet showing the bank's positions in the market. Just as he imagined, it was taking a beating. When markets were falling this far and this fast, it was almost impossible for traders to make any money, no matter how smart they were. Losing money was different, however. They did that all the time. Some of the traders had looked mystified when he put out a message around the floor telling them to start buying up all the call options they could locate in the FTSE, DAX and CAC-40 for noon today; those options would oblige the bank to buy shares in those indexes at pre-set prices. Crazy, a couple of them protested back at him. With the market falling as far and as fast as it is this morning, we will get hammered. Fletcher told them not to worry. He knew what he was doing, and had calculated the odds. He would be grateful if they could just get on and do as they were told. Checking his screen at just after ten, he saw the bank had collected the bulk of the options available in the market. All its rivals were desperate to off-load their obligations, and were selling everything they could to his team of dealers. Just as Tom had suggested it would, their plan was working out.

Fletcher grinned to himself, switched the numbers off the screen, and turned back towards his chess screen. Deep Blue had responded to this morning's move by seeming to place its queen in danger. Why on earth has it done that? thought Fletcher to himself, taking a swig on his Coke. In another hour or two, he decided, he might even have figured out his next move.

Looking at the numbers on the screen, John Dundee reflected it might be good to be back into a bear market. In the last five years, the markets had gone up so far and so fast, it had taken most of the fun out of managing a large portfolio of equities. They all went up anyway, usually regardless of which ones you picked. And if your fund couldn't produce a return of at least thirty per cent, it was regarded as a failure. In a crash, it should be possible to start sorting out the smart from the simply lucky.

His third cup of coffee of the morning was sitting on the edge of his desk, already cold by the time he raised it to his lips. Since arriving at the office this morning, the pace of trading had been frenetic. All of the main European markets were falling heavily, and the Eastern European exchanges had just about closed down. According to the wire reports, the IMF was meeting in emergency session, its officials heading for Eastern European capitals to arrange bail-outs for their bankrupt financial systems. Trading in Eastern European currencies had stopped, and without convertible currencies all trade would soon stop as well. One wire story speculated that the European Central Bank was planning a dramatic rate cut across Europe to try to restore some confidence in the financial system, and was urging European Union finance ministers to put together a rescue package for the East. Fat chance, thought Dundee to himself. It will never happen.

On his screen, he glanced through the performance of his own fund. Dundee's territory included the company's six main unit trust and pension funds, as well as the several hundred pension funds managed on behalf of companies and local authorities. A total of twenty-eight billion pounds, last time he calculated. Probably more like twenty-five billion now. It had been a bad morning. In conditions like these, there was nothing he could do to stop the funds taking huge losses. Right now, he wouldn't even be able to sell most of the stocks and bonds the funds owned. There weren't any buyers. This could be about more than just helping out Tom, Dundee thought to himself. It could be about saving all our skins.

Calling up the e-mail notepad on to his screen, he started typing: 'I have heard a strong rumour the Leopard Fund has taken some terrible hits this morning,' he wrote. 'I'm told it's bust. For our own safety, we should stop trading with them immediately.'

Pressing 'send' on the computer, he waited a couple of minutes, allowing time for the message to flash up on to screens all around the office. Picking up the phone, he punched out the number of one of his rivals. Within about half an hour, he reckoned, this rumour would be running right through the City. Nobody would want to trade with a hedge fund they thought might be out of business by the end of the day.

On hold? thought Lars Frezenburg. Nobody puts the President of the European Central Bank on hold; Alan Greenspan occasionally, perhaps, but that was only when he was feeling mischievous. Telmont had always had a ridiculously inflated view of his own importance, but this was preposterous. 'Yes, I'll wait,' he said to the secretary. 'But tell him it's urgent.'

Frezenburg looked out across the clouds settling into the Frankfurt skyline; a dismal morning, however you looked at it, he decided. The markets were collapsing around them, and the euro had been battered by the markets. He'd already taken three calls from European Prime Ministers asking for an emergency cut in interest rates to salvage confidence in the euro, and the calls were stacking up. Unless it's the German Chancellor or the French President, he told his secretary, don't put anyone through.

'A rare honour, Lars,' said Telmont, his tone smooth and calm. 'It is not often a mere fund manager gets a call from the most powerful central banker in the world.'

Frezenburg sighed. Surely, he reflected, this was not the time for playing rhetorical games. 'Everything I am hearing in the markets disturbs me,' he began. 'There are rumours going around that the Leopard Fund may be responsible for this crisis.'

'You and I have been around too long to listen to rumours,' said Telmont.

'I'd have thought we'd been around long enough to listen mainly to the rumours,' said Frezenburg sharply. 'Sometimes gossip is the most reliable data we have.'

'But this time it is just a rumour, Lars,' said Telmont, his breath quickening. 'Believe me, the Leopard has nothing to do with any of this. Our losses are just as bad as everyone's. Possibly worse.'

'I have your word?' asked Frezenburg.

'You have my word,' answered Telmont, his tone firm and decisive.

'Remember one thing, Jean-Pierre,' said Frezenburg. 'The euro isn't like the pound or the rouble. We won't allow it to be destroyed by speculators.'

Telmont put the phone down. If the President of the European Central Bank was worried enough to call him directly, then his plan must be unfolding better than he could have dared hope.

Tom looked down at the screen of his laptop. Ice had already started to form around the edges of the display, and his fingers, wrapped tight in thick padded gloves, found it slow and cumbersome to press the keys. Otherwise it worked okay; he could almost be back in his office.

A hunger was knawing at the inside of his stomach, mixed with sweat and fear and anxiety, but he could also feel the adrenaline surging through his veins; a potent stimulant, supplying the energy to press on. In a couple of hours, this will all be over, he told himself. One way or another, the issue will have been resolved.

Together with Terah, he had already walked for one hour this morning, trekking down the side of the stream, walking through heavy snow that pulled against his feet, fighting every step. It was in his calf muscles he started to feel the strain first; a slow painful throbbing of the veins and flesh. By now the pain was spreading through his spine, and across his back. I'm not in good enough shape for this kind of exercise, thought Tom. I have spent too much time sitting around in banks.

Terah had suggested they break for a few minutes; the most dangerous thing we can do, he said, is to exhaust ourselves. With a stick he had broken the layer of ice covering the stream, cracking his way through to the small trickle of water flowing underneath. Tom raised the cup to his mouth; the water felt freezing on his lips, but also pure and refreshing, and briefly revived his spirits. I can get through this, he told himself.

By the time he opened up his laptop and connected his modem, there were already five messages waiting. Tom glanced though them. His friends had pulled through for him, he saw. That was something he could be grateful for. They were good, loyal men, and he trusted he would have done the same for them had their positions been reversed. All that they could, they had done, but he could expect no more from them. 'It's up to me now,' he said, looking towards Terah.

The Estonian nodded, taking another sip of water, throwing the rest to the ground. 'It always was up to you, I suppose,' he replied.

Tom looked across at the stream, noticing the cracked ice had already frozen, hiding the water beneath. His eyes drifted down the valley, thick with pines covered in white powder, the trees and snow and hills drifting into the horizon, like clouds viewed from an aeroplane. 'That's true everywhere, isn't it?' he said. 'In the end, we rely only on ourselves.'

CHAPTER 25

Friday, 19 February

THE OXYGEN WITHIN THE BASE HAD BURNT UP, CONSUMED by the constant smoke from Boissant's cigarette; the fresh air, Tatyana decided, had been replaced by a stale mixture of nicotine and carbon monoxide. The smell of rust and iron seeped everywhere, including, she felt sure, every pore of her skin. *Every minute I spend in this place must be adding another wrinkle,* Tatyana reflected. *It could take me weeks to get my skin clean again.*

Across the table, Boissant stubbed out his cigarette, looking straight at Tatyana, peering into her eyes, searching for any sign of resistance. She turned away. The man's gaze, she decided, had become repulsive. 'I am not a doll,' she said sharply. 'You should find something else to look at.'

Boissant leant forward, the flesh around his thick shoulders creasing up around his neck. 'There is not much else to look at around here,' he said. 'Surely it is natural that a man should look at a woman?'

'There is nothing natural about you,' said Tatyana, her eyes retreating behind her dark lashes. 'You are nothing more than an animal.'

'I have stronger muscles than an animal, and a sharper brain,' answered Boissant. 'Come, it's time.'

He jabbed a cigarette into his mouth, drawing deeply on the nicotine. Standing up, he offered Tatyana his hand. She ignored him, following one pace behind as he led her through the corridor, the way lit by Boissant's torch. Beneath the soles of her shoes, Tatyana could feel the dampness of the metal, and along the walls their shadows seemed to merge into the decayed steel. A thick reinforced door protected the control room, its surface pitted with scars of rust. Tatyana could remember the times her father had brought her here as a child; then, it had seemed a place of power, permanently busy and lively, with her father always in charge. Sometimes he would sit her on one of the machines, and the men would salute her as she went by, calling her Commander Tattie, making her giggle every time. To see it now, emptied of all life, sent a shiver of regret sliding through Tatyana's spine. Like a tomb, it now seemed a place designed only to be inhabited by memories.

The hinges to the door were congealed with age, and Boissant had to push it sharply before it swung open. About twenty feet long, by ten feet wide, the narrow metal chamber was fitted with a row of desks and seats and four computer screens. Three bulbs were strung across the ceiling, but only two still worked, casting a dim and pale light through the chamber. At the head of the room, Tatyana could see the chair where her father had always sat. On its back was stencilled a hammer and sickle. Boissant walked towards the terminals, gesturing to them with his hand, ash falling from his cigarette as he did so. Each one consisted of a grey metal box, engineered from a single slab of steel, with a rectangular green screen sticking out several inches. Below, there was a basic metal keypad. On the front of each display, Tatyana could read the words 'SIMD PS-2000: Severodonetsk Computer Plant, Ukraine.'

A single metal switch brought the four machines to life, their screens glowing green in the dim light. 'Crap Russian computers,' said Boissant roughly, looking down at the cursor flashing on the screen. 'A country that produced the greatest chess players in the world should have had the greatest computer technicians,' he continued. 'But I suppose they never had the materials to work with. Have you ever seen one of these before?'

'Only this one,' said Tatyana, her head shaking from side to side. 'You know that.'

'Best of a bad bunch,' said Boissant. 'Designed by Iery Prangishvili at the Moscow Institute of Control Problems. Personal computers the Russians couldn't do. Didn't interest them, I suppose. But networks, they knew something about those. Parallel-processing was working in Russia long before anyone in the West thought of it. In its day, around about the mid-Seventies, the PS-2000 was about as advanced a network computer as you could find anywhere in the world.'

'You forget, I saw it in operation once,' said Tatyana.

Boissant nodded, his expression grave. 'Security, that was the other thing they cared about,' he continued. 'In the Soviet Union, security took priority over everything. You saw that in operation as well, I trust?'

Tatyana nodded, walking closer to the flashing terminal, its green light shining up into her eyes. 'That's why you brought me here, isn't it?'

'Voice and palm print recognition,' said Boissant. 'Completely unbreakable. Unless the right person is here, a person who has been given authorization, then nobody can get into the system. Tapes don't work. Believe me, we tried. Neither does any kind of computer simulation of your palm print. The processors know when they are being conned. You need the actual person in this actual place, otherwise you can't get in.'

'I remember,' said Tatyana. 'It is not something you ever forget.'

Boissant edged closer to where she was standing, no more than an inch away from her, close enough for her to smell the sweat forming on his skin. 'Your father gave you authorization,' he said. 'Your voice and your palm print will get us inside the machine.'

The memory spun into her mind like an old tune, a haunting refrain from a distantly forgotten time. Leonid Draka had been a heavy, tall man, his broad shoulders sloping away from his neck like thick branches from a tree. His manner had been cold and reserved, even among the men on the base. He walked through them with a look of indifference on his face, acknowledging their salutes with only a curt nod of his head. With Tatyana, he had always been tender and kind, treating her with an exaggerated, formal courtesy that became a joke between them. Her visits to the base were irregular – no more than three times in the years her family lived in Tartu – but were always a great treat; at the end of her tours, her father would always order some hot chocolate and cake for her. Was I seven or eight that day? Tatyana asked herself. It was hard to remember now, but she could recollect perfectly eating the cake and drinking the chocolate, looking up towards her father, and noticing the seriousness on his face as he spoke to her. 'There is something I want you to do for me, Tattie,' he had said. She remembered how he had taken her hand and placed it onto a flat electronic screen; it had felt warm beneath her fingers, and she had held it there a fraction longer than necessary. Then he had held a microphone before her, asking her to say something. 'What shall I say, daddy?' she had asked him. 'It doesn't matter,' he replied. 'Can I have some more cake, please?' she had said, before collapsing into a fit of giggles.

The moment had receded from her mind, yet as she stood in the same room, next to the same computer, next to the same microphone, the memory was suddenly as sharp and clear as a piece of crystal. It was years since she had been able to recall her father so closely, or remember the warmth of his embrace; she could feel his eyes on her now, watching her, following her movements around the darkened chamber. 'Never, Tattie, must you tell anyone that your voice can activate this machine,' she could recall him telling her. 'If anyone ever asks you, deny all knowledge of this place. It will be our secret.'

Well, secrets are made to be revealed, thought Tatyana to herself. And I am sure father would not have wanted me to sacrifice my life to preserve this one. 'What does it do?' she asked. 'I can take you inside the machine, but what does it do then?'

Boissant lit up a match, holding it close to the cigarette between his lips, its glow illuminating the sparse wrinkles on his weather-beaten skin. 'The money,' he replied. 'The machine controls the money.'

'What money?'

'The accounts controlled by the Red Army before the fall of the Soviet Union,' said Boissant. 'The greatest hidden fortune of the twentieth century. All the money that was looted from Europe after the war, all the German, Polish and Czech money, all the Tsar's money, all the money made from the labour camps, and all the gold and oil in Russia for seventy years, it all ended up in the hands of the Red Army. Your father, as you might have known, managed the Army's finances. Some of it was laundered through the accounts in your name in Switzerland, and placed with the Leopard Fund. The rest, and there was much, much more of it, was placed in another series of offshore bank accounts. Where it has remained hidden until now.'

'And you can't access it?'

A cloud of cigarette smoke drifted across Boissant's face. 'No, we can't access it,' he said flatly. 'Not without the passwords.' He nodded towards the computer. 'And the passwords are inside that machine.'

'I get the passwords for you,' said Tatyana, the words crawling reluctantly from her lips. 'Then you let me go home.'

Boissant nodded. 'You go home, we complete the covenant,' he said. 'Everybody's happy.'

'The covenant?' said Tatyana, looking into Boissant's eyes.

'Your father didn't tell you about that?' Tatyana shook her head, watching while Boissant used the heel of his shoe to grind his cigarette into the floor. 'The covenant is what we do with the money.'

Vereden used one hand to hold the phone to his ear, the other to light the cigarette he was about to put into his mouth. 'Any progress?' asked Radek.

'Not yet,' wheezed Vereden, exhaling as the words escaped his lips. 'Paris is a big place. We don't even know if she is still in the city.'

'She'll be in the city,' said Radek. 'This is France, remember. Everything happens in Paris.'

'Okay, but where?' said Vereden. 'All we know is that she disappeared in a van. Last night. It isn't much to go on.'

'We have one piece of information,' said Radek. 'We know that the people who took her are connected to the party.'

'To headquarters. No,' said Vereden. 'Too dangerous.'

'Not headquarters, no,' said Radek, taking a sip of the water lying next to his hospital bed. 'But as I remember, the party used to keep a number of safe houses in most major cities, places where they could store people if they needed to.'

Vereden nodded into the phone, taking another cigarette from his packet. 'There were such places, yes,' he said slowly. 'You think they might still be there?'

'It's worth a shot,' said Radek. 'Right now it might be the only clue we have.'

The weight of his equipment felt heavy in Tom's hands. How long they might have been walking on this stretch, he was no longer sure; his watch was buried beneath his gloves. Half an hour, perhaps, he reflected to himself. Maybe less. Time seemed to slow down here in the forest, as if it too was freezing up.

At his side, the path was obscured by the snow, and only a trace of the stream could be seen underneath the thick layer of ice. The branches of the trees seemed to sag under the weight of snow collected on each needle of pine, drooping so low they sometimes brushed the ground. Above him, clouds had formed in the sky, and as he looked into the distance, he was no longer sure where the snow ended and the clouds began. The world, he decided, had turned into one huge blanket of grey and white. Tom stopped, wiped away some frost that was starting to form on the exposed skin of his face, and looked across towards Terah. 'Much further?' he asked.

'A mile or so,' Terah answered. 'No more than that.'

Tom could feel his heart beating in his chest, the blood surging through his veins. 'Your father came to this place?'

'Sometimes,' answered Terah. 'The Russians put their main head-quarters out here in the centre of the forest so that they could be close to the woodsmen. Patrols would come out from the base every day. Mostly, the woodsmen just avoided them. That is the way in a terrorist war. When you are a small power against a big one, you don't fight in the open.'

'But you have seen it?'

Terah nodded, taking a flask of water from his hip and holding it to his lips. 'My father brought me this way a couple of times,' he said. 'He thought it important I knew where it was, and what it represented.'

'It's empty now?' said Tom.

Terah handed the water across. 'Ever since the Russians left Estonia,' he replied. 'These days, the forests are mostly empty. People are moving to the towns. I'd be surprised if anyone has been there for years.'

Tom took a drink from the flask, wincing as the freezing water hit his throat; a shiver ran through him, rattling into the centre of his bones. 'The strange thing is, I am not even sure I want to see her,' he said. 'I want to know where she is, and why. But see her and talk to her, that's different.'

Taking the flask, Terah knelt down, refilling the metal container with more snow, then hooking it back onto his jacket. 'A man is under no obligation to talk to his wife,' he said, pointing down to the bottom of the valley. 'If you want to, you just turn around and walk away.'

The heat in the kitchen was turning oppressive. Sarah could feel the sweat under her clothes starting to clog the pores of her skin. On the radio, she had just been listening to a news bulletin, led by stories of collapsing stock markets right across Europe. As the newsreader rattled out some of the numbers, Sarah could feel her spirits deflating. 'Can't we open a window?' she said, looking across at Jennings.

'Too hot for you?' said Jennings, a puff of smoke emerging from his lips.

Sarah nodded. 'I'm sweating all over,' she said.

'So you should be, like, the situation you're in,' he said.

She could feel the perspiration on her forehead, but hardly had the strength left to reach up and wipe it away. 'You won't do it.'

Jennings shook his head. 'I'm here to give orders, like, not take them,' he answered. 'Not from you.'

'Who are you taking orders from?'

His hand slapped across her cheek, stinging the nerves, sending ripples of pain crashing into her neck. Sarah's muscles tightened, and she could feel her eyes watering. Her eyes flashed shut, then opened again. His breath was hot and buttery as he lent into her face. 'Think that was a slap?' he barked. 'When I start hitting you, then you'll feel it.'

Sarah looked out towards the window, her eyes following the slow drift of a cloud through the sky. Tom is too far away, she thought to herself. And there is no one else to help me now.

Unlike most banks and dealing rooms in the City, the clocks on the wall of the Leopard Fund showed the time in Paris as well as London, New York, Los Angeles, Tokyo and Hong Kong. Paris time is what counts, Telmont would sometimes remark to the dealers; time could be spent in other cities, but that was the only place in which it could be preserved.

Telmont glanced at the row of clocks, watching while the hands clicked to eleven in London, twelve in Paris. Walking purposefully through the floor, judging the air as he went, he stood next to Semple's desk. The numbers on his screen told their own story. The FTSE was now standing at 7290, the CAC at 5340 and the DAX at 6001. All three indexes just needed to move a fraction lower over the next hour and the battle would be his. He leant down over Semple's shoulder, his eyes fixed on the screen, transfixed by the dance of blue and red numbers across the monitor. 'How's it looking?' he whispered.

'Still going down,' muttered Semple, reaching across to the box of Dunkin' Donuts at the side of his desk and offering one to Telmont. 'The market's freaked, turning this into a total collapse. Merrills, Goldmans, UBS and SocGen have all basically stopped trading, too frightened to make a market. The market's so thin right now, the wild men are taking over. At the moment, I reckon it will keep falling.'

'Spook it some more then,' said Telmont, pushing aside the box of doughnuts.

'Like what, boss?' said Semple, sliding a doughnut into his mouth and looking up towards Telmont.

'Take the biggest company in each market – Shell in London, DaimlerChrysler in Frankfurt and BNP in Paris – and start selling as much stock as you can in each one,' said Telmont, his back stiffening as he spoke. 'Every point those companies tick down takes the index further down. For the next hour we must focus our forces on the market's weakest points.'

Tatyana pondered the moment, turning it over in her mind, waiting until she was sure she was ready before she asked the question. The failing half-light of the chamber and the rusted metal of the walls had already exhausted her eyes, and her stomach was feeling queasy from the tension of the past few days. 'What was the covenant?' she asked.

Boissant looked at her closely, examining the contours of her skin. It had wearied in the last three days, he noted, acquiring a leathery, beaten texture. 'The deal between the Red Army and the Leopard Fund,' he said. 'The agreement reached between your father, Leonid Draka, and Jean-Pierre Telmont, some time back in the early Seventies, back when Jean-Pierre was a bright young revolutionary, and I was a young soldier, and you were hardly even out of your nappies.'

'What was the deal?' asked Tatyana, delivering the question with as much poise as she could muster.

'The deal,' repeated Boissant, his eyes moving up towards the ceiling. 'The deal was the Leopard Fund would manage money in the West on behalf of the Red Army. That was how the fund got started. How else might we suppose a kid like Telmont – he was twenty-two or twenty-three then – was going to start up an investment fund? He had no credentials, nothing to his name, a nobody. He was given the money. And, in return, when the time came, he would use the money as the Army directed.' Boissant paused, fishing a cigarette from his packet, placing it between his lips. 'At first, it was part of the softening-up process. If the Red Army had ever received orders to attack Western Europe, the fund would have been part of the enemy within. It would have been used to destroy currencies, plunge companies into financial crisis, and so on.

Economic warfare. For that, the Red Army needed a big presence in Western capital markets, and Telmont was its man. All that changed, of course, after the collapse of the Soviet Union.' Boissant hesitated, flicking up his lighter, its flame shining onto his face, his dark eyes peering out through the light. 'Just before your father died in 1990, he changed the terms of the deal. That was when he created the covenant. Telmont could keep control of the money, the Leopard would carry on, but only if it fought to preserve the Red Army's greatest achievement.'

Tatyana could feel the cold bearing through the thick sheet of metal that formed the husk of the base; above her, she could sense the thick layer of snow and ice beneath which she had been incarcerated. 'The achievement,' she said, the words trembling on her lips, 'was what, exactly?'

Boissant held the flame to his cigarette, inhaling deeply, releasing a thick cloud of smoke. 'The capture of Eastern Europe and its absorption into the Russian Empire by the Red Army was, I suppose, the finest military achievement of the twentieth century. Your father was a loyal soldier. The covenant was that all the money the Army had acquired over the century would be used to destroy Eastern Europe, after which the fund could keep the rest. That is what this is all about. It is time for the money to be put to the use for which it was intended.'

He leant down over the keyboard, looking into the green luminous screen. Made out of steel, the keys were built into the desk, and the cursor had to be moved around by using the tab button. Tatyana watched as he punched a series of commands into the machine, reading the words that scrolled back at him. 'When your father died, most of the Army's money was tied up in offshore accounts. To complete the covenant, we must access it.' He looked back up at her, a thin smile looping over his face. 'So, you see, we are just following your father's wishes.'

Tatyana moved closer, resting her thumbs on the rough metal edge of the desk. 'Whatever you say,' she said, her tone cold and distant. 'I have already agreed to do as I am told. What my father might or might not have wanted does not matter in the least.'

Boissant pointed towards the screen. 'Your palm should be placed just there,' he said.

Tatyana placed her hand on the glass, feeling its soft, electric warmth feed into her fingers. She rested it there, wondering how long the computer might take to verify this was the hand of the small girl who had been brought to this place more than a quarter of a century ago. At her side, she could see Boissant holding out a microphone attached by a length of cord to the innards of the machine. 'Speak into this, please,' he said firmly. 'Use the same words you used when your father imputted your voice.'

Tatyana took the microphone in her free hand, looking first across at Boissant, then down at her palm still stretched out on the flashing screen. Taking a deep breath, she summoned some strength and character into her throat. 'Can I have some more cake, please?' she said.

The ridge stretched out into the distance, sculpted into the contours of the hill like a finely wrought piece of plasterwork. Terah had spotted it immediately during their descent down the edge of the valley. Cover, he explained. The one advantage they would have this morning was that they knew how to make the forests work for them.

The climb had been hard, ripping into Tom's tendons, bolts of pain lodging themselves into his muscles, reminding him that no matter how much you might go to the gym, office life still left you useless for this kind of exercise. They had kept to the edge of the stream, taking them close to the pit of the valley, then banked hard to the right, moving away from the path, climbing upwards, walking through the trees. The natural curve of the land provided a wall, allowing them to look down, but making it unlikely anyone would observe them. The ground was soft and treacherous underfoot, Tom's boots digging into the snow, then cracking on buried twigs, branches and leaves. Twice, his foot stuck in a trench, and had to be yanked free. If I get out of here without at least a broken ankle it will be a miracle, he thought to himself.

Tom stopped by a tree, catching his breath, taking a drink from his

water flask; how quickly he was dehydrating in the cold was already
surprising him. Looking down, he could see the base clearly from here.
Four or five hundred yards away in the foot of the valley, the building rose
from the ground upwards, a giant circular dome of steel and barbed wire.
About eighty yards or so in diameter, Tom estimated, it was built entirely
of metal, its walls and roof painted grey, but most of it now hidden under
a thick layer of snow and ice. Every twenty yards or so, faded lettering
was stencilled onto the side of the dome. Outside, two four-wheel drive
vehicles were parked, a Mitsubushi Shogun and a Land Rover. Neither
of them was occupied, and, judging by the amount of snow on them,
both had been there since last night. Towards the back of the base, a
thin stream of smoke came from a metal chimney rising twenty feet into
the air, above what Tom assumed to be the boiler room. 'I'd guess there
are four guards,' said Terah, keeping his voice low.

Tom tracked Terah's finger down into the valley. The first man was
standing about fifteen yards from the base, in the middle of open snow,
wearing a dark green anorak with a hood strapped over his head, thick
green trousers and high black boots. He was holding what looked to Tom
like a hunting rifle, and was pacing back and forth, endlessly retracing
his steps. Sixty yards away, on the other side of the dome, Tom could see
another man, this time wearing a black coat but also carrying a hunting
rifle. Between them, he calculated, they would be able to see the entire
circumference of the building. 'I only see two guards,' whispered Tom.

'Cold weather tactics,' said Terah. 'A guard can't keep watch over
exposed ground for more than an hour at a stretch. He'll get frostbite.
Those men will do an hour, then be relieved. If they have two guards
out, it means there are another two inside.'

Tom nodded, looking down at the first guard, watching his steady,
unhurried parade around the same stretch of land, focusing on the rifle
that was held between his hands. 'Think we can get past them?' he asked.

Terah lit a cigarette, holding it between his lips, shaking his head from
side to side. 'It's a military base, remember,' he said. 'They built it to
withstand attack. Notice the way it is on a completely open piece of
ground. A few trees are starting to spring up since it was abandoned,

but there is no cover. It is a circle, no walls to slide along, no corners to take advantage of. There is no way you can creep up unnoticed on that building. The guards will see you.'

Tom could feel his heart sinking into the soles of his boots. For a moment, the thought of turning around, going home, flashed through his mind. As Terah had said, a man was under no obligation to talk to his wife. 'We can't get past.'

'No,' said Terah, taking a deep drag on his cigarette. 'If we want to get in there, we will have to fight them.'

'They have guns,' said Tom, gesturing towards the valley.

'True, but they probably don't know the rules.'

'What rules?' asked Tom.

Terah tossed the embers of his cigarette into the snow. 'The rules of the forest,' he replied.

The wall of rough grey pebble dash that clad the sides of the nondescript suburban house was too high to scale. Not even in my younger days, thought Vereden to himself. Certainly not now. He lit a cigarette, coughed, and walked away. This was the second building on the list. A call to Moscow had been all it took to get hold of the addresses of the buildings the party had once used in Paris; one of his former KGB contacts, now living in penury in a dingy one-bedroomed apartment on the outskirts of the city, had been glad of the promise of fifteen hundred euros and had found the addresses in less than an hour. This was the second of them and, as far as Vereden could tell, it looked as empty as the first.

He walked around the thin strip of gravel to the front of the building. Poor girl, he thought to himself. It was now fourteen hours since she had been captured. The fear, he knew from his days as an interrogator back in Prague, would be starting to get to her. The first ten, twelve hours, the victim was usually okay. The adrenaline produced a certain bravado; they thought they could take anything. After ten hours of captivity, bravery started to evaporate, vanishing into thin air. Despair started to offer its suffocating embrace; slowly the victim realized there was no easy escape, and nobody was about to rescue them. It was then the experienced interrogator moved in. It was then, in the bleakest moments of captivity, they were usually most ready to break.

Sarah would be just about getting there, Vereden reflected to himself. Kneeling, he inspected the gravel on the ground. It was cold and moist to the touch. Rubbing it between his fingers, he could feel edges of moss accumulating on the sides. Nobody has walked across it for months, he decided. Standing, he walked to the front door, bending down to peer through the letterbox. A collection of brochures, junk mail and leaflets lay scattered across the grey carpet covering the hallway. Empty, he thought to himself.

Wherever it might be they have taken her, it is not here. Lighting up another cigarette, dragging hard on the nicotine, Vereden walked back towards his car, taking the map from the glove compartment and starting to study the route. Three more houses on the list, he told himself.

Tom opened up his computer, resting it on a small mound of snow he had built. Next to him, a pine tree towered up towards the sky, reaching close to the low clouds drifting through the valley. A shaft of sunlight burst down, illuminating the needles of the tree, lighting it up. For a brief moment, Tom allowed himself to smell the air, absorbing its energy. I need some strength from somewhere, he thought.

At his side, the satellite kit was open, the tiny dish pointing upwards. A single wire connected it to Tom's mobile, another line threading the phone into the modem on his laptop. Powering up the screen, Tom switched on the Reuters display, calling up the headlines of the morning. The market was savagely down: one hundred and eighty points off the FTSE, one hundred and twenty off the DAX, ninety off the CAC-40. Selling had turned into a tidal wave right across Europe. In Tallinn and Riga, the markets had now closed to prevent a complete economic collapse. In Lithuania, a state of emergency had been declared, and all trading in the currency had been stopped. The Polish and Hungarian central banks were reported to be ready to abandon the link with the euro, while in the Slovak Republic two banks had closed this morning. The IMF was meeting in emergency session to organize loans to Eastern Europe, and the board of the European Central Bank was meeting in Frankfurt to discuss a rapid cut in interest rates to try to pump some confidence back into the markets. Chaos, thought Tom to himself. Complete and utter chaos. Unless they act now, it will be too late to do anything.

He switched to a screen showing the prices for all the stocks in the FTSE. Each number on the display was coloured red; so far the biggest losses were in the banking sector; on speculation the clearing banks would be taking huge losses in the market, but every share in the index was trading lower. Cutting the screen in two, he scanned the French and German markets; they told the same grim story. Next, Tom called up details of a trading account lodged at the London office of KrippenBank; an error account with authorization to trade up to one million sterling, to which Jones had messaged through the password this morning. Technically, this might look like theft, legally it might even be so, he reflected. But in reality, he was just borrowing a bit of the bank's money and playing with it for an hour or so. Who knows? If everything works out according to plan, I might even make the bank a profit.

In truth, he realized, that was unlikely. One million against the one thousand billion the Leopard Fund could put into the fight, Tom reflected to himself. The odds were hardly appealing. Switching back to the index, he glanced quickly at the screen, then placed an order for one thousand shares in BP Amoco at 962p; that compared with the price now on the screen of 871p. The screen displayed the progress of the transaction as it sped through the computer's processors, and he could see the share price tick up to the level at which it last traded – 962p. On the screen, the BP symbol turned blue. Above it, Tom could see the impact of that upon the index; the FTSE briefly ticked up four points. He rubbed his hands together, trying to breathe some life back into fingers that were already growing numb from the cold. It may not be much, he decided, but it is at least a start. The fight had begun.

CHAPTER 26

Friday, 19 February

TELMONT LEANT OVER THE SCREEN, HIS GOLD CUFFLINKS gleaming under the hard neon light of the trading floor. His thumb pressed against the share price for BP Amoco, leaving a smeared trace of sweat on the hot glass of the monitor. 'What is happening there?' he asked, his voice turning to a whisper.

'Beats me, sir,' answered Sheldon, standing at his side, moving nervously from one foot to another. 'Some buying of BP, I guess. Perhaps the market thinks all this turmoil will be good for the oil price.'

A thin smile started to crease slowly over Telmont's lips. He pulled back from the screen, adjusting the knot of his tie. 'Even by your own standards, that is a remarkably shallow and stupid answer,' he said. 'The currency crisis in the East means Russia, Georgia and Azerbaijan will have to sell more oil. So too will the Middle East, to pay for weapons. And a recession in the West will reduce the demand for fuel.' He paused, shaking his head slowly. 'No, BP is one of the last stocks you would buy on a morning like this.'

'A rogue trade, perhaps, sir?' said Sheldon quickly, trying to decide whether shallow was worse than stupid.

'Almost a pound above the market price? I don't think so,' said Telmont, his voice growing edgier. 'Somebody is playing games with us.' He pointed to one of the traders, snapping his fingers, summoning his attention. 'Start selling BP, at 750p a share,' he commanded.

Telmont walked closer to the screen, watching while the instructions were fed in to the computer. His eyes remained glued to the screen as the price started to turn red, falling below nine pounds, then eight pounds, resting at 750p. Looking upwards, he saw the FTSE, after taking the sudden fall in BP into account, had now dropped more than two hundred points in the morning. 'That, I think, should make sure they get the message,' he said.

Taking the mobile from his pocket, Telmont punched eleven digits into the phone, tapping his fingers rapidly against the edge of the desk as he waited impatiently for the satellites to locate the person he was calling, then another fifteen seconds while the phone rang three times. 'Her husband is trying to do something, I suspect,' he said quickly.

One of the two tired light-bulbs illuminating the narrow metal chamber had exhausted itself, darkening the room still further and making the green fluorescent glow of the SIMD 2000 seem harsher, more vibrant. Tatyana wiped away the dust accumulated on its surface with her Chanel headscarf, looking down at the numbers displayed on the monitor. At her side, Boissant was nodding into his mobile, pressing the handset close to his ear. He glanced at her furtively, his eyes locking onto hers for no more than a second before turning his back, cupping his hand around his mouth. 'What exactly is he trying to do?' he asked.

'I can't be sure,' said Telmont. 'It was just a single incident, but it looked to me as if someone was trying to drive the market back upwards.'

'Surely that is impossible?'

'This morning, quite so,' said Telmont. 'But you should know he is out there somewhere, and not beaten yet. The woman, she is co-operating?'

Tatyana noticed Boissant glancing in her direction again, his eyes roaming across her face. 'Like a lamb,' he said. 'The computers here recognized her, and they are responding to her commands.'

'How much is in those accounts?'

'Just over fifty billion dollars,' said Boissant, savouring the words on his lips. 'Everything is as Draka said it would be.'

'Then that money must be used as well,' said Telmont sharply. 'We leave nothing to chance. Make sure the woman is ready.'

Boissant snapped the phone shut, replacing it in the pocket of his overcoat. Tatyana noticed his face was drawn and tired, the lines in his skin etched a little deeper, and the jowls of his cheeks hanging lower. He moved closer to her, pointing down towards the screen. 'We will need to use this money in the market, as your father instructed,' he said. 'Once this computer hears your voice, it unlocks the passwords, and starts sending instructions to the offshore banks in which the money is held,' he said. 'Later we will transfer the money to new accounts. For now, there is not enough time.'

Tatyana looked down at the rows of figures displayed on the screen. It was, she reflected, as fabulous a display of entombed and forgotten wealth as it was possible to imagine. A series of fifty separate accounts, lodged in banks in Switzerland, Luxembourg, France, Italy, Gibraltar, London, the Cayman Islands, Bermuda, Hong Kong and Brazil. Every account held a mixture of cash, bonds and equities, and each, thanks to the great bull market of the Nineties, had multiplied its original value many times. 'You want to sell?' said Tatyana. 'To crash the markets?'

'Starting now,' said Boissant. 'If you don't obey, we can pick up your husband in the next hour or two and have him brought right here. You have already seen what we will do to you then.'

Tatyana looked away, her eyes locked on the screen, absorbing its pale green light. 'Where should I start?' she asked.

Terry Semple reached to his left, took a packet of Salt 'n' Vinegar crisps from the pile, and started eating. Still holding the packet, he climbed from his chair, walking across the trading floor to where he could see Telmont holding a discussion with the currency team. He stood next to him, catching the end of a lecture about putting more pressure onto the euro for the next fifteen minutes. 'Something's up,' he said, turning to look at Semple.

Semple crunched a crisp between his teeth. 'A word alone, boss.'

The two men walked in silence towards the long glass window that stretched along the entire north face of the building, looking down onto the river below. Semple could feel the eyes of some of the traders tracking them as they walked slowly away from the crowd. Looking at the red electronic display high above the floor, he could see they were close to their targets: the FTSE was at 7300, the CAC-40 at 5290 and the DAX at 6002. 'The French market is already where we want it,' said Telmont. 'Another fifty points off the FTSE, and another eighty-three points off the DAX, and we have made it. Now, tell me what you wish to speak of.'

Semple scrunched the empty crisp packet in his hand, chucking it towards one of the bins. 'Rumour we're bust, boss,' he said, his lips turning into a grimace as he delivered the words. 'Few of the guys in the market are saying we've done a Barings. Gone pop in the futures market. Some of them are turning nervous about taking our trades. Apparently there is a memo out at Mercury warning their boys not to deal with us.'

The words trailed away, while Telmont's face remained still and impassive, soaking up the information. In the background, Semple could hear the frantic noise of the floor, a sweaty, anxious blend of fear, desperation and hope. 'Not true, is it, boss?' he added, looking up towards Telmont.

'I can see what they are doing,' said Telmont slowly, his eyes peering through the massive sheet of glass. 'They are trying to cut off my supply lines. A rumour of bankruptcy is almost the same as the real thing. Without access to the markets, we are weakened. It is a clever move.' He hesitated, breathing deeply, the lungful of air briefly expanding his chest. 'But it is nothing that cannot be easily deflected. Tell the floor they must reassure the market the Leopard Fund has never been in better financial shape. There will be a statement out on the wire in the next few minutes.'

Vereden approached the house carefully, stopping his car half a block short of the address listed, approaching it on foot. A suburban semi detached, the building was located in the heart of the Paris commuter belt, and the street, at mid-morning on a Friday, was almost empty. Up ahead, he could see a single woman pushing a pram, but no one else. Lighting a cigarette, he walked slowly past the house, reducing his pace to nothing more than a stroll, careful to glance upwards just twice as he went past.

Vereden recognized the white van instantly. A three-year-old unwashed Citroen, it was parked on the gravel driveway. The number plate was the same. No question, he thought to himself. It was here they had taken her. He kept walking, his hands deep in his pockets, a cigarette hanging from his lips, his pace quickening as he reached the end of the road. As soon as he turned the corner into the next street, he took the mobile from his pocket, punching out the number. 'She's here,' he said,

'Are you sure?' asked Radek.

Vereden dragged deeply on his cigarette, drawing the nicotine into his lungs. 'The same van I saw last night,' he said quickly. 'She'll be in there somewhere.'

The sound of Radek's sigh was audible through the static. 'Can you take them?' he asked.

'An old man like me?' said Vereden, releasing a pale, empty laugh. 'Against three or four guys in their twenties or thirties? Who are we kidding, Victor?'

'Brains, not muscle – isn't that what we always used to say?' said Radek. 'In Prague, in the Sixties.'

'Brains *with* muscle, I think,' said Vereden. 'That was the phrase.'

'Okay, the muscles have gone, but the brains are still there,' said Radek.

'It means a lot that she survives?'

'Both of us have a lot of debts,' said Radek. 'It is time we paid them off. You, of all people, should know how to deal with that house.'

Vereden took another lungful of nicotine, breathing out into the cold morning air. 'If you haven't heard from me in an hour, assume I'm dead,' he said.

*   *   *

Tom looked down at the story displayed on his screen. *Leopard Fund insists it is solvent* ran the headline on the Reuters wire copy. He punched up the text.

> *London: 19/2: 11.19 GMT: The Leopard Fund, the giant hedge fund controlled by the French financier Jean-Pierre Telmont, this morning denied rumours it was a victim of the turbulence sweeping through the world's markets. In the City, it was reported some banks had decided to stop trading with the Leopard Fund, on the grounds its losses in the markets in the last few days were so huge, it was no longer solvent. A spokesman for the fund rejected that. 'The Leopard Fund is in a healthy and strong financial position,' he said. 'It is fully able to meet all its obligations.'*

Tom shivered, allowing the cold to rattle through his bones, and looked up towards the sky, searching for the glimmers of sunlight fighting their way through the thick, dark blanket of low-lying cloud. The bankruptcy rumour had obviously started to bite – enough anyway for Telmont to be forced into denying it. That at least would publicize the story, Tom reflected. Those people who hadn't heard the gossip would see the denial on the wires and wonder if it was true. In the last few minutes, while the Leopard's dealers had been finding it hard to trade, the market had started to stabilize; it was still falling, but not quite so quickly. Leaning into his terminal, Tom typed out a message: 'Good work, but we need to tell people the denial is a phoney, that the guy is bust and trying desperately to trade his way out of trouble. Regards Tom.'

He could feel the muscles in his knees aching as he rose to his feet; the combination of the walk, the cold, and the discomfort was starting to weaken him. He walked closer to the ridge overlooking the base, glancing down at the two guards walking a lonely, looping circle through the deep snow. His eyes fixed once again on the black metal of the guns they were holding. 'Think we can take them?' he whispered, his eyes darting up towards Terah.

'By ourselves, you and me, without weapons? No, we can't take them,' said Terah, shaking his head slowly from side to side. 'But with the cold on our side, we might just have a chance.'

Vereden surveyed the shelves of the small local hardware shop six blocks from the house, looking to see if they had the equipment he needed. A dimly remembered memory was running through his mind, a recollection of a lesson taught more than thirty years ago. The details of the man's face he could no longer recapture. A short, balding figure with mean eyes – that was all he could see of him. But the words had stuck. Live off the land, had been the lesson. Use whatever weapons your environment will bring to hand. In suburban Paris, Vereden reflected, living off the land meant the local hardware shop.

From the racks he selected a simple tin pot and a single-flame camping stove, with a tube of gas attached. He then asked the assistant for three kilos of potassium nitrate, usually used as a plaster mixer, and three large plastic lunchboxes. Vereden handed over eighty-two francs, and walked two shops further on. In the grocers, he bought two kilos of sugar, a wooden spoon, a box of matches and an apple. Walking further down the street, he ate the apple while looking for an empty alleyway.

The apple cast aside, he knelt down in the alley, next to a garage, took the stove from its box, and, fishing his lighter from his pocket, lit the flame. He placed the pot on the burner, and carefully mixed the sugar and the potassium nitrate together. As the heat began to melt the two powders into a foamy liquid, Vereden stirred the mixture until it had thickened. He began pouring the heavy liquid into the lunchboxes, taking the matches from the packet and pushing the ends into the hardening liquid.

When he had filled all three boxes, Vereden lit a cigarette, taking a couple of minutes to relax while the liquid hardened and set. Throwing his cigarette butt to the ground, he switched off the burner but left it on the concrete surface of the alleyway. Putting the three boxes in a bag, he started walking back to the car. Those people have probably never seen an old-fashioned smoke bomb before, he thought to himself. They won't know what's hit them.

Telmont looked hard at the screen, his eyes moving swiftly across the lines of red and blue and white pixels, absorbing the information spat out by the computer. His fingers ran down the list of Eastern European bond prices, his brow furrowed, his mind working on a series of calculations. At his side, Sheldon could hear his breath becoming more rapid. 'Why is the bond market starting to shift upwards?' he said, his eyes moving up from the screen.

Sheldon shook his head. 'I don't know, sir,' he said quickly, the words tumbling from his lips.

'Somebody must be buying,' he snapped. 'Find out who!'

Sheldon moved quickly across to the trading floor, whispering the question in the ears of the five men who worked on the bond trading desk. The discussion lasted no more than a minute before he scampered back towards where Telmont was standing, the fingers of his left hand pressed into his brow, his eyes rooted on the window. 'It's Morgan Stanley,' said Sheldon breathlessly. 'Apparently, some guy called Andrew Taylor put out research this morning saying now was the time to buy the bond markets in Eastern Europe. It seems to be having some impact with their clients.'

Telmont remained silent, the furrows on his brow deepening, and he started running his fingers quickly through his thick black hair. Leaning into the computer, he tapped into the keyboard. 'Who Andrew Taylor?' he wrote. It took three seconds for the machine to display the man's photograph and resumé, detailing his degree, the four different places he had worked, and the qualifications he had acquired along the way. 'What do you notice?' asked Telmont, looking across at Sheldon.

Sheldon shook his head anxiously. 'Nothing out of the ordinary, sir,' he replied. 'Fairly typical bond analyst.'

Telmont rested his thumb on the screen, just above the list of jobs. 'Morgan Grenfell, trainee, 1980 to 1982,' he said. 'The same year Tom Bracewell was there. Englishmen and their fucking clubs.'

'You think there is a connection, sir?' said Sheldon.

'Of course there's a fucking connection,' said Telmont, spitting the words from his mouth. 'They're all fucking connected to one another.' He walked quickly to the five bond traders grouped around one desk near the centre of the trading floor. 'Which bond is up most this morning?' he asked.

'The Polish 2008 long-dated,' answered one of the traders quickly. 'Yielding eight point four per cent, up twenty basis points already since the market opened.'

Telmont leant forward into the screen. 'Sell it,' he said sharply. 'Find all you can, buy it at whatever price it takes, then immediately sell it so cheaply people will never want to own it again. Is that clear?'

The five traders picked up their phones in unison, each of them talking at once. Above them, Telmont lingered for a few seconds, listening to a few brief snatches of conversation, making sure his instructions were being followed. 'We will teach that analyst that nobody can play in the markets against the Leopard Fund and survive,' he said sharply.

Traces of ice were starting to form around the edges of Tom's computer screen, freezing into the hinges of the laptop, glazing its black plastic surface, making it even colder to the touch. As his fingers hit the keyboard, Tom could feel the temperature lowering on the surface of his skin.

His eyes scanned across the list of headlines displayed on the Reuters wire. The markets could hardly be looking worse. This morning eight more banks had shut their doors in Hungary, creating complete panic as people rushed to withdraw their money. In Romania, a government bond issue had failed to find a single investor, meaning the state was effectively bankrupt; four Eastern European investment funds had stopped trading, cutting off the flow of money from the developed world; and Lithuania had announced it was introducing emergency capital controls to try to stem the flight of capital from its borders. Already the DAX was down to 5820; Tom was starting to realize they might as well give that up for lost.

The CAC-40 was hovering at 5280, just below the level Telmont needed, but still within reach. The FTSE was up at 7258, just eight points above where Telmont needed it.

Tom started keying out a message to Gibson. 'Are we ready to roll?' He waited, his eyes drifting out into the towering bank of snow rising up on the hillside beside him, its immaculate whiteness undisturbed by any sign of animal life. 'We're ready to try, anyway,' came the reply. 'Thanks,' tapped Tom into his machine. 'We need luck, but we also need courage.'

Gibson walked swiftly across the trading floor, towards where Markham was sitting. A temporary silence seemed to have descended on the six hundred square metres of neon-lit space; a subdued, reverential quiet, Gibson reflected, as though he had suddenly walked out of a dealing room and into a cathedral. Normally, this place was drowning in testosterone-fuelled anxiety, but this morning the noise had crept down to a level where you could almost hear yourself think. Strange, thought Gibson. Thinking was not what the trading floor was about.

Markham looked worse than usual. A man who was not yet forty, three years as head of equity trading at the bank had left him looking ravaged and beaten. His skin had turned a pale, grey colour, his hair was retreating rapidly into his scalp, and his figure was worsening faster than he could find the time to buy new suits. He was sitting back in his chair, the speaker phone on his desk switched off, his fingers playing idly across his keyboard. 'We've taken a horrible beating,' he said looking up at Gibson. 'Christ knows what Jane will say if the bank goes pop. She's pregnant again, you know.'

The traders, Gibson had noticed, moved instantly from total euphoria to an existential moroseness of overwhelming power, without pausing for any emotional stops along the way.

They lived by shuttling between extremes. 'Still hope, apparently,' said Gibson quietly. 'That's what I'm hearing from head office.'

'In a market like this?' said Markham, his shoulders slumped back against the chair, his eyes sinking into his head.

'If we're willing to go to the edge,' said Gibson, lowering his voice to a whisper, and leaning forward.

'Play around with the SETS system, you mean?' said Markham, his eyes crawling up from his desk. 'You were serious this morning then?'

Gibson nodded. SETS was a new trading system the London Stock Exchange had introduced in 1998 which computerized the trading of stocks throughout the City. Whenever a share was traded by one of the main brokers, the order was fed through a central computer, which matched a buyer at every price with a seller. The last price at which each stock was traded, and the volume of stock bought and sold, was automatically recorded, and displayed on the Reuters and Bloomberg screens around the City. But the system, as traders had quickly discovered when it was introduced, could be manipulated. By posting ridiculous prices up on the screen, trading could be briefly brought to a halt, as the other brokers around the City tried to digest what was happening. And the FTSE index, made up of the prices of the one hundred leading stocks, could be sent haywire. It was against Stock Exchange rules. Brokers were meant to trade at sensible prices, and any trades that looked to be aimed at creating a false market could be unwound by Stock Exchange officials and set aside from calculating the index. But that took hours, and often didn't happen until the next day. Right now, decided Gibson, they didn't care about the next day. They just cared about the next thirty minutes.

'That's exactly what I mean,' said Gibson.

'You think that will save us?'

Gibson shrugged, adopting the kind of studied, macho nonchalance that was standard on the trading floor. 'It's our last chance, I reckon.'

Markham leant forward, a glimmer of excitement returning to his eyes. 'We might as well, I suppose,' he said, the breath catching in his words. 'The market is in so much chaos already, I don't suppose the Stock Exchange will notice what we are doing.'

'The DAX is completely fucked this morning,' said Gibson. 'The FTSE still has some life in it. Concentrate your fire.'

Markham nodded, gesturing to three other traders to come to his desk. 'That's what we'll do,' he said roughly, his voice rising as he pronounced the words. 'If we are going down, we may as well go down fighting.' As Gibson walked away, he observed the group of four traders leaning in a huddle over the desk, all of them talking at the same time. Their depression, he noticed, had already evaporated, burnt up by a sudden rush of euphoria.

The shopping bag tucked under his arm, Vereden walked swiftly back along the street, keeping his head low as he passed the house. Looking towards the building, he took a couple of seconds to scan the ground and first-floor windows. Net curtains covered both, through which he could see very little. He paused, looking into the windows, wishing his eyes were younger.

So far as he could tell, nobody was looking back at him. Whoever was inside the house, they were confident enough their location would remain a secret not to guard the front of the building. Burying his hands back in his pockets, fishing around for a fresh packet of cigarettes, he started walking quickly on down the street. About four of them, he decided to himself. If he had been running that operation, four was the number of men he would have chosen for the task. Enough to guard the four walls of any building, and to completely surround the girl if necessary. But not so many that they would start falling over each other in a fight. I've faced worse odds, thought Vereden to himself, taking a cigarette from the packet and placing it between his lips. But not, admittedly, since I turned sixty.

He sat down in the car, blew the smoke into the air, and turned the ignition. Steering the car gently into the road, he turned it past the corner, and drew up behind a green Peugeot 206 parked two buildings from the house. Shutting the door carefully, Vereden stepped out onto the pavement, then opened the boot. Carrying a canister of petrol was never really necessary in the West, he reflected. There was always a filling station every few miles. It was a habit he had acquired back in

the Czech Republic, and it had never left him; the petrol had sat there
in the back of his car unused for the last three years. This morning he
was grateful for it.

Vereden tucked the canister under the folds of his overcoat and started
to walk back down the street. He checked the inside pocket of his jacket.
One good thing about smoking, he reflected. You are never short of a
light. I must remember that the next time I think about giving up.

Ian Fletcher looked thoughtfully at the screen. For most of the morning
he had been pondering queen to bishop four, but he could feel his
confidence starting to drain away from him. The more he looked at
it, the more it seemed to open up the potential for the computer to
bring its castle into play. Deep Blue seemed to favour castle and bishop
strategies. A quirk of its programmers, he supposed. That was the thing
about computer chess programs, he reflected briefly. To understand
them, you had to crawl into the minds of their creators. It was the only
way to find an edge.

Glancing across the screen, he flashed on the message pending icon
flagging in the corner. 'You ready, regards Tom,' it read.

'As ready as we'll ever be,' Fletcher typed into the machine. He looked
up at the trading monitor on the wall. The DAX, he could see, was heavily
underwater, at 5750 and still falling; the CAC-40 was slightly below their
target at 5220, and the FTSE was balanced on a knife edge, trading at
7256. 'What's the stake?' asked Tom's message.

Gibson made the calculation mentally, then called up his spreadsheet
to make sure he had crunched the numbers correctly. 'We're committed
to $12.16 billion on the DAX, $22.41 billion on the FTSE and $36.97
billion on the CAC-40,' he tapped into the machine. 'A total exposure
to the European markets of $71.54 billion.'

'All of it guaranteed by the French government?' came back the
message from Tom.

'Affirmative,' Gibson messaged back.

'Then I think it's time to let them know,' answered Tom.

Gibson nodded into his screen. That was surely right, he thought to himself. It was now approaching eleven-thirty, and if the markets didn't perk up by noon, the bank was going to be facing losses that would make even the French Ministry of Finance, the ultimate shareholder in the bank, pale with terror. As he started composing the message to the chief executive's office, Fletcher pondered for a moment how precisely the bank would respond. Impossible to be sure, he decided. But he was certain it would involve doing everything it could to prop the markets up for the next thirty minutes.

Knight to queen six, Fletcher thought to himself, looking towards the corner of his screen. That might open up some interesting possibilities for putting pressure on her bishop. Yes, he decided. That might well be the best move for today.

Tom folded the screen downwards, cracking the tiny bricks of ice that had lodged themselves into the hinges of his computer. One power warning had already flashed onto the machine and he didn't want to use up any more of the battery than was strictly necessary.

He took a deep breath, filling his lungs with freezing air; he could feel the oxygen from the forest settling into his bloodstream. Fletcher and Gibson were ready to go, he told himself. They were good and loyal men, well aware that in the markets it was your friends you looked out for, not your employers. They would do what they could. Tom raised himself to his feet, painfully aware of the ache in the tendons around his knees. Maybe my flesh is starting to freeze, he thought to himself. Everything else is.

He walked slowly to the edge of the ridge, allowing his eyes to glance down at the guard, tramping his lonely circle around the perimeter of the base. From the idle, reluctant pace of his march through the snow, Tom reckoned he was losing interest. It would be hard, he supposed, to stay alert when you thought you were in the middle of an abandoned wilderness. That, at least, would work in their favour.

Tom walked on to where Terah was digging a small trench in the ground, excavating the snow to a depth of four feet. 'Somebody's grave?' Tom whispered.

Terah looked back at him and smiled. 'Theirs, I hope,' he answered, tossing his head in the direction of the base. He took the end of the cigarette from his lips, crushing it into the snow, then pulled open his rucksack, taking out a canister and a roll of clear plastic kitchen bags. 'Snow weapons,' he said, looking back up at Tom.

Tom opened the lid of the canister, aware immediately of the familiar smell of petrol rising from the flask. 'We're going to burn them?' he hissed. 'In this weather?'

'Petrol is dangerous hot or cold,' said Terah. 'That's why your mother told you never to play with it.' From the roll, he tore a plastic bag, handed it to Tom, along with a strip of tape. 'Fill this with petrol, then seal it up,' he said.

Tom took the bag, poured a thin measure of the liquid into it, before handing the canister back to Terah. He watched as he carefully filled another bag with the liquid, taped it together to seal it firmly, then placed it at the bottom of the trench. 'Snow at the surface is usually around freezing, sometimes a couple of degrees above, sometimes a couple below,' he explained. 'But about four feet below the surface, it is much colder, usually ten degrees below zero.'

'You want to freeze the petrol?' whispered Tom.

'Not quite,' answered Terah. 'Petrol has a lower freezing point than water. Twelve degrees below zero. Put these bags down here for twenty minutes or so, the petrol should be ten degrees below zero. It will stay that way for half an hour at least. Nothing heats up in this weather.' His eyes rooted to the ground, Terah placed the first of the bags neatly into the foot of the short trench. 'When you spent time with the woodsmen, you learnt the kind of tricks the cold can play on people,' he continued. 'Have you ever seen what a liquid frozen to minus ten degrees will do to a person?'

Tom shook his head slowly. In truth, it was not a possibility he had ever contemplated. 'You'll see,' said Terah. 'It is not a pretty sight.'

*   *   *

Terry Semple pushed the KitKat to the edge of his desk. It was not twelve yet, and as a rule he didn't eat any chocolate until noon. Ever since he turned thirty-five, he had been alarmed at the rate at which he had been gaining weight, and he was trying out a no-chocolate-before-lunch diet to see if that made any difference. He pushed back from his chair, watching his screen as he did so, trying to get a better perspective on the constantly changing kaleidoscope of colours and numbers displayed in front of him. In the last five minutes, he calculated, the FTSE had climbed by seventy points, taking it to 7302, fifty-two points above their target level. He signalled to Telmont, standing three desks away, leaning across the desk of one of the junior traders, his finger sliding down the screen. 'Something strange is happening, boss,' he said.

Telmont was leaning so close he could feel the man's breath on his ear. The pale aroma of his sweat and aftershave drifted toward his nostrils. 'Your explanation?' he said curtly.

Semple ran his finger along the screen, pointing to the growing lines of blue figures on the Reuters display; the system always marked out prices on the way up in blue, those on the way down in red. 'About a third of these stocks are moving up again – mostly bigcaps, like Glaxo and Vodafone,' said Semple briskly. 'That's starting to move the index up. But if you look at what is happening in those prices, you see the spreads are widening. One of the brokers is manipulating the SETS system, I reckon, by posting ridiculously high offer prices, completing the trade internally, then feeding the prices out onto the screen. You see it from time to time – ever since they computerized the stock exchange – but not on this kind of scale.'

'They aren't trading to make money,' said Telmont, resting himself on the edge of Semple's desk. 'They are trading to manipulate the index.'

'Looks like that,' said Semple. 'They'll be in trouble if they get found out.'

'What happens to them?'

Semple shrugged. 'Depends on the intention,' he said quickly. 'At the very least the Stock Exchange should go back and unwind the trades, then recalculate the index. If they think there is some kind of attempt at fraud, they'll fine the brokers involved, then kick them out of the City.'

'So who is it?' asked Telmont, his tone hardening as he delivered the sentence.

'Looking at how their spreads are widening, I'd say it was HSBC,' said Semple. 'Very respectable bank. Not the kind of stunt they would usually pull. Not unless they were in some kind of trouble, I suppose.'

Telmont jabbed his thumb towards the screen, his skin touching the glass just where the latest figure for the FTSE was displayed. 'Seven thousand three hundred and thirty,' he whispered, the words so low Semple had to strain to catch them. 'We must get hold of the Stock Exchange, and tell them to do something. This has to stop – and it has to stop right now!'

Sarah wiped her brow, feeling the sweat on her hand. The cigarette smoke of the men opposite was starting to sting her eyes, and her mouth felt dry and stale, the way it might feel waking up with a bad hangover. On the radio, she could hear the opening chords of The Clash's 'London Calling', its beat embedding itself in her mind. 'Maybe we could open a window,' she said, looking up towards where Jennings was sitting.

He shrugged. 'Don't bother me, like,' he answered, a thick grin playing around the edges of his lips. 'Don't mind, like, if it's hot or cold.'

Sarah leant back in her chair, aware of the tension in her muscles as she moved. A cramp had lodged itself into her shoulders, making it painful to move her arms. Tension, she told herself. Tension and raw, brutal unrelenting fear. 'Then perhaps you wouldn't mind if I opened it myself,' she said. 'I can't take the heat much longer.'

'I don't think you ever could,' said Jennings, laughing. 'Take the heat, like.'

Standing uneasily from her chair, Sarah walked slowly towards the window. She could feel her legs stretch uncomfortably beneath her, her calves trembling, and sense the eyes of the men following every movement she made. She stood by the window, looking out into the dismal concrete yard, watching the clouds drift by overhead. The bindings were still strapped to her hands, but she had enough movement to grip onto the frame, starting to yank it upwards. She could feel her muscles straining as she tried to lean into the frame, and the aching in her shoulders grew worse; the throbbing seemed to sear up through her neck, reaching into her jaw. None of the men stood to help. Their eyes remained rooted on her, enjoying the spectacle, smoking their cigarettes, with broad grins playing on their lips. Each time Sarah looked at them, she could only imagine the impact of their fists upon her skin.

A blast of air hit her face as the window sprang open, the sashes rolling suddenly upwards. It felt cool and refreshing, and Sarah drew a deep breath, clearing the remains of nicotine-soaked air from her lungs. The hit of oxygen rushed to her blood, curling through her lungs, flooding her with a surge of energy. Behind her, she could hear one of the men coughing, but none of them rose from their seats. Her eyes scanned the dirty strip of ground leading to the edge of the building, a strip of old and damaged concrete no more than a foot wide, its surface pocketed with cracks and puddles.

To the road, she judged, was about fifteen, maybe twenty yards. A run of ten, perhaps twelve, seconds. Hopeless even to think about it, she decided. Once she got to the road, there was nowhere she could find help. In the time she had been looking out, one car had driven past, and one white-haired old man, the collar of his coat turned up around his neck, had walked by, tossing his cigarette into the ground as he did so. He, Sarah told herself, was unlikely to be much help.

Calling the story up onto his screen, Tom devoured the details of the report.

The Bank of France was this morning reported to be intervening to support the French market, following rumours one of the big French banks could be on the brink of collapse. Traders in Paris said the Bank had been buying equities in the market on its own account, as well as urging French financial institutions and corporations to support the market by buying shares themselves. News of the intervention prompted a bounce in the CAC-40. A spokesman for the Bank of France said it could neither confirm nor deny the rumours, but said it was the policy of the Bank to support the market in moments of crisis. No clear information is yet available on which of the big French banks might be most vulnerable to a collapse. 'It could be almost any of them,' said one trader. 'All the banks have heavy exposure to Eastern Europe, and all of them have taken a horrible beating in the last couple of weeks.'

Tom punched his fist into the snow, enjoying the ripple of cold that ran up through his arm and into his chest. Fletcher had come through, he thought to himself. That piece of the plan, at least, had worked as smoothly as clockwork. His fingers ran quickly across the keyboard, summoning the message pending onto his screen. 'Seems to be working, at least for the moment. Good luck . . .'

On the top right-hand corner of his display, Tom checked the current level of the FTSE: 7331, ran the neat row of red letters. Eighty-one points above our target level, he thought to himself. The DAX was trading at 5871, well below their target, and probably too low to salvage. The CAC was trading at 5422, well above the level they wanted it to reach, thanks to Fletcher's trades in the derivatives market. France is above, Germany below, Tom realized. It all comes down to the level of the London market. That would be their decisive battleground.

He stood up, stretching his muscles, flexing them, trying to restore some warmth to his body. Looking at his screen, he could see that it was now 11:42 back in London. If they could hold the FTSE at this level for another eighteen minutes, then they would have made it. Telmont would be destroyed, and, like snow melting in the spring, his brooding icy presence would vanish completely. Still, Tom corrected himself, I mustn't get ahead of myself. In the markets, eighteen minutes can be a long time.

*   *   *

Telmont checked the numbers on the screen. I might as well forget about France, he thought to himself. Some idiot derivatives trader, according to the rumour mill, had fitted up Credit Lyonnais so that it would go bust if the CAC-40 collapsed this morning. The French Government was not about to let that happen. Nothing to be won by chasing lost causes, he reflected to himself. The secret of successful generalship was to take your losses, re-equip and then move on. Germany was completely defeated. That left London to play for.

So be it, though Telmont to himself. A man seldom has the luxury of choosing his own field of battle. And should I have chosen for myself, I might well have picked this market above all others. No other market was so open to manipulation, nor so prone to sudden and violent swings, as London. Of the arenas in which to fight, this was the best.

Drawing himself to his feet, Telmont took a deep breath, letting the oxygen roar out of his lungs, striding purposefully across the floor. He could smell the anxiety in the air; a stale, lingering odour that mixed sweat and worry with junk food and coffee. The traders looked pale and tense, as if they could sense the game was not unfolding according to plan, and knew time was running against them. At a moment such as this, one must show leadership, Telmont reflected to himself. Just as a man does not always choose the place of battle, so he does not always choose the moment. The moment sometimes chooses the man.

'The Footsie is too high,' he said, his voice ringing out around the room in a loud, deep baritone, his tone commanding the attention of the room. 'By noon, it must be down another eighty points.' He paused, his eyes flashing around the room, resting momentarily on each trader, fixing them with a harsh stare. 'The target is seven thousand two hundred and fifty. The funds at our disposal are unlimited. But we must use every device we can to manipulate that index down. For the next few minutes, each and every one of us must play his part to the full. It will be the decisive, defining moment of our lives. We have travelled a long road together. Let us not fail ourselves now.' Telmont spun on his heels, breaking eye contact, fixing his gaze towards the ceiling. He walked briskly across the floor, looking at no one, moving in the direction of his own office. Eighty points on the index, he thought to himself. A slender thread on which to hang the fate of a man.

CHAPTER 27

Friday, 19 February

THE BASEMENT OF THE KRIPPENBANK HEADQUARTERS JUST off Cheapside in the City had always been the home of the black boxes. A series of network servers, they were stored in a separate room from the bank's mainframes, eighteen feet long and twelve feet wide. The boxes – simple machines that could be bought from any supplier for two thousand each – were kept at a constant temperature of twelve degrees centigrade. Once a month, one of the cleaners came in to wipe away the dust. Otherwise, the boxes remained undisturbed from one year to the next, shuffling billions between each other twenty-four hours a day.

At 11.45, had anyone been present in the room, they might have noticed the boxes were noisier then usual. The room was always filled with the whisper of the computer's fans. But at that moment, the scratching of data being retrieved from the hard drives could also be heard. That was the moment when the KrippenBank's black boxes believed the UK had converted to the euro, and started recalculating their portfolios. At 11.45 and ten seconds, the boxes decided that UK equities were looking dramatically undervalued. Within the next fifteen seconds, a series of twenty-five thousand different buy orders had streamed out of the fibre optic cables buried in the concrete beneath the KrippenBank headquarters, been fed into the telecoms loop that connected all the main banks around the City, and been lodged with other black boxes at different banks. Back down the wires came the information that the buy orders had been received and acted upon, and the information was already stored in the innards of the computers. Within thirty seconds, the black boxes had already spent twenty-two billion pounds buying UK stocks. And they were still bidding for everything in sight.

Vereden glanced down at his watch. Unless I make my move now, it will be too late, he told himself. He dragged deep on his cigarette, flooding his lungs with a rush of nicotine. His pulse was racing, and he could feel his blood pumping furiously through his veins. It's a long time since I have tried anything like this, he thought with a wry smile. Too long and too many cigarettes.

He turned, walking back in the direction of the house. Ten times he had walked past it now, always shuffling by with the same slow, deliberate pace. So far, he was sure they had not noticed him; every time his eyes crept towards the windows, they were always empty. This time, he saw her. There was little mistaking the curls of blonde hair framed by the window, and although he could not catch her eyes at this kind of distance, he felt sure he could picture them in his mind. They would be filled with the same dumb pleading and blind terror he had witnessed on the faces of the prisoners back in Prague. He tossed his cigarette to the ground. It's worth the risk, he said to himself. Even if I were to sacrifice my life, what is that? A few more years, at most, of sad and wasted memories.

The narrow strip of alleyway ran along the front garden, then down the side of the house, leading to a shed where the dustbins were stored. Vereden edged carefully along the side of the fence, staying close to its wooden frame until he reached the dustbins. Taking the petrol canister from his coat, he began to pour the liquid onto the plastic bins. Inside the store, he told himself, they would burn without hurting anyone, but the thick black smoke produced by burning plastic and petrol would be spectacular and terrifying. Crouching on the ground, Vereden crawled along the shabby alleyway and over the rough, uncut grass until he reached the centre of the bay window. He placed one of his three smoke bombs on the ledge, jabbing a box of matches into the cover to act as a ready-made fuse. Crawling further, he left the second bomb outside the side window. Then, crawling along the alleyway, he placed the third bomb directly by the front door, again with a box of matches inside it.

Sitting back, resting against the concrete wall beneath the window, Vereden lit a cigarette, sucking the smoke into his chest. There was enough ammunition there to make them think, for a few minutes at least, they were under heavy bombardment. In the confusion, anything might be possible. One last prayer, he thought to himself. And then I shall be ready.

Sheldon looked up nervously towards Telmont, shifting his weight from his left foot to his right. 'The Stock Exchange are saying they have sent out a warning to all their members not to interfere with the SETS system,' he said. 'Apparently there has been manipulation of the way the Footsie is calculated. They should be resetting it at any moment.'

Telmont nodded, the expression on his face darkening, his lips tightly pressed together. He remained silent. On his screen, displayed inside matt black casing, he glanced down at the level of the FTSE. The numbers flashed for a moment, and for a brief second there was no figure for the index. Then it reappeared, this time at 7270, while an asterisk explained the number had been recalculated to adjust for problems within the SETS system. 'Another twenty points to go,' he muttered archly.

'No so far then, sir,' said Sheldon, his tone brightening.

Telmont looked up, his eyes quickly surveying the young man standing before him. 'I hear that when you climb Everest, it is the last few yards that are the hardest,' he said softly. 'But then it is only the last few yards that count. Whoever heard of anyone climbing *almost* to the top of a mountain?'

Sheldon shook his head vigorously. 'I guess that's true,' he said. 'Nobody remembers the guys who came second.'

'I suppose that's why you're here,' said Telmont. 'You like to be among the winners.'

'Sure,' answered Sheldon, his tone brightening. 'Where the winners are, that's the place to put yourself.'

'But it's not just a game, you know,' said Telmont, looking out from the window. 'The markets are not just an international, three-dimensional chessboard, although sometimes it may appear that way. They have meanings as well. They shape the world around us.' Telmont glanced back up towards Sheldon. He could tell from the half-smile playing on the boy's lips that his words were washing right through him. Sometimes, he reflected, he would be better off talking to the wall than some of the MBAs the fund had hired. 'You probably have no idea what this is about,' he muttered.

Telmont's eyes dropped towards the screen; in the last ten seconds the FTSE had just clicked to 7273, up another three points. 'Rising,' he said under his breath, the tone so low it could hardly be heard. 'The index is not meant to be rising.'

Sheldon looked down at Telmont, and for the first time sensed the fingerprints of anxiety in the quietness of the man's tone. 'The fund is still selling,' he said. 'It should be back down in a moment.'

'Let us hope so,' said Telmont. 'In the next fifteen minutes, let us hope to God that is true.'

Tom scanned the message on his screen one more time, making sure he had digested the information. 'Black boxes in action,' it ran. 'The KrippenBank should be doing our work for us right now. Give Tatyana my love, and tell her we think she's crazy. Mark.'

He checked the FTSE: 7278. They were twenty-eight points above their target with fourteen minutes to go. Right now, Telmont was standing on the edge of the steepest financial precipice ever created. If they could keep this up for just another eight hundred and forty seconds, then

Telmont would be bankrupted. And bankrupted, Tom reflected, the man would be utterly ruined. Without money at his disposal, Telmont would shrink to nothing.

Breathing hard on his hands, trying to snap some warmth back into his fingers, Tom logged back onto his trading screen. In the top right-hand corner, he could see the battery icon flashing, warning him there were now just six minutes' life left on the machine. Keying up his trading account, he took a quick glance at the FTSE, checked the level of his balance, then laid out a series of orders. The little money I have to play with may not be worth much more than a fraction of a point on the index, he reflected. But each of us must do what we can.

The trades were timed to detonate two minutes before noon. If there is just one bullet in your chamber, thought Tom, then you don't use it until your opponent is within sight. He snapped the lid of the laptop firmly shut, took a deep breath, then walked the few yards to the ridge. Terah was leaning against the bank of snow, his eyes peering down on the dome laid out before them. 'How soon?' asked Tom, his voice turned down to a whisper.

Terah glanced at his watch. 'A couple more minutes,' he replied. 'My guess is those men will be changing guard at noon. Catch them when they are most tired.'

Tom paused for a moment, looking down into the pit of the valley, his eyes fixing on the layer of thick sheet metal, huge rusted iron bolts protruding from its seams, its surface iced and glistening in the midday light. Somewhere beneath that metal skin, Tatyana was waiting. What she might be doing, he could not imagine; nor could he summon up any idea of the look on her face when she saw him again. 'The moment of maximum vulnerability,' whispered Tom, looking across at Terah.

'The best way,' he answered, his tone hardening.

Tom nodded, looking back down at the two guards circling through the snow. I can't fault the tactic, he thought to himself. If we are going to strike, this is the moment.

*　　*　　*

Terry Semple reached forward and grabbed the KitKat from his desk, tearing away the wrapper and jabbing the first of the four fingers into his mouth. He chewed hard on the chocolate, letting the sugar sink into his veins. Anxiously, he glanced first at the screen, now showing the FTSE trading at 7315, then up at Telmont. 'Black boxes, sir,' he said quickly. 'It's the bloody black boxes.'

'Boxes?' said Telmont archly.

For the last three minutes he had been pacing furiously through the trading floor, watching whilst the index clocked steadily upwards. It was now nine minutes before noon, and the index had pushed past 7300, more than fifty points from their target. The CAC-40 was way past where they needed it to be. Even the DAX was starting to tick upwards again.

'KrippenBank boxes have just gone crazy, that's the word in the market,' continued Semple, his breath smelling of biscuit and chocolate. 'Bloody boxes. Nobody should ever try to automate trading. Not natural. It's one of those jobs you need a man to do.'

'The KrippenBank boxes are buying the market,' repeated Telmont, his eyes rolling up towards the ceiling. 'The boxes will have been reprogrammed, I am sure of it. By her husband.'

'Doesn't matter whose husband,' answered Semple, stuffing the last of the KitKat into his mouth. 'Right now, the boxes are burning us to pieces.'

Telmont glanced up towards the screen. The FTSE was now trading at 7327, rising steadily as the black boxes bought every equity they could find in the market. The clock was ticking closer to seven minutes before noon. Across the dealing floor, the traders had now rolled up their sleeves, but most of them were just staring listlessly into their screens, their eyes transfixed by the financial catastrophe being played out before their eyes. None of them knew precisely how much the fund had bet on the futures contracts expiring at noon today, but all of them sensed it was enough to make them start photocopying their CVs if the target was missed. 'Have you ever seen a wall of money?' asked Telmont, looking down at Semple. Semple shook his head, swallowing the last of his chocolate. 'Then watch and learn,' said Telmont. He turned away, walking quickly back towards the window, his eyes averted from those following him across the floor. Show no fear, he told himself. A leader must never be weak, not in the eyes of his men.

Telmont reached for his mobile, punching out the familiar row of digits into the slim Nokia. Boissant answered on the second ring. 'You have Strich's number,' said Telmont. 'His bank has started buying the market. Tell him it has to stop in the next three minutes. Otherwise we ruin him.'

'He already agreed to sell,' said Boissant, his tone questioning.

'His computers are buying,' snapped Telmont. 'Probably fixed by her husband.'

Boissant glanced in Tatyana's direction. She was sitting, almost motionless, in front of the antique screen, her faced bathed in its pale green light, her legs crossed neatly in front of her, the angle calculated to display the elegance of her calves and ankles. 'I'm onto it,' said Boissant.

'And start moving the money,' Telmont growled.

Boissant nodded into the phone. 'To where?' he said, his tone quickening.

'Against the FTSE. That is where we need the wall,' said Telmont. 'Use every last billion in those accounts. The woman is co-operating?'

'Perfectly,' answered Boissant. 'We will have no trouble from her, at least. One of the few obedient females I have ever met.'

The sound of the explosion rocked through the walls of the building, its echo resounding deafeningly across the room. The plaster shook from the ceiling, a thin film of dust falling into the room, while the crack of noise rolled across the house like a wave breaking against the rocks.

A bolt of terror shot through Sarah's spine, seizing her in its grip, and for a moment she was unable to move; her nerves froze, her limbs ignoring her commands. The noise shook through her, blocking out anything apart from the fear. Half in fascination, half in dread, she waited for the roof to start falling down, and for the flames to consume her, whilst her hands started to struggle against the rope binding her.

She coughed violently, vomit rising to her throat, its smell filling her nostrils. Anxiously, she started to look about, listening, watching for the next move. At the sound of the explosion, the four men in the room all ducked for cover, diving for the floor, using the table as protection, leaving Sarah the only person exposed to its next impact. As the sound rolled away, Comtes emerged from the floor, looked anxiously about him, then started shouting to the men. 'What the fuck is going on?' shouted Jennings, his voice raw and harsh.

'She has friends somewhere,' said Comtes.

A gun pulled from his jacket was pointed directly at Sarah's face, its barrel just three feet away, and she could see the grooves and twists on its metal surface. 'Don't think about moving,' he barked.

The sound of another explosion rolled through the room, closer this time, its impact more immediate. It sounded to Sarah as if a bomb had struck the side of the building, maybe at the front of the house by the sitting room. The window immediately shattered, sending shards of broken glass tumbling to the floor. Comtes moved backwards, cowering against the wall like a trapped animal, looking across at Jennings. 'How'd anyone find this place?' he said.

'How the fuck would I know?' Jennings snapped.

On his hands and knees, Jennings crawled along the floor, edging his way towards the open window. Thick clouds of smoke were starting to rise from the ground, moving around the house, and lifting up towards the sky. The smell had already drifted into the room, hitting the back of Sarah's throat. On the ground, Jennings and the two other men started to shield their eyes from the fumes.

'I can't see a fucking thing,' shouted Comtes, his head reaching up towards the edge of the window. Sarah watched, her eyes fixed upon him, whilst his eyes peered up through the shattered glass. The look of swaggering machismo, she noted, had been replaced by abject fear, and all it had taken was a loud bang.

'Can we make it to the van?' shouted Jennings, his voice breathless, the tone broken and cracked with fear.

'Don't know how many of them are out there,' said Comtes, his face edging closer to the window. 'The place is burning up.'

Sarah could smell the fumes in the air. A thick, foul, gut-wrenching cloud of smoke had already started to float into the room, a smoke that could only be produced by plastic and polyester and plasterboard. It was swimming through her nostrils and eyes, stinging her nerve endings. Jennings was already raising his fists to his face to clear his eyes. She watched his expression, examining how he wrestled with the dilemma: stay here and burn, or move out and face whatever might be out there?

'I'm not burning to death,' shouted Comtes, his face red with fear, his eyes turned upon Jennings.

There was a moment of hesitation, a moment during which the thick cloud of smoke grew heavier, and when Jennings lost the support of the other three men. On their knees, the two other Frenchmen started crawling over the floor towards Comtes. Their decisions, Sarah realized, were already made. 'Grab the girl,' shouted Jennings roughly, the fibre returning to his voice. 'We'll make a run for the van.'

The message flashed up on Jones's screen. 'Please store all your work immediately. The computer system will be shut down completely in two minutes. Repeat: the entire KrippenBank system will be shut down in two minutes.'

Bugger it, he muttered beneath his breath; if the entire system was shut down, the black boxes would be turned off as well. He looked towards the clock on his screen. Six minutes to twelve. If the boxes were going down in two minutes, the market would be on its own for four minutes. He checked the level of the index: 7331 on the FTSE. It would have to hold onto those eighty-one points by itself. 'What the heck is happening to the system?' he asked Peter Daniels, one of the analysts who sat closest to him.

'It seems the black boxes have gone crazy,' said Daniels, a mischievous grin playing on his face. 'Seems the only way to stop them is to shut the whole computer operation down. Otherwise they'll bankrupt the whole bank.'

'Never did like those things,' said Jones. 'Takes out the human element. All calculation and no judgement, that's the trouble with computers.'

Daniels nodded. 'It really is the strangest morning,' he said. 'First the markets take the biggest roller-coaster ride any of us have ever seen. Then the boxes flip out. Weirdest day I've ever seen.'

Jones grinned, and started walking back towards his desk. 'And you don't even know the half of it,' he said.

'It's done,' whispered Boissant into the phone. 'Strich says the entire computer system at KrippenBank will be shut down in the next minute. You'll have the market to yourself.'

'Fine,' muttered Telmont. 'Make sure the woman keeps selling.'

Boissant snapped his mobile shut, the soles of his shoes echoing across the bare tiled surface of the floor. Tatyana winced at the sound of his arrival, leaning closer into the pale green light rising from the screen. She could smell his breath against her ear. 'How much have you transferred?' he asked.

She turned to face him. 'So far, eighteen billion euros,' Tatyana answered, her voice flat and sullen, emptied of any emotion.

'Every last centime an instruction to sell the market?'

'Just as you said,' replied Tatyana.

Boissant seemed to swell out his chest, she noticed, as she pronounced the words; he was a man who loved to be obeyed. The order, she judged, was of no significance to him. The fact it was his, and it was followed, puffed up his sense of importance, bringing a smile to his lips and a shine to his eyes. 'Move faster,' he said sharply. 'You must have deployed fifty billion in the markets by noon.'

She watched as he turned on his heels and began walking away from her, the echo of his feet against the floor ringing through her ears. He moved at a steady pace, his hips swaggering. Tatyana turned back, looking down at the screen. She placed her palm in position, and began reciting a series of commands into the microphone. Another fifty billion, she thought to herself. More money than anyone could possibly imagine.

Tom looked up at the corner of the screen. The icon flashing in the corner told him he had one minute to go before the battery ran down. He glanced at his clock. Three minutes to twelve. Unless the battery had some unexpected life left in it, he would not find out what happened to the market.

He checked the index. In the last sixty seconds, prices had begun to deflate like the air from a burst balloon. The FTSE was now down at 7295. Three minutes, thought Tom to himself. He had one order left in his locker, but otherwise he was just about out of ammunition. 'What's going on?' he messaged Jones.

'Computers turned off,' came back the reply. 'An order from Frankfurt. They must have found out about the boxes.'

'Do we have any hope?' Tom messaged back. He glanced at the index again: 7287.

'It's in the balance,' came the reply in the message box in the top left-hand corner of the screen. 'Telmont's pushing against an open door. Just a question of how fast he can bring it down. Good luck.'

His laptop was fading fast now, the light from the screen ebbing with each second. The pixels started to pop, one by one, the power switching itself off in stages. The image became blurred, the colours disappearing; the reds first, followed by the blues, then the greens. In nothing but stark black and white, Tom looked at the last number on the screen. The FTSE was now down to 7271. Twenty-one points, Tom thought to himself. If we can just hold those twenty-one points for the next hundred and fifty seconds, the day might still be ours.

He stared at the empty screen, his mind hurtling through a series of alternative scenarios. Telmont had taken the index down by more than forty points in less than two minutes. With another two minutes to play with, he could bring it down further. Of all the defeats life could serve up, he reflected, it was the last-minute defeats that inflicted the greatest damage to the soul.

'We're ready,' said Terah.

He took a series of plastic pouches, each one filled with frozen petrol, from his pockets. Tom placed each one in a different compartment of his jacket, standing warily to his feet. He could feel the vibrations in his legs as he stood. Nerves, I suppose, he thought to himself. Nerves and pure undiluted fear. 'You don't have to do this,' he said, placing a hand on Terah's shoulders. 'It was good enough of you to bring me this far. This isn't your battle.'

Terah shook his head. 'My father always wanted to take out this base,' he answered. 'I think he would have wanted me to come with you.'

Tom could feel the trembling in the man's shoulder blades, and he could see the fear in the movement of his eyes. He could tell he was as crippled by anxiety as himself. 'We make our own choices,' he said, his tone dropping to a whisper. 'And then we have to learn to live with the consequences.'

Semple popped the last of the M&Ms into his mouth, slammed down the phone, and let his gaze flicker up towards the screen high above the trading floor. The FTSE was now trading at 7261, and it was now 11: 57:45. Another hundred and thirty-five seconds, and only another eleven points to take off the index.

'What did you sell?' growled Telmont, his voice rasped and hoarse.

'Twenty million Lloyds TSB, good for four points off the index,' said Semple. 'We're getting there.'

Sheldon was at his side, holding a mobile in his hand. 'I have both the Governor of the Bank of England and the President of the ECB on hold,' he said anxiously. 'They are demanding to speak to you at once.'

'Tell them I will call back after lunch,' replied Telmont. He allowed a brief flicker of a smile to move across his features, creasing up the lines of skin around his face. His eyes descended upon one of the traders on the line. 'Start selling Reuters,' he barked. 'Short it as quickly as you can. Let people think they'll lose a fortune if the financial markets are wiped out.' He moved on down the line, his pace quickening along the tiled floor. 'Sell the banks, sell all the banks,' he snapped to a group of four dealers. 'Take one of them each, and mark them down as hard as you can.' He moved on, a single bead of sweat starting to drop from his forehead. His hand rested heavily on the shoulder of one trader, making the man swivel nervously in his chair. Telmont bent over, looking directly into his eyes, no more than an inch from his face. 'Unload all the stock you can in Vodafone,' he said, his breath escaping in a gust. 'Everyone knows mobiles give you cancer. The shares should be worthless. Dump all the stock you can find.'

Semple took a long, deep slug of coffee, waiting for the caffeine to wash into his system. He could see Telmont drawing up, his chest bulging forward, his expression so resolute it looked as if it had been carved from solid granite. He could see him looking towards the display; the FTSE was now at 7257 and still falling. 'Victory is ours,' Semple could hear Telmont muttering, the words grinding from his lips. 'The day will soon be won.'

The smoke stung Sarah's eyes. She could feel it burning through her retina, making it impossible to see anything. It filled her throat and lungs, choking her, making her stomach churn and heave. At the side of the house, she could feel the heat from the flames reaching high up into the sky. Beneath her, she could feel her legs starting to weaken and buckle as Jennings dragged her from the door and out into the alleyway.

The four Frenchmen, led by Comtes, had left the room first, bursting out of the door, their guns cocked, disappearing into the smoke. Where they might have got to, she could not tell, but she could hear their voices just a few feet away, shouting at one another. Jennings had grabbed her by the wrist, dragging her into the smoke. The sunlight was now completely blocked, and even if she could open her eyes, it was impossible to see anything further than two inches from her face.

She could just see Jennings moving ahead of her, pulling her arm behind him, dragging her into the darkness. Sarah heard, but could not see, the blow. It was the sound of wood cracking against human flesh, and she could hear Jennings screaming before he fell to the ground, releasing her hand from his grip. 'Here,' said a voice from the darkness. 'Take my hand and run.'

Sarah lunged forwards, recognizing Vereden's voice. He took her wrist and started running, his feet moving swiftly along the ground. She could hear him panting, his breath starting to weaken, as they lunged into the thickening smoke, but she could not see where they were going. Behind her she could hear a shot ringing out, violent swearing in French, then another shot. Her pulse was exploding, and she could feel the smoke starting to make her vomit, retching through her throat. 'Just keep moving,' hissed Vereden. 'If I stumble, just keep moving.'

Cepartinu dragged heavily on his cigarette, tossing the butt into the snow. 'You think he might be out there?' he said, looking across at Boissant.

'I'm sure of it,' said Boissant. 'Your men must stay alert.'

'He must have local help then,' said Cepartinu, his eyes scanning the woods running into the horizon. 'Otherwise he would never find this place.'

'Who?' asked Boissant.

Cepartinu shrugged. 'Who knows?' he answered. 'Estonia is full of men who hire their lives out by the hour.'

Boissant lit a cigarette, blowing the smoke out roughly. He walked out from the base, pulling his collar up around his neck. His feet sank deep into the snow, rising up to the ankles of his boots. The clouds had opened a fraction, sending a shaft of weak sunlight down into the valley, its reflection caught in the clean snow. The trees in the hills sparkled, the light bouncing from their branches. Raising his hand to his forehead, Boissant looked out into the distance, examining the landscape for any sign of movement. He smelt the air and listened, but, for the moment, could sense nothing apart from the emptiness and the untouched snow.

'Does the woman know he might be close?' asked Cepartinu.

Boissant shook his head. 'No,' he replied. 'And she doesn't need to know. It would be of no interest to her.'

Sarah looked down at the clock on the dashboard. Twelve fifty-eight, it read. That meant it was eleven fifty-eight in London. Still two minutes left to play with.

The run to the car took just fifteen seconds, but to Sarah it stretched into an eternity. The clouds of smoke had been swelling up around her, burning all the oxygen from the atmosphere, making it impossible for her to breathe. Twice she had almost stumbled in the darkness, pulled along by Vereden. Behind her, she could hear gunshots blasting through the air; each one ricocheted through her eardrums, the deafening noise of the gunfire filling her with dread. Only the darkness of the smoke, she realized, was saving them from an immediate execution.

By the time they stumbled into the car, the smoke was starting to loosen. The clouds were drifting up into the sky, blown upwards by the wind. As Sarah looked behind, she could see two figures starting to emerge from the dense fog surrounding the house, guns held high over their heads, their eyes swerving from side to side as they looked down the street.

Vereden turned on the engine and pulled the car sharply away from the kerb. His foot snapped onto the accelerator, the tyres screeching against the tarmac. Sarah could feel the force of its sudden movement pinning her back into her seat. 'In the glove compartment,' he said, his voice trembling. 'You'll find some cigarettes.'

Sarah took the packet, pulled open the polythene wrapping, and placed one in her lips. Using the car's cigarette lighter, she took one drag to get it alight, then placed it between Vereden's lips. 'Thanks,' he said, turning to her and smiling. 'I've always loved smoke.'

Sarah smiled back. Her hands and legs were still trembling, but the adrenaline was starting to ebb from her veins. 'Your mobile,' she said quickly, the words tumbling from her lips. 'I need your mobile.'

*   *   *

The climb down the bank was steeper than Tom had expected. Terah was walking one pace ahead of him, edging silently down the side of the ridge, his feet planted firmly in the snow. Tom could feel his feet struggling to keep their grip on the iced surface of the hillside. The deep grooves on the soles of his boots dug hard into the snow, but at moments he could feel himself starting to slide into the pit of the valley.

For their descent, they had chosen a point midway between the two guards. A circle, Terah had explained, is always the shape chosen for any defensive encampment, since it provides the maximum visibility for the minimum number of guards. But there is always a point, ninety degrees to either side of the guards, where you become invisible. No more than a few feet wide, it was a narrow opening through which they could slip.

Tom found his grip on the flat surface of the valley. Ahead of him, there was a twenty-five yard strip of snow-covered ground reaching out to the base, ground over which he hoped he could move unobserved. Terah went first, moving as swiftly as he could, turning sharply as he hit the metal wall, signalling to Tom to follow. In less than five seconds Tom threw his back gratefully against the base. 'That way,' said Terah, nodding to the left. 'Good luck.'

Time started to slow down, each second stretching out into minutes, the minutes into hours. He could feel the contours of every snow-flake as his feet moved slowly forwards. Tom kept himself tight to the perimeter of the base, edging around the cold metal. His pulse, he noticed, beating furiously as they scrambled down the bank, had started to slow, turning itself down as he moved closer to his tar-get. A numbness had started to overcome him, as if his body was already anaesthetizing itself from the violence it was about to con-front.

He had discussed the plan carefully with Terah. The guards, they reasoned, would be looking for an attack from the front, not from behind. If they could slip unnoticed to the wall of the base, they could then edge along it until they were close enough to attack the guards from behind. Throw the petrol bags directly into their faces, Terah had told him. Keep moving while you throw it; that way, when they shoot, they'll miss. And make sure you get them with the first shot. You won't get another chance.

Tom dug his hands deeper into his pockets, brushing his gloved fingertips against the edge of the plastic bags; five were packed into either side of his jacket. He looked up from the pristine snow, keeping his ears alert. Up ahead, he could hear the wheezing of the guard, his breath heavy on his lips. And as he moved forward, clinging tight to the wall of the base, on the far periphery of his vision he could just see the edge of a figure walking in a tight circle through the snow. The target, thought Tom to himself. I'll get just one shot at this.

Radek could feel his confidence start to drain away. The clock on the Ceefax screen of the television in his hospital room was reading 11:58, and the FTSE, according to the financial page, was now at 7257. Seven more points in the next two minutes. For Telmont that would be nothing.

For the first time, despair was starting to overcome him, rattling through his spine and eating into his stomach. If she was going to call, she would have done so, he decided. Their plan had failed. Briefly he contemplated the chaos Telmont would unleash on Eastern Europe once he was victorious in the markets. The money he would have at his disposal would be practically unlimited, and the turmoil would destroy each of those countries' fragile hopes of freedom. Another wasted generation, he reflected bitterly.

The thought was still with him, rumbling darkly in his mind like a cloud that was about to break. So fierce was the emotion, he ignored the phone until it had rung three times. 'Sarah!' he exclaimed, as he put the mobile to his ear. 'Are you all right?'

'Just about,' she answered. 'You have the system set up?'

Radek looked across to the laptop he had requested for his room. The machine was switched on, the software loaded, and the modem already connected to an outside line. 'Of course,' he answered softly. 'All I need is the password for the Leopard's system.'

'Maurice Chevalier,' answered Sarah. 'Don't ask me why. Just use it and the system will work the way I said it would.'

Radek reached across to the computer by his bed, tapping the sixteen letters of the code into the machine. Within less than a second, he was inside the computer system feeding prices into the Leopard Fund's offices. He glanced back at the clock. 11:58:45. The FTSE was standing at 7251. Who knows? thought Radek to himself. Perhaps there is still time.

Telmont might be a good general, he reflected, his fingers moving swiftly across the keyboard of his laptop. But even the greatest general was only as good as his information.

The shot echoed through Tom's ears, louder and more violent than he expected. He turned, instinctively looking back in the direction of the noise, but the metal wall of the base blinded him from seeing what had happened to Terah. Another shot rang out, this time echoing through the valley. Tom's eyes darted ahead. Already the guard was starting to edge slowly forwards, moving towards the sound of the gunfire, his gun cocked in front of him, his eyes moving out across the snow. Briefly, Tom wondered if he had been seen. Impossible, he realized. If I had been seen I would already be dead. He took a deep breath, filling his lungs with air. Move, he told himself.

Panic started to grip his mind, a swirling confusion that descended upon him with the suddenness of a lightning strike, blurring his vision and blocking his thoughts. He could feel his legs trembling beneath him. And he could feel his muscles starting to freeze.

Up above, the guard was starting to advance steadily forward, each step bringing him a foot closer to Tom. The gun was held steady in his hand, its barrel pointing forward. Move, Tom repeated to himself. If you don't move now, you are nothing but a piece of dead meat in a slaughterhouse. Yet no matter how hard he willed it, he remained frozen and immobile on the ground, his muscles refusing to work.

CHAPTER 28

Friday, 19 February

TATYANA TURNED AWAY FROM THE SCREEN, LOOKING DOWN the corridor. She could see no sign of him. A thick smell of smoke mixed with rusting cold metal filled the room, clogging her lungs, but for the moment the silence of the place was a relief. The animal trusts me, she thought to herself. Enough to leave me alone at a moment such as this.

She swivelled back towards the SIMD 2000, a chill curling through her shoulder blades. Each time a door was opened in the base, a cool draft would catch her, whistling through the empty corridors, wrapping itself around her limbs and striking at her bones. My father must have spent too long working in this cold, she decided. The thought made her pause. The moment you realize your parents spent most of their lives dedicated to lost and broken causes was always going to be sad, she reflected. But that does not mean I have to sacrifice myself to the same emptiness. I have, like everyone else, the right to break free.

Tatyana looked towards the screen, putting her palm back down on the glass. Her fingers started to run delicately and smoothly across the keyboard. A sell order could be changed to a buy order with no more than the flick of a wrist. All it took was the resolve and strength to press the right buttons on the right keyboard.

*   *   *

Well, thought Semple to himself. A morning like this deserves a Yorkie bar. He looked up towards the screen. The clock had just clicked past 11:59 and the FTSE index was now at 7251. One point short of the target, thought Semple to himself, with less than a minute to go. They couldn't miss now. The momentum of the market was with them, and when you had that on your side, nothing could stop you.

The second drawer to the left of his desk was where he stashed the good stuff; a hoard that he reserved only for moments of the greatest stress or the greatest triumphs. Unlocking the door, he took out a chocolate and raisin Yorkie, carefully removing the wrapper, placing the thick wedge of the bar into his mouth. He could already feel the sugar in his blood as he looked through the office. All the eyes across the trading floor were fixed on the screen, necks craning towards the display showing the level of the FTSE. A hush had descended on the floor, a quiet that reflected not fear but anticipation; a collective holding of breath that reminded Semple of the terraces at White Hart Lane just before a penalty was taken.

He looked across at Telmont, now standing with his shoulder resting against the window, his expression brooding and pained. The lines on his face had grown deeper, the beads of sweat on his forehead larger. His fists were clenched so tightly together it looked as if the blood was about to drain from his fingers. Semple started to walk towards the window. He looked back at the display on the wall: 11:59:32 ran the numbers on the clock. The FTSE was standing at 7253. Slipped back two points, thought Semple. They could make that up over the next thirty seconds.

Across the trading floor, a few of the dealers were still talking into their phones, the expressions on their faces growing more animated. The others had fallen silent, their faces fixed on the screen. They knew they were close enough now, Semple decided. There was little more they needed to do. He stood behind Telmont, watching the flesh on the back of the man's neck tense as he stood transfixed by the glittering array of computer pixels displayed before him. 11:59:45, noted Semple. The FTSE was at 7251. At his side, he could see Sheldon starting to rise from his feet, his fists held tight at his side. Telmont stood absolutely still, completely motionless, his spirit deadening the space around him, his energy focused on willing the index down one more point. For a moment, Semple wondered if he had stopped breathing.

11:59:48 ran the numbers on the clock. Semple glanced upwards. The FTSE had hit 7250. For a second, perhaps two, the room remained perfectly quiet. A few of the dealers turned and looked towards Telmont. A flicker of a smile was playing on his lips, as he slowly raised the palm of his right hand into the air. 'Another twelve seconds to go, gentlemen,' he said quietly, his tone reduced to a whisper. 'Let us not celebrate prematurely.'

Across the room, the traders looked back towards the screen. 11:59:53 ticked onto the clock. 7247 on the FTSE. Semple edged slightly closer. The momentum was definitely with them now, no question about that, he decided. 11:59:56. The FTSE had clicked down to 7241. Around the room, the dealers had put down their phones. No point in trading any more. The game was already won.

For the last four seconds, nobody moved, nobody spoke. It was if they were collectively counting down to their target, all of them mouthing out the numbers under their breath. The index was clicking down by the second. 7239, then 7235, then 7229. The room remained silent as the clock rolled over. Noon, precisely. Somewhere over the river, Semple could hear the bells of St. Paul's starting to chime, the sound rolling up over the water and smashing against the glass. He looked towards the screen. The CAC-40 stood at 5327. The DAX at 5861. And the FTSE stood at 7229. Two targets out of three, reflected Semple. They had made it.

A cheer rolled through the room, gathering strength as it moved from one set of lungs to another. The traders were standing up, stamping their feet against the floor and clapping. In front of him, Semple could see Sheldon throwing his fist high above his head in triumph. He rested a hand on Telmont's shoulder. 'Well done, boss,' he said firmly.

Telmont turned around, wiping the bead of sweat from his forehead, and rubbing the stain of a tear from his eye. 'You have no idea,' he said, his voice hoarse and broken. 'You have no idea how much this has taken to achieve.'

Tom could feel the wave of energy starting to roll through his body.

Like a bird just released from its cage, he took flight suddenly and fantastically, his feet darting out across the snow. His mind was suddenly emptied, hollow of every thought aside from the immediacy of survival. To his left, the guard was clearly in view, but his eyes were trained on the bank of ground rising ahead of him, expecting an attack from above or from his side. Tom started to run, willing his feet to move faster through the thick snow. The guard turned, started to level his rifle to his eye, loosening off a single bullet that exploded through the air. The noise hardly registered in Tom's ears. He kept moving, reaching into his pocket, taking a bag of petrol. Steadying himself, he paused for a brief second, long enough to hurl the missile into the face of his target. The guard had already raised the gun back to his eye, his face squinting tight into the barrel. Tom hurled himself forward, running with total commitment, his feet forcing their way through the ground. The shot rang out, and Tom sensed the bullet rushing through the air. He watched as the bag collided with the barrel of the gun, bursting open on impact. The liquid, frozen far below zero, spilt out onto the metal, dripping onto the man's hands, splashing up onto his face and into his eyes. He could see his hands rising up to his skin, the gun dropping from his fist. Already the colour of his face was starting to change. Tom moved closer, throwing another bag. This time it hit him directly on the nose, tearing open, the liquid pouring onto his eyes and neck, soaking through the thin material of his scarf. His knees buckled first, cracking beneath him. The man fell to the ground, writhing in agony, a cry of pain escaping from his lips.

Tom slowed, his pace suddenly evaporating. He tried to change direction, but slipped, falling to the ground. Scrambling back to his feet, his hands scratching on the deep snow, he rushed towards the gun, collecting it from the ground, gripping it with both hands. The cold of the metal seared through his gloves. How you might use it, he had no idea. Pull the trigger, I suppose, he told himself with a sudden rush of elation. Point and pull the trigger.

In the distance, forty, perhaps fifty, feet away, he could hear the sound of a man shouting. The language, he was not sure about; it might be Estonian, it might be Russian. Whatever, he wasn't about to reply.

He walked closer to where the guard was lying on the ground. The sight of sudden, total frostbite was horrible, worse than Tom could have imagined. The skin on the man's face had turned a pale grey, the colour of broken concrete, its surface pitted with lines, his mouth held open as if a wedge had been stuck in his jaw. His eyes were closed, the hair around his eyebrows turned to ice and set hard. Two of his fingers had snapped when he crashed to the ground, and now lay next to him in the snow. By his side was a patch of red, stained snow where blood had trickled into the ground before the wound froze up.

A heave of vomit rose up from Tom's stomach. He clutched his chest, looking away from the man, trying to fight it back down. He spat the foul-tasting sick down into the snow, tucked the gun back under his arm, and started running towards the side of the base. He could see another figure starting to emerge from the distance, his shadow captured by the sun and cast out across the pristine white snow as he edged his way towards the sound of the gunfire. In the hands of the shadow, Tom could see a gun.

Tatyana gripped the keyboard as she heard the sound of gunfire.

It echoed through the base, bouncing from wall to wall until each shot was multiplied a hundredfold. Impossible to tell whether there was one man outside, two men, or a whole platoon.

She looked down at the screen. In the last two minutes, on her instructions, the machine had told the accounts it controlled to spend seventy-two billion dollars buying equities throughout the Western European market, mainly in France and Britain. The clock on the side of the screen told her it was now fifteen seconds past noon. The machines could keep on trading if they wanted to; it mattered little to her, anyway. The deadline was passed now, and there was nothing she could do any more.

Another shot rang out through the valley, louder this time, the volley rattling through her ears. Instinctively, Tatyana ducked, her hands gripping tight to the metal desk. Who can it be? she asked herself. Who else could there possibly be in this godforsaken spot? Please God, she thought to herself. Let it not be Tom.

'That way!' shouted Boissant, his voice harsh and strained. 'That way, now!'

Cepartinu took the gun from his shoulder, held it close to his chest and started walking along the perimeter of the base. The sound of gunfire had taken both him and Boissant by total surprise. They had been standing by the entrance to the base, smoking, staring out into the sun, when the shots had broken through the valley. Cepartinu had cried out into empty space, telling both the guards to respond immediately if they were okay. The silence that hung through the valley was its own reply. They had been attacked. And since they hadn't responded, he could only assume they had not won the battle.

'I'll hold the entrance,' said Boissant. 'You find them. Shoot on sight.'

His feet felt heavy in the ground. Cepartinu could feel himself shaking as he walked carefully along the perimeter of the base, his back close to the metal wall. Not the cold, he thought, with a sorrowful shake of his head. It is not the cold that is making me shake. It is fear.

He edged closely forward, his gun held out in front of him, the trigger poised for action. Out in the valley, he could see a figure lying face down in the snow, one of the two men he had brought here. Cepartinu looked to see if the rifle was at his side, but it had disappeared. They are armed, he thought to himself. And they have already killed two of us.

On the surface of the snow, he could see the edge of a shadow. Christ, he thought. There may well be several of them. I might be well paid, but nothing is worth my life. He tossed his gun to the ground, stood up straight, took a deep breath, stretched his arms out wide, and started to walk firmly forward. When you are surrendering, he told himself, you have to make sure they know you are surrendering. No point in getting shot by mistake.

Twenty yards away, Tom studied the shape of the shadow. The gun was no longer visible, and the man's hands were outstretched. He was walking towards him. Tom held the gun out, his finger poised on the trigger. 'No further,' he said firmly.

Whether the man understood or not, Tom had no way of knowing. The words seemed to have the intended effect, bringing him to a sharp halt. Tom strode up to the man, digging the barrel of his gun sharply into his chest. Quickly, he searched his pockets, taking a knife and a small pistol, and placing them in his own pocket. A captive, he thought. A corpse, I could handle. But what the hell do I do with a captive?

Up ahead, he could see the outline of a figure emerging from the side of the base. Inwardly, his heart started to beat faster. He grabbed Cepartinu's arm, then started walking forward, his gun ready. The figure raised one hand and waved, and Tom could feel the relief surge through him. 'Terah,' he breathed. 'Thank God you're all right.'

The limp was evident from the painful way he dragged his right foot across the snow. 'What happened?' Tom asked, when Terah was standing next to him.

'A flesh wound,' said Terah, gritting his teeth, his face wincing each time he moved his foot. 'The bullet caught my calf as I was putting the petrol in his face. I'll be okay.' He looked up towards Tom. 'One casualty and one prisoner. You did better than me.'

'You did well enough,' said Tom.

'How many left?' he asked.

Tom shrugged. 'No idea,' he answered. He pushed Cepartinu towards Terah. 'He might have the answers.'

Terah pulled the man close to him, looking into his eyes. He could smell the fear on the man's breath, and feel it on his skin. 'How many?' he barked in Estonian. One, Cepartinu answered quickly. 'And the woman?' snapped Terah. 'The woman is inside the base?' Cepartinu nodded. 'Okay?' said Terah. 'She's all right?' Cepartinu's head moved swiftly up and down. 'Okay, yes,' he answered in Estonian.

Tom moved closer to where they were standing. 'He says she's there,' said Terah. 'One more man to get past.'

'He'll do it for us, then,' said Tom, the rage evident in the tone of his voice. 'We have no time to waste on a fair fight.'

Radek looked first at the Ceefax display on the hospital television, then at the Bloomberg display on his laptop. Both of them told the same story. In the last couple of minutes, the FTSE had surged, rising back up above 7250. Someone, somewhere, he reflected, had been buying equities in vast, limitless quantities. The clock on the screen read 12:01:30 and the FTSE was now at 7261. According to both sources, at 12.00 precisely, it had been trading 7253. Three points above their target. Telmont might not know it yet, he thought to himself with a smile, but he was about to become the most spectacular bankrupt in financial history.

'It worked,' he said into the phone propped up against the side of his pillow.

'How high?' asked Sarah.

'Seven thousand, two hundred and fifty three,' said Radek.

Sarah sat back in the seat of the car. She felt suddenly exhausted and afraid, more afraid than she had been during her escape, as if she had been storing up the fear within herself, and now it was flooding through her in an uncontrollable wave. She shivered, looking across at Vereden, then out at the road. Where they were driving, she had no idea. Somewhere with a hot bath, she hoped. 'Will he know yet?' she asked.

Radek shook his head. 'The password you gave me is still switched on,' he replied. 'The Leopard Fund's computer feeds are still rigged so that all their Bloomberg and Reuters screens are showing false numbers. They think the FTSE is still trading below seven thousand, two hundred and fifty. They stopped trading in the last couple of minutes, just as we thought they would. Natural human instinct. When you think the fight is over, you ease back. In the last ninety seconds some huge buy orders started arriving in the London market, and Telmont did nothing about it.' He paused, wondering how to shape the next sentence. 'We can't be sure where they came from,' he continued. 'But we could probably take a fair guess.'

'Tom,' said Sarah, her tone turning harder. 'Is Tom all right?'

'I haven't been able to speak to him,' said Radek. 'We have no way of telling.'

Sarah hesitated, choking back the words starting to form on the back of her throat. 'How long will the fund be fooled?' she asked.

'A few minutes perhaps,' Radek replied. 'They are bound to realize soon.'

'I should be the person to break the news,' said Sarah.

'I think so, yes,' answered Radek. 'That would be the right thing to do.'

Cepartinu's tread was uncertain through the snow, his feet struggling to get a grip on the icy surface. He walked slowly, swaying each time his foot slipped, his eyes nervously scanning the ground in front of him. He kept his hands dug deep into his pockets, leaving the gun slung loose over his shoulder.

If I go back, those two men will kill me, he thought to himself. If I go forward, I will have to confront Boissant. Fate has been bitterly hard on me, he decided. Bitterly hard and cruel. The sight of Boissant standing ahead of him did nothing to steady his nerves. He was standing at the entrance to the base, his gun held in front of him, his finger nestling on its trigger. His head moved slowly from side to side, making sure he watched the entire horizon. 'It's done,' shouted Cepartinu.

Boissant raised the rifle to his eye, levelling its sights onto Cepartinu, checking he recognized the man before lowering the gun from his shoulder. 'What's done?' he shouted, his voice echoing through the valley.

'They're dead,' said Cepartinu, speaking as he approach Boissant, his voice breaking into gasps. 'Two of them attacked both of my men. They're dead as well.'

Boissant lowered the gun, took the cigarette packet from his pocket, placed one in his own lips, offering another to Cepartinu. His hands cupped over the lighter, torching his own cigarette first, then Cepartinu's. 'You have done well,' he said slowly. 'What kind of men were they?'

Cepartinu shrugged. 'Dead men,' he answered. 'They all look much the same.' He allowed the nicotine to mix with the freezing air in his lungs. I must make my move, he told himself. Catch him now when he is at his most relaxed. It is my only chance of survival. He could feel the weight of the two plastic bags in his pockets, digging into the side of his coat like icebergs. Two seconds, he told himself. That is all it will take.

'Take me to them,' said Boissant, starting to walk away from the entrance to the base.

Cepartinu's gloved hand reached into his pocket, grabbing hold of a bag of frozen petrol. With one swift movement, he raised it into the air. Briefly his eyes locked into Boissant's, and he could see the look of bewilderment and confusion on the man's face. Within a second, it was replaced by an expression of brutal realization. His hand crashed into Boissant's face, then drew swiftly back. The bag burst open, spilling petrol into Boissant's skin. His eyes closed, and his head bent down, a scream starting to emerge from his lips. Cepartinu jumped backwards, avoiding the fist Boissant had started to hurl violently in his direction. His balance lost, he fell to the ground, crashing into the snow. Above him, he could see Boissant, already blinded, swinging his fists in the air. His mouth was stuck open, the jaw frozen solid, but no sound was escaping from his lips. Falling, he collided with the snow, his head scraping the edge of Cepartinu's boot. His hand started to reach out, crawling slowly across the snow, but Cepartinu kicked it away contemptuously. He could see that Boissant's strength was starting to evaporate. Now Cepartinu was becoming the stronger man, and his confidence was starting to return.

He was evil, decided Cepartinu, picking himself up from the ground, and dusting some of the snow from his jacket. I have done the right thing.

'Is he finished?' asked Terah.

In the noise of the struggle, he had not noticed the two men making their way along the edge of the base. He looked towards Terah, his eyes hardening. 'He won't trouble us in that state,' he said quickly, trying to break his lips into a smile.

Tom looked down at the man. The skin on his face had started to harden, turning grey. His eyes were closed, the lashes frozen into his lower eyelids. The smell of liquefied petrol hung over him, like a broken engine. Tom jabbed the end of his gun into Boissant's side, feeling the metal smash into his ribs. The flesh twitched, and some air escaped from Boissant's lips, but he remained silent. 'Can he speak?' he asked, looking across at Terah.

'The jaw has frozen, and so have his lips,' Terah answered. 'He can say nothing.'

'But he can hear?'

Terah nodded, grabbing the packet of cigarettes that had fallen at Boissant's side and putting one to his lips. 'Of course, so long as he is still conscious.'

Tom knelt down beside him, looking into his face, examining his shut eyes. An overpowering stench of petrol rose up into his nostrils, flooding his stomach, churning his guts. 'I would have liked you to have seen me,' he said softly, lowering his lips close to Boissant's ear. 'I would have liked you to watch Tatyana walking out of here.'

He sensed the man's mouth was starting to twitch, and he could see the end of his boot starting to move across the snow. His hand started to move, then the thumb snapped away, left lying in the snow, while the rest of the hand inched carefully forward towards Tom's knee. Tom watched it, then moved away. The words that had formed in his mind had already abandoned him, and he was starting to feel sorry for the pitiful, frozen carcass with just minutes to live. Tom looked up towards Terah. 'Should we end his pain?' he said.

Terah shrugged. 'Each man has the right to dispose of his own enemies,' he replied.

*   *   *

'Our victory has indeed been a great one,' said Telmont. 'And although the battle has been hard and at times dangerous, none of you has let me down. Your courage and perseverance have been a monument to the fighting spirit of this fund.'

He was standing on one of the trading desks at the back of the hall, his figure framed by the expansive glass window, the sunlight bursting through the glass and streaming down onto the floor. In the three minutes since the noon deadline had passed, and their targets successfully met, the dealers and analysts of the Leopard Fund had all left their desks, surging forward like a football crowd. The mood was joyful and relieved and powerful; each and every one of them was exhilarated by sharing some minor particle of the ability to make the markets buckle to their will.

'Our enemies have been everywhere, surrounding us, both inside and outside the markets,' continued Telmont, his voice deepening as the sentences rolled fluently from his lips. 'At times it may have looked as if they would overwhelm us, but with guile, and wit and ingenuity, we have managed to outflank them at every turn. Now we are the masters of everything we survey.' Telmont paused, allowing the impact of his words time to sink in, leaning back on his heels, absorbing the energy of the crowd. It was moments such as this that made the enterprise worthwhile; the delicate flavour of manipulation and control was unimaginably sweet to his lips. 'The ability to take the random chaos of the markets and shape it to our own ends is a fierce and terrible power, and a power that only the Leopard Fund now possesses,' continued Telmont, his eyebrows drawing closer together as he spoke. 'It is a power that will be multiplied fiftyfold by our victories this morning.'

Semple popped a Smartie into his mouth. It was quite hard to see what the boss was on about sometimes, he reflected, but it always had a sense of violent poetry about it. And there was one thing you could be sure about from all the stuff about controlling the markets: bigger bonuses, for him and the rest of the boys. He glanced at the television screen hanging from the wall, wondering if there might be something about the fund on the one o'clock news. 'Look at that,' he said to Sheldon, his voice quickening. 'On Ceefax it says the FTSE was 7253 at noon.'

Sheldon looked across at the screen, then pointed to the Bloomberg and Reuters displays. 'Amazing,' he said, breaking into a broad grin. 'Ceefax got it wrong. Someone over there is going to be in big trouble.'

Semple looked back at Telmont, now pausing for breath in the middle of a long sentence. Walking away from the crowd, he strode back to his desk, picking up his ringing phone.

'Is the Leopard bust?'

Semple recognized the voice: Mike Cornwell, a friend from the trading desk at HSBC. 'Where was the FTSE at noon, Mike?' he said.

There was a pause. 'You don't have a Reuters screen over there?' Cornwell laughed.

'Just tell me,' repeated Semple.

'Seven thousand, two hundred and fifty-three,' said Cornwell.

'Shit,' said Semple. 'We're bust all right. Probably more bust than anyone in history.'

He put the phone down softly, then looked up towards Telmont. The numbers were still ringing in his ears, and he could catch nothing more than the end of a sentence about the need for a new financial architecture in Europe. Reaching down into the bottom drawer of the desk, he collected four Yorkie bars, two KitKats and a packet of Smarties, stuffed them into the pockets of his overcoat, put the picture of his wife beneath his arm, and started walking towards the door. 'It's all gone pear-shaped, Jerry,' he said to the dealer standing closest to him. 'We're finished. I'm off. I'd do the same if I were you. Get out before the sodding vultures show up.'

Perhaps I should go and say something to the boss, thought Semple to himself. He shook his head swiftly, dismissing the thought. Sod it, he told himself. When you're broke, you're on your own. Telmont could look after himself from now on.

Tatyana glanced at her watch. It was three minutes past twelve, she noted. Well past the deadline. Whether her last-minute buying had done any good, it was impossible for her to tell. The machine could tell her how much she had spent. It could not tell her what kind of impact it might have had on the markets. I have done what I can, and I was capable of nothing else, she told herself. That should be all that is asked of me.

Leaning forward into the machine, she took her palm from the screen, switching off the display. It took more than a minute for the valves powering the screen to fade, and the glow hung silently in the air, reflecting from the metal surface of the ceiling. Five shots in total, Tatyana had counted. But who they had been fired at, or who they might have struck, she could not imagine.

Standing up, she could feel her knees trembling beneath her. Taking her shawl, she wrapped it around her shoulders, shivering in the cold, and started to walk uneasily through the hallway. The glow of the screen had faded now, and it was becoming darker. Tatyana's hand reached out to the wall, to steady herself, and she could feel the ice clinging to its surface. 'Who's there?' she shouted, listening to the words rattle through the narrow, iron chamber. She waited nervously for a reply, but for the moment could hear only the echo of her own voice.

Time to stop playing with them, thought Sarah to herself.

She leant into the screen of Vereden's laptop, entered the password, and looked at the display for the Leopard Fund's computer system. Just as she would have expected, it showed numbers for all the main indexes, all of which were completely fictitious, just as they had been for her on her first day. The system had fooled them just as it fooled me, she decided, except this time the game was for real. She looked at her watch; it was now five minutes past twelve. It need fool them no longer.

She hesitated only momentarily, then instructed the computer to set the Fund's Reuters and Bloomberg displays back to normal. Her hands moved swiftly across the keyboard as she tapped a message into the system. 'It's over,' she said, looking across at Vereden, a pale smile reaching across her lips.

The catch was audible in Telmont's voice.

A word had caught in his throat, midway through a sentence, forcing him to stumble, throwing the sentence off-balance. There was a restiveness among the dealers, a feeling he could sense in the air, as if he was starting to lose their attention. At the back, several people were whispering to one another, their faces telling another story from the one he had been outlining for the last few minutes – a story with a different and darker ending. He caught the eye of one of the dealers, saw the panic in his eyes, and moved his gaze through the rest of the crowd. The whispering was growing in strength now, gathering in volume as it moved through the ranks of people assembled before him. 'As I was saying,' Telmont continued, hardening the tone of his voice. 'The fund will need to move forward from this day with new strength.'

He stopped again, the words on his lips evaporating into the air. All the eyes in the room had now turned up towards the bright red neon display that ran across the centre of the dealing floor. Telmont paused before looking, fearful of what he might see there. Slowly, his eyes crept up to the screen. FTSE at 12:00 GMT: 7,253, it read. Next to the words, a message was displayed: 'Capital is the hardest thing in the world to create, and the easiest thing in the world to destroy. Regards, S.'

Silence had now descended upon the dealers and traders. Some were starting to walk back towards their phones, others were looking towards Telmont. 'It can't be true,' he muttered, looking towards Sheldon. 'Tell me it can't be true.'

'Looks like the system has got itself all garbled up,' said Sheldon brightly. 'We'll get it working again in a moment.'

One of the traders was pointing towards the Ceefax numbers on the television. 'They're using the same figure,' he said.

Telmont shook his head, wiping his brow with his hand. 'They can't all be wrong,' he said, his voice sounding strained.

Across the room, he could see some of the dealers talking into their phones. Their expressions told their own story. Their shoulders were sagging, and their faces wore the exhausted, weary look of defeat. Telmont looked up at the screen again, slowly digesting the message. He turned, walking towards the window, looking back down to the river. This is too awful to contemplate, he thought to himself. Complete and utter humiliation on a scale he could never have even imagined.

At his side, he could see Sheldon approaching him with a mobile phone in hand. 'It's a reporter from Reuters, sir,' he was saying. 'He wants to know if the fund has been liquidated yet.'

The words rang out in Tom's ears – the same crystal sharp clarity, the same mellow tone, the same mysterious, embracing strength. It was surprising, he reflected, how much of a woman's character could be conveyed by the sound of her voice. And how close you could come to forgetting it within just three weeks.

Who's there? he asked himself, repeating the question that had echoed through the metal chamber. Who else might it be? Surely she knows it is me?

He looked at the entrance to the base. The arch of the doorway was cut from a single sheet of iron. With the door locked into place, it would be like the door to a submarine. Boissant had left it ajar. Tom pushed, listening as the rusty metal hinges creaked under the pressure. The door swung reluctantly open, light streaming through the corridor.

He looked inside. The corridor was dank and still, moss growing on some of the rivets in the wall, a single bulb some twenty feet away casting a dim and pale light onto the floor below. Three different doorways broke off from the main entrance, leading to separate parts of the base. It was, Tom realized, impossible to tell where her voice had come from. 'It's me,' he shouted.

He heard his voice echo through the chamber, repeating itself over and over again. By the third or fourth echo, he was already wishing he had chosen some other words. So much time had gone into imagining this moment, yet, now it had arrived, he hardly knew what he was going to say.

Tom stepped forward, his feet unsteady on the frozen metal surface of the floor. He gripped the handles along the wall, steadying himself, reluctant to walk more than a few feet into the base. His voice had died away now, the echo turning down to a murmur then disappearing completely. In the distance, he could hear the sound of shoes against metal. Tom listened, gripped harder onto the wall handle to steady himself, and waited.

The flashing of the solitary diamond in her engagement ring caught his eye first, capturing the light from the bulb and sparkling through the corridor. He heard her shoes approaching, then watched as Tatyana emerged from the darkness, her coat wrapped tightly around her shoulders, a shawl covering her head. A few strands of her long black hair were tumbling down the back of her neck. She walked closer, remaining silent as she moved down the corridor, stopping one foot short of where Tom stood. She was so close he could smell the scent on her neck.

She looked tired and worn, he realized. Her skin was pale, and her lips, though still covered in traces of lipstick, were chapped and broken. His eyes locked onto hers, a tide of emotion washing through him. 'You didn't listen to the song,' she said.

'What song?' asked Tom, the beat of his heart thumping through his eardrums.

'The one I left for you on the CD player,' continued Tatyana, her eyes moving rapidly across his face. 'Don't look for me, I'll get ahead, remember darling.' She paused and hesitated, as if searching for the fragments of the tune. 'Don't smoke in bed.'

'That was meant for me?' said Tom.

'Of course,' answered Tatyana. Her eyes looked up at him, the anger evident in her enlarged pupils. 'I can't believe you risked your life to come to this place.' She began to walk out towards the sunshine streaming through the door of the base. 'Don't you understand? The whole point of my leaving was to save you from danger.'

'You left me for another man,' said Tom, stepping a pace away from her. 'You left for this Boissant person.'

Tatyana shook her head, a lock of her hair breaking free. 'I left because I had to deal with this myself,' she said, the anger starting to subside from her voice, her tone turning sad. 'It is part of my history, not yours, and it is something I had to deal with myself. I could cope with the thought of sacrificing my own life. Not with the thought of sacrificing yours as well.'

She started to walk from the chamber, out towards the sunlit valley. As she walked past him, Tom noticed she was wiping a tear from her eye. 'What else was I meant to do?' she asked. The words were delivered without making eye contact.

Tom strode past her, walking quickly towards Cepartinu. Taking his mobile from him, he checked quickly that it was hooked up to a satellite, then put a call through to Radek, asking him immediately if he had Sarah's number, then phoning her. 'Thank God you're safe,' he said, through a burst of static on the line. 'I have been so worried about you.'

'I'm okay,' said Sarah. 'Shook up, but okay. And you?'

Tom allowed himself to laugh. As the sound rattled through his chest, he realized how good it was to be alive. 'Shook up, but okay,' he answered.

'We won,' said Sarah. 'The index didn't collapse. Telmont's broke.'

Tom felt a brief burst of elation – a surge of pride that his plans had worked. 'I'm coming straight back. We'll celebrate when I return.'

Sarah hesitated, nervous about asking the next question. 'Did you find her?'

'Yes,' answered Tom flatly, his voice conveying nothing. 'She's okay. But you and me, we'll get back together in London.'

'I'm so glad you're safe,' said Sarah.

'Everything's okay now,' said Tom firmly. 'We've both survived.'

He snapped the phone shut and handed it back to Cepartinu. He watched while Tatyana walked out into the snow, her boots wading through it. She knelt close to where Boissant was lying, his face turned into the ground, his hands stretched out before him. Her hand reached out to touch his wrist, looking for a pulse, but it had already stopped. He had died quietly some time in the last minute, but nobody had noticed. A fitting end for the man, Tatyana reflected.

His mobile, connected to the same satellite as Cepartinu's, lay next to him, its hollow insistent ring the only sound interrupting the peace of the valley. Tatyana took the phone and put it to her ear, standing up as she did so. 'What the hell is happening?' shouted Telmont, as soon as she switched the answer button. 'The money has been used to buy the market.'

Tatyana had never heard his voice before, but she recognized it instinctively. 'The money has been used as it always should have been,' she said, making sure she kept her voice level and calm.

'Who is this?' said Telmont abruptly.

'Tatyana Bracewell,' she answered. 'Formerly Tatyana Draka. You are familiar with the name, I think.'

A pause lingered on the line. 'Where is Henri?'

Tatyana permitted herself a brief smile. 'The bears got to him,' she said. 'Just as they are about to get to you.' She snapped the phone shut and tossed it down into the snow next to Boissant. She and Telmont would probably never meet, she reflected, and that was just as well. Sometimes there was nothing left to be said. To have spoken once was enough. As long as you got the last word.

She looked up into the hills rising from the forest, drawing a deep breath of freshly scented pine, then walked back towards where the men were standing. Taking a mirror from her handbag, she dabbed some fresh lipstick on. Then she walked slowly towards her husband. 'Thank you for coming,' she said, looking towards Tom, her eyes warming.

'Coming home?' said Tom.

'I'm certainly not staying here,' she answered.

Tom walked at her side, his head down, towards the Shogun that Boissant had left parked next to the entrance to the base. 'Who were you talking to?' asked Tatyana.

'A woman I met while you were away,' said Tom. 'She has been a great help.'

'Will you be going back to her?'

Tom nodded, looking into her eyes, wondering how much there might be left of the woman he married. 'I thought you'd left me,' he said. 'I didn't think I would ever see you again.'

Tatyana looked away. 'I am still the woman you married,' she whispered softly.

Tom shook his head, rubbing his hands together, aware of the damp, harsh cold seeping through his clothes. 'The woman I married was a fiction,' he said. 'An invented character.'

Tatyana turned around, the brightness of her scarf shimmering against the frozen hillside. 'A fiction?' she said, her tone rising. 'Is this skin an invention of your imagination? These eyes, these lips?' She paused, the hot breath flaring from her nostrils visible in the still air. 'Even if to nobody else, I would have thought I would have been real to you.'

Tom could feel the blood quickening through his veins. 'I came here for you,' he said. 'What more can you ask?'

'That you should love me the way you find me,' Tatyana replied. 'What else should any woman ask for?'

Tom could feel his hands slipping deep into the corners of his pockets, and his shoulders drew together, the muscles rippling with anger. He remained silent, the words frozen on his lips. He pulled open the door of the jeep, gesturing to Tatyana to get inside, wondering how they might survive the journey back to Tartu together.

Tatyana looked at him and smiled. 'I don't blame you, Tom,' she said. 'I just did what I had to do, that's all. Now I'll just have to live with it.' She paused, climbing up into the seat of the car, loosening the scarf from around her neck, allowing a thick lock of black hair to roll in front of her eyes. 'At least we survived.'

EPILOGUE

To him I was just a fuse, thought Tom, as he watched the coffin being lowered into the ground. A touch paper you lit when you wanted to detonate an explosion. For that reason alone, I should be pleased to be here today.

A light drizzle was falling on Highgate Cemetery, and Tom tightened his scarf up around his neck. I hardly feel the cold anymore, he decided – not since returning from Estonia – but there is no point in getting wet. He looked along the thin line of people. The number of mourners was not great, but then you would not expect it to be. Telmont had been a man who acquired money rather than friends, and when his money had disappeared there had been few people left to grieve for him. After the Leopard Fund had collapsed six months ago, he was not just finished financially but faced the prospect of spending what remained of his time embroiled in litigation before beginning an inevitable jail sentence. That he took his own life should have surprised no one, Tom reflected. The man was evil, but he was not a coward.

Tom was standing back from the grave, watching from what he felt was a safe distance. Even in death, Telmont was not a man you wanted to get too close to. The familiar words of the service washed over him, their drab familiarity shutting out his own thoughts. 'We'll miss him somehow,' said

Tom, his tone hushed. 'The markets need a human face, and, for better or worse, he was that.'

'But he cracked towards the end,' answered Radek. 'The markets and the economy are like an ocean. A skilled sailor can steer his way through it profitably. But to think you can control it is madness. Dangerous madness.'

Tatyana was standing about twenty yards away, on the other side of the grave. By nature, she likes to stand back from the action too, thought Tom. It was one of the many things we have in common. And one of the many things that made February so strange and uncomfortable for both of us. For a brief moment, the action spun around us.

'Do you think she has come to see him buried?' said Radek, glancing across at Tom. 'Or to look at *her*.'

Tom glanced over to where Sarah stood. Her blonde hair fell loose from her hat, tumbling down the back of her shoulders. It was a month now since she had moved out of the house, and, if Tom was being honest with himself, this was the first pang of remorse he had felt. The space to himself had been welcome. He needed the freedom and the loneliness to work through everything that had happened. His new job as an Emerging Europe economist at Morgan Stanley kept him busy during the day, but for the past four weeks he had spent the nights mostly alone, turning over different possibilities and scenarios in his mind.

'To see her, don't you think?' answered Tom.

Radek nodded. 'Women like to meet the opposition,' he replied, instinctively crossing himself as he watched the first spade of dirt thrown into the grave. 'And you?' he continued. 'Who have you come to see?'

Tom smiled. 'Tatyana, I suppose,' he replied. 'One way or another, I'm always looking for Tatyana.'

Over on the other side of the grave, he could see Sarah and Tatyana exchanging looks at each other, neither allowing her eyes to linger for more than a fraction of a second. Their expressions suggested both were equally puzzled by what he could possibly see in the other.

Tom started walking around the edge of the cemetery, deciding as he

JAMES HARLAND

did so there was no point in preparing anything to say. Sometimes it was better just to go with the moment; your first thought, he reflected, was usually your truest.

Sarah smiled as he approached, tossing her hair back. She looked away from the man she had been talking to, now emptying a tube of Smarties into his mouth. 'Terry used to work with me at the fund,' she said brightly. 'We've been catching up.'

'I hope you found something else,' said Tom.

'Doing some futures trading at Dresdner,' answered Semple. 'Blokes like me always find a port we can dock at for a time. Most of the chaps have done all right. I was just saying to Sarah here, even this complete tosser of a Yank called Sheldon who used to hang around with the boss got a job with the wankers over at Goldmans.'

'How have you been?' said Sarah, as Semple started to walk away.

'Not bad,' answered Tom quietly. 'And you?'

'Not so bad,' replied Sarah. Her head was bowed and she was looking down at the ground. 'Is Radek okay? I'll go and say hello. And Vereden?' she asked.

'Fine, just fine,' said Tom. 'Even Terah's leg is better, and we managed to slip him some of the money Tatyana controlled. The rest went back to the governments it was looted from, just the way we said it should.'

'I'm glad he's finally gone,' said Sarah, looking down at the grave. She looked back up at Tom, a question playing in her wide blue eyes. 'Are you missing me?'

Tom's expression remained immobile. 'Of course,' he answered.

'That's nice,' she replied. 'I like hearing that.' Her glance moved across to where Tatyana was standing. 'But I think we both know that in February we needed each other, and now we don't any more. I was figuring out why Telmont hired me, and you were looking for your wife, and we mistook that for love.' She hesitated, the words catching in her throat. 'Fun while it lasted, though.'

He leant forward, brushing his lips against her cheek. 'Thanks for everything.'

Tom paused momentarily, letting his lips rest on Sarah's cheek for a second, then turned away from her. Tatyana was still standing twenty feet from the grave, her head bowed beneath the wide brim of her black hat. Her eyeliner, Tom noticed, was slightly smudged – evidence, he supposed, that at least one tear must have fallen. 'You're looking well,' he said.

She looked up, a smile spreading across her face. 'So are you,' she said.

'Do you think six months might be enough?'

'For what?'

'For the wounds to start to heal,' said Tom.

'I suppose so, yes,' answered Tatyana. 'We should talk.'

Tom nodded, allowing the words to hang in the air. He watched as the last of the mourners turned away from the grave and started to walk back along the concrete path towards the gates of the cemetery. Then he offered Tatyana his arm. She slipped her hand over it, and together they began to walk. 'He's buried now,' said Tom. 'We can forget about him.'

AUTHOR'S NOTE

This is a work of fiction, and the characters and story are pure invention. Most of the incidental details, however, in so far as is possible, are accurate. The Red Army had substantial investments in the western capital markets: some of its laundered money started turning up in Channel Islands bank accounts in the mid-1990s. The operations of a hedge fund are portrayed as accurately as possible – some readers will recall that the collapse of one such fund, Long Term Capital Management, in 1998, with debts of more than one trillion dollars, provoked a global financial panic. And the Estonian woodsmen, that minuscule country's own liberation movement, fought the Red Army for more than thirty years from the forests near Tartu. The last of its warriors, August Sabe, was killed by Soviet troops in 1978.

James Harland
London
2000